'One of the masters of the short story'
Nicholas Lezard, *Guardian*

'Stefan Zweig… was a talented writer and ultimately another tragic victim of wartime despair. This rich collection… confirms how good he could be'
Eileen Battersby, *Irish Times*

'An unjustly neglected literary master'
The Times

'Zweig is at once the literary heir of Chekhov, Conrad, and Maupassant, with something of Schopenhauer's observational meditations on psychology thrown in'
Harvard Review

'The stories are as page-turning as they are subtle… Compelling'
Guardian

'Stefan Zweig's time of oblivion is over for good… it's good to have him back'
Salman Rushdie, *The New York Times*

'Zweig, prolific storyteller and embodiment of a vanished Mitteleuropa, seems to be back, and in a big way'
The New York Times

'Zweig is the most adult of writers; civilised, urbane, but never jaded or cynical; a realist who nonetheless believed in the possibility—the necessity—of empathy'
Independent

'He was capable of making the reader live other people's deepest experience—which is a moral education in itself. My advice is that you should go out at once and buy his books'
Sunday Telegraph

STEFAN ZWEIG was born in 1881 in Vienna, into a wealthy Austrian-Jewish family. He studied in Berlin and Vienna and was first known as a poet and translator, then as a biographer. Zweig travelled widely, living in Salzburg between the wars, and was an international bestseller with a string of hugely popular novellas including *Letter from an Unknown Woman*, *Amok* and *Fear*. In 1934, with the rise of Nazism, he moved to London, and later on to Bath, taking British citizenship after the outbreak of the Second World War. With the fall of France in 1940 Zweig left Britain for New York, before settling in Brazil, where in 1942 he and his wife were found dead in an apparent double suicide. Much of his work is available from Pushkin Press.

STEFAN ZWEIG

FANTASTIC NIGHT

Tales of
Longing and Liberation

Translated from the German by
Anthea Bell

PUSHKIN PRESS

LONDON

Pushkin Press
71–75 Shelton Street
London WC2H 9JQ

Original texts © Williams Verlag AG Zurich
English translations © Anthea Bell

This edition first published by Pushkin Press in 2015

0 0 1

ISBN 978 1 782271 48 2

Set in 10.25 on 14 Monotype Baskerville
by Tetragon, London

Printed and bound by CPI Group (UK) Ltd, Croydon CR0 4YY

www.pushkinpress.com

CONTENTS

FANTASTIC
NIGHT

A SEALED PACKET *containing the following pages was found in the desk of Baron Friedrich Michael von R... after he fell at the battle of Rawaruska in the autumn of 1914, fighting with a regiment of dragoons as a lieutenant in the Austrian reserve. His family, assuming from the title and a fleeting glance at the contents that this was merely a literary work by their relative, gave it to me to assess and entrusted me with its publication. I myself do not by any means regard these papers as fiction; instead, I believe them to be a record of the dead man's own experience, faithful in every detail, and I therefore publish his psychological self-revelation without any alteration or addition, suppressing only his surname.*

This morning I suddenly conceived the notion of writing, for my own benefit, an account of my experiences on that fantastic night, in order to survey the entire incident in its natural order of occurrence. And ever since that abrupt moment of decision I have felt an inexplicable compulsion to set my adventure down in words, although I doubt whether I can describe its strange nature at all adequately. I have not a trace of what people call artistic talent, nor any literary experience, and apart from a few rather light-hearted squibs for the *Theresianum* I have never tried to write anything. I don't even know, for instance, if there is some special technique to be learnt for arranging the sequence of outward events and their simultaneous inner reflection in order, and I wonder whether I am capable of always finding the right word for a certain meaning and the right meaning for a certain word, so as to achieve the equilibrium which I have always subconsciously felt in reading the work of every true storyteller. But I write these lines solely for my own satisfaction, and they are certainly not intended to make something that I can hardly explain even to myself intelligible to others. They are merely an attempt to confront an incident which constantly occupies my mind, keeping it in a state of painfully active fermentation, and to draw a line under it at last: to set it all down, place it before me, and cover it from every angle.

I have not told any of my friends about the incident, first because I felt that I could not make them understand its essential aspects, and then out of a certain sense of shame at having been so shattered and agitated by something that happened quite by chance. For the whole thing is really just a small episode. But even as I write this, I begin to realise how difficult it is for an amateur to choose words of the right significance when he is writing, and what ambiguity, what possibilities of misunderstanding can attach to the simplest of terms. For if I describe the episode as small, of course I mean it only as relatively small, by comparison with those mighty dramatic events that sweep whole nations and human destinies along with them, and then again I mean it as small in terms of time, since the whole sequence of events occupied no more than a bare six hours. To me, however, that experience—which in the general sense was minor, insignificant, unimportant—meant so extraordinarily much that even today, four months after that fantastic night, I still burn with the memory of it, and must exert all my intellectual powers to keep it to myself. Daily, hourly, I go over all the details again, for in a way it has become the pivot on which my whole existence turns; everything I do and say is unconsciously determined by it, my thoughts are solely concerned with going over and over its sudden intrusion into my life, and thereby confirming that it really did happen to me. And now I suddenly know, too, what I certainly had not yet guessed ten minutes ago when I picked up my pen: that I am recording my experience only in order to have it securely and, so to speak, objectively fixed before me, to enjoy it again in my emotions while at the same time understanding it intellectually. It was quite wrong, quite untrue when I said just now that I wanted to draw a line under it by writing it down; on the contrary, I want to make what I lived through all too quickly even more alive, to have it warm and breathing beside me, so that I can clasp it to me again and again. Oh, I am not afraid of forgetting so much as a second of that sultry afternoon, that fantastic night, I need no markers or milestones to help me trace the path I took in those hours step by step in memory: like a sleepwalker I find myself back under its spell at any time, in the middle of the day or the middle of the night, seeing every detail with that clarity of vision that only the heart and not the feeble memory knows. I could draw the outline of every single leaf in that green spring landscape on this paper, even now in autumn I feel the mild air, the soft and pollen-laden wafts of chestnut blossom. So if I am about to describe those hours again, it is done not for fear of forgetting them but for the joy of bringing them to life again. And if I now describe the changes that took place that night, all exactly as they occurred, then I must control myself for the sake of an orderly account, for whenever I begin to think of the details of my experience ecstasy wells up from my emotions, a kind of intoxication overcomes me, and I have to hold back the images of memory to keep them from tumbling over one another in wild confusion, colourful and frenzied. With passionate ardour, I still relive what I experienced on that day, the 7th of June, 1913, when I took a cab at noon...

But once more I feel I must pause, for yet again, and with some alarm, I become aware of the double-edged ambiguity of a single word. Only now that, for the first time, I am to tell a story in its full context do I understand the difficulty of expressing the ever-changing aspect of all that lives in concentrated form. I have just written "I", and said that I took a cab at noon on the 7th of

June, 1913. But the word itself is not really straightforward, for I am by no means still the "I" of that time, that 7th of June, although only four months have passed since that day, although I live in the apartment of that former "I" and write at his desk, with his pen, and with his own hand. I am quite distinct from the man I was then, because of this experience of mine, I see him now from the outside, looking coolly at a stranger, and I can describe him like a playmate, a comrade, a friend whom I know well and whose essential nature I also know, but I am not that man any longer. I could speak of him, blame or condemn him, without any sense that he was once a part of me.

The man I was then differed very little, either outwardly or inwardly, from most of his social class, which we usually describe here in Vienna, without any particular pride but as something to be taken entirely for granted, as 'fashionable society'. I was entering my thirty-sixth year, my parents had died prematurely just before I came of age, leaving me a fortune which proved large enough to make it entirely superfluous for me to think thereafter of earning a living or pursuing a career. I was thus unexpectedly spared a decision which weighed on my mind a great deal at the time. For I had just finished my university studies and was facing the choice of a future profession. Thanks to our family connections and my own early inclination for a contemplative existence proceeding at a tranquil pace, I would probably have opted for the civil service, when this parental fortune came to me as sole heir, suddenly assuring me of an independence sufficient to satisfy extensive and even luxurious wishes without working. Ambition had never troubled me, so I decided to begin by watching life at my leisure for a few years, waiting until I finally felt tempted to find some circle of influence for myself. However, I never got beyond this watching and waiting, for as there was nothing in particular that I wanted, I could have anything within the narrow scope of my wishes: the mellow and sensuous city of Vienna, which excels like no other in bringing leisurely strolls, idle observation and the cultivation of elegance to a peak of positively artistic perfection, a purpose in life of itself, enabled me to forget entirely my intention of taking up some real activity. I had all the satisfactions an elegant, noble, well-to-do, good-looking young man without ambition could desire: the harmless excitement of gambling, hunting, the regular refreshment of travels and excursions, and soon I began cultivating this peaceful way of life more and more elaborately, with expertise and artistic inclination. I collected rare glasses, not so much from a true passion for them as for the pleasure of acquiring solid knowledge in the context of an undemanding hobby, I hung my apartment with a particular kind of Italian Baroque engravings and landscapes in the style of Canaletto—acquiring them from second-hand shops or bidding for them at auction provided the excitement of the chase without any dangers—I followed many other pursuits out of a liking for them and always with good taste, and I was seldom absent from performances of good music or the studios of our painters. I did not lack for success with women, and here too, with the secret collector's urge which in a way indicates a lack of real involvement, I chalked up many memorable and precious hours of varied experience. In this field I gradually moved from being a mere sensualist to the status of a knowledgeable connoisseur. All things considered, I had enjoyed many experiences which occupied my days pleasantly and allowed me to feel that my life was a full one, and increasingly I began to relish the easygoing, pleasant atmosphere of a youthful existence that was lively but never agitated. I formed almost no new wishes, for quite small things could blossom into pleasures in the calm climate of my days. A well-chosen tie could make me almost merry; a good book, an excursion in a motor car or an hour with a woman left me fully satisfied. It particularly pleased me to ensure that this way of life, like a faultlessly correct suit of English tailoring, did not make me conspicuous in any way. I believe I was considered pleasant company, I was popular and welcome in society, and most who knew me called me a happy man.

I cannot now say whether the man of that time, whom I am trying to conjure up here, thought himself as happy as those others did, for now that this experience of mine has made me expect a much fuller and more fulfilled significance in every emotion, I find it almost impossible to assess his happiness in retrospect. But I can say with certainty that I felt myself by no means unhappy at the time, for my wishes almost never went unsatisfied and nothing I required of life was withheld. But the very fact that I had become accustomed to getting all I asked from destiny, and demanded no more, led gradually to a certain absence of excitement, a lifelessness in life itself. Those yearnings that then stirred unconsciously in me at many moments of half-realisation were not really wishes, but only the wish for wishes, a craving for desires that would be stronger, wilder, more ambitious, less easily satisfied, a wish to live more and perhaps to suffer more as well. I had removed all obstacles from my life by a method that was only too reasonable, and my vitality was sapped by that absence of obstacles. I noticed that I wanted fewer things and did not want them so much, that a kind of paralysis had come over my feelings, so that—perhaps this is the best way to express it—so that I was suffering from emotional impotence, an inability to take passionate possession of life. I recognised this defect from small signs at first. I noticed that I was absent more and more often from the theatre and society on certain occasions of great note, that I ordered books which had been praised to me and then left them lying on my desk for weeks with their pages still uncut, that although I automatically continued to pursue my hobbies, buying glasses and antiques, I did not trouble to classify them once they were mine, nor did I feel any particular pleasure in unexpectedly acquiring a rare piece which it had taken me a long time to find.

However, I became really aware of this lessening of my emotional vigour, slight but indicative of change, on a certain occasion which

I still remember clearly. I had stayed in Vienna for the summer—again, as a result of that curious lethargy which left me feeling no lively attraction to anything new—when I suddenly received a letter written in a spa resort. It was from a woman with whom I had had an intimate relationship for three years, and I even truly thought I loved her. She wrote fourteen agitated pages to tell me that in her weeks at the spa she had met a man who meant a great deal to her, indeed everything, she was going to marry him in the autumn, and the relationship between us must now come to an end. She said that she thought of our time together without regret, indeed with happiness, the memory of me would accompany her into her marriage as the dearest of her past life, and she hoped I would forgive her for her sudden decision. After this factual information, her agitated missive surpassed itself in truly moving entreaties, begging me not to be angry with her, not to feel too much pain at her sudden termination of our relationship; I mustn't try to get her back by force, or do anything foolish to myself. Her lines ran on, becoming more and more passionate: I must and would find comfort with someone better, I must write to her at once, for she was very anxious about my reception of her message. And as a postscript she had hastily scribbled, in pencil: "*Don't do anything stupid, understand me, forgive me!*" I read this letter, surprised at first by her news, and then, when I had skimmed all through it, I read it a second time, now with a certain shame which, on making itself felt, soon became a sense of inner alarm. For none of the strong yet natural feelings which my lover supposed were to be taken for granted had even suggested themselves to me. I had not suffered on hearing her news, I had not been angry with her, and I had certainly not for a second contemplated any violence against either her or myself, and this coldness of my emotions was too strange not to alarm me. A woman was leaving me, a woman who had been my companion for years, whose warm and supple body had offered itself to me, whose breath had mingled with mine in long nights together, and nothing stirred in me, nothing protested, nothing sought to get her back, I had none of those feelings that this woman's pure instinct assumed were natural in any human being. At that moment I was fully aware for the first time how far advanced the process of paralysis already was in me—it was as if I were moving through flowing, bright water without being halted or taking root anywhere, and I knew very well that this chill was something dead and corpse-like, not yet surrounded by the foul breath of decomposition but already numbed beyond recovery, a grimly cold lack of emotion. It was the moment that precedes real, physical death and outwardly visible decay.

After that episode I began carefully observing myself and this curious paralysis of my feelings, as a sick man observes his sickness. When, shortly afterwards, a friend of mine died and I followed his coffin to the grave, I listened to myself to see if I did not feel grief, if some emotion did not move in me at the knowledge that this man, who had been close to me since our childhood, was now lost to me for ever. But nothing stirred, I felt as if I were made of glass, with the world outside shining straight through me and never lingering within, and hard as I attempted on this and many similar occasions to feel something, however much I tried, through reasonable argument, to make myself feel emotion, no response came from my rigid state of mind. People parted from me, women came and went, and I felt much like a man sitting in a room with rain beating on the window panes; there was a kind of sheet of glass between me and my immediate surroundings, and my will was not strong enough to break it.

Although I felt this clearly, the realisation caused me no real uneasiness, for as I have said, I took even what affected myself with indifference. I no longer had feeling enough to suffer. It was enough for me that this internal flaw was hardly perceptible from the outside, in the same way as a man's physical impotence becomes obvious only at the moment of intimacy, and in company I often put on a certain elaborate show, employing artificially passionate admiration and spontaneous exaggeration to hide the extent to which I knew I was dead and unfeeling inside. Outwardly I continued my old comfortable, unconstrained way of life without any change of direction; weeks, months passed easily by and slowly, gathering darkly into years. One morning when I looked in the glass I saw a streak of grey at my temple, and felt that my youth was slowly departing. But what others call youth had long ago ended in me, so taking leave of it did not hurt very much, since I did not love even my own youth enough for that. My refractory emotions preserved their silence even to me.

This inner rigidity made my days more and more similar, despite all the varied occupations and events that filled them, they ranged themselves side by side without emphasis, they grew and faded like the leaves of a tree. And the single day I am about to describe for my own benefit began in a perfectly ordinary way too, without anything odd to mark it, without any internal premonition. On that day, the 7th of June, 1913, I had got up later than usual because of a subconscious Sunday feeling, something that lingered from my childhood and schooldays. I had taken my bath, read the paper, dipped into some books, and then, lured out by the warm summer day that compassionately made its way into my room, I went for a walk. I crossed the Graben in my usual way, greeted friends and acquaintances and conducted brief conversations with some of them, and then I lunched with friends. I had avoided any engagement for the afternoon, since I particularly liked to have a few uninterrupted hours on Sunday which I could use just as my mood, my pleasure or some spontaneous decision dictated. As I left my friends and crossed the Ringstrasse, I felt the beauty of the sunny city doing me good, and enjoyed its early summer finery. All the people seemed cheerful, as if they were in love with the Sunday atmosphere of the lively street, and many details struck me, in particular the way the broad, bushy trees rose from the middle of the asphalt wearing their new green foliage. Although I went this way almost daily, I suddenly became aware of the Sunday crowd as if it were a miracle, and involuntarily I felt a longing for a great deal of greenery, brightness and colour. I thought with a certain interest of the Prater, where in late spring and early summer the great trees stand to right and left of the main avenue down which the carriages drive, motionless like huge green footmen as they hold up their white candles of blossom to the many well-groomed and elegant passers-by. Used as I was to indulging the most fleeting whim at once, I hailed the first cab I saw, and when the cabby asked where I was going I told him the Prater. "Ah, to the races, Baron, am I right?" he replied obsequiously, as if that was to be taken for granted. Only then did I remember that there was a fashionable race meeting today, a preview of the local Derby, where Viennese high society foregathered. How strange, I thought as I got into the cab, only a few years ago how could I possibly have forgotten or failed to attend such a day? When I thought of my forgetfulness I once again felt all the rigidity of the indifference to which I had fallen victim, just as a sick man feels his injury when he moves.

The main avenue was quite empty when we arrived, and the racing must have begun long ago, for I did not see what was usually a handsome procession of carriages; there were only a few cabs racing along, hooves clattering, as if catching up with some invisible omission. The driver turned on his box and asked whether he should make the horses trot faster, but I told him to let them walk slowly, I didn't mind arriving late. I had seen too many races, and had seen the racegoers too often as well, to mind about arriving on time, and as the vehicle rocked gently along it matched my idle mood better to feel the blue air, with a soft rushing sound in it like the sea when you are on board ship, and at my leisure to view the handsome, broad and bushy chestnut trees which sometimes gave up a few flower petals as playthings to the warm, coaxing wind, which then raised them gently and sent them whirling through the air before letting them fall like white flakes on the avenue. It was pleasant to be rocked like that, to sense the presence of spring with eyes closed, to feel carried away and elated without any effort at all. I was quite sorry when the cab reached the Freudenau and stopped at the entrance. I would have liked to turn round and let the soft, early summer day continue to cradle me. But it was already too late, the cab was drawing up outside the racecourse. A muffled roar came to meet me. It re-echoed with a dull, hollow sound on the far side of the tiers of seats, and although I could not see the excited crowd making that concentrated noise I couldn't help thinking of Ostend, where if you walk up the small side streets from the low-lying town to the beach promenade you feel the keen, salty wind blowing over you, and hear a hollow boom before you ever set eyes on the broad, grey, foaming expanse of the sea with its roaring waves. There must be a race going on at the moment, but between me and the turf on which the horses were probably galloping stood a colourful, noisy, dense mass swaying back and forth as if shaken by some inner turmoil: the crowd of spectators and gamblers. I couldn't see the track, but I followed every stage of the race as their heightened excitement reflected it. The jockeys must have started some time ago, the bunched formation at the beginning of the race had thinned out, and a couple of horses were disputing the lead, for already shouts and excited cries were coming from the people who mysteriously, as it seemed, were watching the progress of a race which was invisible to me. The turn of their heads indicated the bend which the horses and jockeys must just have reached on the long oval of turf, for the whole chaotic crowd was now moving its gaze as if craning a single neck to see something out of my line of vision, and its single taut throat roared and gurgled with thousands of hoarse, individual sounds, like a great breaker foaming as it rises higher and higher. And the wave rose and swelled, it already filled the whole space right up to the blue indifferent sky. I looked at a few of the faces. They were distorted as if by some inner spasm, their eyes were fixed and sparkling, they were biting their lips, chins avidly thrust forwards, nostrils flaring like a horse's. Sober as I was, I found their frenzied intemperance both a comic and a dreadful sight. Beside me a man was standing on a chair. He was elegantly dressed, and had what was probably a good-looking face in the usual way, but now he was raving, possessed by an invisible demon, waving his cane in the air as if lashing something forwards; his whole body—in a manner unspeakably ridiculous to a specta-tor—passionately mimed the movement of rapid riding. He kept bobbing his heels up and down on the chair, as if standing in the stirrups, his right hand constantly whipped the air like a riding crop, his left hand convulsively clutched a slip of white card. And there were more and more of those white slips fluttering around, like sparkling wine spraying above the grey and stormy tide that swelled so noisily. A few horses must be very close to each other on the bend now, for suddenly the shouting divided into three or four individual names roared out like battle cries again and again by separate groups, and the shouts seemed like an outlet for their delirious state of possession.

I stood amidst this roaring frenzy cold as a rock in the raging sea, and I remember to this day exactly what I felt at that moment. First I thought how ridiculous those grotesque gestures were, I felt ironic contempt for the vulgarity of the outburst, but there was something else too, something that I was unwilling to admit to myself—a kind of quiet envy of such excitement, such heated passion, envy of the life in this display of fervour. What, I thought, would have to happen to excite me so much, rouse me to such fever pitch that my body would burn so ardently, my voice would issue from my mouth against my own will? I could not imagine any sum of money that would so spur me on to possess it, any woman who could excite me so much, there was nothing, nothing that could kindle such fire within me in my emotional apathy! If I faced a pistol suddenly aimed at me, my heart would not thud as wildly in the second before I froze as did the hearts of these people around me, a thousand, ten thousand of them, just for a handful of money. But now one horse must be very near the finishing line, for a certain name rang out above the tumult like a string stretched taut, uttered by a thousand voices and rising higher and higher, only to end all at once on an abrupt, shrill note. The music began to play, the crowd suddenly dispersed. One of the races was over, the contest was decided, their tension was resolved into swirling movement as the excited vibrations died down. The throng, just a moment ago a fervent concentration of passion, broke up into many individuals walking, laughing, talking; calm faces emerged from behind the Maenad mask of frenzy; social groups formed again out of the chaos of the game that for seconds on end had forged these thousands of racegoers into a single ardent whole, those groups came together, they parted, I saw people I knew who hailed me, and strangers who scrutinised and observed each other with cool courtesy. The women assessed one another's new outfits, the men cast avid glances, that fashionable curiosity which is the real occupation of the indifferent began to show, the racegoers looked around, counted others, checked up on their presence and their degree of elegance. Scarcely brought down to earth again from their delirium, none of them knew whether the real object of their meeting in company here was the races themselves or this interlude of walking about the racecourse.

I walked through this relaxed, milling crowd, offering and returning greetings, and breathing in with pleasure—for this was the world in which I lived—the aura of perfume and elegance that wafted around the kaleidoscopic confusion. With even more pleasure I felt the soft breeze that sometimes blew out of the summery warmth of the woods from the direction of the Prater meadows, sometimes rippling like a wave among the racegoers and fingering the women's white muslins as if in amorous play.

A couple of acquaintances hailed me; the pretty actress Diane nodded invitingly to me from a box, but I joined no one. I was not interested in talking to any of these fashionable folk today; I found it tedious to see myself reflected in them. All I wanted was to experience the spectacle, the crackling, sensuous excitement that pervaded the heightened emotion of the hour (for the excitement of others is the most delightful of spectacles to a man who himself is in a state of indifference). A couple of pretty women passed by, I boldly but without any inward desire scrutinised the breasts under the thin gauze they wore, moving at every step they took, and smiled to myself to see their half-awkward, half-gratified embarrassment when they felt that I was assessing them sensuously and undressing them with my eyes. In fact none of the women aroused me, it simply gave me a certain satisfaction to pretend to them that they did; it pleased me to play with their idea that I wanted to touch them physically and felt a magnetic attraction of the eye, for like all who are cold at heart I found more intense erotic enjoyment in arousing warmth and restlessness in others than in waxing ardent myself. It was only the downy warmth lent to sensuality by the presence of women that I loved to feel, not any genuine arousal, only stimulation and not real excitement. So I walked through the promenading crowd as usual, caught glances, tossed them back as lightly as a shuttlecock, took my pleasure without reaching out a hand, fondled women without physical contact, warmed only slightly by the mildly amorous game.

But soon I found this tedious too. The same people kept passing; I knew their faces and gestures by heart now. There was a chair nearby, and I took it. A new turbulence began in the groups around me, passers-by moved and pushed more restively in the confusion; obviously another race was about to start. I was not interested in that, but sat at my ease and as if submerged beneath the smoke from my cigarette, which rose in white rings against the sky, turning brighter and brighter and disintegrating like a little cloud in the springtime blue. And at that very second the extraordinary, unique experience that still rules my life today began. I can fix the moment exactly, because it so happens that I had just looked at my watch: the hands were crossing, and I watched with idle curiosity as they overlapped for a second. It was sixteen minutes past three on the afternoon of the 7th of June, 1913. With cigarette in hand, then, I was looking at the white dial of the watch, entirely absorbed in this childish and ridiculous contemplation, when I heard a woman laugh out loud just behind my back with the ringing, excited laughter that I love in women, springing warm and startled out of the hot thickets of the senses. I instinctively leant my head back to see the woman whose sensuality, boldly proclaimed aloud, was forcing its way into my carefree reverie like a sparkling white stone dropped into a dull and muddy pond—and then I controlled myself. A curious fancy for an intellectual game, a fancy of the kind I often felt for a small and harmless psychological experiment, held me back. I didn't want to see the laughing woman just yet; it intrigued me to let my imagination work on her first in a kind of anticipation of pleasure, to conjure up her appearance, giving that laughter a face, a mouth, a throat, a neck, a breast, making a whole living, breathing woman of her.

At this moment she was obviously standing directly behind me. Her laughter had turned to conversation again. I listened intently. She spoke with a slight Hungarian accent, very fast and expressively, her vowels soaring as if in song. It amused me to speculate on the figure that went with her voice, elaborating my imaginary picture as richly as I could. I gave her dark hair, dark eyes, a wide and sensuously curving mouth with strong, very white teeth, a little nose that was very narrow but had flared, quivering nostrils. I put a beauty spot on her left cheek and a riding crop in her hand; as she laughed she slapped it lightly against her thigh. She talked on and on. And each of her words added some new detail to my rapidly formed image of her: a slender, girlish breast, a dark-green dress with a diamond brooch pinned to it at a slant, a pale hat with a white feather. The picture became clearer and clearer, and I already felt as if this stranger standing invisible behind my back was also on a lit photographic plate in the pupil of my eye. But I didn't want to turn round yet, I preferred to enhance my imaginary game further. A touch of lust mingled with my audacious reverie, and I closed both eyes, certain that when I opened them again and turned to her my imagined picture would coincide exactly with her real appearance.

At that moment she stepped forwards. Instinctively I opened my eyes—and felt disappointment. I had guessed quite wrong. Everything was different from my imaginary idea, and indeed was distressingly at odds with it. She wore not a green but a white dress, she was not slim but voluptuous and broad-hipped, the beauty spot I had dreamt up was nowhere to be seen on her plump cheek, her hair under her helmet-shaped hat was pale red, not black. None of my details fitted her real appearance; however, this woman was beautiful, challengingly beautiful, although with my psychological vanity injured, foolishly overweening as it was, I would not acknowledge her beauty. I looked up at her almost with hostility, but even in my resistance to it I felt the strong sensuous attraction emanating from this woman, the enticing, demanding, animal desirability in her firm yet softly plump opulence. Now she laughed aloud again, showing her strong white teeth, and I had to admit that this warm, sensuous laughter was in harmony with her voluptuous appearance; everything about her was vehement and challenging, the curve of her breasts, the way she thrust her chin out as she laughed, her keen glance, her curved nose, the hand pressing her parasol firmly to the ground. Here was the feminine element incarnate, a primeval power, deliberate, pervasive entice-ment, a beacon of lust made flesh. Beside her stood an elegant, rather colourless officer talking earnestly to her. She listened to him, smiled, laughed, contradicted him, but all this was only by the way, for at the same time her nostrils were quivering as her glance wandered here and there as if to light on everyone; she attracted attention, smiles, glances from every passing man, and from the whole male part of the crowd standing around her too. Her eyes moved all the time, sometimes searching the tiers of seats and suddenly, with joyful recognition, responding to someone's wave, turning now to right, now to left as she listened to the officer, smiling idly. But they had not yet rested on me, for I was outside her field of vision, hidden from her by her companion. I felt some annoyance and stood up—she did not see me. I came closer—now she looked up at the tiers of seats again. I stepped firmly up to her, raised my hat to her companion, and offered her my chair. She looked at me in surprise, a smiling light flickered in her eyes, and she curved her lips into a cajoling smile. But then she simply thanked me briefly and took the chair without sitting down. She merely leant her voluptuous arm, which was bare to the elbow, lightly on the back of the chair, employing this slight bending movement to show off her figure more visibly.

My vexation over my psychological failure was long forgotten; now I was intrigued by the game I was playing with this woman. I retreated slightly, moving to the side of the stand, where I could look at her freely but unobtrusively, leaning on my cane and trying to meet her eyes. She noticed, turned slightly towards my observation post, but in such a way that the movement seemed to be made quite by chance, did not avoid my glance and now and then answered it, but non-committally. Her eyes kept moving, touching on everything, never resting anywhere—was it I alone whose gaze she met with a dark smile, or did she give that smile to everyone? There was no telling, and that very uncertainty piqued me. At the moments when her own gaze fell on me like a flashing light it seemed full of promise, although she responded indiscriminately and with the same steely gleam of her pupils to every other glance that came her way, out of sheer flirtatious pleasure in the game, but without letting her apparent interest in her companion's conversation lapse for an instant. There was something dazzlingly audacious about that passionate display, which was either virtuoso dalliance or an outburst of overflowing sensuality. Involuntarily, I came a step closer: her cold audacity had transferred itself to me. I no longer gazed into her eyes but looked her up and down like a connoisseur, undressed her in my mind and felt her naked. She followed my glance without appearing insulted in any way, smiled at the loquacious officer with the corners of her mouth, but I noticed that her knowing smile was acknowledging my intentions. And now, when I looked at her small, delicate foot just peeping out from under the hem of her white dress, she checked it and smoothed her skirt down with a casual air. Next moment, as if by chance, she raised the same foot and placed it on the first rung of the chair I had offered her, so that through the open-work fabric of her dress I could see her stockings up to the knee. At the same time, the smile she gave her companion seemed to take on a touch of irony or malice. She was obviously playing with me as impersonally as I with her, and I was obliged, with some animosity, to admire the subtle technique of her bold conduct, for while she was offering me the sensuousness of her body in pretended secrecy, she appeared to be flattered by and immersing herself in her companion's whispered remarks at the same time, giving and taking in the game she was playing with both of us. In fact I felt vexed, for in other women I disliked this kind of cold, viciously calculating sensuality, feeling that it was incestuously related to the absence of feeling of which I was conscious in myself. Yet I was aroused, perhaps more in dislike than in desire. I boldly came closer and made a brutal assault on her with my eyes. My gestures clearly said, "I want you, you beautiful animal", and I must involuntarily have moved my lips, for she smiled with faint contempt, turning her head away from me, and draped her skirt over the foot she had just revealed. Next moment, however, those flashing black eyes were wandering here and there again. It was quite obvious that she was as cold as I myself and was a match for me, that we were both playing coolly with a strange arousal that itself was only a pretence of ardour, though it was a pretty sight and amusing to play with on a dull day.

Suddenly the intent look left her face, her sparkling eyes clouded over, and a small line of annoyance appeared around her still smiling mouth. I followed the direction of her gaze; a small, stout gentleman, his garments rumpled, was steering a rapid course towards her, his face and brow, which he was nervously drying with his handkerchief, damp with agitation. His hat, which he had perched askew on his head in his hurry, revealed a large bald patch on one side (I could not help thinking that when he took the hat off there were sure to be large beads of sweat gathering on it, and I found him repulsive). His ringed hand held a whole bundle of betting slips. He was puffing and blowing excitedly, and paying no attention to his wife, addressed the officer at once in loud Hungarian. I immediately recognised him as an aficionado of the turf, some horse-dealer of the better kind for whom the sport was the only form of ecstasy he knew, a surrogate for sublimity. His wife must obviously have admonished him in some way (she was evidently irked, and disturbed in her elemental confidence by his presence), for he straightened his hat, apparently at her behest, then laughed jovially and clapped her on the shoulder with good-natured affection. She angrily raised her eyebrows, repelled by this marital familiarity, which embarrassed her in the officer's presence and perhaps even more in mine. He seemed to be apologising, said a few more words in Hungarian to the officer, who replied with an agreeable smile, and then took her arm, tenderly and a little deferentially. I felt that she was ashamed of his intimacy in front of us, and with mingled feelings of derision and disgust I relished her humiliation. But she was soon in control of herself again, and as she pressed softly against his arm she gave me an ironic sideways glance, as if to say, "There, you see, he has me and you don't." I felt both anger and distaste. I really wanted to turn my back on her and walk away, showing her that I was no longer interested in the wife of such a vulgar, fat fellow. But the attraction was too strong. I stayed.

At that moment the shrill starting signal was heard, and all of a sudden it was as if the whole chattering, dull, sluggish crowd had been shaken into life. Once again, and from all directions, it surged forwards to the barrier in wild turmoil. It cost me some effort not to be carried along with it, for I wanted to stay near her in all this confusion; there might be an opportunity for a meaningful glance, for a touch, a chance for me to take some spontaneous liberty, though just what I didn't yet know, so I doggedly made my way towards her through the hurrying people. At that very moment the stout husband was forging his own path through the crowd, obviously to get a good place in the stand, and so it was that the pair of us, each impelled by a different passion, collided with each other so violently that his hat flew to the ground, and the betting slips loosely tucked into the hatband were scattered wide, drifting like red, blue, yellow and white butterflies. He stared at me for a moment. I was about to offer an automatic apology, but some kind of perverse ill will sealed my lips, and instead I looked coolly at him with a slight but bold, offensive touch of provocation. As red-hot anger rose in him but then timidly gave way, his glance flickered uncertainly for a moment and then cravenly sank before mine. With unforgettable, almost touching anxiety he looked me in the eye for just a second, then turned away, suddenly seemed to remember his betting slips, and bent to pick them and his hat up from the ground. His wife, who had let go of his arm, flashed me a glance of unconcealed fury, her face flushed with agitation, and I saw with a kind of erotic pleasure that she would have liked to strike me. But I stood there very cool and nonchalant, watched the fat husband, smiling and offering no help as he bent, puffing and panting, and crawled around at my feet picking up his betting slips. When he bent over his collar stood away from him like the ruffled feathers of a chicken, a broad roll of fat was visible at the nape of his red neck and he gasped asthmatically at every movement he made. Seeing him panting like that, I involuntarily entertained an improper and distasteful idea: I imagined him alone with his wife engaged in conjugal relations, and this thought put me in such high spirits that I smiled in her face at the sight of the anger she could barely rein in. There she stood, impatient and pale again now, scarcely able to control herself—at last I had wrested a real, genuine feeling from her: hatred, unbridled rage! I would have liked to prolong this distressing scene to infinity; I watched with cold relish as he struggled to gather his betting slips together one by one. Some kind of devil of amusement was in my throat, chuckling continuously and trying to burst into laughter; I would have liked to laugh heartily at that soft, scrabbling mass of flesh, or to tickle him up a little with my cane. I really couldn't remember ever before being so possessed by an evil demon as I was in that delightful moment of triumph at his bold wife's humiliation. Now the unfortunate man finally seemed to have picked up all his slips except one, a blue betting slip which had fallen a little further away and was lying on the ground just in front of me. He turned, puffing and panting, looked round with his short-sighted eyes—his pince-nez had slipped to the end of his damp, sweating nose—and my sense of mischief used that second to prolong his ridiculous search. Obeying the boyish high spirits that had seized on me without my own volition, I quickly moved my foot forwards and placed the sole of my shoe on the slip, so that for all his efforts he couldn't find it as long as it pleased me to let him go on looking. And he did go on looking for it, on and on, now and then counting the coloured slips of card again and again, panting as he did so; it was obvious that he knew one of them—mine!—was still missing, and he was about to start searching again in the middle of the noisy crowd when his wife, deliberately avoiding my scornful gaze and with a grim expression on her face, could no longer restrain her angry impatience. "Lajos!" she suddenly and imperiously called, and he started like a horse hearing the sound of the trumpet, cast one last searching glance at the ground—I felt as if the slip hidden under the sole of my shoe were tickling me, and could hardly conceal an urge to laugh—and then turned obediently to his wife, who led him away from me with a certain ostentatious haste and into the tumultuous crowd, where excitement was rising higher and higher.

I stayed behind, feeling no wish to follow the two of them. The episode was over as far as I was concerned, the sense of erotic tension had resolved into mirth, doing me good. I was no longer aroused, nothing was left but a sense of sound satisfaction after following my sudden mischievous impulse, a jaunty, almost boisterous complacency at the thought of the trick I had played. Ahead of me the crowd was thronging close together, waves of excitement were beginning to rise, surging up to the barrier in a single black, murky mass, but I did not watch, it bored me now. I thought of walking over to the Krieau or going home. But as soon as I instinctively raised my foot to step forwards I noticed the blue betting slip lying forgotten on the ground. I picked it up and held it idly between my fingers, not sure what to do with the thing. I vaguely thought of returning it to 'Lajos', which might serve as an excellent excuse to be introduced to his wife, but I realised that she no longer interested me, that the fleeting ardour this adventure had made me feel had long since cooled into my old apathy. I wanted no more of Lajos's wife than that single combative, challenging exchange of glances—I found the fat man too unappetising to wish to share anything physical with him. I had experienced a tingling of the nerves, but now felt only mild curiosity and a pleasant sense of relaxation.

There was the chair, abandoned and alone. I made myself comfortable on it and lit a cigarette. Ahead of me the breakers of excitement were rising again, but I did not even listen; repetition held no charms for me. I watched the pale smoke rising and thought of the Merano golf course promenade where I had sat two months ago, looking down at the spray of the waterfall. It was just like this: at Merano too you heard a strongly swelling roar that was neither hot nor cold, meaningless sound rising in the silent blue landscape. But now impassioned enthusiasm for the race had reached its climax again; once more parasols, hats, handkerchiefs and loud cries were flying like sea-spray above the black breakers of the throng, once again the voices were swirling together, once again a shout—but of a different kind—issued from the crowd's gigantic mouth. I heard a name called out a thousand, ten thousand times, exultantly, piercing, ecstatically, frantically. "*Cressy! Cressy! Cressy!*" And once again the sound was suddenly cut short, as if it were a taut string breaking (ah, how repetition makes even passion monotonous!). The music began to play, the crowd dispersed. Boards were raised aloft showing the numbers of the winning horses. I looked at them, without conscious intent. The first number was a distinct *SEVEN*. Automatically, I glanced at the blue slip I was still holding and had forgotten. It said *SEVEN* too. I couldn't help laughing. The slip had won; friend Lajos had placed a lucky bet. So my mischief had actually tricked the fat husband out of money: all of a sudden my exuberant mood had returned, and I felt interested to know how much my jealous intervention had cost him. I looked at the piece of blue card more closely for the first time: it was a twenty-crown bet, and Lajos had put it on the horse to win. That could amount to a considerable sum. Without thinking more about it, merely obeying my itch of curiosity, I let myself be carried along with the hurrying crowd to the tote windows. I was pushed into some kind of queue, put down the betting slip, and next moment two busy, bony hands—I couldn't see the face that went with them behind the window—were counting out nine twenty-crown notes on the marble slab in front of me.

At that moment, when the money, real money in blue banknotes was paid out to me, the laughter died in my throat. I immediately felt an unpleasant sensation. Involuntarily, I withdrew my hands so as not to touch the money which was not mine. I would have liked to leave the blue notes lying on the marble slab, but people were pushing forwards behind me, impatient to cash their winnings. So there was nothing I could do but, feeling very awkward, take the notes with reluctant fingers: the banknotes burned like blue fire, and I unconsciously held my spread fingers well away from me, as if the hand that had taken them was not my own any more than the money was. I immediately saw all the difficulty of the situation. Without my own volition, the joke had turned to something that a decent man, a gentleman, an officer in the reserve ought not to have done, and I hesitated to call it by its true name even to myself. For this was not money that had been withheld; it had been obtained by cunning. It was stolen money.

Voices hummed and buzzed around me, people came thronging up on their way to and from the tote windows. I still stood there motionless, my spread hand held away from me. What was I to do? I thought first of the most natural solution: to find the real winner, apologise, and give him back the money. But that wouldn't do, least of all in front of that officer. After all, I was a lieutenant in the reserve, and such a confession would have cost me my commission at once, for even if I had found the betting slip by chance, cashing it in was a dishonest act. I also thought of obeying the instinct of my twitching fingers, crumpling up the notes and throwing them away, although that would also be too easily visible in the middle of such a crowd of people, and would look suspicious. However, I didn't want to keep the money that was not mine on me for a moment, let alone put it in my wallet and give it to someone later: the sense of cleanliness instilled into me from childhood, like the habit of wearing clean underclothes, was revolted by any contact, however fleeting, with those banknotes. I must get rid of the money, I thought feverishly, I must get rid of it somewhere, anywhere! I instinctively looked around me, at a loss, wondering if I could see a hiding place anywhere, a chance of concealing it unobserved; I noticed that people were beginning to flock to the tote windows again, but this time with banknotes in their hands. The idea was my salvation. I would throw the money back to the malicious chance that had given it to me, back into the all-consuming maw that was now greedily swallowing up new bets in notes and silver—yes, that was the thing to do, that was the way to free myself of it.

I impetuously hurried, indeed ran as I pushed my way in among the crowd. But by the time I realised that I didn't know the name of any horse on which to bet there were only two men in front of me, and the first was already at the tote window. I listened avidly to the conversation around me. "Are you backing Ravachol?" one man asked. "Yes, of course, Ravachol," his companion replied. "Don't you think Teddy has a chance?" "Teddy? Not a hope. He failed miserably in his maiden race. All show, no substance."

I drank in these words. So Teddy was a bad horse. Teddy was sure to lose. I immediately decided to bet on him. I pushed the money over, put it on Teddy, the horse I had only just heard of, to win, and a hand gave me the betting slips. All of a sudden I now had nine pieces of card in my fingers instead of just the one, this time red and white. I still felt awkward, but at least the slips didn't burn in so fiery, so humiliating a way as the crumpled banknotes.

I felt light at heart again, almost carefree: the money was gone now, the unpleasant part of the adventure was over, it had begun as a joke and now it was all a joke again. I leant back at ease in my chair, lit a cigarette and blew the smoke into the air at my leisure. But I did not stay there long; I rose, walked around, sat down again. How odd: my sense of pleasant reverie was gone. Some kind of nervousness was tingling in my limbs. At first I thought it was discomfort at the idea that I might meet Lajos and his wife in the crowd of people walking by, but how could they guess that these new betting slips were really theirs? Nor did the restlessness of the crowd disturb me; on the contrary, I watched closely to see when they would begin pressing forwards again, indeed I caught myself getting to my feet again and again to look for the flag that would be hoisted at the beginning of the race. So that was it—impatience, a leaping inward fever of expectation as I wished the race would begin soon and the tiresome affair be over for good.

A boy ran past with a racing paper. I stopped him, bought the programme of today's meeting, and began searching the text and the tips, written in a strange and incomprehensible jargon, until I finally found Teddy, the names of his jockey and the owner of the racing stables, and the information that his colours were red and white. But why was I so interested? Annoyed, I crumpled up the newspaper and tossed it away, stood up, sat down again. I suddenly felt hot, I had to pass my handkerchief over my damp brow, my collar felt tight. And still the race did not begin.

At last the bell rang, people came surging up, and at that moment I felt, to my horror, that the ringing of that bell, like an alarm clock, had woken me from some kind of sleep. I jumped up from the chair so abruptly that it fell over, and eagerly hurried—no, ran forwards into the crowd, betting slips held firmly between my fingers, as if consumed by a frantic fear of arriving too late, of missing something very important. I reached the barrier at the front of the stand by forcibly pushing people aside, and ruthlessly seized a chair on which a lady was about to sit down. Her glance of astonishment showed me just how wild and discourteous my conduct was—she was a lady I knew well, Countess R, and I saw her brows raised in anger—but out of shame and defiance I coldly ignored her and climbed up on the chair to get a good view of the field.

Somewhere in the distance, at the start, several horses were standing close together on the turf, kept in line with difficulty by small jockeys who looked like brightly clad versions of Punchinello. I immediately looked for my horse's colours among them, but my eyes were unpractised, and everything was swimming before them in such a hot, strange blur that I couldn't make out the red-and-white figure among all the other splashes of colour. At that moment the bell rang for the second time, and the horses shot off down the green racetrack like six coloured arrows flying from a bow. It would surely have been a fine sight to watch calmly, purely from an aesthetic point of view, as the slender animals stretched their legs in the gallop, hardly touching the ground as they skimmed the turf, but I felt none of that, I was making desperate attempts to pick out my horse, my jockey, and cursing myself for not bringing a pair of field glasses with me. Lean forwards and crane my neck as I might, I saw nothing but four or five insects tangled together in a blurred, flying knot; however, at last I saw its shape begin to change as the small group reached the bend and strung out into a wedge shape, leaders came to the front while some of the other horses were already falling away at the back. It was a close race: three or four horses galloping full speed stuck together like coloured strips of paper, now one and now another getting its nose ahead. I instinctively stretched and tensed my whole body as if my imitative, springy and impassioned movement could increase their speed and carry them along.

The excitement was rising around me. Some of the more knowledgeable racegoers must have recognised the colours as the horses came round the bend, for names were now flying up like bright rockets from the murky tumult below. A man with his hands raised in a frenzy was standing beside me, and as one horse got its head forwards he stamped his feet and yelled in an ear-splitting tone of triumph, "Ravachol! Ravachol!" I saw that the jockey riding this horse did indeed wear blue, and I felt furious that my horse wasn't winning. I found the piercing cries of "Ravachol! Ravachol!" from the idiot beside me more and more intolerable, I felt cold fury, I would have liked to slam my fist into the wide, black hole of his shouting mouth. I quivered with rage, I was in a fever, and felt I might do something senseless at any moment. But here came another horse, sticking close behind the first. Perhaps it was Teddy, perhaps, perhaps—and that hope spurred my enthusiasm again. I really did think it was a red arm now rising above the saddle and bringing something down on the horse's crupper—it could be red, it must be, it must, it must! But why wasn't the fool of a jockey urging him on? The whip again! Go on, again! Now, now he was quite close to the first horse. Hardly anything between them now. Why should Ravachol win? Ravachol! No, not Ravachol! Not Ravachol! Teddy! Teddy! Come on, Teddy! Teddy!

Suddenly and violently, I caught myself up. What on earth was all this? Who was shouting like that? Who was yelling "Teddy! Teddy!" I was shouting the name! And in the midst of my impassioned outburst I felt afraid of myself. I wanted to stop, control myself, in the middle of my fever I felt a sudden shame. But I couldn't tear my eyes away, for the two horses were sticking very close to each other, and it must really be Teddy hanging on to Ravachol, the wretched horse Ravachol that I fervently hated, for others were now shouting louder around me, many voices in a piercing descant: "Teddy, Teddy!" The yells plunged me back into the frenzy from which I had emerged for one sober second. He should, he must win, and now, now a head did push forwards past the flying horse ridden by the other jockey, just by the span of a hand, and then another, and now—now you could see the neck—and then the shrill bell rang, and there was a great cry of jubilation, despair and fury. For a second the name I longed to hear filled the whole vault of the blue sky above. Then it died away, and somewhere music started playing.

Hot, drenched in sweat, my heart thudding, I got off the chair. I had to sit down for a moment, so confused had my excited enthusiasm left me. Ecstasy such as I had never known before flooded through me, a mindless joy at seeing chance bow to my challenge with such slavish obedience; I tried in vain to pretend to myself it was against my will that the horse had won, I had really wanted to lose the money. But I didn't believe it myself, and I already felt a terrible ache in my limbs urging me, as if magically, to be off somewhere, and I knew where: I wanted to see my triumph, feel it, hold it, money, a great deal of money, I wanted to feel the crisp blue notes in my fingers and sense that tingling of my nerves. A strange and pernicious lust had come over me, and no sense of shame now stood in its way. As soon as I stood up I was hurrying, running to the tote window, I pushed brusquely in among the people waiting in the queue, using my elbows, I impatiently pushed others aside just to see the money, the money itself. "Oaf!" muttered someone whom I had jostled behind me; I heard him, but I had no intention of picking a quarrel. I was shaking with a strange, pathological impatience. At last my turn came, my hands greedily seized a blue bundle of banknotes. I counted them, both trembling and delighted. I had won six hundred and forty crowns.

I clutched them avidly. My first thought was to go on betting, to win more, much more. What had I done with my racing paper? Oh yes, I'd thrown it away in all the excitement. I looked round to see where I could buy another. Then, to my inexpressible dismay, I saw that the people around me were suddenly dispersing, making for the exit, the tote windows were closing, the fluttering flag came down. The meeting was over. That had been the last race. I stood there frozen for a moment. Then anger flared in me as if I had suffered some injustice. I couldn't reconcile myself to the fact that it was all over, not now that all my nerves were tense and quivering, the blood was coursing through my veins, hot as I hadn't felt it for years. But it was no use feeding hope artificially with the deceptive idea that I might have been mistaken, that was just wishful thinking, for the motley crowd was flowing away faster and faster, and the well-trodden turf already showed green among the few people still left. I gradually felt it ridiculous to be lingering here in a state of tension, so I took my hat—I had obviously left my cane at the tote turnstile in my excitement—and went towards the exit. A servant with cap obsequiously raised hurried to meet me, I told him the number of my cab, he shouted it across the open space through his cupped hands, and soon the horses came trotting smartly up. I told the cabby to drive slowly down the main avenue. For now that the excitement was beginning to fade, leaving a pleasurable sensation behind, I felt an almost prurient desire to go over the whole scene again in my thoughts.

At that moment another carriage drove past; I instinctively looked at it, only to look away again very deliberately. It was the woman and her stout husband. They had not noticed me, but I felt a horrible choking sensation, as if I had been caught in the guilty act. I could almost have told the cabby to urge the horses on, just to get away from them quickly.

The cab moved smoothly along on its rubber tyres among all the other carriages, swaying along with their brightly clad cargoes of women like boats full of flowers passing the green banks of the chestnut-lined avenue. The air was mild and sweet, the first cool evening breeze was already wafting faint perfume through the dust. But my pleasant mood of reverie refused to return; the meeting with the man I had swindled had struck me a painful blow. In my overheated and impassioned state it suddenly went through me like a draught of cold air blowing through a crack. I now thought through the whole scene again soberly, and could not understand myself: for no good reason I, a gentleman, a member of fashionable society, an officer in the reserve, highly esteemed in general, had taken money which I did not need, had put it in my wallet, had even done so with a greedy and lustful pleasure that rendered any excuse invalid. An hour ago I had been a man of upright and blameless character; now I had stolen. I was a thief. And as if to frighten myself I spoke my condemnation half-aloud under my breath as the cab gently trotted on, the words unconsciously falling into the rhythm of the horses' hooves: "Thief! Thief! Thief! Thief!"

But strange to say—oh, how am I to describe what happened now? It is so inexplicable, so very odd, and yet I know that I am not deceiving myself in retrospect. I am aware of every second's feelings in those moments, every oscillation of my mind, with a supernatural clarity, more clearly than almost any other experience in my thirty-six years, yet I hardly dare reveal that absurd chain of events, those baffling mood swings, and I really don't know whether any writer or psychologist could describe them logically at all. I can only set them down in order, faithfully reflecting the way they unexpectedly flared up within me. Well, so I was saying to myself, "Thief, thief, thief." Then came a very strange moment, as it were an empty one, a moment when nothing happened, when I was only—oh, how difficult it is to express this!—when I was only listening, listening to my inner voice. I had summoned myself before the court, I had accused myself, and now it was for the plaintiff to answer the judge. So I listened—and nothing happened. The whiplash of that word 'thief', which I had expected to terrify me and then fill me with inexpressible shame and remorse, had no effect. I waited patiently for several minutes, I then bent, as it were, yet closer to myself—for I could feel something moving beneath that defiant silence—and listened with feverish expectation for the echo that did not come, for the cry of disgust, horror, and despair that must follow my self-accusation. And still nothing happened. There was no answer. I said the word "Thief" to myself again, I said it out loud, "Thief", to rouse my numbed conscience at last, hard of hearing as it was. Again there was no answer. And sud-denly—in a bright lightning flash of awareness, as if a match had suddenly been struck and held above the twilit depths—I realised that I only wanted to feel shame, I was not really ashamed, that down in those depths I was in some mysterious way proud of my foolish action, even pleased with it.

How was that possible? I resisted this unexpected revelation, for now I really did feel afraid of myself, but it broke over me with too strong and impetuous a force. No, it was not shame seething in my blood with such warmth, not indignation or self-disgust—it was joy, intoxicated joy blazing up in me, sparkling with bright, darting, exuberant flames, for I felt that in those moments I had been truly alive for the first time in many years, that my feelings had only been numb and were not yet dead, that somewhere under the arid surface of my indifference the hot springs of passion still mysteriously flowed, and now, touched by the magic wand of chance, had leapt high, reaching my heart. In me too, in me too, part as I was of the living, breathing universe, there still glowed the mysterious volcanic core of all earthly things, a volcano that sometimes erupts in whirling spasms of desire. I too lived, I was alive, I was a human being with hot, pernicious lusts. The storm of passion had flung wide a door, depths had opened up in me, and I was staring down at the unknown in myself with vertiginous joy. It frightened and at the same time delighted me. And slowly—as the carriage wheeled my dreaming body easily along through the world of bourgeois society—I climbed down, step by step, into the depths of my own humanity, inexpressibly alone in my silent progress, with nothing above me but the bright torch of my suddenly rekindled awareness. And as a thousand people surged around me, laughing and talking, I sought for my lost self in myself, I felt for past years in the magical process of contemplation. Things entirely lost suddenly emerged from the dusty, blank mirrors of my life. I remembered once, as a schoolboy, stealing a penknife from a classmate and then watching, with just the same demonic glee, as he looked for it everywhere, asking everyone if they had seen it, going to great pains to find it; I suddenly understood the mysteriously stormy nature of many sexual encounters, I realised that my passions had been only atrophied, only crushed by social delusions, by the lordly ideal of the perfect gentleman—but that in me too, although deep, deep down in clogged pipes and wellsprings, the hot streams of life flowed as they flowed in everyone else. I had always lived without daring to live to the full, I had restrained myself and hidden from myself, but now a concentrated force had broken out, I was overwhelmed by rich and inexpressibly powerful life. And now I knew that I still valued it; I knew it with the blissful emotion of a woman who feels her child move within her for the first time. I felt—how else can I put it?—real, true, genuine life burgeon within me, I felt—and I am almost ashamed to write this—I felt myself, desiccated as I was, suddenly flowering again, I felt red blood coursing restlessly through my veins, feelings gently unfolded in the warmth, and I matured into an unknown fruit which might be sweet or bitter. The miracle of Tannhäuser had come to me in the bright light of a racecourse, among the buzz of thousands of people enjoying their leisure; I had begun to feel again, the dry staff was putting out green leaves and buds.

A gentleman waved to me from a passing carriage and called my name—obviously I had failed to notice his first greeting. I gave an abrupt start, angry to be disturbed in the sweet flow of the stream pouring forth within me, in the deepest dream I had ever known. But a glance at the man hailing me brought me out of myself; it was my friend Alfons, a dear schoolmate of mine and now a public prosecutor. Suddenly a thought ran through me: now, for the first time, this man who greets you like a brother has power over you; you will be his quarry as soon as he is aware of your crime. If he knew about you and what you have done, he would be bound to snatch you out of this carriage, take you away from your whole comfortable bourgeois life, and thrust you down for three to five years into a dismal world behind barred windows, amidst the dregs of human life, other thieves driven to their dirty cells only by the lash of destitution. But it was only for a moment that cold fear grasped the wrist of my trembling hand, only for a moment did it halt my heartbeat—then this idea too turned to warmth of feeling, to a fantastic, audacious pride that now scrutinised everyone else around me with confidence, almost with contempt. How your sweet, friendly smiles, I thought, how the smiles with which you all greet me as one of yourselves would freeze on your lips if you guessed what I really am! You would wipe away my own greeting with a scornful, angry hand, as if it were a splash of excrement. But before you reject me I have already rejected you; this afternoon I broke out of your chilly, skeletal world, where I was a cogwheel performing its silent function in the great machine that coldly drives its pistons, circling vainly around itself—I have fallen to depths that I do not know, but I was more alive in that one hour than in all the frozen years I spent among you. I am not one of you any more, no, I am outside you somewhere, on some height or in some depth, but never to tread the flat plain of your bourgeois comfort again. For the first time I have felt all mankind's desire for good and evil, but you will never know where I have been, you will never recognise me: what do any of you know about my secret?

How could I express what I felt in that moment as I, an elegantly clad gentleman, drove past the rows of carriages greeting acquaintances and returning greetings, my face impassive? For while my larva, the outward man of the past, still saw and recognised faces, so delirious a music was playing inside me that I had to control myself to keep from shouting something of that raging tumult aloud. I was so full of emotion that its inner swell hurt me physically, like a man choking I had to press my hand hard to the place on my chest beneath which my heart was painfully seething. But pain, desire, alarm, horror or regret—I felt none of these separately and apart from the others, they were all merged and I felt only that I was alive, that I was breathing and feeling. And this simplest, most primeval of feelings, one I had not known for years, intoxicated me. I have never felt myself as ecstatically alive for even a second of my thirty-six years as I did in the airy lightness of that hour.

With a slight jolt, the cab stopped: the driver had reined in his horses, turned on the box and asked if he should drive me home. I came back to myself, feeling dizzy, looked at the avenue, and was dismayed to see how long I had been dreaming, how far my delirium had spread out over the hours. It was growing dark, a soft wind stirred the tops of the trees, the chestnut blossom was beginning to waft its evening perfume through the cool air. And behind the treetops a veiled glimpse of the moon already shone silver. It was enough, it must be enough. But I would not go home yet, not back to my usual world! I paid the cabby. As I took out my wallet and counted the banknotes, holding them in my fingers, something like a slight electric shock ran from my wrist to my fingertips. So there must be something of my old self left in me, the man who was ashamed. The dying conscience of a gentleman was still twitching, but my hand dipped cheerfully into the stolen money again, and in my joy I was generous with a tip. The driver thanked me so fervently that I had to smile, thinking: if only you knew! The horses began to move, the cab rolled away. I watched it go as you might look back from shipboard at a shore where you have been happy.

For a moment I stood dreamy and undecided in the midst of the murmuring, laughing crowd, with music drifting above it. It was about seven o'clock, and I instinctively turned towards the Sachergarten, where I usually ate with companions after going to the Prater. The cabby had probably set me down here on purpose. But no sooner did I touch the handle of the door in the fence of that superior garden restaurant than I felt a scruple: no, I still did not want to go back to my own world yet, I didn't want to let the wonderful fermentation so mysteriously filling me disperse in the flow of casual conversation, I didn't want to detach myself from the sparkling magic of the adventure in which I had been involved for hours.

The confused music echoed faintly somewhere, and I instinctively went that way, for everything tempted me today. I felt it delightful to give myself up entirely to chance, and there was something extraordinarily intriguing in being aimlessly adrift in this gently moving crowd of people. My blood was seething in this thick, swirling, hot and human mass: I was suddenly on the alert, all my senses stimulated and intensified by that acrid, smoky aroma of human breath, dust, sweat and tobacco. All that even yesterday used to repel me because it seemed vulgar, common, plebeian, all that the elegant gentleman in me had haughtily avoided for a lifetime now magically attracted my new responses as if, for the first time, I felt some relationship in myself with what was animal, instinctive, common. Here among the dregs of the city, mixing with soldiers, servant girls, ruffians, I felt at ease in a way I could not understand at all; I almost greedily drank in the acridity of the air, I found the pushing and shoving of the crowd gathered around me pleasant, and with delighted curiosity I waited to see where this hour would take me, devoid as I was of any will of my own. The cymbals crashed and the brass band blared closer now, the mechanical orchestrions thumped out staccato polkas and boisterous waltzes with insistent monotony, and now and then I heard dull thuds from the sideshows, ripples of laughter, drunken shouting. Now I saw the carousels of my childhood going round and round among the trees, with lights crazily flashing. I stood in the middle of the square, letting all the tumult break over me, filling my eyes and ears: these cascades of sound, the infernal confusion of it all did me good, for there was something in this hurly-burly that stilled my own inner torrent of feeling. I watched the servant girls, skirts flying, getting themselves pushed up in the air on the swings with loud cries of glee that might have issued from their sexual orifices, I saw butchers' boys laughing as they brought heavy hammers down on the try-your-strength machine, barkers with hoarse voices and ape-like gestures cried their wares above the noise of the orchestrions, and all this whirling activity mingled with the thousand sounds and constant movement of the crowd, which was inebriated, as if it had imbibed cheap spirits, on the music of the brass band, the flickering of the light, and their own warm pleasure in company. Now that I myself had been awakened, I suddenly felt other people's lives, I felt the heated arousal of the city as, hot and pent-up, it poured out with its millions in the few leisure hours of a Sunday, as its own fullness spurred it on to sultry, animal, yet somehow healthy and instinctive enjoyment. And gradually, feeling people rub against me, feeling the constant touch of their hot bodies passionately pressing close, I sensed their warm arousal passing into me too: my nerves, stimulated by the sharp aroma, tensed and reached out of me, my senses played deliriously with the roar of the crowd and felt that vague stupor that inevitably mingles with all strong sensual gratification. For the first time in years, perhaps for the first time in my life, I felt the crowd, I felt human beings as a force from which lust passed into my own once separate being; some dam had been burst, and what was in my veins passed out into this world, flowed rhythmically back, and I felt a new desire, to break down that last barrier between me and them, a passionate longing to copulate with this hot, strange press of humanity. With male lust I longed to plunge into the gushing vulva of that hot, giant body; with female lust I was open to every touch, every cry, every allurement, every embrace—and now I knew that love was in me, and a need for love such as I had not felt since my twilight boyhood days. Oh, to plunge in, into the living entity, to be linked somehow to the convulsive, laughing, breathing passion of others, to stream on, to pour my fluids into their veins; to become a small and nameless part of the hurly-burly, something infused into the dirt of the world, a creature quivering with lust, sparkling in the slough with those myriads of beings—oh, to plunge into that fullness, down into the circling ripples, shot like an arrow from the bow of my own tension into the unknown, into some heaven of collective experience.

I know now that I was drunk at the time. Everything was roaring
in my blood at once, the ringing bells on the carousel, the high lusty
laughter of the women as the men swung them up in the air, the
chaotic music, the whirling skirts. Every single sound fell sharply
into me and then flickered up again, red and quivering, past my
temples, I felt every touch, every glance with fantastically stimulated
nerves (it was rather like sea-sickness), yet it came all together in
a delirious whole. I cannot possibly explain my complex state in
words, it can perhaps best be done by means of a comparison if
I say I was brimming over with sound, noise, feeling, overheated
like a machine operating with all its wheels racing to escape the
monstrous pressure that must surely burst the boiler of my chest
any moment. My fingertips twitched, my temples thudded, my
heated blood pressed in my throat, surged in my temples—from
a state of half-hearted apathy lasting many years I had suddenly
plunged into a fever that consumed me. I felt that I must open up,
come out of myself with a word, with a glance, unburden myself,
flow out of myself, give my inner self away, bring myself down to
the common level, be resolved—save myself somehow from the
hard barrier of silence dividing me from the warm, flowing, living
element. I had not spoken for hours, had pressed no one's hand,
felt no one's glance rest on me, questioning and sympathetic, and
now, under the pressure of events, this excitement was building
up against the dam of silence. Never, never had I so strongly felt
a need for communication, for another human being than now,
when I was in the middle of a surging throng of thousands and
tens of thousands, warmth and words washing around me, yet
cut off from the circulating blood of that abundance. I was like a
man dying of thirst out at sea. And at the same time, this torment
increasing with every glance, I saw strangers meeting at every
moment to right and left, touching lightly, coming together and
parting in play like little balls of quicksilver. Envy came over me
when I saw young men addressing strange girls as they passed by,

taking their arms after the first word, seeing people find each other and join forces: a word exchanged beside the carousel, a glance as they brushed past each other was enough, and strangeness melted away in conversation, which might be broken off again after a few minutes, but still it was a link, a union, communication, and all my nerves burned for it now. But practised as I was in social intercourse, a popular purveyor of small talk and confident in all the social forms, I was now afraid, ashamed to address one of these broad-hipped servant girls for fear that she might laugh at me. Indeed, I cast my eyes down when someone looked at me by chance, yet inside I was dying of desire for a word. What I wanted from these people was not clear even to myself, but I could no longer endure to be alone and consumed by my fever. However, they all looked past me, every glance moved away from me, no one wanted to be with me. Once a lad of about twelve in ragged clothes did come near me, his eyes bright in the reflected lights as he stared longingly at the wooden horses going up and down. His narrow mouth was open as if with thirst; he obviously had no money left for a ride, and was simply enjoying the screams and laughter of others. I made my way up to him and asked—though why did my voice tremble and break, ending on a high note?—I asked: "Wouldn't you like a ride?" He looked up, took fright—why? why?—turned bright red and ran away without a word. Not even a barefoot child would let me give him pleasure; I felt there must be something terribly strange about me that meant I could never mingle with anyone, but was separate from the dense mass, floating like a drop of oil on moving water.

However, I did not give in; I could no longer be alone. My feet were burning in my dusty patent leather shoes, my throat was sore from the turbulent air. I looked round me: small islands of green stood to right and left among the flowing human crowds, taverns with red tablecloths and bare wooden benches where ordinary citizens sat with their glasses of beer and Sunday cigarettes. The sight was enticing: strangers could sit together here and fall into conversation, there was a little peace here among the wild frenzy. I went into one such tavern, looked round the tables until I found one where a family was sitting: a stout, sturdy artisan with his wife, two cheerful daughters and a little boy. They were nodding their heads together, joking with each other, and their happy, carefree glances did me good. I greeted them civilly, moved to a chair and asked if I might sit down. Their laughter stopped at once, for a moment they were silent as if each was waiting for another to give consent, and then the woman, in tones almost of dismay, said, "Oh yes, certainly, do." I sat down and then felt that in doing so I had spoilt their carefree mood, for an uncomfortable silence immediately fell around the table. Without daring to take my eyes off the red check tablecloth where salt and pepper had been untidily spilt, I felt that they were all watching me uneasily, and at once—but too late!—it struck me that I was too elegant for this servants' tavern in my race-going suit, my top hat from Paris and the pearl pin in my dove-grey tie, that my elegance, the aura of luxury about me at once enveloped me in an invisible layer of hostility and confusion. The silence of these five people made me sink my head lower and lower to look at the table, grimly, desperately counting the red squares on the cloth again and again, kept where I was by the shame of suddenly standing up again, yet too cowardly to raise my tormented glance. It was a relief when the waiter finally came and put the heavy beer glass down in front of me. Then I could at last move a hand and glance timidly over the rim of the glass as I drank: sure enough, all five were watching me, not as if they disliked me but in silent embarrassment. They recognised an intruder into the musty atmosphere of their world, with the naive instinct of their class they felt that I wanted something here, was looking for something that did not belong in my own environment, that I was brought here not by love or liking, not by the simple pleasure of a waltz, a beer, a wish to sit quietly in a tavern on a Sunday, but by some kind of desire which they did not understand and which they distrusted, just as the boy by the carousel had distrusted my offer, just as the thousands of others out there in the throng avoided my elegance and sophistication with unconscious hostility. Yet I felt that if I could find something careless, easy, heartfelt, truly human to say, the father or mother would respond to me, the daughters would smile back, flattered, I could go to a shooting range with the boy and play childish games with him. Within five, ten minutes I would be released from myself, immersed in the carefree atmosphere of simple conversation, of readily granted, even gratified familiarity—but I could not think of that simple remark, that first step in the conversation. A false, foolish, but overpowering shame stuck in my throat, and I sat with my eyes downcast like a criminal at the table with these simple folk, immersed in the torment of feeling that my grim presence had spoilt the last hour of their Sunday. And as I doggedly sat there, I did penance for all the years of haughty indifference when I had passed thousands and thousands of such tables and millions and millions of my fellow men without a glance, thinking only of ingratiating myself or succeeding in the narrow circles of elegant society, and I felt that the direct way to reach these people and talk to them easily, now that I was cast out and wanted contact in my hour of need, was barred to me on the inside.

So I sat, once a free man, now painfully inward-looking, still counting the red squares on the tablecloth until at last the waiter came by. I called him over, paid, left my almost untouched glass of beer and said a civil good evening. They thanked me in tones of friendly surprise; I knew, without turning round, that as soon as my back was turned they would resume their lively cheerfulness, and the warm circle of their conversation would close in as soon as I, the foreign body, had been thrust out of it.

Once again, but now more greedily, fervently and desperately, I threw myself back into the human whirlpool. The crowd had thinned out under the black trees that merged with the sky, there was not so dense and restless a torrent of people in the circle of light around the carousel, only shadowy forms scurrying around on the outskirts of the square. And the deep roar of the crowd, a noise like breathing in desire, was separating into many little sounds, always ringing out when the music somewhere grew strong and frenzied, as if to snatch back the people who were leaving. Faces of another kind emerged now: the children with their balloons and paper confetti had gone home, and so had families on a leisurely Sunday outing. Now there were loud-mouthed drunks about; shabby characters with a sauntering yet purposeful gait came out of side alleys. During the hour when I had sat transfixed at the strangers' table, this curious world had descended to a lower plane. But in itself this phosphorescent atmosphere of audacity and danger somehow pleased me more than the earlier Sunday respectability. The instinct that had been aroused in me scented a similarly intent desire; I felt myself somehow reflected in the sauntering of these dubious figures, these social outcasts who were also roaming here with restless expectation in search of an adventure, of sudden excitement, and I envied even these ragged fellows the way they roamed so freely and openly, for I was standing beside the wooden post of a carousel and breathing with difficulty, impatient to thrust the pressure of silence and the pain of my isolation away from me and yet incapable of a movement, of a cry, of a word. I just stood there staring at the square that was illuminated by the flickering reflection of the circling lights, looking out from my island of light into the darkness, glancing with foolish hope at any human being who, attracted by the bright light, turned my way for a moment. But all eyes moved coldly away from me. No one wanted me, no one would release me.

I know it would be mad to try to describe or actually explain to anyone how I, a cultured and elegant man, a figure in high society, rich, independent, acquainted with the most distinguished figures of a city with a population of millions, spent a whole hour that night standing by the post of a tunelessly squeaking, constantly rocking carousel in the Prater, hearing the same thumping polka, the same slowly dragging waltz circle past me with the same silly horses' heads of painted wood, twenty, forty, a hundred times, never moving from the spot out of dogged defiance, a magical feeling that I could force fate to do my will. I know I was acting senselessly, but there was a tension of feeling in that senseless persistence, a steely spasm of all the muscles such as people usually feel, perhaps, only at the moment of a fatal fall and just before death. My whole life, a life that had passed so emptily, had suddenly come flooding back and was building up in me like pent-up water behind a dam. And tormented as I was by my pointless delusion, my intention of staying, holding out there until some word or glance from a human being released me, yet I relished it too. In standing at the stake like that I did penance not so much for the theft as for the dull, lethargic vacuity of my earlier life, and I had sworn to myself not to leave until I received a sign that fate had let me go free.

And the more that hour progressed, the more night came on. Lights went out in one after another of the sideshows, and then there was always a kind of rising tide of darkness, swallowing up the light patch of that particular booth on the grass. The bright island where I stood was more and more isolated, and I looked at the time, trembling. Another quarter of an hour and then the dappled wooden horses would stand still, the red and green lights on their foolish foreheads would be switched off, the bloated orchestrion would stop thumping out its music. Then I would be wholly in the dark, all alone here in the faintly rustling night, entirely outcast, entirely desolate. I looked with increasing uneasiness at the now dimly lit square, where a couple on their way home now hurried past or a few drunken fellows staggered about only very occasionally: but over in the shadows hidden life quivered, restless and enticing. Sometimes there was a quiet whistle or a snap of the fingers when a couple of men passed by. And if the men, lured by the sound, moved into the darkness you would hear women's voices whispering in the shadows, and sometimes the wind blew scraps of shrill laughter my way. Gradually that hidden life emerged more boldly from the dark outskirts, coming closer to the circle of light in the illuminated square, only to plunge back into the shadows again as soon as the spiked helmet of a passing policeman shone in the reflected street light. But no sooner had he continued on his beat than the ghostly shadows returned, and now I could see their outlines clearly, so close did they venture to the light. They were the last dregs of that nocturnal world, the mud left behind now that the flowing torrent of humanity had subsided: a couple of whores, the poorest and most despised who have no bedstead of their own, sleep on a mattress by day and by night walk the streets restlessly, giving their worn, abused, thin bodies to any man here in the dark for a small silver coin, with the police after them, driven by hunger or by some ruffian, always roaming the darkness, hunters and hunted alike. They gradually emerged like hungry dogs, sniffing about near the lit square for something male, for a forgotten denizen of the night whose lust they could slake for a crown or so to buy a Glühwein in a café and keep the flickering candle-end of life going; it would soon enough be extinguished in a hospice or a prison. These girls were the refuse, the last liquid muck left after the sensuous tide of the Sunday crowd had ebbed away—it was with boundless horror that I now saw those hungry figures flitting out of the dark. But my horror was also mingled with a magical desire, for even in this dirtiest of mirrors I recognised something forgotten and now dimly felt again: here was the swamp-like world of the depths through which I had passed many years ago, and it now rose in my mind again with a phosphorescent glow. How strange was what this fantastic night offered me, suddenly revealing matters closed to me before, so that the darkest of my past, the most secret of my urges now lay open to me! Dim feelings revived from my forgotten boyhood years, when my timid glance was curiously attracted to such figures, yet felt afraid of them, a memory of the first time I followed one of them up a damp and creaking staircase to her bed—and suddenly, as if lightning had riven the night sky, I sharply saw every detail of that forgotten hour, the bad print of an oil painting over the bed, the good-luck charm she wore round her neck, I felt every fibre of that moment, the uncertain heat of it, the disgust, my first boyish pride. All that surged through my body at once. I was suddenly flooded with immeasurable clarity of vision, and—how can I say it, this infinite thing?—I suddenly understood all that bound me to these people with such burning pity, for the very reason that they were the last dregs of life, and my instinct, once aroused by my crime, felt for this hungry sauntering, so like my own on this fantastic night, felt for that criminal availability to any touch, any strange, chance-come desire. I was magnetically drawn to them, the wallet full of stolen money suddenly burned hot on my breast as at last I sensed beings over there, human beings, soft, breathing, speaking, wanting something from others, perhaps from me, only waiting as I was to offer myself up, burning in my fervent desire for human contact. And suddenly I understood what drives men to such creatures, I saw that it is seldom just the heat in the blood, a growing itch, but is usually simply the fear of loneliness, of the terrible strangeness that otherwise rises between us, as my inflamed emotions felt for the first time today. I remembered when I had last dimly felt something like this: it was in England, in Manchester, one of those steely cities that roar under a lightless sky with a noise like an underground railway, and yet at the same time are frozen with a loneliness that seeps through the pores and into the blood. I had been staying there with relatives for three weeks, but spent all my evenings wandering around bars and clubs, visiting the glittering music hall again and again just to feel some human warmth. And then, one evening, I had found such a woman, whose

gutter English I could scarcely understand, but suddenly I was in a
room, drinking in laughter from a strange mouth, there was a warm
body there, something of this earth, close and soft. Suddenly the
cold, black city melted away, the dark and raucous lonely space: a
being you did not know, who just stood there waiting for all comers,
could release you, thaw the frost; you could breathe freely again,
feel life, all light and bright in the middle of the steely dungeon.
How wonderful for those who are lonely, shut up in themselves, to
know or guess that there is something to support them in their fear,
something to cling to, though it may be dirty from much handling,
stiff with age, eaten away by corrosion. And this, this of all things
I had forgotten in that hour of ultimate loneliness from which,
staggering, I rose that night. I had forgotten that somewhere, in
one final corner, there are always these creatures waiting to accept
any devotion, let any desolation rest in their breath, cool any heat
for a small coin, which is never enough for the great gift they give
with their eternal readiness, the gift of their human presence.

Beside me the orchestrion of the carousel started droning away
again. This was the last ride, the last fanfare of the circling light
going round in the darkness before Sunday passed into the workaday
week. But no one was riding now, the horses went round empty
in their crazy circle, the tired woman at the cash desk was raking
together the day's takings and counting them, the errand boy was
ready with a hook to bring the shutters rattling down over the booth
after this last ride. Only I stood there alone, still leaning against the
post, and looked out at the empty square where nothing but those
figures moved, fluttering like bats, seeking something just as I was
seeking, waiting as I was waiting, yet with an impassably strange
space between us. Now, however, one of them must have noticed
me, for she slowly made her way forwards, and I looked closely
at her from under my lowered eyelids: a small, crippled, rickety
creature without a hat, wearing a tasteless and showy cheap dress
with worn dancing shoes peeping out from under it, the whole

outfit probably bought bit by bit from a street stall or junk shop at third-hand, crumpled by the rain or some indecent adventure in the grass. She came over with an ingratiating look and stopped beside me, casting out a sharp glance like a fishing line and showing her bad teeth in an inviting smile. My breath stopped short. I could not move, could not look at her, and yet I could not tear myself away: as if I were under hypnosis, I felt that a human being was walking around me hopefully, that someone was wooing me, that with a word, with a gesture I could finally rid myself of my terrible loneliness, my painful sense of being an outcast. But I could not move, I was wooden as the post against which I was leaning, and in a kind of lascivious powerlessness I felt only—as the melody of the carousel wearily wound down—this close presence, the will to attract me, and I closed my eyes for a moment, to feel to the full this magnetic attraction of something human coming out of the darkness of the world and flowing over me.

The carousel stopped, the waltz tune was cut short with a last groaning sound. I opened my eyes just in time to see the figure beside me turn away. Obviously she felt it tedious to wait beside a man standing here like a block of wood. I was horrified. I suddenly felt very cold. Why had I let her go, the only human being who had approached me this fantastic night, who was receptive to me? Behind me the lights were going out; the shutters rolled down with a rattle and a clatter. It was over.

And suddenly—oh, how can I describe to myself that warm sense like spindrift suddenly spraying up?—suddenly—and it was as abrupt, as hot, as red as if a vein had burst in my breast—suddenly something broke out of me, a proud, haughty man fully armoured with cool social dignity, something like a silent prayer, a spasm, a cry: it was my childish yet overpowering wish for this dirty, rickety little whore to turn her head again so that I could speak to her. For I was not too proud to follow her—my pride was all crushed, trodden underfoot, swept away by very new feelings—no, I was too weak, too much at a loss. So I stood there, trembling and in turmoil, alone at the martyr's stake of darkness, waiting as I had never waited since my boyhood years, as I had waited only once before, standing by a window in the evening as a strange woman slowly began undressing, and I kept lingering and hesitating as she unwittingly stripped herself naked—I stood crying out to God with a voice I did not recognise as my own for a miracle, for this crippled thing, this last scum of humanity, to try me once more, to turn her eyes to me again.

And yes—she did turn. Once more, quite automatically, she looked back. But so strong must my convulsive start have been, so strong the leaping of intense feeling into my eyes, that she stopped and observed me. She half-turned again, looked at me through the darkness, smiled and nodded her head invitingly over to the shadowy side of the square. And at last I felt the terrible spell of rigidity in me give way. I could move again. I nodded my consent.

The invisible pact was made. Now she went ahead over the dimly lit square, turning from time to time to see if I was following. And I did follow: the leaden feeling had left my legs, I could move my feet again. I was magnetically impelled forwards, I did not consciously walk but flowed along behind her, so to speak, drawn by a mysterious power. In the dark of the alley between the booths of sideshows she slowed her pace. Now I was beside her.

She looked at me for a few seconds, scrutinising me distrustfully; something made her uncertain. Obviously my curiously timid lingering there, the contrast between the place and my elegance, seemed to her somehow suspicious. She looked round several times, hesitated. Then, pointing down the street that was black as a mine shaft: "Let's go there. It's dark behind the circus."

I could not answer. The dreadful vulgarity of this encounter numbed me. I would have liked to tear myself away somehow, bought myself off with a coin, an excuse, but my will had no more power over me. I felt as if I were on a toboggan run flinging myself round a bend, racing at high speed down a steep incline of snow, when the fear of death somehow mingles pleasantly with the intoxication of speed, and instead of braking you give yourself up to the sense of falling without your own volition, with delirious yet conscious weakness. I could not go back now, and perhaps I didn't want to. She pressed herself intimately against me, and I instinctively took her arm. It was a very thin arm, the arm not of a woman but of an underdeveloped, scrofulous child, and no sooner did I feel it through her lightweight coat than I was overcome, in the midst of my intense access of feeling, by gentle, overwhelming pity for this wretched, downtrodden scrap of life washed up against me by the night. And instinctively my fingers caressed the weak, feeble joints of her hand more respectfully and purely than I had ever touched a woman before.

We crossed a dimly lit road and entered a little grove where huge treetops held the sombre, evil-smelling darkness in their embrace. At that moment, and although you could hardly make out an outline any more, I noticed that she turned very carefully on my arm, and did the same thing again a few steps later. And strangely enough, while I was, as it were, numbed and rigid as I slipped into this indecent adventure, my senses were perfectly bright and alert. With clear vision that nothing escaped, that took conscious note of every movement, I realised that something was following quietly behind us on the borders of the path we had crossed, and I thought I heard a dragging step. And suddenly—as when a crackling, white flash of lightning leaps across a landscape—I guessed, I knew it all: I was to be lured into a trap, this whore's pimps were lurking behind us, and in the dark she was taking me to the appointed place where I was to be their victim. I saw it all, with the supernatural clarity that one is said to have only in the concentrated seconds between life and death, and I considered every possibility. There was still time to get away, the main road must be close, for I could hear the electric tram rattling along its rails, a shout or a whistle could summon aid. All the possibilities of flight and rescue leapt up in my mind, in sharply outlined images.

But how strange—this alarming realisation did not cool me but only further inflamed me. Today, awake in the clear light of an autumn day, I cannot explain the absurdity of my actions to myself: I knew, I knew at once with every fibre of my being that I was going into danger unnecessarily, but the anticipation of danger ran through my nerves like a fine madness. I knew there was something terrible and perhaps deadly ahead, I trembled with disgust at the idea of being forced into a criminal, mean and dirty incident somewhere here, but even death itself aroused a dark curiosity in me in my present state of life-induced intoxication, an intoxication I had never known or guessed at before, but now it was streaming over me, numbing me. Something—was it that I was ashamed to show fear, or was it weakness?—something drove me on. I felt intrigued to climb down to this last sewer of life, to squander my whole past, gamble it away. A reckless lust of the spirit mingled with the low vulgarity of this adventure. And although all my nerves scented danger, and I understood it clearly with my senses and my reason, I still went on into the grove arm-in-arm with this dirty little Prater tart who physically repelled rather than attracted me, and who I knew was bringing me this way just for her accomplices. Yet I could not go back. The gravitational pull of criminality, having taken hold of me that afternoon during my adventure on the racecourse, was dragging me further and further down. And now I felt only the daze, the eddying frenzy of my fall into new depths, perhaps into the last depths of all, into death.

After a few steps I stopped. Once again her glance flew uncertainly around. Then she looked expectantly at me.

"Well—what are you going to give me?"

Oh yes. I'd forgotten that. But the question did not sober me, far from it. I was so glad to give her something, to make her a present, to be able to waste my substance. I hastily reached into my pocket and tipped all the silver in it and a few crumpled banknotes into her outstretched hand. And now something so wonderful happened that even today my blood warms when I think of it: either this poor creature was surprised by the size of the sum—she must have been used to getting only small change for her indecent services—or there was something new and unusual to her in the way I gave it readily, quickly, almost with delight, for she stepped back, and through the dense and evil-smelling darkness I felt her gaze seeking me in great astonishment. And at last I felt what I had not found all evening: someone was interested in me, was seeking me, for the first time I was alive to someone else in the world. The fact that it should be this outcast, this creature who carried her poor abused body round in the darkness, offering it for sale, and who had thrust herself on me without even looking at the buyer, who now turned her eyes to mine, the fact that she was wondering about the human being in me only heightened my strange sense of intoxication, clear-sighted and dizzy as I was at one and the same time, both fully conscious and dissolving into a magical apathy. And already the stranger was pressing closer to me, but not in the businesslike way of a woman doing a duty that had been paid for. Instead, I thought I felt unconscious gratitude in it, a feminine desire for closeness. I gently took her thin, rickety, childish arm, felt her small, twisted body, and suddenly, looking beyond all that, I saw her whole life: the borrowed, smeared bedstead in a suburban yard where she slept from morning to noon among a crowd of other people's children; her pimp throttling her; belching drunks falling on her in the dark; the special hospital ward; the lecture hall where her abused body was put on show, sick and naked, as a teaching aid to cheerful young medical students; and the end somewhere in a poorhouse to which she would be carted off in a batch of women and left to die like an animal. Infinite pity for her, for all of them came over me, a warmth that was tenderness

59

without sensuality. Again and again I patted her small, thin arm.
And then I bent down and kissed the astounded girl.

At that moment there was a rustle behind me. A twig cracked.
I jumped back. And a coarse, vulgar male voice was laughing.
"There we are. I thought so."

Even before I saw them I knew who they were. Not for one
second, dazed and confused as I was, had I forgotten that I was
surrounded, and indeed this was what my mysteriously lively curiosity had been waiting for. A figure now emerged from the bushes,
and a second behind it: a couple of rough fellows boldly taking
up their positions. The coarse laugh came again. "Turning a trick
here, eh? A fine gentleman, of course! Well, we'll see to him now."
I stood perfectly still, the blood beating in my temples. I felt no fear.
I was simply waiting for what came next. Now I was in the very
depths at last, in the final abyss of ignominy. Now the blow must
come, the shattering end towards which I had half-intentionally
been moving.

The girl had moved quickly away from me, but not to join them.
She was in a way standing between us; it seemed that she did not
entirely like the ambush prepared for me. The men, for their part,
were vexed because I did not move. They looked at each other,
obviously expecting some protest from me, a plea, some display of
fear. "Oh, so he's not talking!" said one of them at last, threateningly. The other approached me and said in commanding tones,
"You'll have to come down to the police station with us."

I still did not answer. One of the men put his hand on my
shoulder and gave me a slight push. "Move," he said.

I began to move. I did not defend myself, for I did not want to:
the extraordinary, degraded, dangerous nature of the situation
left me dazed. But my brain remained perfectly clear: I knew that
these fellows must fear the police more than I did, that I could
buy myself off for a few crowns—but I wanted to relish the depths
of horror to the full, I was enjoying the dreadful humiliation of

the situation, in a kind of waking swoon. Without haste, entirely automatically, I went the way they had pushed me.

But the very fact that I moved towards the light so obediently and without a word seemed to confuse the men. They whispered softly, and then began to talk to each other again in deliberately raised voices. "Let him go," said one (a pockmarked little fellow), but the other replied, with apparent decision: "No, that won't do. If poor starving devils like us do such things they put us behind bars. But a fine gentleman like this—he really deserves punishment." I heard every word, and in their voices I detected their clumsily expressed request for me to begin negotiating with them; the criminal in me understood the criminal in them, understood that they wanted to torment me with fears, while I was tormenting them with my docility. It was a silent battle between us, and—oh, how rich in experience this night was!—and in the midst of deadly danger, here in this insalubrious grove on the Prater, in the company of a couple of ruffians and a whore, I felt the frenzied enchantment of gambling for the second time in twelve hours, but this time for the highest of stakes, for my whole comfortable existence, even my life. And with all the force of my quivering nerves, tensed as they were to breaking point, I abandoned myself to this great game, to the sparkling magic of chance.

"Hey, there goes the cop," said a voice behind me. "Our fine gentleman won't like this, he'll be behind bars a week or more." It was meant to sound like a grim threat, but I heard the man's hesitant uncertainty. I went placidly towards the dim light, where I did indeed see light glint on a police officer's spiked helmet. Twenty more paces and I would have reached him. Behind me, the men had fallen silent. I realised they were slowing down. Next moment, I knew, they must retreat like cowards into the dark, into their own world, embittered by the failure of their trick, perhaps to vent their anger on the poor woman. The game was over: again, for the second time today, I had won, I had cheated other strangers of their malicious designs. Pale lantern light was already flickering ahead, and when I turned I looked for the first time into the two ruffians' faces: bitterness and a craven shame looked out of their uncertain eyes. They still stood there, but downcast and disappointed, ready to slink back into the dark. For their power was gone: it was *me* they feared now.

At that moment I was suddenly overcome—and it was like fermentation within me, bursting the staves in the barrel of my breast to pour out hot feeling into my blood—I was suddenly overcome by an infinite, fraternal sympathy for these two men. What had they wanted from me, these poor hungry, ragged fellows, what had they wanted from me, a satiated parasite, but a few miserable crowns? They could have strangled me there in the dark, they could have robbed me, killed me, but they had not; they had only tried to frighten me in a clumsy, amateurish way for the sake of the loose silver in my pocket. How could I, who had become a thief on a whim, out of a sense of audacity, who had turned criminal for the pleasure of my nerves, how could I dare to torment these poor devils further? And my infinite sympathy was mingled with infinite shame at having toyed with their fear and impatience for my own amusement. I pulled myself together: now that I was safe and the light of the nearby street protected me, I must go along with them and banish the disappointment from those bitter, hungry eyes.

With a sudden movement I stepped up to one of them. "Why would you want to report me to the police?" I said, taking care to inject a touch of stress and fear into my voice. "What good will it do you? Perhaps I'll be locked up, perhaps not. But it won't do you any good. Why do you want to make my life a misery?"

They both stared at me in embarrassment. They must have expected anything: cries, threats to make them cringe like growling dogs, not this subservience. At last one of them said, not threateningly at all, but as it were apologetically: "Justice have got to be done! We're only doing our duty, right?"

This comment was obviously prepared for such cases, yet it rang false. Neither of the pair dared look at me. They were waiting. And I knew what they were waiting for. They were waiting for me to beg for mercy and offer them money.

I still remember everything about those seconds. I recollect every nerve that stirred in me, every thought that shot through my mind. And I know what I maliciously wanted at first: I wanted to make them wait, torment them a little longer, relish the pleasure of keeping them on tenterhooks. But soon I forced myself to beg, because I knew it was time for me to relieve these two of their anxiety. I began putting on a show of being terrified, I begged for mercy, asked them to keep all this quiet and not make me wretched. I saw these poor amateur blackmailers begin to feel awkward, and the silence between us was milder now.

And then at last, at last I said what they had been longing to hear all this time. "I'll... I'll give you... I'll give you a hundred crowns."

All three started and looked at each other. They had not expected so much, not now that all was really lost for them. At last one of them, the pockmarked man with the shifty eyes, pulled himself together. He started to speak twice, but couldn't get it out. Then he said—and I felt that he was ashamed as he spoke—"Two hundred crowns."

"Oh, shut it!" the girl suddenly intervened. "You be glad he gives you anything. He ain't done nothing, he didn't hardly touch me. This is too much."

She was shouting at them in genuinely embittered tones. And my heart sang. Someone was sorry for me, someone was speaking up for me, kindness was born of something low and mean, blackmail gave rise to some dim desire for justice. How good it felt, how it responded to the swelling tide of my feelings! No, I must not play with these people or torment them in their fear and shame any longer—enough, enough!

"Very well, two hundred crowns."

All three fell silent. I took out my wallet. Slowly, very openly I held it in my hand. With one move they could have snatched it from me and fled into the dark. But they looked shyly away. There was some kind of secret pact between them and me, not a conflict and a gamble any more but a condition of trust and justice, a human relationship. I took the two notes from the bundle of stolen money and handed them to one of the men.

"Thank you," he said automatically, and turned away. He himself obviously felt how ridiculous it was to thank me for money obtained by blackmail. He was ashamed, and his shame—for I could feel everything that night, I could read the meaning of every gesture—his shame distressed me. I did not want a human being to feel ashamed in front of me, one of his own kind, a thief like him, weak, cowardly, lacking in willpower. I felt pain for his humiliation, and wanted to lift it from him. So I refused his thanks.

"No, it is for me to thank you," I said, surprised at the amount of true feeling in my voice. "If you had reported me to the police I'd have been done for. I'd have had to shoot myself, and you'd have gained nothing by that. It's better this way. I will go right over there, and perhaps you will go the other way. Goodnight."

They stood silent for a moment longer. Then one man said: "Goodnight," and then the other, and last the whore, who had stayed in the dark all this time. The words sounded warm and heartfelt, like true good wishes. I sensed in their voices that somewhere deep in their dark natures they liked me, they would never forget this strange moment. It might perhaps return to their minds again in the penitentiary or the hospice; something of me lived on in them, I had given them something. And the pleasure of giving it filled me as no emotion had ever done before.

I walked alone through the night to the exit from the Prater. All inhibition had left me, I had been like a man missing, presumed dead, but now I felt my nature flowing out into the whole infinite world in a plenitude I had never known before. I sensed everything as if it lived for me alone, and as if in its own turn it linked me with that flow. The black trees stood around me, rustling, and I loved them. Stars shone down from above, and I breathed in their white salutation. I heard singing voices somewhere, and I felt they were singing for me. Now that I had torn away the carapace from my breast everything was suddenly mine, and the joy of lavish abandonment swept me on. Oh, how easy it is, I thought, to give pleasure and rejoice in that pleasure yourself: you have only to open yourself up and the living current will flow from one human being to another, falling from the heights to the depths, rising up again like spindrift from the depths into infinity.

At the exit of the Prater, beside a cab rank, I saw a street trader, tired and bowed over her paltry wares. She had baked goods for sale, covered with dust, and a few fruits; she had probably been sitting there since morning bending over the few coins she had earned, and weariness bent her back. Why not make her happy too, I thought, now that I am happy? I chose a small pastry and put a banknote down in front of her. She began busily looking for change, but I was already walking on and saw only her start of delight, saw the bent back suddenly straighten, while her open mouth, frozen in amazement, sent a thousand good wishes after me. Holding the pastry, I went up to a horse standing wearily in the shafts. It turned and gave me a friendly snort, and its dark eyes showed gratitude when I stroked its pink nostrils and gave it the sweet morsel. And as soon as I had done that I wanted more: to give more pleasure, to feel how a few silver coins, a few notes printed on coloured paper can conquer fear, kill want, kindle merriment. Why were there no beggars here? Why no children who would have liked to have the bunches of balloons on strings which a surly, white-haired cripple was taking home, disappointed by the poor business he had done all this long, hot day. I went up to him. "I'll take the balloons." "Ten hellers each," he said suspiciously, for what would this elegant gentleman of leisure want with his coloured balloons at midnight? "I'll take them all," I said, giving him a ten-crown note. He swayed on his feet, looked at me as if something had dazzled him, and then, trembling, gave me the string that held the whole bunch together. I felt the taut string tug at my finger; the balloons wanted to be gone, to be free, to fly through the air. Go then, fly where you like, be free! I let go of the strings, and up they suddenly rose like so many coloured moons. Laughing people came up from all sides, lovers emerged from the shadows, drivers cracked their whips and called to each other, pointing out the freed balloons drifting over the trees towards the houses and rooftops. The onlookers all glanced cheerfully at each other, enjoying my happy folly.

Why did I never know before how easy and how good it is to give pleasure? All of a sudden the banknotes were burning a hole in my wallet again, twitching in my fingers like the strings of the balloons just now. They wanted to fly away from me into the unknown too. And I took them, those I had stolen from Lajos and my own—for I felt no difference between them now and no guilt—and kept them ready to be given to any who wanted one. I approached a street-sweeper morosely sweeping the deserted Praterstrasse. He thought I wanted to ask him the way, and looked up with a surly expression; I smiled and held out a twenty-crown note. He started, uncomprehending, then finally took it and waited to see what I wanted in return. But I just smiled at him again, said: "Buy something you like," and went on. I kept looking around to see if anyone wanted something from me, and when no one came up I just handed the money out myself: I gave a note to a whore who accosted me, two notes to a lamplighter, I threw one into the open hatch of a basement bakery, and so I went on, leaving behind me a wake of amazement, thanks and pleasure, I walked on and on. Finally I crumpled notes up and scattered them around the empty street and on the steps of a church, liking the idea of the old ladies who would come to morning service, find all those banknotes and thank God, or of a poor student, a girl or a workman on their way out coming upon the money in amazement and delight, just as I had discovered myself in amazement and delight that night.

I couldn't say now where and how I scattered all those banknotes, and finally my silver too. There was some kind of delirium in me, an outpouring like lovemaking, and when the last pieces of paper had fluttered away I felt light, as if I could fly, and I knew a freedom I had never known before. The street, the sky, the buildings, all seemed to flow together and towards me, giving me an entirely new sense of possession and of belonging: never, even in the most warmly experienced moments of my life, had I felt so strongly that all these things were really present, that they were alive, that I was alive, and that their lives and mine were one and the same, that life is a great and mighty phenomenon and can never be hailed with too much delight. It is something that only love grasps, only devotion comprehends.

There was one last dark moment, and that came when, having walked happily home, I put the key in my door and the corridor leading to my rooms opened up black before me. I was suddenly overcome by fear that I would be returning to my old life if I entered the apartment of the man I had been until this moment, if I lay down in his bed and found myself once more connected with everything from which this night had so wonderfully released me. No, I must not be what I had been before, remote from the real world, I must not be the correct, unfeeling gentleman of yesterday and all the days before. I would rather plunge into any depths of crime and horror, but I must have the reality of life! I was tired, inexpressibly tired, yet I feared that sleep might close over me, and then its black silt would sweep away all the hot, glowing, living emotions that this night had aroused in me, and I might find that the whole experience had been as fleeting and without foundation as a fantastic dream.

But I woke cheerfully to a new morning next day, and none of that gratefully flowing emotion had run away into the sand. Four months have passed since then, and my old paralysis of feeling has not returned. I still bloom warmly as I face the day. The magical intoxication of my experience when the ground of my old world suddenly gave way under my feet, plunging me into the unknown, when I felt the delirium of speed mingled with the profundity of all life as I fell into my own abyss—yes, that flowing heat is gone, but since that hour I have been conscious of my own warm blood with every breath I take, and I daily feel new lust for life. I know I am a different man now, with different senses; different things arouse me, and I am more aware than before. I dare not say, of course, that I have become a better man; I know only that I am a happier man because I have found some kind of meaning in an existence that had been so cold, a meaning for which I can find no term but life itself. Since then I hold back from nothing, for I feel the norms and formalities of the society in which I live are meaningless, and I am not ashamed in front of others or myself. Words like honour, crime, vice, have suddenly acquired a cold, metallic note, I cannot speak them without horror. I live by letting myself draw on the power I so magically felt for the first time on that night. I do not ask where it will carry me: perhaps to some new abyss, into what others call vice, or perhaps to somewhere sublime. I don't know and I don't want to know. *For only he who lives his life as a mystery is truly alive.*

But never—and I am sure of this—have I loved life more fervently, and now I know that all who are indifferent to any of the shapes and forms it takes, commit a crime (the only crime there is!). Since I began to understand myself, I have understood much of many other things: someone's avid glance into a shop window can distress me, the playfulness of a dog can delight me. I suddenly care for everything; I am indifferent to nothing now. In the paper (which I used to consult only in search of entertainment and auction sales) I read of a hundred things that excite me every day; books that once bored me suddenly reveal their meaning to me. And the strangest thing of all is that I can suddenly talk to people outside the bounds of polite conversation. My manservant, who has been with me for seven years, interests me and I often talk to him; the caretaker whom I used to pass by, thinking no more of him than if he were a moving pillar, recently told me about his little daughter's death, and it affected me more than the tragedies of Shakespeare. And this change—although I continue to lead my life in circles of polite tedium so as not to give myself away—this change seems to be gradually becoming evident. I find that many people are suddenly on terms of warm good friendship with me; for the third time this week a strange dog ran up to me in the street. And friends tell me with a certain pleasure, as if speaking to one who has recovered from an illness, that I am quite rejuvenated.

Rejuvenated? I alone know that I am only just beginning to live. Well, it is a common delusion to think the past was nothing but error and preparation for the present, and I can well see that it is presumptuous of me to think that taking a cold pen in a warm, living hand and recording my feelings on dry paper means that I am really alive. But if it is a delusion, then it is the first ever to delight me, the first to warm my blood and open my senses to me. And if I write about the miracle of my awakening here, then I do it for myself alone, for I know the truth of this more profoundly than any words can say. I have spoken to no friend about it; my friends never knew how dead to the world I was, and they will never know how I live and flourish now. And should death strike me in the middle of this life of mine, and these lines should fall into another's hands, that idea does not alarm or distress me. For he who has never known the magic of such an hour will not understand, as I myself could not have understood half-a-year ago, that a few fleeting, apparently disconnected incidents on a single evening could so magically rekindle a life already extinguished. I feel no shame before such a man, for he will not understand me. But he who knows how those incidents are linked will not judge or feel pride. And I feel no shame before him, for he *will* understand me. Once a man has found himself there is nothing in this world that he can lose. And once he has understood the humanity in himself, he will understand all human beings.

FORGOTTEN DREAMS

T HE VILLA LAY CLOSE TO THE SEA.

The quiet avenues, lined with pine trees, breathed out the rich strength of salty sea air, and a slight breeze constantly played around the orange trees, now and then removing a colourful bloom from flowering shrubs as if with careful fingers. The sunlit distance, where attractive houses built on hillsides gleamed like white pearls, a lighthouse miles away rose steeply and straight as a candle—the whole scene shone, its contours sharp and clearly outlined, and was set in the deep azure of the sky like a bright mosaic. The waves of the sea, marked by only the few white specks that were the distant sails of isolated ships, lapped against the tiered terrace on which the villa stood; the ground then rose on and on to the green of a broad, shady garden and merged with the rest of the park, a scene drowsy and still, as if under some fairy-tale enchantment.

Outside the sleeping house on which the morning heat lay heavily, a narrow gravel path ran like a white line to the cool viewing point. The waves tossed wildly beneath it, and here and there shimmering spray rose, sparkling in rainbow colours as brightly as diamonds in the strong sunlight. There the shining rays of the sun broke on the small groups of Vistulian pines standing close together, as if in intimate conversation, they also fell on a Japanese parasol with amusing pictures on it in bright, glaring colours, now open wide.

A woman was leaning back in a soft basket chair in the shade of this parasol, her beautiful form comfortably lounging in the yielding weave of the wicker. One slender hand, wearing no rings, dangled down as if forgotten, petting the gleaming, silky coat of a dog with gentle, pleasing movements, while the other hand held a book on

which her dark eyes, with their black lashes and the suggestion of
a smile in them, were concentrating. They were large and restless
eyes, their beauty enhanced by a dark, veiled glow. Altogether the
strong, attractive effect of the oval, sharply outlined face did not
give the natural impression of simple beauty, but expressed the
refinement of certain details tended with careful, delicate coquetry.
The apparently unruly confusion of her fragrant, shining curls
was the careful construction of an artist, and in the same way the
slight smile that hovered around her lips as she read, revealing her
white teeth, was the result of many years of practice in front of
the mirror, but had already become a firmly established part of
the whole design and could not be laid aside now.

There was a slight crunch on the sand.

She looks without changing her position, like a cat lying bask-
ing in the dazzling torrent of warm sunlight and merely blinking
apathetically at the newcomer with phosphorescent eyes.

The steps quickly come closer, and a servant in livery stands in
front of her to hand her a small visiting card, then stands back a
little way to wait.

She reads the name with that expression of surprise on her
features that appears when you are greeted in the street with great
familiarity by someone you do not know. For a moment, small lines
appear above her sharply traced black eyebrows, showing how hard
she is thinking, and then a happy light plays over her whole face
all of a sudden, her eyes sparkle with high spirits as she thinks of
the long-ago days of her youth, almost forgotten now. The name
has aroused pleasant images in her again. Figures and dreams
take on distinct shape once more, and become as clear as reality.

"Ah, yes," she said as she remembered, suddenly turning to the
servant, "yes, of course show the gentleman up here."

The servant left, with a soft and obsequious tread. For a moment
there was silence except for the never-tiring wind singing softly in
the treetops, now full of the heavy golden midday light.

Then vigorous, energetic footsteps were heard on the gravel path, a long shadow fell at her feet, and a tall man stood before her. She had risen from her chair with a lively movement.

Their eyes met first. With a quick glance he took in the elegance of her figure, while a slight ironic smile came into her eyes. "It's really good of you to have thought of me," she began, offering him her slender and well-tended hand, which he touched respectfully with his lips.

"Dear lady, I will be honest with you, since this is our first meeting for years, and also, I fear, the last for many years to come. It is something of a coincidence that I am here; the name of the owner of the castle about which I was enquiring because of its magnificent position recalled you to my mind. So I am really here under false pretences."

"But nonetheless welcome for that, and in fact I myself could not remember your existence at first, although it was once of some significance to me."

Now they both smiled. The sweet, light fragrance of a first youthful, half-unspoken love, with all its intoxicating tenderness, had awoken in them like a dream on which you reflect ironically when you wake, although you really wish for nothing more than to dream it again, to live in the dream. The beautiful dream of young love that ventures only on half-measures, that desires and dares not ask, promises and does not give.

They went on talking. But there was already a warmth in their voices, an affectionate familiarity, that only a rosy if already half-faded secret like theirs can allow. In quiet words, broken by a peal of happy laughter now and then, they talked about the past, or forgotten poems, faded flowers, lost ribbons—little love tokens that they had exchanged in the little town where they spent their youth. The old stories that, like half-remembered legends, rang bells in their hearts that had long ago fallen silent, stifled by dust, were slowly, very slowly invested with a melancholy solemnity; the

STEFAN ZWEIG

final notes of their youthful love, now dead, brought profound and almost sad gravity to their conversation.

His darkly melodious voice shook slightly as he said, "All that way across the ocean in America, I heard the news that you were engaged—I heard it at a time when the marriage itself had probably taken place."

She did not reply to that. Her thoughts were ten years back in the past. For several long minutes, a sultry silence hung in the air between them.

Then she asked, almost under her breath, "What did you think of me at the time?"

He looked up in surprise. "I can tell you frankly, since I am going back to my new country tomorrow. I didn't feel angry with you, I had no moments of confused, hostile indecision, since life had cooled the bright blaze of love to a dying glow of friendship by that time. I didn't understand you—I just felt sorry for you."

A faint tinge of red flew to her cheeks, and there was a bright glint in her eyes as she cried, in agitation, "Sorry for me! I can't imagine why."

"Because I was thinking of your future husband, that indolent financier with his mind always bent on making money—don't interrupt me, I really don't mean to insult your husband, whom I always respected in his way—and because I was thinking of you, the girl I had left behind. Because I couldn't see you, the independent idealist who had only ironic contempt for humdrum everyday life, as the conventional wife of an ordinary person."

"Then why would I have married him if it was as you say?"

"I didn't know exactly. Perhaps he had hidden qualities that escaped a superficial glance and came to light only in the intimacy of your life together. And I saw that as the easy solution to the riddle, because one thing I could not and would not believe."

"And that was?"

"That you had accepted him for his aristocratic title of Count and his millions. That was the one thing I considered impossible."

It was as if she had failed to hear those last words, for she was looking through her fingers, which glowed deep rose like a murex shell, staring far into the distance, all the way to the veils of mist on the horizon where the sky dipped its pale-blue garment into the dark magnificence of the waves.

He too was lost in thought, and had almost forgotten that last remark of his when, suddenly and almost inaudibly, she turned away from him and said, "And yet that is what happened."

He looked at her in surprise, almost alarm. She had settled back into her chair with slow and obviously artificial composure, and she went on in a soft melancholy undertone, barely moving her lips.

"None of you understood me when I was still a girl, shy and easily intimidated, not even you who were so close to me. Perhaps not even I myself. I think of it often now, and I don't understand myself at that time, because what do women still know about their girlish hearts that believed in miracles, whose dreams are like delicate little white flowers that will be blown away at the first breath of reality? And I was not like all the other girls who dreamt of virile, strong young heroes who would turn their yearnings into radiant happiness, their quiet guesses into delightful knowledge, and bring them release from the uncertain, ill-defined suffering that they cannot grasp, but that casts its shadow on their girlhood, becoming more menacing as it lies in wait for them. I never felt such things, my soul steered other dreams towards the hidden grove of the future that lay behind the enveloping mists of the coming days. My dreams were my own. I always dreamt of myself as a royal child out of one of the old books of fairy tales, playing with sparkling, radiant jewels, wearing sweeping dresses of great value—I dreamt of luxury and magnificence, because I loved them both. Ah, the pleasure of letting my hands pass over trembling, softly rustling silk, or laying my fingers down in the soft, darkly dreaming pile of a heavy velvet fabric, as if they were asleep! I was happy when I could wear jewels on my slender fingers as they trembled with happiness, when pale gemstones looked out of the thick torrent of my hair, like pearls of foam; my highest aim was to rest in the soft upholstery of an elegant vehicle. At the time I was caught up in a frenzied love of artistic beauty that made me despise my real, everyday life. I hated myself in my ordinary clothes, looking simple and modest as a nun, and I often stayed at home for days on end because I was ashamed of my humdrum appearance, I hid myself in my cramped, ugly room, and my dearest dream was to live alone beside the sea, on a property both magnificent and artistic, in shady, green garden walks that were never touched by the dirty hands of the common workaday world, where rich peace reigned—much like this place, in fact. My husband made my dreams come true, and because he could do that I married him."

She has fallen silent now, and her face is suffused with Bacchanalian beauty. The glow in her eyes has become deep and menacing, and the red in her cheeks burns more and more warmly.

There is a profound silence, broken only by the monotonous rhythmical song of the glittering waves breaking on the tiers of the terrace below, as if casting itself on a beloved breast.

Then he says softly, as if to himself, "But what about love?"

She heard that. A slight smile comes to her lips.

"Do you still have all the ideals, *all* the ideals that you took to that distant world with you? Are they all still intact, or have some of them died or withered away? Haven't they been torn out of you by force and flung in the dirt, where thousands of wheels carrying vehicles to their owners' destination in life crushed them? Or have you lost none of them?"

He nods sadly, and says no more.

Suddenly he carries her hand to his lips and kisses it in silence. Then he says, in a warm voice, "Goodbye, and I wish you well."

She returns his farewell firmly and honestly. She feels no shame at having unveiled her deepest secret and shown her soul to a man who has been a stranger to her for years. Smiling, she watches him go, thinks of the words he said about love, and the past comes up with quiet, inaudible steps to intervene between her and the present. And suddenly she thinks that *he* could have given her life its direction, and her ideas paint that strange notion in bright colours.

And slowly, slowly, imperceptibly, the smile on her dreaming lips dies away.

IN THE SNOW

A SMALL MEDIEVAL German town close to the Polish border, with the sturdy solidity of fourteenth-century building: the colourful, lively picture that it usually presents has faded to a single impression of dazzling, shimmering white. Snow is piled high on the broad walls and weighs down on the tops of the towers, around which night has already cast veils of opaque grey mist.

Darkness is falling fast. The hurry and bustle of the streets, the activity of a crowd of busy people, is dying down to a continuous murmur of sound that seems to come from far away, broken only by the rhythmic, monotonous chime of evening bells. The day's business is over for the weary workers who are longing for sleep, lights become few and far between, and finally they all go out. The town lies there like a single mighty creature fast asleep.

Every sound has died away, even the trembling voice of the wind over the moors is only a gentle lullaby now, and you can hear the soft whisper of snowflakes dusting down on the surfaces where their wandering ends...

But suddenly a faint sound is heard.

It is like the distant, hasty beat of hoofs coming closer. The startled man in the guardhouse at the gate, drowsy with sleep, goes to the window in surprise to listen. And sure enough, a horseman is approaching at full gallop, making straight for the gate, and a minute later a brusque voice, hoarse from the cold, demands entrance. The gate is opened. A man steps through it, leading in a steaming horse which he immediately hands to the gatekeeper. He swiftly allays the man's doubts with a few words and a sizeable sum of money, and then, his confident and rapid strides showing that he knows the place, he crosses the deserted white market place, and goes down quiet streets and along alleys deep in snow, making for the far end of the little town.

Several small houses stand there, crowding close together as if they needed each other's support. They are all plain, unassuming, smoky and crooked, and they stand in eternal silence in these secluded streets. They might never have known cheerful festivities bubbling over with merriment, no cries of delight might ever have shaken those blank, hidden windows, no bright sunshine might ever have been reflected in their panes. Alone, like shy children intimidated by others, the houses press together in the narrow confines of the Jewish quarter.

The stranger stops outside one of these houses, the largest and relatively speaking the finest. It belongs to the richest man in the little community, and also serves as a synagogue.

Bright light filters through the crack between the drawn curtains, and voices are raised in religious song inside the lighted room. This is the peaceful celebration of Chanukah, a festival of rejoicing in memory of the victory of the Maccabaeans, a day that reminds these exiled people, reduced to servitude by Fate, of their former great power. It is one of the few happy days that life and the law will allow them. But the song sounds melancholy, yearning, and the bright metal of the voices singing it has rusted with all the thousands of tears that have been shed. Out in the lonely street, the singing echoes like a hopeless lament, and is blown away on the wind.

The stranger stands outside the house for some time, inactive, lost in thought and dreams, and tears rise in his throat as he instinctively joins in the ancient, sacred melodies that flow from deep within his heart. His soul is full of profound devotion.

Then he pulls himself together. His steps faltering now, he goes to the closed doorway and brings the knocker down heavily, with a dull thud that shakes the door.

The vibration is felt through the entire building as the sound echoes on.

At once the singing in the room above stops dead, as if at an agreed signal. The people inside have turned pale and are looking at one another in alarm. Their festive mood has instantly evaporated. Dreams of the victorious power of such men as Judas Maccabaeus, by whose side they were all standing in spirit a moment ago, have fled; the bright vision of Israel that they saw before their eyes has gone, they are poor, trembling, helpless Jews again. Reality has asserted itself.

There is a terrible silence. The trembling hand of the prayer leader has sunk to his prayer book, the pale lips of his congregation will not obey them. A dreadful sense of foreboding has fallen on the room, seizing all throats in an iron grip.

They well know why.

Some while ago they heard an ominous word, a new and terrible word, but they were aware of its murderous meaning for their own people. The Flagellants were abroad in Germany, wild, fanatically religious men who flailed their own bodies with scourges in Bacchanalian orgies of lust and delight, deranged and drunken hordes who had already slaughtered and tortured thousands of Jews, intending to deprive them of what they held most holy, their age-old belief in the Father. That was their worst fear. With blind, stoical patience they had accepted exile, beatings, robbery, enslavement; they had all known late-night raids with burning and looting, and they shuddered to think of living in such times.

Then, only a few days earlier, rumours had begun spreading that one company of Flagellants was on its way to their own part of the country, which so far had known them only by hearsay, and it was said to be not far off. Perhaps the Flagellants have already arrived?

Terrible fear has seized on them all, making their hearts falter. They already see those forces, greedy for blood, men with faces flushed by wine, brandishing blazing torches and breaking violently into their homes. Already the stifled cries of their women ring in their ears, crying out for help as they pay the price of the murderers' wild lust; they already feel the flashing weapons strike. It is like a clear and vivid dream.

The stranger listens for sounds in the room above, and when no one lets him in he knocks again. Once more the dull echo of his knock resounds through the silence and distress inside the building.

By now the master of the house, the prayer leader, whose flowing white beard and great age give him the look of a patriarch, has been the first to recover some composure. He quietly murmurs, "God's will be done," and then bends down to his granddaughter. She is a pretty girl and, in her fear resembles a deer turning its great, pleading eyes on the huntsman. "Look out and see who's there, Lea."

All eyes are on the girl's face as she goes timidly to the window, and draws back the curtain with pale, trembling fingers. Then comes a cry from the depths of her heart. "Thank God, it's only one man."

"Praise the Lord." It is a sound like a sigh of relief on all sides. Now movement returns to the still figures who had been oppressed by the dreadful nightmare. Separate groups form, some standing in silent prayer, others talking in frightened, uncertain voices, discussing the unexpected arrival of the stranger, who is now being let in through the front gate.

The whole room is full of the hot, stuffy aroma of logs burning and a large crowd of people, all of them gathered around the richly laid festive table on which the sign and symbol of this holy evening stands, the seven-branched candlestick. The candles shine with a dull light in the smouldering vapours. The women wear dresses adorned with jewellery, the men voluminous robes with white prayer bands. There is a sense of deep solemnity in the crowded room, a solemnity such as only genuine piety can bring.

Now the stranger's quick footsteps are coming up the steps, and he enters the room.

At the same time a sharp gust of biting wind blows into the warm room through the open door. Icy cold streams in with the snow-scented air, chilling everyone. The draught puts out the flickering candles on the candlestick; only one of them still wavers unsteadily as it dies down. Suddenly the room is full of a heavy, oppressive twilight, as if cold night might suddenly fall within these walls. All at once the peace and comfort are gone. Everyone feels that the extinguishing of the sacred candles is a bad omen, and superstition makes them shiver again. But no one dares to say a word.

A tall, black-bearded man, who can hardly be more than thirty years old, stands at the door. He quickly divests himself of the scarves and coats in which he had been muffled up against the cold, and as soon as his face is revealed in the faint light of that last little flickering candle flame, Lea runs to him and embraces him.

This is Josua, her fiancé from the neighbouring town.

The others also crowd eagerly around him, greeting him happily, only to fall silent next moment, for he frees himself from his fiancée's arms with a grave, sad expression, and the weight of his terrible knowledge has dug deep furrows on his brow. All eyes are anxiously turned on him, and he cannot defend himself and what he has to say from the raging torrent of his own emotions. He takes the girl's hands as she stands beside him, and quietly forces himself to utter the fateful news.

"The Flagellants are here."

The eyes that had been turned questioningly to him stare, fixed on his face, and he feels the pulse of the hands he is holding falter suddenly. The prayer leader clutches the edge of the heavy table, his fingers trembling, so that the crystal glasses begin to sing softly, sending quavering notes through the air. Fear digs its claws into desperate hearts again, draining the last drops of blood from the frightened, devastated faces staring at the bearer of the news.

The last candle flickers once more and goes out.

Only the lamp hanging from the ceiling now casts a faint light on the dismayed, distraught people; the news has struck them like a thunderbolt.

One voice softly murmurs the resigned phrase with which Fate has made them familiar. "It is God's will."

But the others still cannot grasp it.

However, the newcomer is continuing, his words brusque and disconnected, as if he could hardly bear to hear them himself.

"They're coming—many of them—hundreds. And crowds of people with them—blood on their hands—they've murdered thousands—all our people in the East. They've been in my town already..."

He is interrupted by a woman's dreadful scream. Her floods of tears cannot soften its force. Still young, only recently married, she falls to the floor in front of him.

"They're there? Oh, my parents, my brothers and sisters! Has any harm come to them?"

He bends down to her, and there is grief in his voice as he tells her quietly, making it sound like a consolation, "They can feel no human harm any more."

And once again all is still, perfectly still. The awesome spectre of the fear of death is in the room with them, making them tremble. There is no one present here who did not have a loved one in that town, someone who is now dead.

At this the prayer leader, tears running into his silver beard and unable to control his shaking voice, begins to chant, disjointedly, the ancient, solemn prayer for the dead. They all join in. They are not even aware that they are singing, their minds are not on the words and melody that they utter mechanically; each is thinking only of his dear ones. And the chant grows ever stronger, they breathe more and more deeply, it is increasingly difficult for them to suppress their rising feelings. The words become confused until at last they are all sobbing in wild, uncomprehending sorrow.

Infinite pain, a pain beyond words, has brought them all together like brothers.

Deep silence descends. But now and then a great sob can no longer be suppressed. And then comes the heavy, numbing voice of the messenger telling his tale again.

"They are all at rest with the Lord. Not one of them escaped, only I, through the providence of God…"

"Praise be to his name," murmurs the whole circle with instinctive piety. In the mouths of these broken, trembling people, the words sound like a worn-out formula.

"I came home late from a journey, and the Jewish quarter was already full of looters. I wasn't recognized, I could have run for it—but I had to go in, I couldn't help going to my place, my own people, I was among them as they fell under flailing fists. Suddenly a man came riding my way, struck out at me—but he missed, swaying in the saddle. Then all at once the will to live took hold of me, that strange chain that binds us to our misery—passion gave me strength and courage. I pulled him off his horse, mounted it, and rode away on it myself through the dark night, here to you. I've been riding for a day and a night."

He stops for a moment. Then he says, in a firmer voice, "But enough of all that now! First of all, what shall we do?"

The answer comes from all sides.

"Escape!"—"We must get away!"—"Over the border to Poland!"

It is the one way they all know to help themselves, age-old and shameful, yet the only way for the weaker to oppose the strong. No one dreams of physical resistance. Can a Jew defend himself or fight back? As they see it, the idea is ridiculous, unimaginable; they are not living in the time of the Maccabaeans now, they are enslaved again. The Egyptians are back, stamping the mark of eternal weakness and servitude on the people. Even the torrent of the passing years over many centuries cannot wash it away.

Flight, then.

One man did suggest, timidly, that they might appeal to the other citizens of the town for protection, but a scornful smile was all the answer he got. Again and again, their fate has always brought the oppressed back to the necessity of relying on themselves and on their God. No third party could be trusted.

They discussed the practical details. Men who had regarded making money as their sole aim in life, who saw wealth as the peak of human happiness and power, now agreed that they must not shrink from any sacrifice if it could speed their flight. All possessions must be converted into cash, however unfavourable the rate of exchange. There were carts and teams of horses to be bought, the most essential protection from the cold to be found. All at once the fear of death had obliterated what was supposed to be the salient quality of their race, just as their individual characters had been forged together into a single will. In all the pale, weary faces, their thoughts were working towards one aim.

And when morning lit its blazing torches, it had all been discussed and decided. With the flexibility of their people, used to wandering through the world, they adjusted to their sad situation, and their final decisions and arrangements ended in another prayer.

Then each of them went to do his part of the work.

And many sighs died away in the soft singing of the snowflakes, which had already built high walls towering up in the shimmering whiteness of the streets.

The great gates of the town closed with a hollow clang behind the last of the fugitives' carts.

The moon shone only faintly in the sky, but it turned the myriad flakes whirling in their lively dance to silver as they clung to clothes, fluttered around the nostrils of the snorting horses, and crunched under wheels making their way with difficulty through the dense snowdrifts.

Quiet voices whispered in the carts. Women exchanged reminiscences of their home town, which still seemed so close in its security and self-confidence. They spoke in soft, musical and melancholy tones. Children had a thousand things to ask in their clear voices, although their questions grew quieter and less frequent, and finally gave way to regular breathing. The men's voices struck a deeper note as they anxiously discussed the future and murmured quiet prayers. They all pressed close to one another, out of their awareness that they belonged together and instinctive fear of the cold. It blew through all the gaps and cracks in the carts with its icy breath, freezing the drivers' fingers.

The leading cart came to a halt.

Immediately the whole line of carts following behind it stopped too. Pale faces peered out from the tarpaulin covers of these moving tents, wondering what had caused the delay. The patriarch had climbed out of the first cart, and all the others followed his example, understanding the reason for this halt.

They were not far from the town yet; through the falling white flakes you could still, if indistinctly, make out the tower rising from the broad plain as if were a menacing hand, with a light shining from its spire like a jewel on its ringed finger.

Everything here was smooth and white, like the still surface of a lake, broken only by a few small, regular mounds surmounted by fenced-in trees here and there. They knew that this was where their dear ones lay in quiet, everlasting beds, rejected, alone and far from home, like all their kind.

Now the deep silence is broken by quiet sobbing, and although they are so used to suffering hot tears run down their rigid faces, freezing into droplets of bright ice on the snow.

As they contemplate this deep and silent peace, their mortal fears are gone, forgotten. Suddenly, eyes heavy with tears, they all feel an infinite, wild longing for this eternal, quiet peace in the 'good place' with their loved ones. So much of their childhood sleeps under this white blanket, so many good memories, so much happiness that they will never know again. Everyone senses it; everyone longs to be in the 'good place'.

But time is short, and they must go on.

They climb back into the carts, huddling close to each other, for although they did not feel the biting cold while they were out in the open, the icy frost now steals over their shaking, shivering bodies again, making them grit their teeth. And in the darkness of the carts their eyes express unspeakable fear and endless sorrow.

Their thoughts, however, keep going back the way they have come, along the path of broad furrows left by the horse-drawn carts in the snow, back to the 'good place', the place of their desires.

It is past midnight now, and the carts have travelled a long way from the town. They are in the middle of the great plain which lies flooded by bright moonlight, while white, drifting veils seem to hover over it, the shimmering reflections of the snow. The strong horses trudge laboriously through the thick snow, which clings tenaciously, and the carts jolt slowly, almost imperceptibly on, as if they might stop at any moment.

The cold is terrible, like icy knives cutting into limbs that have already lost much of their mobility. And gradually a strong wind rises as well, singing wild songs and howling around the carts. As if with greedy hands reaching out for prey, it tears at the covers of the carts which are constantly shaking loose, and frozen fingers find it hard to fasten them back in place more firmly.

The storm sings louder and louder, and in its song the quiet voices of the men murmuring prayers die away. It is an effort for their frozen lips to form the words. In the shrill whistling of the wind the hopeless sobs of the women, fearful for the future, also fall silent, and so does the persistent crying of children woken from their weariness by the cold.

Creaking, the wheels roll through the snow.

In the cart that brings up the rear, Lea presses close to her fiancé, who is telling her of the terrible things he has seen in a sad, toneless voice. He puts his strong arm firmly around her slender, girlish waist as if to protect her from the assault of the cold and from all pain. She looks at him gratefully, and a few tender, longing words are exchanged through the sounds of wailing and the storm, making them both forget death and danger.

Suddenly an abrupt jolt makes them all sway.

Then the cart stops.

Indistinctly, through the roaring of the storm, they hear loud shouts from the teams of horse-drawn carts in front, the crack of whips, the murmuring of agitated voices. The sounds will not die down. They leave the cart and hurry forward through the biting cold to the place where one horse in a team has fallen, carrying the other down with it. Around the two horses stand men who want to help but can do nothing; the wind blows them about like puppets with no will of their own, the snowflakes blind their eyes, and their hands are frozen, with no strength left in them. Their fingers lie side by side like stiff pieces of wood. And there is no help anywhere in sight, only the plain that runs on and on, a smooth expanse, proudly aware of its vast extent as it loses itself in the dim light from the snow and in the unheeding storm that swallows up their cries.

Once again the full, sad awareness of their situation comes home to them. Death reaches out for them once more in a new and terrible form as they stand together, helpless and defenceless against the irresistible, invincible forces of nature, facing the pitiless weapon of the frost.

Again and again the storm trumpets their doom in their ears. You must die here—you must die here.

And their fear of death turns to hopeless resignation.

No one has spoken the thought out loud, but it came to them all at the same time. Clumsily, stiff-limbed, they climb back into the carts and huddle close together again, waiting to die.

They no longer hope for any help.

They press close, all with their own loved ones, to be with one another in death. Outside, their constant companion the storm sings a song of death, and the flakes build a huge, shining coffin around the carts.

Death comes slowly. The icy, biting cold penetrates every corner of the carts and all their pores, like poison seizing on limb after limb, gently, but never doubting that it will prevail.

The minutes slowly run away, as if giving death time to complete its great work of release. Long and heavy hours pass, carrying these desperate souls away into eternity.

The storm wind sings cheerfully, laughing in wild derision at this everyday drama, and the heedless moon sheds its silver light over life and death.

There is deep silence in the last cart of all. Several of those in it are dead already, others are under the spell of hallucinations brought on by the bitter cold to make death seem kinder. But they are all still and lifeless, only their thoughts still darting in confusion, like sudden hot flashes of lightning.

Josua holds his fiancée with cold hands. She is dead already, although he does not know it.

He dreams.

He is sitting with her in that room with its warm fragrance, the seven candles in the golden candlestick are burning, they are all sitting together as they once used to. The glowing light of the happy festival rests on smiling faces speaking friendly words and prayers. And others, long dead, come in through the doorway, among them his dead parents, but that no longer surprises him. They kiss tenderly, they exchange familiar words. More and more approach, Jews in the bleached garments of their forefathers' time, and now come the heroes, Judas Maccabaeus and all the others; they all sit down together to talk and make merry. More come, and still more. The room is full of figures, his eyes are tiring with the sight of so many, changing more and more quickly, giving way to one another, his ear echoes to the confusion of sounds. There is a hammering and droning in his pulse, hotter and hotter—

And suddenly it is over. All is quiet now.

By this time the sun has risen, and the snowflakes, still falling, shine like diamonds. The sun makes the broad mounds that have risen overnight, covered over and over with snow, gleam as if they were jewels.

It is a strong, joyful sun that has suddenly begun to shine, almost a springtime sun. And sure enough, spring is not far away. Soon it will be bringing buds and green leaves back again, and will lift the white shrouds from the grave of the poor, lost, frozen Jews who have never known true spring in their lives.

A SUMMER
NOVELLA

I SPENT THE MONTH OF AUGUST last summer in Cadenabbia, one of those little places on Lake Como that nestle so charmingly between white villas and dark woods. Probably quiet and peaceful even in the livelier days of spring, when travellers from Bellagio and Menaggio gather in crowds on the narrow strip of beach, in these warm summer weeks the little town was fragrant, sunny and isolated. The hotel was almost entirely deserted: a few occasional guests, each an object of curiosity to the others by virtue of having chosen to spend a summer holiday in this remote place, surprised every morning to find anyone else still here. Most surprising of all to me was the continued presence of an elderly gentleman, very distinguished in appearance and very cultivated—he looked something like a cross between a very correct English statesman and a Parisian man of the world—who, instead of amusing himself by enjoying some lakeside sporting activity, spent his days thought-fully watching the smoke from his cigarettes dispersing in the air, or now and then leafing through a book.

The oppressive isolation of two rainy days, and his frank, open manner, soon gave our acquaintanceship a warmth that almost entirely bridged the gap in years between us. Born in Estonia, brought up in France and later in England, a man who had never practised any profession and for years had not lived in any one place, he was homeless in the noble sense of those who, like the Vikings and pirates of beauty, have collected in their intellectual raids all that is most precious in many great cities. He was close to all the arts in the manner of a dilettante, but stronger than his love for them was his sublime disdain to serve them. He had them to thank for a thousand delightful hours, but had never devoted a single creative impulse to any of them. He lived one of those lives that seem otiose because they are not linked to any community of interest, because all the riches stored in them by a thousand separate valuable experiences will pass when their last breath is drawn, without anyone to inherit them.

I said as much to him one evening when we were sitting outside the hotel after dinner, watching the bright lake slowly darken before our eyes. He smiled. "You may be right. I don't believe in memoirs; what you have experienced is in the past as soon as its moment is over. And as for literature: doesn't that perish as well twenty, fifty, a hundred years later? However, I'll tell you something today that I think would make a pretty novella. Come with me—such things are better told as one walks along."

So we set off on the beautiful path along the beach, overshadowed by the eternal cypresses and tangled chestnut trees, with the lake casting restless reflections through their branches. Over there lay the white cloud of Bellagio, softly tinted by sunset colours, and high, high above the dark hill gleamed the sparkling crown of the walls of the Villa Serbelloni. The atmosphere was still slightly sultry, but not oppressive; like a woman's gentle arm, it leant tenderly on the shadows and filled the night with the fragrance of invisible flowers. Then he began his tale.

"I will introduce the story with a confession. Until now I haven't told you that I have been in Cadenabbia before, last year, at the same season and in the same hotel. That may surprise you, especially as I have mentioned that I always avoid doing anything twice. But listen to my story. Last year this place was, of course, as deserted as it is now. The same gentleman from Milan was here—the one who spends all day catching fish and throws them back into the lake in the evening, only to catch them again next day; there were two old Englishwomen whose quietly vegetative existence one hardly noticed, and in addition a handsome young man with a pretty, pale girl, who I don't believe to this day was his wife, because they seemed far too fond of each other for that. Finally, there was also a German family, the most typical kind of north Germans. A flaxen-haired, raw-boned woman getting on in years, with angular, graceless movements, piercing steely eyes and a sharp, quarrelsome mouth like a cut made with a knife. She had a sister with her, unmistakably her sister because she had the same features, only lined and somehow softened; the two of them were always together, yet never seemed to talk to each other, and were always intent on their embroidery, into which they seemed to weave all their absence of thought, implacable Fates in a restricted world of tedium. And between them a young girl some sixteen years old, the daughter of one of them, I don't know which, for the pronounced immaturity of her features was already mingling with a slight indication of feminine curves. She was not really pretty, too thin, not fully grown yet, but there was something touching in her look of helpless yearning. Her eyes were large, and probably full of dark light, but they always shyly avoided the glance of others, their glow dispersed into fitful glints. She too always had some needlework with her, but her hands often moved slowly, her fingers slackened, and then she would sit still, looking out over the lake.

"I don't know what it was about that sight that so strangely attracted my attention. Was it the banal yet inevitable idea that struck me, on seeing the faded mother beside her daughter coming into the bloom of youth? Was it the shadow behind her figure, the thought that lines wait hidden in every cheek, weariness in all laughter, disappointment in every dream? Or was it that wild, unfocused longing just breaking out, giving away everything about the girl, every wonderful moment in her life when her eyes were fixed on the whole universe in desire, because they had not yet found one desirable object to cling to, then to remain there rotting like algae on a piece of floating wood? I found it infinitely fascinating to watch her, to see her dreamy, dewy-eyed glance, the wildly exuberant caresses she lavished on every dog and cat, the restlessness that made her begin so many projects and then leave them unfinished. And then the ardent haste with which she raced through the few wretched books in the hotel library in the evening, or leafed through the two volumes of poetry, worn with much reading, that she had brought with her, books containing the poetry of Goethe and Baumbach... but why do you smile?

I had to apologize. "It's the juxtaposition of Goethe and Baumbach."

"I see! Yes, of course, it's comical. And then again, it isn't. You may believe me when I say that it is immaterial to young girls of that age whether the poetry they read is good or bad, the real essence of poetry or an imitation. To them, poems are only vessels for quenching their thirst, and they pay no attention to the quality of the wine in those vessels; it is intoxicating even before it is drunk. And this girl was like that, so full to the brim of longing that it glowed in her eyes, made her fingertips tremble on the table, and she moved in a manner somewhere between awkwardness and elation. You could see she was hungry to talk to someone, to give away something of all that filled her mind, but there was no one there, only a void, only the slight sound of the embroidery needles to right and left of her, and the cold, deliberate glances of the two older ladies.

"I felt a great sense of pity for her. And yet I could not approach her, for first, what does a man of my age mean to a girl at this moment in her life, and secondly, my dislike of becoming acquainted with family groups, and in particular ageing middle-class ladies, stood in the way of any opportunity to do so. Then an odd approach occurred to me. I thought: here is a young girl, unfledged, inexperienced, probably visiting Italy for the first time, a country that in Germany, thanks to Shakespeare, the Englishman who never went there, is regarded as the land of romantic love—the land of Romeos, secret adventures, dropped fans, flashing daggers, of masks, duennas and tender letters. She surely dreams of such adventures, I thought, and who knows a girl's dreams? They are white, wafting clouds hovering aimlessly in the blue sky, and like real clouds always more intensely coloured in the evening, glowing pink and then an ardent red. Nothing will strike her as improbable or unlikely here. So I decided to invent a secret lover for her.

"And that same evening I wrote a long letter, humbly and respectfully tender, full of strange hints, and unsigned. A letter demanding nothing, promising nothing, exuberant and restrained at the same time—in short a romantic letter that would not have been out of place in a verse drama. As I knew that she was the first to come down to breakfast every day, driven by her restlessness, I folded it into her napkin. Morning came. Watching from the garden, I saw her incredulous surprise, her sudden alarm, the red flame that shot into her pale cheeks and quickly spread down her throat. I saw her looking around helplessly, fidgeting, I saw the nervous movement with which she hid the letter, and then I saw her sit there, nervous and uneasy, scarcely touching her breakfast and soon running away, out of the dining room, to somewhere in the dark, deserted corridors of the hotel, to find a place where she could decipher her mysterious letter... Did you want to say something?"

I had made an involuntary movement, and now I had to explain it. "Wasn't that a bold step to take? Didn't you stop to think she might want to find out how the letter came to be in her napkin, or simplest of all ask the waiter? Or show it to her mother?"

"Of course I thought of that. But if you had seen the girl, that timid, scared, sweet creature who was always looking around anxiously if for once she had raised her voice, any doubts would have been dispelled. There are girls whose modesty is so great that you can go to considerable lengths with them, because they are so helpless and would rather put up with anything than confide so much as a word about it to others. I smiled as I watched her going, and was pleased with the success of my little game. Then she came back, and I felt the blood rush suddenly to my temples; this was another girl, moving in a different way. She came in, looking restless and confused, a glowing wave of red had suffused her face, and a sweet awkwardness made her clumsy. And it was the same all day. Her glance flew to every window as if to find the answer to the mystery there, circled around every passer-by, and once fell on me. I carefully avoided it, so as not to give myself away by any sign, but in that fleeting second I had felt a fiery questioning that almost alarmed me; and it struck me again, from years of experience, that there is no more dangerous, tempting and corrupt desire than to light that first spark in a girl's eyes. Then I saw her sitting between the two older ladies, her fingers idle, and noticed that she sometimes quickly felt a place in her dress, where I was sure she was hiding the letter.

"Now the game really did tempt me. That very evening I wrote her a second letter, and so on over the next few days; I found it exciting to be playing the part of a young man in love in my letters, exaggerating an imaginary passion. It became a fascinating sport such as I suppose huntsmen feel when they set snares or entice game to within the firing line of their guns. And my own success was so indescribable, almost frightening me, that I was thinking of putting an end to it, but temptation now bound me ardently to the game I had begun. It was so easy. Her bearing became light, wildly confused as if by dancing, her features radiated a hectic beauty all their own; her sleep must have been a matter of watching and waiting for next morning's letter, for her eyes were darkly shadowed early in the day, and the fire in them unsteady. She began looking after herself, wore flowers in her hair, a wonderful tenderness for everything calmed her hands, and there was always a question in her eyes, for she sensed, from a thousand small indications in my letters, that the writer of them must be near her—an Ariel filling the air with music, hovering nearby, listening for the sound of the slightest things she did, yet invisible by his own will. She became so cheerful that even the two dull-witted ladies noticed the change, for sometimes they let their eyes linger with kindly curiosity on her hurrying form and her budding cheeks, and then looked at her with a surreptitious smile. There was a new sound in her voice, louder, brighter, bolder, and her throat often vibrated and swelled as if she were about to burst into a song full of joyous trills, as if… but there you go, smiling again!"

"No, no, please go on. I only mean that you tell a very good story. You have—forgive me for taking the liberty—you have talent, you could tell as good a tale as one of our novelists."

"You say that, I suppose, for the sake of courtesy, suggesting that I tell a story like your German novelists, that's to say with lyrical fancies, broad, sentimental, tedious. Very well, I'll cut it short! The marionette was dancing, and I pulled the strings with care. To divert any suspicion from me—for sometimes I felt her eyes resting on mine with a question in them—I had suggested that the writer was not staying here but in one of the nearby spa resorts, and came over the lake in a boat or on the steamer every day. And now I saw that when the bell of the approaching steamer rang, she would always escape her mother's supervision on some pretext, hurry away, and keep watch, with bated breath, on the passengers disembarking from a corner of the pier.

"And then one day it happened. It was a gloomy afternoon, and I had nothing better to do than to watch her, when something remarkable occurred. One of the passengers was a handsome young man with the showy elegance of young Italians, and as he scanned the place as if in search of something, the desperately enquiring, questioning, intent look in the young girl's face met his eye. And at once, flooding wildly over her gentle smile, a modest blush swiftly rose in her face. The young man stopped in surprise, his attention drawn to her—something easily understood when you are the recipient of so warm a glance, full of a thousand unsaid things—and he smiled and tried to follow her. She fled, came to a halt in the certainty that this was the man she had been looking out for so long—hurried on again, but looked round once more. It was the eternal interplay of wanting and fearing, longing and shame, in which the sweet, weak partner is always really the stronger. Obviously encouraged, if surprised, he hurried after her, and was getting close. I was feeling, apprehensively, that all this must surely collapse into an alarming state of chaos—when the two older ladies came along the path. The girl flew to them like a shy bird, the young man cautiously withdrew, but still their eyes met once more as they turned to look back, feverishly fixed on one another. This incident was a warning to me to bring my game to an end, yet the temptation was still too strong, and I made up my mind to make use of this coincidence as an aid. I wrote her an unusually long letter that evening, one that was bound to confirm her assumption. It intrigued me to be directing two characters in my play.

"Next morning the quivering confusion of her features alarmed me. Her pretty unrest had given way to nervous agitation that I did not understand; her eyes were moist and red-rimmed, as if by tears, and she seemed to feel a piercing pain. It was as if all her silence were trying to emerge in a wild scream. Darkness lay on her brow, and there was a gloomy astringency in her eyes, while this time above all I had expected bright joy. I was frightened. For the first time a strange element had entered the game; the marionette didn't obey me and wouldn't dance as I had planned. I thought of all possible reasons, and couldn't find one. I began to be afraid of the play I myself had staged, and I did not return to the hotel until evening, to avoid the accusation in her eyes.

"When I did get back, I understood it all. The family's table was no longer laid. They had left. She had been obliged to go away without a chance to say a word to him, and she could not let her family see how her heart was still attached to that one day, that single hour—she had been dragged away from a sweet dream and back to some miserable small town. I had forgotten to think of that. And I still feel that last look of hers as an accusation, its terrible force of mingled anger, torment, despair and the most bitter pain—something that I had brought into her life, and who knew how long it would last?"

He fell silent. The night had been walking with us, and the moon, partly covered with clouds, was shedding a fitful light. Sparkling stars seemed to hang between the trees and the pale surface of the lake. We went on without a word. At last my companion broke our silence. "Well, that was my story. Don't you think it would make a novella?"

"I don't know. At any rate, it's a story that I will remember, along with the others for which I already have to thank you. But a novella? A good opening for one that might perhaps tempt me. For these people are only ships passing in the night, they are not entirely in control of themselves, they mark the beginning of human stories, but there is no real story. You would have to think it out to the end."

"I see what you mean. The young girl's life, her return to the small town, the dreadful tragedy of ordinary life…"

"No, that's not quite it. The girl doesn't interest me so much. Young girls are never interesting, remarkable as they may think themselves, because all that they've experienced is negative, and so their stories are all the same. In this case the girl marries some good solid citizen at home when the time for it comes, and this affair remains a flower petal among her memories. I'm not, as I said, interested in the girl."

"That's strange. I don't know what you can find in the young man to interest you. Everyone catches such glances in his youth, a fire kindled between one pair of eyes and another, most don't even notice it, others quickly forget. You have to grow older to know that this is perhaps the noblest and deepest thing you ever receive, the sacred privilege of youth."

"I'm not interested in the young man either..."

"Then?"

"I'd develop the character of the older man, the letter-writer, trace it all the way through the story. I don't think that you write ardent letters with impunity at any age, or meddle with the feelings of someone else's love. I would try to show how the game becomes serious, how he thinks he is in control of it, when the game now controls him. The girl's awakening beauty, beauty that he thinks he sees only as an observer, intrigues him and fascinates him more deeply. And the moment when it all slips away from him makes him feel a wild longing for the game—and his plaything. I would be intrigued by the reversal in love that is bound to make an old man's passion very like a boy's, because neither feels entirely adequate as a lover, I would give him the fears and expectations of that state of mind. I would make him uncertain, I'd have him travelling after her to see her, yet at the last minute not venturing near her, I'd have him coming back to the same place in the hope of seeing her again, imploring coincidence, which is always cruel in such cases. I would plan my novella along those lines, and then it would be..."

"A lie, false, impossible!"

I was startled. His voice interrupted me harshly, hoarse and shaking, almost menacing. I had never seen my companion so agitated before. Instantly I realized what note I had incautiously struck in him. And when he stopped suddenly, I was painfully moved to see his white hair in the moonlight.

I wanted to change the subject quickly, broach another. But then he spoke again, this time warmly and softly in his calm, deep voice, pleasantly tinged with slight melancholy. "Or you may be right. Yes, it's more interesting: *L'amour coûte cher aux vieillards*—I think that was the title of one of Balzac's most moving stories, and many could be written on the subject. But the old people who know most about it are happy to talk only about their successes, not their failures. They are afraid of looking ridiculous in circumstances that only, so to speak, illustrate the pendulum of eternity swinging. Do you really think it was chance that the 'lost' chapters of Casanova's memoirs are those describing him in later life, when the cockerel becomes a cuckold, the betrayer the betrayed? Maybe his hand was too reluctant and his heart too heavy to write about that."

He offered me his own hand. Now his voice was cool, calm and placid again. "Goodnight! I see it's dangerous to tell young people stories on summer nights. It easily leads to foolish thoughts and all kinds of unnecessary dreams. Goodnight to you!"

And he walked back into the dark, his step still with a spring in it, but slower now. It was late, but the weariness that usually came over me early in the warmth of these mild nights had been dispersed today by the agitation that rings in the blood when something strange happens, or for a moment you feel another man's experience as if it were your own. So I went along the quiet, dark path to the Villa Carlotta with its marble stairway leading down to the lake, and sat on the cool steps. It was a wonderful night. The lights of Bellagio that had been sparkling among the trees like fireflies earlier now seemed endlessly far away across the water, and slowly, one by one, they fell back into the deep darkness. The lake lay there silent, shining like a black jewel, yet edged with sparkling fire. And the splashing waves, like white hands on the pale keys of an instrument, moved up and down the marble steps with a slight swell. The pale sky seemed endlessly high above, decked with thousands of sparkling stars. They stood there calmly, in bright silence; only occasionally did one suddenly break free of that diamantine dance and fall into the summer night, into the dark, into valleys, ravines, mountains or distant water, knowing nothing of it, slung like a human life into the steep depths of unknown destinies.

THE
GOVERNESS

T HE TWO CHILDREN are alone in their room. The light has been put out; they are surrounded by darkness except for the faint white shimmer showing where their beds are. They are both breathing so quietly that you might think they were asleep.

One of them speaks up. "I say..." she begins. It is the twelve-year-old, and her voice is quiet, almost anxious in the dark.

"What is it?" asks her sister from the other bed. She is only a year older.

"Good, you're still awake. I... there's something I want to tell you."

No answer from across the room, only a rustle of bedclothes. The elder sister is sitting up, looking expectant. Her eyes are sparkling.

"Listen... I wanted to ask you... but no, you tell me first, haven't you noticed anything about our Fräulein in the last few days?"

The other girl hesitates, thinking it over. Then she says, "Yes, but I'm not sure what it is. She isn't as strict as usual. I didn't do any school homework for two whole days recently, and she never told me off. And then she's so... oh, I don't know exactly how to put it. I don't think she's bothering about us any more. She sits somewhere all the time, she doesn't play with us the way she used to."

"I think she's feeling sad, she just doesn't want to show it. She doesn't even play the piano any more."

Silence descends again.

"You wanted to tell me something," the elder girl reminds her sister.

"Yes, but you mustn't tell anyone else, really not anyone, not Mama and not your best friend."

"No, no, I won't!" She is impatient now. "Come on, what is it?"

"Well, when we were going to bed just now, I suddenly remembered that I hadn't said goodnight to Fräulein. I'd taken my shoes off, but I went to her room all the same, ever so quietly, to give her a surprise. And I opened the door of her room very carefully too. I thought at first she wasn't there. There was a light on, but I couldn't see her. Then all at once—it gave me a terrible fright—I heard somebody crying, and I suddenly saw her lying on the bed with all her clothes on and her head in the pillows. She was sobbing so hard that it made me jump. But she didn't notice me. And then I closed the door very quietly again. I had to stand there outside it for a little while because I was trembling so much. And then that sobbing sound came through the door again, quite clearly, and I ran back down here."

The girls keep quiet for a while. Then one of them says, very softly, "Oh, poor Fräulein!" The words linger in the air of the room like a lost, low musical phrase, and then die away again.

"I do wish I knew why she was crying," says the younger sister. "She hasn't quarrelled with anyone these last few days. Mama's leaving her in peace at last instead of scolding her all the time, and I'm sure we haven't done anything bad, not to her. So why was she crying like that?"

"I can think of a reason," says the elder girl.

"What is it? Go on, tell me."

Her sister hesitates, but at last she says, "I think she's in love."

"In love?" The younger girl is baffled. "In love? Who with?"

"Haven't you noticed anything?"

"You don't mean in love with Otto!"

"Oh, don't I? And isn't he in love with her? He's been staying with us for three years while he studies at the university, so why do you think he's suddenly taken to going out with us every day these last few months? Did he ever bother with you or me before Fräulein came to be our governess? He's been hanging around us all the time lately. We keep meeting him by accident in the

People's Garden or the City Park or the Prater when we go out with Fräulein. Didn't you notice?"

Startled, the younger girl stammers, "Yes... yes, of course I noticed. Only I always thought it was..."

Her voice fails her. She doesn't go on.

"So did I at first," says her elder sister. "You know how people always say girls are silly. Then I realised that he was only using us as an excuse."

Now they are both silent. It sounds as if the conversation is over. Both girls seem to be deep in thought, or already far away in their dreams.

Then the younger sister breaks the silence in the darkness again. Her voice sounds helpless. "But then why was she crying? He likes her, doesn't he? And I always thought being in love must be wonderful."

"I don't know," says her elder sister, dreamily. "I thought it must be wonderful too."

And once again sleepy lips say, softly and sorrowfully, "Oh, poor Fräulein!"

Then all is quiet in the room.

Next morning they do not discuss the subject again, and yet they are both aware that their thoughts are circling around it. They walk past one another, avoid each other, yet their eyes involuntarily meet when they are glancing surreptitiously at their governess. At mealtimes they watch their cousin Otto as if he were a stranger, although he has been living here with them for years. They do not talk to him, but they keep looking at him from under lowered eyelids to see if he is communicating with Fräulein in some way. Both sisters feel uneasy. They do not play today, and instead do useless, unnecessary things in their nervous anxiety to fathom the mystery. That evening, however, one of them asks the other in a cool tone, as if it were of no importance to her, "Did you notice anything else today?" To which her sister says, "No," and turns away. They are both somehow afraid of talking about it. And so it goes on for a few days, both children silently observing as their minds go round in circles, feeling restlessly and unconsciously close to some sparkling secret.

At last, after a few days, one of them, the younger girl, notices the governess discreetly giving Otto a look full of meaning. He nods in answer. The child quietly takes her sister's hand under the table. When her sister turns to her, she flashes her a meaning glance of her own. The elder girl understands at once, and she too is on the alert.

As soon as they rise from table, the governess tells the girls, "Go to your room and occupy yourselves quietly with something. I have a headache, I'd like to rest for half-an-hour." The children look down. Cautiously, they communicate by touching hands. And as soon as the governess has left, the younger girl hurries over to her sister. "You wait and see—Otto will go to her room now."

"Of course! That's why she sent us to ours."

"We must listen outside her door."

"But suppose someone comes along?"

"Who?"

"Well, Mama."

The younger girl takes fright. "Yes, then…"

"I tell you what. I'll listen at the door, you stay further along the corridor and warn me if there's anyone coming. That way we'll be safe."

The smaller girl looks cross. "But then you won't tell me anything!"

"Yes, I will. I'll tell you all about it."

"Really *all* about it?"

"Yes, I promise. You must cough as a signal if you hear someone coming."

They wait in the corridor, trembling with excitement. Their hearts are beating fast. What will happen? They press close to each other.

Footsteps are approaching. The girls retreat into the shadows. Sure enough, it is Otto. He takes hold of the door handle, and the door closes after him. The elder girl shoots up to it like an arrow from the bow, pressing close to the door, holding her breath as she listens. The younger sister looks wistfully at her from a distance. She is burning with curiosity, and it tears her away from her post. She creeps up, but her sister angrily pushes her away. So she waits at a distance for two or three more minutes that seem to her like an eternity. She is quivering with impatience, stepping from foot to foot as if the floor were burning hot. In her excitement and anger she is near tears—to think that her sister can hear it all and she can't hear anything! Then, in a third room, a door closes. She coughs. And both girls hurry away back to their room. They stand there for a moment breathless, their hearts thudding.

"Come on then, tell me all about it," demands the younger girl avidly.

Her elder sister looks thoughtful. At last she says, dreamily, as if to herself, "I can't make it out!"

"What?"

"It's so strange."

"What? What's so strange?" The younger girl is impatient to know. Her sister tries to collect her thoughts. The smaller girl is pressing very close to her so as not to miss a word.

"It was really funny… not at all what I expected. I think when he came into the room he was going to hug her or kiss her, but then she said, 'Don't do that, I have something serious to discuss with you.' I couldn't see anything, because the key was in the lock on the inside of the door, but I could hear every word. 'Well, what is it?' asked Otto, but I've never heard him speak like that before. You know his usual cheerful, loud way of talking, but he sounded uncertain of himself when he said that, and I felt at once that he was somehow scared. And she must have noticed that he was pretending, too, because she just said very quietly, 'You know what it is.' 'No, I don't, I have no idea,' he said. 'Oh,' she said, so sadly, so terribly sadly, 'then why are you avoiding me all of a sudden? It's a week since you spoke a word to me, you avoid me whenever you can, you don't go out with the children or to the park with us any more. Am I such a stranger all at once? Oh, you know very well why you're keeping away from me.' He said nothing for a bit, then he said, 'I'm about to sit my examinations, I have a great deal of work to do and no time for anything else. It can't be helped.' Then she began crying, and she said to him, through her tears but so kindly, she wasn't angry, 'Otto, why are you lying to me? Tell the truth. I really haven't deserved this from you. I never asked for anything, but now the two of us have to discuss something after all. You know what I am going to say to you, I can see it from your eyes.' And then he said, 'Well, what is it?' But very faintly. And she said…"

Suddenly the girl began trembling, and in her emotion she could get no further. Her younger sister pressed close, saying, "And then what?"

"Then she said, 'What am I going to do about our baby?'"

The smaller girl started with surprise, and cried, "Their baby? What baby? That's not possible!"

"But she said it."

"You can't have heard properly."

"I did, I did. And he repeated it, he sounded just as surprised as you, he cried, 'A baby!' She didn't say anything for quite a time, and then she asked, 'What's to become of me now?' And then…"

"And then?"

"Then you coughed, and I had to run away."

The younger girl stares ahead of her, dismayed. "A baby! But that's impossible. Where *is* the baby?"

"I don't know. That's what I don't understand."

"Maybe at home where... well, where she was living before she came to be our governess. Mama probably wouldn't let her bring the baby with her because of us. And that's why she's so sad."

They both fall silent again, baffled, brooding, unable to come to any conclusions. The thought of the baby is weighing on their minds. Once again it is the smaller girl who speaks first. "A baby, I mean it isn't possible! How can she have a baby? She isn't married, and only married people have babies, I know that!"

"Perhaps she *was* married."

"Don't be so silly. Not to Otto."

"Then how?..."

They stare at each other, at a loss.

"Oh, poor Fräulein," says one of the girls very sadly. They keep repeating the same phrase, and it dies away into a sigh of sympathy. But their curiosity also keeps flaring up.

"I wonder if it's a girl or a boy?"

"How could we find out?"

"Suppose I asked her some time, very, very carefully... What do you think?"

"I think you're crazy!"

"Why? She's so nice to us."

"Oh, do stop and think! No one tells us *that* sort of thing. They hush everything up. When we come into a room they break off their conversation and start talking to us in a silly way as if we were little children. And I'm thirteen already! What's the point of asking? Grown-ups always tell lies."

"But I really, really would like to know."

"Do you think I wouldn't?"

"I tell you what, the bit I understand least is why Otto didn't sound as if he knew about it. You know if you have a baby, the way you know that you have a mother and a father."

"He was only pretending not to know. He's horrid. Otto is always pretending."

"But you wouldn't pretend about something like that. Perhaps he's just trying to fool people…"

However, at this point the governess comes in. They stop talking at once and seem to be doing homework. However, they surreptitiously glance at her. Her eyes look reddened, her voice is rather huskier and more vibrant than usual. The children keep very quiet, suddenly regarding her with awed timidity. She has a baby, they keep thinking, that's why she's so sad. And soon they are feeling sad themselves.

At the dining-room table next day they hear unexpected news. Otto is leaving the family apartment. He has told his uncle that with his examinations so close he has to work very hard, and there are too many distractions here. He will rent a room somewhere for the next month or so, he says, until the exams are over.

The children are very interested to hear this. They guess there is a secret connection with yesterday's conversation, and alert as their instincts now are they pick up the scent of cowardice and flight. When Otto comes to say goodbye to them, they sulk and turn their backs. But they watch surreptitiously as he faces their governess. Her lips are trembling, but she offers him her hand calmly, without a word.

The children have changed a great deal over the last few days. They have lost their playfulness and laughter, the old happy, carefree light has left their eyes. They are full of uneasiness and uncertainty, deeply suspicious of everyone around them. They no longer believe what they are told, they think they detect deliberate lies behind every word. They keep their eyes and ears open all day long, watching every movement, picking up any sudden start of surprise or tone of voice. They haunt the place like shadows in search of clues, listening at doors to overhear anything of interest, possessed by a passionate desire to shake the dark net of secrets off their reluctant shoulders, or at least see through some gap in it and get a glimpse of the real world outside. They have lost their childish trustfulness, their blindly carefree merriment. Moreover, they guess that the tense, sultry atmosphere resulting from recent events will discharge itself in some unexpected way, and they don't want to miss it. Ever since discovering that the people around them are liars they have become persistent and watchful; they are sly and deceitful themselves. With their parents, they take refuge in pretended childishness flaring up into hectic activity. They are a prey to nervous restlessness; their eyes, once shining with a soft, gentle glow, now look deeper and are more likely to flash. In all this constant watching and spying, they feel so helpless that their love for each other is stronger. Sometimes they hug stormily, abandoning themselves to a need for affection suddenly welling up in them, sometimes they burst into tears. All at once, and for no apparent reason, life seems to be in a state of crisis.

Among the many emotional injuries that they now realise they have suffered, there is one that they feel particularly deeply. Seeing how sad Fräulein is these days, they have set out silently, without a word, to please her as much as they possibly can. They do their school exercises carefully and industriously, they help each other, they are quiet and uncomplaining, they try to anticipate her every wish. But Fräulein doesn't even notice, and that hurts them badly. She is entirely different these days. Sometimes, when one of the girls speaks to her, she starts as if woken from sleep. And then her gaze, at first searching, returns from some distant horizon. She will often sit for hours looking dreamily into space, and then the girls go about on tiptoe so as not to disturb her. They have a vague, mysterious idea that she is thinking about her baby who is somewhere far away. And out of the depths of their own awakening femininity they love Fräulein more and more. She is so kind and gentle, her once brisk, high-spirited manner is more thoughtful now, her movements more careful, and the children guess at a secret sadness in all this. They have never seen her shed tears, but her eyelids are often red. They realise that Fräulein is trying to keep her pain secret from them, and are in despair to think that they cannot help her.

And once, when Fräulein has turned to the window and is dabbing her eyes with her handkerchief, the younger girl suddenly plucks up her courage, takes the governess's hand gently, and says, "Fräulein, you're so sad these days. It isn't our fault, is it?"

Much moved, the governess looks at her and caresses her soft hair. "No, my dear, no," she says. "It certainly is not your fault." And she gently kisses the girl's forehead.

It is at this time, when they are keeping watch, letting nothing that moves within their field of vision pass unnoticed, that one of them picks up a remark when she suddenly enters a room. It is only a few words, because the girls' parents break off their conversation at once, but anything they hear now can make them suspicious. "I thought I'd noticed something of that sort myself," their mother was saying. "Well, I'll question her." The child thinks at first that this means her, and almost anxiously runs to her sister for advice and help. But at mid-day they realise that their parents' eyes are resting enquiringly on the governess's dreamy, abstracted face, and then their mother and father look at each other.

After lunch their mother says casually to Fräulein, "Will you come to my room, please? I want to speak to you." Fräulein bows her head slightly. The girls are trembling violently. They can feel that something is brewing.

As soon as the governess goes into their mother's room they hurry after her. This eavesdropping, rummaging about in nooks and crannies, listening and lying in wait has become second nature to them. They are no longer even aware that their conduct is improperly bold and sly, they have just one idea in their heads—to get possession of all the secrets being kept from them. They listen. But all they hear is whispered words, and a soft but angry tone of voice. Their bodies tremble nervously. They are afraid of failing to catch something important.

Then one of the voices inside the room rises higher. It is their mother's. She sounds angry and cantankerous.

"Did you really think everyone's blind, and no one would notice anything? I can well imagine how you've carried out your duties with such ideas in your head, and with morals like that! And it is to such a woman that I have entrusted the upbringing of my children, my daughters, a task that God knows you have neglected…"

Fräulein seems to be saying something in reply, but too quietly for the children to make out what it is.

"Excuses, excuses! Every promiscuous girl will offer that excuse! She'll blame the first man who comes to mind and think nothing of it, hoping the good Lord will come to her aid. And a woman like that claims to be a governess and fit to educate girls. It's outrageous. You surely don't imagine that, in your condition, I shall keep you in my household any longer?"

The children listen intently outside the door. Shivers run through them. They don't understand what their mother is saying, but it is terrible to hear her voice raised in such anger—and the only answer is their governess's quiet, uncontrollable sobbing. Tears come to their own eyes. But the sobbing only seems to make their mother angrier.

"So all you can do now is burst into tears! You don't touch my heart like that. I have no sympathy for such females. What becomes of you now is none of my business. You'll know where to turn, I'm sure, I'm not asking you for the details. All I know is that I shall not tolerate the presence of someone who has so shamefully neglected her duty in my house a day longer."

Only sobs answered her, desperate, wild, animal sobs that shake the children outside the door like a fever. They have never heard anyone cry so hard. And they feel, vaguely, that someone crying like that can't be in the wrong. Their mother is silent now, waiting. Then she says suddenly, brusquely, "Very well, that's all I wanted to say to you. Pack your bags today and come to collect your wages first thing tomorrow. Goodbye."

The children scurry away from the door, and take refuge in their room. What was all that about? They feel as if a bolt of lightning has struck them. Standing there pale and shuddering, for the first time they somehow guess the truth. For the first time, too, they dare to feel hostile to their parents.

"It was wrong of Mama to speak to her like that," says the elder girl, biting her lower lip.

Her younger sister still shrinks from such a bold statement. "But we don't know what she did," she stammers plaintively.

"It can't have been anything bad. Fräulein can't have done anything bad. Mama doesn't know what she's really like."

"And the way she cried—it scared me."

"Yes, it was terrible. So was the way Mama shouted at her. It was wrong of Mama, I tell you it was wrong."

She stamps her foot. Her eyes are blurred with tears. Then the governess comes in, looking very tired.

"Children, there are things I have to do this afternoon. You can be left on your own, can't you? I'm sure I can rely on you, and then I'll see you this evening."

She goes out without noticing how upset the children are.

"Did you see her eyes? They were all red with crying. I can't understand how Mama could treat her like that."

"Oh, poor Fräulein!"

That deep, tearful sigh of sympathy again. The children are standing there in distress when their mother comes in to ask if they would like to go for a walk with her. The girls are evasive. They are afraid of their mother. In addition they are indignant; no one has said a word to them about their governess's departure. They would rather be on their own. Like two swallows in a small cage they swoop back and forth, upset by this atmosphere of lies and silence. They wonder whether to go and see Fräulein in her room and ask her questions, talk to her about it all, tell her they want her to stay and Mama is wrong. But they are afraid of hurting her feelings. And they are also ashamed of themselves for having found out all they know on the sly, by dint of eavesdropping. They must pretend to be stupid, as stupid as they were two or three weeks ago. So they spend the long, endless afternoon on their own, brooding over what they have heard and crying, always with those terrible voices ringing in their ears, their mother's vicious, heartless fury and the desperate sobs of their governess.

Fräulein looks in on them fleetingly that evening and says goodnight. The children tremble when they see her going out; they would like to say something to her. But when Fräulein reaches the door she turns back suddenly, as if their silent wish has brought her back once more of her own accord. Something is gleaming in her eyes; they are moist and clouded. She hugs both children, who begin sobbing wildly, kisses them once again, and then quickly goes out.

The children are in tears. They sense that she was saying goodbye.

"We won't see her any more!" wails one of the girls.

"No, when we get back from school at mid-day tomorrow she's sure to have gone."

"Maybe we can go and visit her later. And then I'm sure she'll show us her baby."

"Oh yes, she's so nice."

"Oh, poor Fräulein!" It is a sigh for their own loss again.

"Can you imagine what it will be like now without her?"

"I'll never be able to take to another governess."

"Nor me."

"No one else will be so kind to us. And then…"

She dares not say it. But an unconscious sense of femininity has made them revere Fräulein even more since they found out about her baby. They both keep thinking about it, and no longer with mere childish curiosity, but deeply moved and sympathetic.

"Listen," says one of the girls. "I know what!"

"Yes?"

"I'd like to do something nice for Fräulein before she goes. So that she'll know we love her and we're not like Mama. What about you?"

"How can you ask?"

"What I thought was, she's always liked white roses so much. Suppose we go out to buy her some first thing tomorrow, before we go to school, and then we can put them in her room."

"But when?"

"At mid-day when we come home."

"She'll be gone by then. I tell you what, suppose I run out very early and buy them before anyone notices I'm gone? And then we can take them to her in her room before we go to school."

"Yes, and we'll get up really early."

They fetch their money boxes, shake out the contents and put all their money together. They feel happier now they know that they can still give Fräulein proof of their silent, devoted love.

They get up very early in the morning. They stand outside the governess's door holding the beautiful double white roses—their hands tremble slightly—but when they knock there is no answer. They think Fräulein must be asleep, and cautiously slip into the room. But it is empty, and the bed has not been slept in. Everything lies scattered around in disorder. A couple of letters in white envelopes lie on the dark tabletop.

The two children take fright. What has happened?

"I'm going to see Mama," says the elder girl with determination. And defiantly, her eyes sombre and entirely fearless, she faces her mother head on and asks, "Where is our Fräulein?"

"She'll be in her room," says her mother, surprised.

"Her room's empty and she hasn't slept in her bed. She must have gone away yesterday evening. Why didn't anyone tell us?"

Her mother doesn't even notice the harsh, challenging tone of the girl's voice. She has turned pale, and goes to see her husband, who quickly disappears into the governess's room.

He stays there for a long time. The child watches her mother, who seems to be upset, with a steady angry gaze that the mother's eyes dare not meet.

Then her father comes back. He is very pale in the face, and is carrying a letter. He goes into the sitting room with her mother and talks to her quietly. The children stand outside, not venturing to listen at the door any more. They are afraid of their father's wrath. Just now he looked as they have never seen him before.

Their mother comes out of the sitting room, her eyes red with tears and appearing distressed. Instinctively, as if attracted to her fear, the children go to meet her, wanting to ask questions. But she says brusquely, "Off you go to school. You're late already."

And the children have to go. As if in a dream they sit there for four or five hours among all the other girls, hearing not a word. They rush home when lessons are over.

Home would be the same as usual except that everyone seems to be in the grip of a terrible idea. No one says anything, but they all, even the servants, look so strange. The children's mother comes to meet them. She seems to have prepared something to tell them. She begins, "Girls, your Fräulein will not be coming back, she has..."

But she does not venture to finish what she was going to say. As her children's eyes meet hers, they flash with such dangerous menace that she dares not tell them a lie. She turns and leaves them, taking refuge in her room.

Otto suddenly turns up that afternoon. He has been summoned; one of the letters left was for him. He too is pale and stands around looking upset. No one speaks to him. They all avoid him. Then he sees the two children huddled together in a corner and goes over to say hello.

"Don't you touch me!" says one of the girls, shuddering with disgust. Her sister actually spits on the floor in front of him. He wanders around for a little longer, looking confused and embarrassed. Then he disappears.

No one talks to the children. They themselves do not exchange a word with anyone. They pace around like caged animals, palefaced, restless and agitated; they keep coming together, meeting one another's tear-stained gaze, but saying nothing. They know all about it now. They know that they have been told lies, all human beings can be bad and despicable. They do not love their parents any more, they don't believe in them. They know that they can never trust anyone, the whole monstrous weight of life will weigh down on their slender shoulders. They have been cast out of the cheerful comfort of their childhood, as if into an abyss. They cannot quite grasp the terrible nature of what has happened, but the thought of it makes them choke and threatens to stifle them. Their cheeks burn feverishly, and they have an angry, agitated look in their eyes. As if freezing in their isolation, they wander up and down. No one, not even their parents, dares speak to them, they look at everyone with such ill will, and their constant pacing back and forth reflects the agitation working inside them. Although the two girls do not talk to each other about it, they have something dreadful in common. Their impenetrable, unquestioning silence and viciously self-contained pain makes them seem strange and dangerous to everyone. No one comes close to them; access to their minds has been cut off, perhaps for many years to come. Everyone around them feels that they are enemies, and determined enemies at that who will not easily forgive again. For yesterday their childhood came to an end.

That afternoon they grow many years older. And only when they are alone in the darkness of their room in the evening do childish fears surface in them, the fear of loneliness, of images of dead people, as well as a presentiment of indistinct terrors. In the general agitation of the house, no one has remembered to heat the rooms. So they get into one bed together, freezing, holding each other tightly in their thin childish arms, pressing their slender bodies, not yet in the full bloom of youth, close to each other as if seeking help in their fear. They still dare not talk freely. But now the younger girl at last bursts into tears, and her elder sister joins her, sobbing wildly. They weep, closely entwined, warm tears rolling down their faces hesitantly at first, then falling faster, hugging one another breast to breast, shaking as they share their sobs. They are united in pain, a single weeping body in the darkness. They are not crying for the governess now, or for the parents who are lost to them; they are shaken by a sudden horror and fear of the unknown world lying ahead of them, after the first terrifying glimpse that they had of it today. They are afraid of the life ahead of them into which they will now pass, dark and menacing like a gloomy forest through which they must go. Their confused fears become dimmer, almost dreamlike, their sobbing is softer and softer. Their breath mingles gently now, as their tears mingled before. And so at last they fall asleep.

COMPULSION

To Pierre J Jouve
in fraternal friendship

THE WOMAN WAS STILL fast asleep, her breath coming full and strong. Her mouth, slightly open, seemed to be on the verge of smiling or speaking, and her curved young breasts rose softly under the covers. The first glimmer of dawn showed at the windows, but the light was poor this winter morning. Somewhere between darkness and day, it hovered uncertainly over sleeping things, veiling their forms.

Ferdinand had risen and dressed quietly, he himself did not know why. It often happened these days that, in the middle of working, he would suddenly pick up his hat and hurry out of the house, into the fields, striding faster and faster until he had walked to the point of exhaustion, and all at once found himself somewhere far away, in a place he did not know, his knees shaking and the pulse throbbing at his temples. Or he would suddenly freeze in the middle of an animated conversation and lose track of the words, failing to hear questions, and he would have to force himself back into awareness. Then again, he might forget what he was doing when he undressed in the evening, and would sit perfectly still on the edge of the bed, holding the shoe he had just taken off, until a word from his wife startled him out of his reverie or the shoe fell to the floor with a bang.

As he now left the slightly close atmosphere of the bedroom and stepped out on to the balcony, he shivered. Instinctively he drew his elbows in, closer to the warmth of his body. The landscape deep below him was still enveloped in mist. Dense, milky vapours hovered over the Lake of Zürich, which from his little house, perched high up here, usually looked as smooth as a mirror, reflecting every white cloud that hurried past in the sky.

Wherever his eyes looked, whatever his hands felt, it was all damp, dark, slippery and grey. Water dripped from the trees, moisture trickled from the rafters of the house. The world rising from the mists was like a man who has just emerged from a river with water streaming off him. The murmur of human voices came through the misty night, but muted and disjointed like the stertorous breathing of a drunk. Sometimes he also heard hammer blows and the distant chime of the bell from the church tower, but its usually clear tone sounded damp and rusty. Dank darkness stood between him and his world.

He shivered. Yet he stayed there, his hands thrust deeper into his pockets, waiting for the view to clear. The mist began slowly rolling up from below, like a sheet of grey paper, and he longed to see the beloved landscape that, he knew, lay down there in its usual orderly fashion, with its clear lines that normally brought clarity and order to his own life, although now it was hidden by these morning mists. He had so often gone to the window here in a mood of inner turmoil to find reassurance in the peaceful view: the houses over on the opposite bank of the lake, turning to each other as if in friendship, a steamer dividing the blue water with delicate precision, gulls flocking cheerfully over the banks, smoke rising in silver coils from red chimneys as the noonday chimes rang out. Peace! Peace! was the message it conveyed for all to see. At such moments, in the face of his own knowledge and despite the madness of the world, he believed in the beautiful signal it gave him, and for hours could forget his own homeland as he looked at this new one that he had chosen. Months ago, in flight from the present times and from other human beings, coming away from a country at war and arriving in Switzerland, he had felt his soul, crumpled, furrowed and ploughed into disorder as it was by horror and dismay, smoothing out here and growing scar tissue as the landscape softly welcomed him in, and its pure lines and colours called on his art to set to work. As a result he always felt alienated from himself, an exile once again, when the sight was obscured, as it was by the mist hiding everything from him at this time of the morning. He felt infinite pity for everyone shut up down in the dark, and for the people in the world of his old home, far away now—infinite pity, and a longing to be linked to them and their fate.

Somewhere out in the mist, the bell in the church tower gave four strokes and then, telling itself the time of day, chimed eight in clearer tones that pealed out into the March morning. He felt as if he were on top of a tower himself, indescribably isolated, with the world before him and his wife behind him in the darkness of her slumbers. His innermost will strained to tear that soft wall of mist apart and to sense, somewhere, the message of awakening, the certainty of life. And as he sent his eyes out into the mist, so to speak, he thought he did see something, either a man or an animal, moving slowly down there in the grey penumbra where the village ended and the winding path climbed up the hill to this house. Small, softly veiled in mist, it was coming towards him. He felt first pleasure to see something awake besides himself, then curiosity too, an avid and unhealthy curiosity. The grey figure of a man was making its way to a crossroads, with tracks leading to the next village in one direction and up here in the other. For a moment the stranger seemed to hesitate and draw breath at the crossroads. Then, slowly, he began climbing the bridle path.

Ferdinand felt uneasy. Who is this man, he wondered, what compulsion drives him out of the warmth of his dark bedroom and into the morning as mine has driven me? Is he coming up to see me, and if so what does he want? Then, through the mist which was thinner at close quarters now, he recognized the post-man. He climbed up here every morning on the stroke of eight, and Ferdinand knew and pictured the man's rough-hewn face, his red seaman's beard turning grey at the ends, and his blue-framed glasses. His name was Nussbaum, meaning 'nut tree', and to himself

Ferdinand called him Nutcracker because of his stiff movements and the ceremony with which he always swung his big, black leather bag over to the right before delivering the post with an air of self-importance. Ferdinand could not help smiling as he saw him trudging up, step by step, bag at the moment slung over his left shoulder, careful to impart great dignity to his short-legged gait.

But suddenly he felt weak at the knees. His hand, which had been shielding his eyes, dropped as if suddenly numb. His uneasiness today, yesterday, all these last weeks was back. He thought he sensed that the man was coming step by step inexorably towards him, coming to him alone. Without knowing just what he was about, he opened the bedroom door, stole past his sleeping wife, and hurried downstairs to intercept the postman on his way up the fenced path. They met at the garden gate.

"Do you have... do you have..."—he had to try again three times—"do you have any post for me?"

The postman pushed up his wet glasses to look at him. "Let's have a look." He hauled the black bag round to his right, and his fingers—they were like large worms, damp and red with the frosty mist—rummaged among the letters. Ferdinand was shivering. In the end the postman took one letter out. It was in a large brown envelope, with the word '*Official*' stamped in large letters on it, and his name underneath. "To be signed for," said the postman, moistening his indelible pencil and holding out the book to Ferdinand, who signed his name with a flourish. In his agitation the signature was illegible.

Then he took the letter that the sturdy red hand was offering him. But his fingers were so awkward that it slipped out of them, and fell to the ground to lie on the wet soil and damp leaves. And as he bent to pick it up, a bitter smell of decomposition and decay rose to his nostrils.

*

This, he now knew for certain, was what had been lurking under the surface for weeks, destroying his peace: the thought of this letter, which he had expected and was reluctant to receive, sent to him from far away, from a pointless, formless distance. Its rigid, typewritten words were groping for him, his warm life and his freedom. He had felt it approaching from somewhere or other, like a mounted man on patrol who senses the cold steel tube invisibly aimed at him from green forest undergrowth, and the little piece of lead in it that wants to penetrate the darkness beneath his skin. So resistance had been useless, and so had the little tricks he had practised to occupy his mind for nights on end. They had caught up with him. Barely eight months ago he had been standing naked, shivering with cold and revulsion, in front of an army doctor who felt the muscles in his arms like a horse-dealer. The humiliation of it illustrated the human indignity of the times and the slavery into which Europe had declined. He bore life in the stifling atmosphere of the patriotic phase of the war for two months, but after a while he found the air too difficult to breathe, and when the people around him opened their lips to speak he thought he saw their lies lying yellow on their tongues. The sight of the women, shivering with cold, who sat on the marketplace steps with their empty potato sacks in the first light of dawn broke his heart; he went around with his fists clenched, he felt that he was turning mean-minded and spiteful, he hated himself in his powerless rage. At last, thanks to a good word that someone put in for him, he succeeded in moving to Switzerland with his wife, and when he crossed the border the blood suddenly returned to his cheeks. He was swaying so much that he had to hold on to a post for support, but he felt like a human being again at last, full of life, will, strength, and capable of action. His lungs opened to breathe the air of freedom. All his fatherland meant to him now was prison and compulsion. His home in the world was outside his country, Europe was humanity.

But that light-hearted happiness did not last long. The fear came back. He felt that somehow or other his name had hooked him from behind to haul him back into that bloodstained thicket, that something he didn't know, although it knew him, was not about to let him go. He retreated inside himself, read no newspapers in order to avoid anything about men being called up, moved house to blur his trail, had letters sent to his wife *poste restante*, and avoided company so as to be asked no questions. He never went into town, he sent his wife to buy canvas and paints. He hid away in anonymity in this little village on the Lake of Zürich, where he had rented a small house from a farming family. But still he knew that in a drawer somewhere, among hundreds of thousands of other sheets of paper, there was one with his name on it. And one day, somewhere, some time, they would be bound to open that drawer—he could hear it being pulled out, he imagined the staccato hammer of his name being typed, and he knew that the letter would be sent on its travels until at last it found him.

Now here it was, crackling and cold, physically present in his fingers. Ferdinand made an effort to keep calm. What does this letter matter to me? he asked himself. Why should I take out the sheet of paper inside the envelope and read what it says overleaf? Tomorrow and the day after tomorrow the bushes will bear a thousand, ten thousand, a hundred thousand leaves, and this is no more to me than any of them. What does that word '*Official*' mean? Does that say I *have* to read it? I hold no office anywhere, and no one holds office over me. What's my name there for—is that really me? Who can compel me to say it means me, who can force me to read what's written on the paper? If I just tear it up unread, the scraps will flutter down to the lake, I won't know anything about it and nor will the world; it will be gone as fast as a drop of water falling from a tree to the ground, as fast as every breath that passes my lips! Why should this piece of paper make me uneasy? I won't know anything about it unless I want to. And I don't want to. All I want is my freedom.

His fingers tensed, ready to tear the stout envelope into small scraps. But oddly enough, his muscles would not do it. Something or other had taken over his own hands against his own will, for they did not obey him. And as he wished with all his heart that they would tear up the envelope, they very carefully opened it and, trembling, unfolded the white sheet of paper. It said what he already knew.

'No 34.729F. On the orders of District Headquarters at M, your honour is hereby requested hereby to present yourself in Room Number 8, District Headquarters at M, by 22nd March at the latest for a further medical examination with a view to establishing your fitness for service in the army. You will be issued with the military papers by the Consulate in Zürich, where you are to go for that purpose.'

When he went back indoors an hour later his wife came to meet him, smiling, a bunch of spring flowers loosely held in her hand. She was radiant with carefree delight. "Look," she said, "look what I've found! They're already flowering in the meadow behind the house, even though the snow still lies in the shade among the trees." He took the flowers to please her, bent over them so as not to catch his beloved wife's untroubled gaze, and was quick to take refuge in the little attic room that he had made into a studio.

But his work did not go well. No sooner did he face his blank canvas than the typewritten words of the letter suddenly stood there as if hammered out on it. The colours on his palette seemed to him like mud and blood. He kept thinking of pus and wounds. His self-portrait, painted in half-shade, showed him a military collar under his chin. "Madness! Madness!" he said out loud, stamping his foot to dispel these deranged images. But his hands trembled and the floor shook beneath his feet. He had to sit down, and he went on sitting there on his small stool, overwhelmed by his thoughts, until his wife called him to luncheon.

Every morsel choked him. Something bitter was stuck high up in his throat, it had to be swallowed with every mouthful, and it always came up again. Hunched there in silence, he realized that his wife was watching him. Suddenly he felt her hand softly placed on his own.

"What's the matter, Ferdinand?" He did not reply. "Have you had bad news?"

He just nodded, and gulped.

"From the army?"

He nodded again. She said no more, and nor did he. The looming, oppressive idea of it was suddenly there in the room, pushing everything else aside. It weighed down, broad and sticky, on the food they had begun to eat. It crawled, a damp slug, over the backs of their necks and made them shudder. They dared not look at each other, but just sat there in silence with their shoulders bent, and the intolerable burden of that thought pressing down on them.

There was a faltering note in her voice when at last she asked, "Have they told you to go to the Consulate?"

"Yes."

"And will you go?"

He was trembling. "I don't know. But I have to."

"Why do you have to? They can't order you about here in Switzerland. You're a free man here."

"Free!" he said savagely, through gritted teeth. "Who's still free today?"

"Anyone who wants to be. You most of all. What *is* this?" Contemptuously, she snatched away the sheet of paper that he had placed in front of him. "What power does this scrap of paper have over you, scribbled by some wretched clerk in an office—what power does it have over you? You're a free, living man! What can it do to you?"

140

"In itself it can't do anything, but the people who sent it can."

"So who sent it? What human being does it come from? It's from no one but a machine, a vast, murderous machine. But it can't touch you."

"It's touched millions, so why not me?"

"Because you don't want to go?"

"Nor did all the others."

"But they weren't free. They were caught between the guns, that's why they went. Not of their own free will, not one of them. No one would willingly have left Switzerland to go back to that hell."

But when she saw how he was tormenting himself, she checked her wildness. Pity welled up in her, as if for a child. "Ferdinand," she said, leaning against him, "try to think perfectly clearly now. You're afraid, and I understand how distressing it is to have this evil beast suddenly pouncing on you. But remember, we were expecting this letter. We've discussed what to do in this event hundreds of times, and I was proud of you because I knew you'd just tear it to pieces, you wouldn't give yourself up to go and murder people. Don't you remember?"

"I know, Paula, I know, but..."

"Don't say any more now," she urged him. "Somehow or other, this thing has got its teeth into you. But think of our conversations, of the statement you drew up—it's there in the left-hand drawer of the desk—saying that you would never carry arms. You had firmly decided..."

He reacted to that. "No, I hadn't firmly decided! I was never sure! All that was lies. I was hiding from my own fear. I intoxicated myself with those words. But it was all true only as long as I was free, and I always knew that if I was summoned I'd be weak. Do you think I trembled before them? They're nothing as long as their ideas aren't really in my heart, otherwise they're just air, words, nothing. But I trembled before myself, because I always knew that as soon as they called me up I'd go."

"Ferdinand, do you *want* to go?"

"No, no, no," he cried, stamping his foot, "I don't want to, I don't, nothing in me wants to. But I *shall* go, against my own will. That's the terrible part of these people's power, you serve them against your will, against your own convictions. If you still had a will of your own—but the moment you have a letter like that in your hands, your free will is gone. You obey. You're a schoolboy, the teacher's calling to you, you stand up and tremble."

"But Ferdinand, who's calling you? The Fatherland? Some clerk in an office! Some bored bureaucrat! And what's more, even the state has no right to force a man to commit murder, no right…"

"I know, I know. Why not quote Tolstoy too? I know all the arguments: don't you understand, I myself don't believe they have any right to call me up, I don't believe it's my duty to obey them. I acknowledge only one kind of duty: to act as a human being and to work. I have no Fatherland beyond mankind in general, no ambition to kill other people, I know all that, Paula, I see it as clearly as you do—except that they've caught me already, they're summoning me and I know, in spite of everything, I shall go."

"But why? Why? I ask you, why?"

He groaned. "I don't know why. Perhaps because madness is stronger than reason in the world these days. Perhaps it's just because I'm no hero and I daren't run away… there's no explaining it. It's a kind of compulsion; I can't break the chain that is throttling twenty million people. I can't do it."

He hid his face in his hands. The clock above them ticked on and on, a guard on duty outside the sentry-box of time. She was trembling slightly. "It's calling to you, yes, I can understand that, although… well, I don't *really* understand it. But can't you hear anything here calling to you as well? Is there nothing to keep you here?"

He flared up. "My pictures? My work? No! I can't paint any more. I realized that today. I'm already living over there, not here any more. It's a crime to work for your own pleasure now while the world falls into ruin. You can't feel and live for yourself alone!"

She stood up and turned away. "I never thought you lived for yourself alone. I thought... I thought I was part of your world too." She couldn't go on; her tears were forcing their way out along with her words. He tried to soothe her. But there was anger behind her tears, and he shrank from that. "Go, then," she said, "you'd better go! What do I mean to you? Less than a scrap of paper. So go if you want to."

"I don't want to!" He struck the table with his fists in helpless rage. "I don't want to. But they want me to. They are strong and I'm weak. They've forged their iron will over thousands of years, they're well-organized and subtle, they've made preparations and now it breaks over us like a thunderstorm. Their will is strong and my nerves are weak. It's an unequal battle. You can't fight back against a machine. You could resist men, yes, but this is a machine, a slaughtering machine, a soulless tool without a heart or mind. There's nothing you can do to oppose it."

"Yes, you can if you must." She was shouting like a madwoman now. "I can do it if you can't. If you're weak I'm not, I don't knuckle under to a piece of paper, I don't give up any living creature for a word. You won't go as long as I have any power over you. You're sick, I can swear it. You're highly strung. If a plate so much as clinks you jump nervously. Any doctor must see that. Get yourself examined here, I'll go with you, I'll tell the doctor everything. He's sure to say you're unfit. You just have to defend yourself, take the bit between your teeth—the bit of your own will. Remember your friend Jeannot in Paris, who had himself put under observation in the psychiatric hospital for three months—and how they tormented him with their investigations, but he held out until they discharged him. You just have to show that you're not going along with them. You can't give up. This means everything; don't forget, they want your life, your liberty, everything. You have to fight back."

"Fight back! How can I fight back? They're stronger than anyone, they're stronger than anything in the whole world."

"That's not true! They're only strong as long as the world allows it. The individual is always stronger than any idea, he just has to be true to himself and his own will. He just has to know that he's a human being and wants to stay human, and then those words they use to anaesthetize people these days—the Fatherland, duty, heroism—then they're simply phrases stinking of blood, warm, living human blood. Be honest, is your Fatherland as important to you as your life? Is a province that will switch overnight from one Serene Highness to another as dear to you as the hand you paint with? Do you believe in some kind of justice beyond the invisible knowledge of what's just and right that we build into ourselves with our thoughts, our blood? No, I know you don't, no! You're lying to yourself if you say you want to go..."

"I don't want to."

"But you don't feel that strongly enough! You don't want to stay any more. You're letting yourself want to do this thing, that's your crime. You're giving yourself up to something you hate and staking your life on it. Why not on something you really believe in? Shedding blood for your own ideas is one thing, but why do it for someone else's? Ferdinand, don't forget, if you really want strongly enough to stay free, what are those people over the border but wicked fools? If you *don't* want it enough, and they get hold of you, then you're the fool. You always said..."

"Yes, I said, I said it all, I talked and talked just to give myself courage. I was boasting, the way children sing in a dark wood because they're afraid of their own fears. It was all a lie, that's cruelly clear to me now. Because I always knew that if they sent for me I'd go..."

"You're really going? Oh, Ferdinand, Ferdinand!"

"Not me! Not me! It's something else in me that's going—has gone already. Something or other stands up in me like the schoolboy obediently standing up for the teacher, I told you so. It trembles and obeys! Yet at the same time I hear all you say, and I know it's right and true and human and necessary—it's the one thing I ought to do, I must do—I know that, I know it, that's why it's so despicable of me to go. But I *am* going, something compels me. Despise me! I despise myself. But there's nothing else I can do, nothing!"

He hammered on the table with both fists. There was a dull, animal, captive expression in his eyes. She couldn't bear to look at him. In her love, she was afraid that she might indeed despise him. The table was still laid, the meat standing on it was cold now and looked like carrion, the bread was black and crumbling; it might have been slag. The heavy smell of food filled the room. Nausea rose to her throat in her disgust at all this. She pushed the window open to let in some fresh air. Her shoulders were shaking slightly, and above them rose the blue March sky, with its white clouds caressing her hair.

"Look," she said more quietly, "look out there! Just once, I beg you. Perhaps all I'm saying isn't entirely true. Words always miss the mark. But what I can see is true all the same. That doesn't lie. There's a farmer down there following the plough. He's young and strong. Why doesn't *he* go off to be murdered? Because his country isn't at war, because his fields lie a little way beyond the border, so the law doesn't apply to him. And now that you're in this country it doesn't apply to you either. Can an invisible law that's in force only as far as a few milestones and then not beyond them be true? Don't you feel how senseless it is when you look at the peace here? Look, Ferdinand, look, see how clear the sky is above the lake, see how the colours wait for us to enjoy them, come here to the window and then tell me just once more that you want to go…"

"I don't want to go! I don't want to! You know I don't! Why should I look out at this scene? I know all about it, everything, everything! You're just tormenting me! Every word you say hurts. And nothing, nothing, nothing can help me!"

She felt weak in the face of his pain. Pity broke her strength. She quietly turned around.

"So when... oh, Ferdinand... when do you have to go to the Consulate?"

"Tomorrow. Well, it ought to have been yesterday, but the letter didn't reach me in time. They didn't track me down until today. So I'll have to go tomorrow."

"But suppose you don't go tomorrow? Keep them waiting. They can't do anything to you here. And there's no hurry. Let them wait a week. I'll write and tell them you were ill, you were in bed. My brother did that and gained two weeks' grace. At the worst they won't believe you and they'll send the doctor from the Consulate up here. Perhaps we could talk to him. People are still human beings if they don't wear a uniform. Maybe he'll look at your pictures and see that someone like you is right out of place at the front. And even if that doesn't work we'll have gained a week."

He said nothing, and she felt that his silence was opposing her.

"Ferdinand, promise me not to go tomorrow! Let them wait. You need to be well prepared in your mind. At the moment you're upset, and they're doing what they like with you. They'd be stronger than you tomorrow, but in a week's time you'll be stronger than them. Think of the happy days we'll enjoy then. Oh, Ferdinand, Ferdinand, are you listening to me?"

She shook him. He looked at her, empty-eyed. That apathetic, lost gaze showed no response to her words, only horror and fear from a depth that she could not plumb. He pulled himself together only slowly.

"You're right," he said at last. "You're right, there's no hurry. What can they do to me? Has the letter necessarily reached me? Couldn't I have gone away for a little while? Or I could have been ill. No—I signed a receipt for the postman. But that makes no difference. We have to think things over. You're right, you're right."

He had risen to his feet and began pacing up and down the room. "You're right, you're right," he mechanically repeated, but there was no conviction in his voice. "You're right, you're right"—it sounded abstracted, he was repeating the words vacantly. She felt that his thoughts were somewhere else, far away, still with the people over the border, still heading for disaster. She couldn't bear to hear his constant "You're right, you're right" any more. Quietly, she went out of the room, and then heard him walking up and down it for hours on end, like a prisoner in his dungeon.

He did not touch dinner that evening either. There was something far away and frozen in him. It was only that night that she felt her living husband's fear as he lay beside her, clasping her soft, warm body as if taking refuge in it, embracing her passionately, convulsively. But this, she knew, was not love but escape. It was a spasmodic reaction, and under his kisses she sensed bitter, salty tears. Then he lay in silence again. Sometimes she heard him groan. Then she held her hand out to him, and he took it as if he could cling to it. They did not talk. Only once, when she heard him sob, did she try to comfort him. "You still have a week. Don't think about it." But then she was ashamed of herself for advising him to think of something else, for she felt from the chill of his hand, the pulsing of his heart, that this one idea possessed and commanded him. And there was no miracle to release him from it.

Never before had silence and the dark weighed so heavily in this house. The horror of the whole world stood there within its walls, cold and chilly. Only the clock, undeterred, ticked on, an iron sentry marching up, marching down, and she knew that with every marching step of that clock the living man at her side, the man she loved, was moving further away from her. She couldn't bear it any more; she jumped out of bed and stopped the pendulum. Now there was no time any more, only terror and silence.

And they both lay mute and wakeful, side by side, until the new day dawned, with the idea of what was to come marching up and down in their hearts.

It was still wintry twilight. Hoarfrost was hovering over the lake in heavy drifts of mist when he got up, quickly threw on his clothes, hurried hesitantly and uncertainly from room to room and back again, until he suddenly took his hat and coat and quietly opened the front door. Later, he often remembered how his hand had trembled when it touched the bolt, which was cold with frost, and he turned furtively to see if anyone was watching him. Sure enough, the dog rushed at him as if he were a thief stealing in, but on recognizing him got down, responded affectionately to his patting, and then raced around wagging his tail, eager to go for a walk with him. However, he shooed the dog away with his hand—he dared not speak. Then, not sure himself why he was in such haste, he suddenly hurried down the bridle path. Sometimes he stopped and looked back at his house as it slowly disappeared from sight in the mist, but then the urge to go on came over him once more and he ran downhill to the station, stumbling over stones as if someone were after him. Only when he arrived did he stop, warm vapour rising from his moist clothes, sweat on his forehead.

A few farmers and other folk who knew him were standing there. They wished him good morning, and one or two seemed inclined to strike up a conversation with him, but he turned away from them. He felt a bashful fear of having to talk to other people at this moment, and yet waiting idly beside the wet rails was painful. Without attending to what he was doing he stood on the scales, put a coin in the slot, stared into his pale, sweating face in the little mirror above the dial that showed his weight, and only when he got off and his coin clinked down inside the machine did he notice that he had failed to register what the pointers said. "I'm going out of my mind, right out of my mind," he murmured quietly, and felt a chill of horror at himself. He sat down on a bench and tried to force himself to think everything over clearly. But then the signal bell rang, very close to him, a harsh, jangling sound, and he jumped, startled. The locomotive was already whistling in the distance. The train raced in, and he sat down in a compartment. A dirty newspaper lay on the floor. He picked the newspaper up and stared at it without taking in what he was reading, seeing only his own hands holding it and shaking more and more all the time.

The train stopped. Zürich. He staggered out. He knew where he was going, and sensed his own reluctance to go there, but it was growing weaker all the time. Now and then he set himself small trials of strength. He stopped in front of a poster and, to prove that he was in command of himself, forced himself to read it from top to bottom. "There's no hurry," he told himself in an undertone, but even as his lips murmured the words he was overcome by haste again. His frantic, thrusting impatience was like an engine driving him on. Helplessly, he looked around for a cab. His legs were trembling. A taxi drove by and he hailed it, flinging himself into it like a suicide plunging into the river. He gave a name; the street where the Consulate stood.

The car engine hummed. He leaned back with his eyes closed. He felt as if he were racing into an abyss, and even took some slight pleasure in the speed of the cab carrying him to his doom. It felt good to observe himself passively. But the car was already stopping. He got out, paid the driver, and entered the lift of the building where the Consulate had its offices. In an odd way he again felt a sense of pleasure at being mechanically raised up and carried onwards. As if it were not himself doing all this, but the unknown, unimaginable power of his compulsion forcing him to go on his way.

The door of the Consulate was locked. He rang the bell. No answer. A thought flashed urgently through his mind: go back, get away from here quickly, go down the stairs and out! But he rang the bell again. Steps came slowly dragging along inside. A servant in his shirt-sleeves, duster in hand, made a great business of opening the door. Obviously he was tidying the offices. "Yes, what do you want?" he growled.

"I—I was told to come to the Consulate,' he managed to say, retreating, and ashamed of stammering in front of this servant.

The man turned, sounding peevish and annoyed. "Can't you read what it says on the plate? Office hours ten to twelve. There's nobody here yet." And without waiting for any answer he closed the door.

Ferdinand stood there, flinching, as a sense of boundless shame struck him to the heart. He looked at his watch. It was ten-past seven. "This is mad! I'm out of my mind!" he stammered, and went down the steps trembling like an old man.

Two-and-a-half hours—this dead, empty time was terrible to him, for he felt that with every minute of waiting some of his strength slipped away. Just now he had been braced and prepared, he had worked out what he would say in advance, every word was ready, the whole scene was constructed in his mind, and now this iron curtain of two hours had fallen between him and the strength he had screwed to the sticking-point. Afraid, he sensed all the warmth in him dissipating, obliterating word after word from his memory as they tumbled over one another and nervously took to flight.

He had worked it out like this: he would go to the Consulate and have himself announced there at once to the military attaché, whom he knew slightly. They had once met and made casual conversation at the house of mutual friends. So he would at least know the man he faced: an aristocrat, elegant, worldly, proud of his joviality, a man who liked to appear generous-minded and did not want to be thought a mere bureaucrat. They all had that ambition, they wanted to figure as diplomats, men of importance, and he planned to work on that: he would have himself announced, speak of general things at first in a civil, sociable tone, ask after the health of the attaché's wife. The attaché would be sure to ask him to sit down, offer him a cigarette, and finally, as silence fell, would say politely, "Well, how can I help you?" The other man must ask him first, that was very important, that was not to be forgotten. In answer he would say, very cool and casual, "I've had a letter asking me to go to M for a medical examination. There must be some mistake; I've already been expressly declared unfit for military service." He must say that very calmly, it must be immediately obvious that he regarded the whole thing as a mere trifle.

At this point the attaché—he remembered the man's casual manner—would take the piece of paper and explain that this was to be a new examination; surely, he would say, he must have seen in the newspapers, some time ago, that even those previously exempted must now report again.

To this, still very coolly, he would say, "Ah, I see! The fact is I don't read the papers, I just don't have time for it. I have work to do." He wanted the other man to see at once how indifferent he was to the whole war, how much he felt himself a free agent.

Of course the attaché would then explain that Ferdinand must comply with this call-up order, he himself was sorry, but the military authorities... and so on and so forth. That would be his moment to speak more forcefully. "Yes, I understand that," he must say, "but the fact is, it's quite impossible for me to interrupt my work just now. I've agreed to have an exhibition of my paintings held, and I can't let the curator down. I've given my word." And then he would suggest to the attaché that he should either be given a longer deadline, or have himself re-examined here by the Consulate doctor.

So far he was sure he knew how it would go. Only after this point were there a number of possibilities. The attaché might agree at once, and then at least he would have gained time. But if the attaché said politely—with cold, evasive civility, suddenly sounding official—that such decisions were inadmissible and outside his jurisdiction, then he had to be resolute. First he must stand up, go over to the desk and say firmly, very, very firmly, his manner conveying an inner sense of inflexible determination, "I understand that, but I would like to put it on record that my economic obligations prevent me from complying with this call-up immediately. I will take it upon myself to postpone matters for three weeks, until I have satisfied my moral liabilities. Naturally I have no intention of failing in my duty to the Fatherland." He was particularly proud of these remarks, which he had planned with care. "I would like to put it on record", "economic obligations"—it all sounded so objective and official. If the attaché then pointed out that there might be legal consequences, that would be the time to make his tone a little sharper and reply coldly, "I know the law, I am well aware of the consequences. But once I have given my word, I regard keeping it the highest law of all, and I must accept any difficulty in order to do so." Then he must be quick to bow, thus cutting the conversation short, and go to the door. He'd show them that he was no workman or apprentice to wait for dismissal, but a man who decided for himself when a conversation was over.

He acted out this scene in his mind three times, pacing up and down. He liked the whole structure, the entire tone of it, he was waiting impatiently for the moment to come like an actor waiting for his cue. There was just one passage that still didn't seem quite right to him. "I have no intention of failing in my duty to the Fatherland." There absolutely had to be some kind of sop to patriotic values in the conversation, it was necessary to show that he was not being purposely obstructive, but he wasn't ready to go either. He would acknowledge the necessity of showing patriotism,

for their ears only, of course, not for himself. However, that "duty
to the Fatherland"—the phrase was too literary, it came too pat.
He thought it over again. Perhaps: "I know that the Fatherland
needs me." No, that was even more ridiculous. Or better: "I have
no intention of shirking my responsibility to answer the call of
the Fatherland." Yes, that was an improvement. But he still didn't
like this part of the scene; it was too servile. He was bowing just a
little too low. He thought yet again. He had better keep it perfectly
simple. "I know my duty"—yes, that was it, you could turn the
phrase this way and that, understand or misunderstand it. And it
sounded clear and brief. You could say it in a masterful tone—"I
know my duty"—almost like a threat. Now it was all perfect. Yet he
glanced nervously at his watch again. Time refused to go forward.
It was only eight o'clock.

People jostled him in the street, he didn't know which way to
turn. He went into a café and tried to read the papers. But he
felt the words disturbing him; they were all about duty and the
Fatherland here too, and the phrases left him confused. He drank a
cognac and then another, to get rid of the bitter taste in his throat.
Frantically, he wondered how he could get the better of time,
and kept reassembling the pieces of his imaginary conversation
in his head. Suddenly he put a hand to his cheek—"Unshaved! I
haven't shaved!" He hurried to a barber's, where he also had his
hair cut and washed. That disposed of half-an-hour of waiting.
And then, it occurred to him, he ought to look elegant. That was
important in such offices. They took an arrogant tone only with
the riffraff, they'd snap at people like that, but if you appeared
looking elegant, a man of the world, at ease, they'd soon change
their tune. The idea went to his head. He had his coat brushed and
went to buy a pair of gloves, taking a long time over his choice.
Yellow gloves somehow seemed too striking, something a gigolo
might wear; a discreet pearl-grey pair would be better. Then he
went up and down the street again, looked at himself in a tailor's

mirror, adjusted his tie. His hand felt too empty—a walking-stick, it occurred to him, a walking-stick would impart a sense of occasion, a touch of worldliness to his visit. He quickly went into the shop and bought one. When he came out again the clock in the tower was striking quarter-to-ten. He recited his lines to himself once more. The new version, with the words, "I know my duty," was now the strongest part of it. Very sure of himself, very firmly he strode out and ran up the stairs to the Consulate, as light on his feet as a boy.

A minute later, as soon as the servant opened the door, a sudden presentiment that his calculations might be all wrong descended on him. And indeed, nothing went as he had expected. When he asked to see the attaché he was told that His Honour the Secretary was with a visitor, and he must wait. A not particularly civil gesture showed him to a chair in the middle of a row where three men of downcast appearance were already sitting. Reluctantly, he sat down, feeling with annoyance that his was just an ordinary affair here, he was a case, something to be dealt with. The men beside him were exchanging their own little stories; one of them was saying, in plaintive and depressed tones, that he had been interned in France for two years and now the people here wouldn't give him the money for his fare home; another complained that no one would help him to find a job, even though he had three children. Privately, Ferdinand was quivering with fury; they had left him on a bench with common petitioners, yet he noticed that somehow he was also irritated by the petty, fault-finding tone of these ordinary people. He wanted to rehearse his conversation once more, but their fatuous remarks put him off his stroke. He felt like shouting at them, "Be quiet, you fools!" or bringing money out of his pocket and sending them home, but his will was crippled and he just sat there with them, hat in hand like his companions. The constant coming and going of people opening and closing doors also confused him; all the time he was afraid that someone he knew might see him here with the petitioners, and yet whenever a door opened he was ready to leap up, only to sit back again disappointed. Once he pulled himself together and told the servant, who was standing beside them like a sentry on duty, "I can always come back tomorrow, you know." But the man reassured him—"His Honour the Secretary will be able to see you soon"—and his knees gave way again. He was trapped here; there was nothing he could do about it.

At last a lady came out, skirts rustling, smiling and preening, passed the waiting petitioners with an air of superiority, and the servant called, "His Honour the Secretary can see you now."

Ferdinand stood up. Only when it was too late did he realize that he had left his walking-stick and gloves on the window-sill, but he couldn't go back for them now, the door was already open. Half looking back, confused by these random thoughts, he went in. The attaché sat at his desk reading. Now he looked up, nodded to Ferdinand, and gave him a courteous but cold smile, without asking him to sit down. "Ah, our *magister artium*. Just a minute." He rose and called to someone in the next room. "The Ferdinand R file, please, you remember, the one that came the day before yesterday, his call-up papers were sent on here." Sitting down again, he said, "So you're another one who's leaving us again! Well, I hope you've enjoyed your stay here in Switzerland. You're looking very well," and then he was leafing through the file that a clerk brought him. "Report to M… yes… yes, that's right… all in order. I've had the papers made out… I don't suppose you want to claim travel expenses, do you?"

Ferdinand stood up and heard his own voice stammering, "No… no."

The attaché signed the call-up order and handed it to him. "You're really supposed to leave tomorrow, but I don't suppose it's all that urgent. Let the paint dry on your latest masterpiece. If you need another day or so to put your affairs in order, I'll take the responsibility for that. A couple of days won't matter to the Fatherland."

Ferdinand sensed that this was a joke, and he ought to smile. To his private horror, he actually did feel his lips stretching in a polite grimace. Say something, he told himself, I must say something now, not just stand around like a dolt. And at last he managed to get out, "Is the call-up letter enough... I don't need anything else... some kind of special pass?"

"No, no," smiled the attaché. "They won't make any trouble for you at the border. They'll be expecting you anyway. Well, *bon voyage*." And he offered his hand.

Ferdinand felt that he had been dismissed. Everything went dark before his eyes as he quickly made his way to the door. Nausea rose in his throat.

"The door on the right, please, the one on the right," said the voice behind him. He had tried the wrong door, and now—with a slight smile, as he thought he saw in the dim light of his bewildered senses—the attaché was holding the correct door open for him.

"Thank you, thank you, please don't trouble yourself," he stammered, furious with himself for this unnecessary civility. And no sooner was he out of the room, with the servant handing him his stick and gloves, than he remembered all he had planned to say. "Economic obligations... put it on the record." He felt more ashamed than ever before in his life, and he had even thanked the man, thanked him politely! But his emotional capacity would no longer suffice even for rage. Pale-faced, he went down the stairs, feeling only that this man walking along couldn't be himself, and that he had been defeated by force, a strange and pitiless force treading a whole world underfoot.

*

It was not until late in the afternoon that he arrived home. The soles of his feet were sore; he had been walking aimlessly around for hours, and had turned back from his own door three times. Finally he tried stealing up to it from the back, along hidden paths through the vineyards. However, the faithful dog had detected him. Barking wildly, he jumped up at him, tail wagging passionately. His wife stood at the door, and he saw at first glance that she knew everything. He followed her without a word, shame weighing heavily on the back of his neck.

But she was not harsh. She did not look at him, she was visibly avoiding anything that would upset him. She placed some cold meat on the table, and when he obediently sat down she went to his side. "Ferdinand," she said, and her voice was shaking badly, "you're not well. This is not the time for me to talk to you. I won't blame you, you're not acting of your own free will, and I feel how much you're suffering. But promise me one thing: don't do anything else in this business without discussing it first with me."

He said nothing. Her voice became more agitated.

"I've never interfered in your personal affairs, I always aimed to leave you the freedom to make your own decisions absolutely. But now you're playing not just with your life, you're playing with mine too. It took us years to find our happiness, and I'm not giving it up as easily as you. Not to the state, not to murder, not to your vanity and weakness. Not to anyone, do you hear? Not to anyone! If you are weak when you face them, I'm not. I know what this is all about, and I'm not giving up."

He still remained silent, and his servile, guilty silence began to make her bitter. "I'm not letting this scrap of paper take something away from me, I don't acknowledge any law that ends in murder. I'm not bowing to any bureaucracy. You men are all ruined by ideologies now, you think in terms of politics and ethics, we women still have straightforward feelings. I know what the word Fatherland means too, but I know what our Fatherland means today: murder and enslavement. You can feel a sense of belonging to your own nation, but that doesn't mean that when the nations have run mad you have to join them. You may be just a number to them, a tool, cannon-fodder, but to me you're still a living man and I won't let them have you. I'm not giving you up. I've never ventured to decide anything for you, but now it's my duty to protect you. You've always been a clear-minded, responsible human being who knew what he wanted; now you're a broken, disturbed, dutiful mechanism without any will of your own—it's dead, like those millions of victims out there. They've worked on you through your nerves, but they forgot me. I was never stronger than I am now."

He still remained silent, lost in gloomy thought. There was no ability in him to resist either his adversary or her.

She stood up very straight, like someone arming for battle. Her voice was hard, tense, braced.

"What did they say to you at the Consulate? I want to know." It was an order. Wearily, he took out the paper and handed it to her. She read it, frowning. Then she tossed it scornfully on to the table.

"What a hurry those good gentlemen are in! Tomorrow! And I expect you even thanked them, clicked your heels, obedient already. 'Ordered to make yourself available at once.' Available! They should have said make yourself a slave. We haven't fallen so low yet, that point hasn't come, not by a long way!"

Ferdinand stood up. He was pale, and his hand clutched the chair convulsively. "Paula, let's not deceive ourselves. That point *has* come. We can't escape it. I tried to defend myself, and it was no use. I'm—I *am* this piece of paper. Even if I tear it up, I still am. Don't make it difficult for me. There'd be no freedom here. Every hour I'd feel something out there calling, groping for me, pulling and tugging at me. It will be easier for me there. There's freedom to be found in the dungeon itself. It's only while I still feel I'm a fugitive, evading them, that I'm not free. And anyway, why jump to the worst conclusions? They rejected me once, why not this time too? Or perhaps they won't give me a weapon, in fact I feel sure they won't, I'll be employed on some lighter kind of service. Why think the worst now? It may not be so dangerous, perhaps I'll be lucky."

She did not relent. "That's not the point any more, Ferdinand. It makes no difference whether they give you light or heavy work to do. It's a case of whether you have to go into service under what you hate, whether you're willing to lend yourself to the greatest crime in the world against your own convictions. Because everyone who isn't against them is with them. And you *can* reject them, you can do it, so you must."

"I can do it? I can't do anything! Not any more. Everything that once made me strong—my abhorrence of this absurdity, my hatred for it, my indignation—all that is such a burden on me now. Don't torment me, please, don't torment me, don't tell me that."

"I'm not. You have to tell yourself: they have no rights over a living man."

"Rights! Rights! Where are there any rights in the world? We've murdered rights. Every individual person has his rights, but they have power, and nothing else matters any more."

"And why do they have power? Because the rest of you hand it to them. And they'll have it only while you're still cowards. What humanity now calls monstrous consists of ten men with strong wills in the countries concerned, and ten men can destroy the monstrosity again. A man, a single living man can destroy their power by saying no to them. But while you and those like you cower, thinking perhaps you'll muddle through, while you dodge and duck and hope to slip through their fingers instead of striking them to the heart, you'll be their servants and you'll deserve no better. A man ought not to crawl away, he ought to say no, that's the only duty there is today, there's no duty to go and get yourself killed."

"But Paula... what do you think... what should I..."

"You should say no if something says no inside you. You know I love life, I love your freedom, I love your work. And if you tell me today: I have to go there, I have to lay down the law with a gun, and if I know you truly believe you must, then I'll say: Go! But if you go for the sake of a lie that you don't believe yourself, out of weakness and lack of nerve and just hoping you can muddle through, then I despise you, yes, I despise you! If you want to go as a man standing for humanity, for what you believe in, then I won't try to stop you. But if you go to be a beast among beasts, a slave among slaves, I shall stand up to you. It's all right for people to sacrifice themselves for their own ideas, not for the madness of others. Let those who believe in the Fatherland die for it."

"Paula!" Instinctively, he rose to his feet.

"Oh, am I speaking too freely for you? Do you feel the corporal's stick behind you already? Never fear! We're still in Switzerland. You'd like me to keep quiet, or tell you you'll be all right, nothing will happen to you. But this is no time for sentimentality. Everything is at stake now. You and I are at stake."

"Paula!" he said, trying to interrupt again.

"No, I have no more sympathy with you. I chose you and lived with you as a free human being. And I despise weaklings and those who lie to themselves. Why should I sympathize with you? What do I mean to you? A sergeant hands you a few words on a piece of paper, and you cast me aside and run after him. But I'm not to be cast aside and then picked up again: you must decide now. Decide between them and me! Despise them or despise me. I know there are hard times ahead for us if you stay; I'll never see my parents and family again, we shall never be allowed to go back, but I can face that if you are with me. If you tear us apart now, though, then it's for ever."

He merely groaned, but she was blazing with angry strength.

"Choose them or me! There's no third choice. Ferdinand, think better of it while there's still time. I've often felt sorry we have no child. Now, for the first time, I'm glad of it. I don't want a weakling's child, and I don't want to bring up a war orphan. I've never stood by you more than I do now that I'm making it hard for you. But I tell you: this is not a trial separation, this is goodbye for ever. If you leave me to join the army and follow those uniformed murderers, there's no coming back. I don't share my life with criminals, I don't share a man with that vampire the state. It or me—you must choose now."

He still stood there shivering as she went to the door and slammed it behind her. The loud slam brought him to his knees. He had to sit down, and collapsed there, sombre, at a loss. And at last he broke down and cried like a small child.

She did not come back into the room all afternoon, but he felt that her strong will stood outside it, hostile and armed. And at the same time he knew about that other will, with a steel driving-wheel set cold under its breast, forcing him on. Sometimes he tried to think about this or that, but his thoughts slipped away, and as he sat there still, apparently thoughtful, the last of his peace flowed away into a state of burning nervous agitation. He felt the two ends of his life taken and tugged both ways by superhuman powers, and wished only that it would split like a rope in the middle.

To occupy himself he went through the desk drawers, tore up some letters, stared at others without taking in a word, stumbled round the room, sat down again, forced up by restlessness and down again by exhaustion. And suddenly he saw his hands putting together necessities for the journey, bringing out his rucksack from under the sofa. He stared at his own hands doing all this deliberately and against his own will. When the rucksack was packed he began to tremble, and suddenly there it was on the table. His shoulders felt weighed down, as if it were already resting on them, and with it the whole weight of these times.

The door opened, and his wife came in with a paraffin lamp. When she placed it on the table, the circle of light it cast fell on the packed rucksack. His secret ignominy, thus brightly lit, emerged starkly from the darkness. He stammered, "It's only in case... I still have time... I..." But a glance, fixed, stony, mask-like, met his words and crushed them. She stared at him for several minutes, her lips tightly pressed over her teeth. She stood motionless at first, then swayed slightly as if she might faint, while her eyes bored into him. The tension of her lips relaxed, but she turned, a shudder ran over her shoulders, and she left him without looking back.

A few minutes later the maid came in, bringing supper for him alone. The usual place at his side was empty, and when, full of incoherent emotion, he looked at it, he saw the cruel symbol of the rucksack placed there. He felt as if he had left already, was already dead to this house; its walls were dark, the circle of light from the lamp did not reach all the way to them, and outside, beyond the lights in other houses, night and the *föhn* wind pressed down. All was still in the distance, and the height of the sky, its vast expanse spanning the depths below, only increased his sense of isolation. He felt everything around him gradually dying, dropping away from him: the house, the landscape, his work, his wife, as the broad sea of his life suddenly dried up, compressing his beating heart. A great need for love overcame him, for warm and kindly words. He felt ready to agree to anything, if he could only somehow get back to the past. Melancholy prevailed over his nervous restlessness, and the strong emotions of his imminent farewell were lost in childish longing for a little tenderness.

He went to the bedroom door and softly tried the handle. It did not move; it was locked. He knocked, hesitantly. No answer. He knocked again. His heart beat in time with his knocking. Still silence. Now he knew it was all over and he had lost; the chilly knowledge came home to him. He put out the lamp, lay down on the sofa in his clothes and wrapped himself in a rug. Everything in him now longed to fall into sleep and oblivion. Once more he listened, and thought he had heard something close. He strained his ears, looking at the door, but it was solid wood. Nothing. His head fell back again.

Then something low down touched him. He started up in alarm, but it soon changed to emotion. The dog, who had slipped in with the maid and hidden under the sofa, came up to him and licked his hand with a warm tongue. And the animal's instinctive love touched him deeply because it came from the world now dead to him, and was all of his past life that still was his. He bent down and hugged the dog like a human being. Something on this earth still loves me and does not despise me, he felt, to him I am not a machine yet, not just a tool of murder, not a willing weakling, only a creature linked to him by love. Again and again, his hand tenderly stroked the soft coat. The dog moved closer to him, as if he knew his master was lonely, and both of them, breathing softly, began to fall asleep.

When he woke up he felt fresher, and the morning was bright and clear outside the shining window. The *föhn* wind had blown away the darkness, and the white silhouette of the distant mountain chain gleamed above the lake. Ferdinand got up, still a little unsteady from the hours he had slept away, and when he was fully awake his eyes fell on the fastened rucksack. Suddenly he remembered it all, but now, in bright daylight, it did not weigh so heavily on his mind.

Why did I pack it? he asked himself. Why? I have no intention of going away. The spring is just beginning. I want to paint. There's no great hurry. He told me himself I could take a couple of days. Even animals don't run to the slaughter. My wife is right: it's a crime against her, against myself, against everyone. Nothing can happen to me, after all. A few weeks under arrest, maybe, if I report for duty late, but isn't military service a prison in itself? I have no ambition to cut a fine figure in society, in fact I'd feel it an honour to have disobeyed at this time of slavery. I've no idea of setting out now. I'll stay here. I want to paint the landscape first, so that some day I'll remember where I was happy. And I won't go until the picture is in its frame. They can't herd me like a cow. I'm in no hurry.

He took the rucksack, swung it up in the air and tossed it into a corner. He enjoyed trying his own strength as he did so. And his new mood made him feel a need for a quick test of his will power. He took the call-up order from his wallet to tear it into pieces, and unfolded it.

But strangely, the military jargon cast its spell over him again. He began to read. "You are under orders to…". The words struck him to the heart. This was an order that would not be denied. Somehow he felt himself wavering; that unknown sensation was back. His hands began to shake. His strength faded. Cold came from somewhere, like a draught of wind blowing around him, uneasiness returned, inside him the steel clockwork of the alien will began to stir, tensing all his nerves and making its way to his joints. Instinctively he looked at his watch. "Plenty of time," he murmured, but he no longer knew what he himself meant: time to catch the morning train to the border, or did he mean the extended deadline he had granted himself? And now it came back, that mysterious internal compulsion, the ebb tide carrying him away, stronger than ever because it faced both his last resistance and his fear, his surely hopeless fear of succumbing. He knew that if no one held fast to him now he would be lost.

He made his way to the door of his wife's room and listened intently. Nothing moved. Hesitantly, he knocked with his knuckles. Silence. He knocked again. Still silence. He cautiously tried the handle. The door was not locked, and opened, but the room was empty, the bed empty too and unmade. He felt alarmed. Softly, he called her name, and when there was no reply repeated, more uneasily, "Paula!" Then, like a man under attack, he shouted at the top of his voice, "Paula! Paula! Paula!" Nothing moved. He tried the kitchen, which was empty. The terrible sense of abandonment asserted its rights over him, and he trembled. He groped his way up to the studio, not knowing what he wanted to do: say goodbye or be prevented from leaving. But here again there was no one. There wasn't even any trace of the faithful dog. Everything was deserting him, loneliness washed around him and broke the last of his strength.

He went back through the empty house and picked up the rucksack. In giving way to the compulsion he somehow felt relieved of the burden of himself. It's her fault, he told himself, her fault. Why has she gone? She ought to have kept me here, it was her duty. She could have saved me from myself, but she didn't want to. She despises me. She doesn't love me any more. She's let me down, so I'll let myself down too. My blood will be on her conscience! It's her fault, not mine, all her fault.

Outside the house, he turned once more. Would no call come from somewhere, no word of love? Would nothing raise its fists against that steely mechanism of obedience inside him and smash it? But nothing spoke. Nothing called. Nothing showed itself. Everything was deserting him, and already he felt himself falling into an abyss. And the thought came to him: might it not be better to take another ten steps towards the lake, let himself fall from the bridge and find peace?

The clock in the church tower struck, a ponderous, heavy sound. Its severe call out of the clear sky he had once loved so much goaded him on like a whiplash. Ten more minutes: then the train would come in, then it would all be over, finally, hopelessly over. Ten more minutes: but he no longer felt they were minutes of freedom. Like a hunted man he raced forward, staggered, hesitated, ran on, gasped in frantic fear of being late, went faster and faster until suddenly, just before reaching the platform, he almost collided with someone standing at the barrier.

He started in alarm. The rucksack fell from his trembling hand. It was his wife standing there, pale, as if she hadn't slept, her grave, sad eyes turned on him again.

"I knew you'd come. For the last three days I've known you would do it. But I'm not leaving you. I've been waiting here since early in the morning, since the first trains came in, and I'll wait until the last have left. As long as I breathe they won't lay hands on you, Ferdinand, remember that. You said yourself there was plenty of time. Why are you in such a hurry?"

He looked at her uncertainly.

"It's just that... my name's been sent in... they're expecting me..."

"Who are expecting you? Slavery and death, maybe, no one else! Wake up, Ferdinand, realize that you're free, entirely free, no one has power over you, no one can give you orders—listen, you're free, free, free! I'll tell you so a thousand times, ten thousand times, every hour, every minute, until you feel it yourself! You're free. Free! Free!"

"Please," he said quietly, as two farmers turned curiously to glance at them in passing. "Please, not so loud. People are looking..."

"People! People!" she cried in a rage. "What do I care about people? How will they help me when you're shot dead, or limping home, a broken man? What do I care for people, their pity, their love, their gratitude? I want you as a human being, a free, living human being. I want you free, free, as a man should be, not cannon-fodder."

"Paula!" He tried to calm her fury. She pushed him away.

"Let me alone, you and your stupid, cowardly fear! I'm in a free country here, I can say what I like, I'm not a servant and I won't give you up to servitude! Ferdinand, if you go I'll throw myself in front of the locomotive."

"Paula!" He took hold of her again, but her face was suddenly bitter.

"But no," she said, "I won't lie. I may be too cowardly to do it. Millions of women have been too cowardly when their husbands and children were dragged away—not one of them did what she ought to have done. Your cowardice poisons us. What will I do if you go away? Weep and wail, go to church and ask God to let you off with some light kind of service. And then perhaps I'll mock men who didn't go. Anything's possible these days."

"Paula." He held her hands. "Why are you making it so hard for me, when you know it must be done?"

"Am I to make it easy for you? It ought to be hard for you, very, very hard, as hard as I can make it. Here I am, you'll have to push me away by force, use your fists, you'll have to kick me when I'm down. I'm not giving you up."

The signals clattered. He straightened up, pale and agitated, and reached for his rucksack. But she had already snatched it and was standing foursquare in front of him.

"Give me that!" he groaned.

"Never! Never!" she gasped, wrestling with him. The farmers gathered around, laughing out loud. There was shouting as the bystanders egged them on, encouraging one or the other, children ran from their games to look. But the pair were struggling for possession of the rucksack with the strength of bitter despair, as if fighting for their lives.

At that moment the locomotive was heard as the train steamed in. Suddenly he let go of the rucksack and ran, without turning back. He hurried on, stumbling over the rails to reach a carriage and fling himself into it. Loud laughter broke out as the farmers roared with glee, pursuing him with shouts of, "You'll have to jump out again, mister, the missus has got it!" Their raucous laughter lashed at his shame. And now the train was moving out.

She stood there holding the rucksack, with the laughter of the crowd all around her, and stared at the train vanishing faster and faster into the distance. He did not wave from the window,

he gave her no sign. Sudden tears veiled her eyes, and she saw
no more.

He sat hunched in the corner of the carriage, and did not venture
to look out of the window as the train gathered speed. Outside,
torn to a thousand pieces by the speed of the train, everything
he owned passed by: the little house on the hill with his pictures,
his table and chair and bed, his wife, the dog, many days of happiness. And the wide landscape at which he had often gazed, his
eyes shining, was gone as if hurled away, like his freedom and his
whole life. He seemed to feel his life's blood streaming out of all
his veins; he was nothing now but the white call-up order crackling
in his pocket, and he was driven on with it by the ill will of Fate.

In dull bewilderment, he merely registered events as they happened. The conductor asked for his ticket; he had none, but in
the voice of a sleepwalker named the town on the border as his
destination, and passively changed to another train. The mechanism inside him did everything, and it had stopped hurting. At the
Swiss customs office they asked to see his papers. He showed them
what he had: only that one sheet of paper. Now and then some
lost remnant of himself made a slight effort to think, murmuring
as if in a dream, "Turn back! You're still free! You don't have to
go." But the mechanism in his blood that did not speak, and yet
made his nerves and limbs move by force, thrust him implacably
on with its invisible command, "You must."

He was standing on the platform of the transit station where he
had to change trains again for his native land. Over there, clearly
visible in the dull light, a bridge crossed the river which was the
border. His weary mind tried to understand the meaning of the
word; on this side of the border you could still live, breathe, and

speak freely, act as you liked, do work that mattered. Eight hundred paces further on, once over that bridge, your will would be removed from your body like an animal's entrails being gutted, you would have to obey strangers and stab other strangers to death. And the little bridge there, a structure of just ten dozen wooden posts and two crossbeams meant all those things. That was why two men, each in a different, colourful and pointless uniform, stood one at each end with guns to guard the bridge. A sombre sensation tormented him, he knew he couldn't think clearly any more, but his thoughts rolled on. What exactly were they guarding in the form of that wooden structure? They were preventing anyone passing from one country to the other, making sure no one got out of the country where men's wills were gutted, and went to the country on the other side of the border. And was he himself going to cross the bridge? Yes, but the other way, out of freedom into...

He stood still, musing, hypnotized by the idea of the border. Now that he saw its intrinsic nature, a physical object guarded by two bored citizens in military uniforms, there was something in himself that he could no longer entirely understand. He tried to stand back and think: there was a war going on. But only in the country over there—the war was going on a kilometre away, or rather a kilometre minus two hundred metres away. Or perhaps, it occurred to him, it was ten metres closer than that, say a kilometre minus eight hundred metres minus ten metres away. He felt some kind of odd urge to find out whether there was still a war in progress on those last ten metres or not. The comical aspect of the idea amused him. There ought to be a line drawn somewhere, the dividing line. Suppose when you reached the border you had one foot on the bridge and one on the ground, what were you then—were you still free, or already a soldier? You'd have to be wearing a civilian boot on one foot and a military boot on the other. His confused thoughts became more and more childish. Suppose you were standing on the bridge, you were already over it, and then you ran back, were you a deserter? And the water under the bridge—was it warlike or peaceful? And *was* there a line drawn somewhere in the national colours? What about the fish, were they allowed to swim across into the war zone? What about the animals? He thought of his dog. If the dog had come along too, they'd probably have called him up as well, he'd have had to fire machine guns or go tracking down wounded men under a hail of bullets. Thank God the dog had stayed at home.

Thank God! The thought gave him a shock, and he shook himself. He sensed that since he had seen the border in physical form, a bridge between life and death, something in him that was not the mechanism was beginning to work, understanding and resistance were coming back to life in him. The train that had brought him in still stood on the opposite track, except that the locomotive had been moved and its gigantic glass eyes were now looking the other way, ready to pull the carriages back into Switzerland. It was a reminder that there was still time. He felt painful life return to the numbed nerve of his longing for his lost home, and the man he had once been began to revive. Over there, on the far side of bridge, he saw a soldier strapped into a strange uniform, he saw him marching pointlessly up and down with his gun over his shoulder, and he saw himself reflected in this stranger. Only now was his destiny clear to him, and now that he understood it he saw that it meant death and destruction. And life cried out in his soul.

Then the signals clattered, and the harsh sound shattered his still tentative feelings. Now, he knew, all was lost—if he got into the train just coming in and spent three minutes in it, travelling to the bridge and over it. And he knew that he would. Another quarter-of-an-hour and he would have been saved. He stood there feeling dizzy.

But the train did not come in from the distance into which he looked as he stood there trembling; it rumbled slowly over the bridge from the other side. And suddenly the station concourse was full of movement, people were streaming out of the waiting rooms, women crowded forward, crying out, pushing, Swiss soldiers quickly lined up. And all at once music began to play—he listened, amazed, he couldn't believe it. But there it was, blaring out, unmistakeable: the Marseillaise. The enemy's national anthem, sung on a train coming out of German territory!

The train thundered up, puffing, and stopped. And now everything was fast and frantic: carriage doors were flung open, pale-faced men stumbled out, delight in their glowing eyes—Frenchmen in uniform, wounded Frenchmen, enemies, enemies! In his dreamlike state, it was some seconds before he realized that this was a train with wounded prisoners being exchanged, freed from captivity over there, saved from the madness of the war. And they knew it, they all felt it; how they waved and shouted and laughed, although even laughter still hurt many of them! One man, staggering and hesitant, stumbled out on a wooden leg, clung to a post and shouted, "*La Suisse! La Suisse! Dieu soit béni!*" Sobbing women hurried from window to window until they found the beloved faces they were looking for, voices called out in confusion, sobbing, shouting, but all of them rising high in the golden moment of rejoicing. The music died away, and for some time nothing could be heard but great waves of emotion breaking over these people as they shouted and cried out.

Then they gradually calmed down. Groups formed, happily united in quiet joy and rapid talk. A few women were still wandering around, calling out names. Nurses brought refreshment and presents. The very sick were carried out on their stretchers, pale in white bandages, tenderly surrounded by care and comfort. The whole debris of suffering could be seen concentrated in those forms: maimed men with empty sleeves, the emaciated and half-burnt, the lingering remnants of youth gone to seed and growing old. But all eyes gleamed happily as they looked up at the sky; they all sensed that they were near the end of their pilgrimage.

Ferdinand stood as if paralysed amidst this unexpected throng of new arrivals; his heart was suddenly beating strongly again under the sheet of paper in his breast pocket. Standing alone and apart from the others, with no one expecting him, he saw a stretcher come to a halt. Slowly, with unsteady steps, he went over to the wounded man, who seemed to have been forgotten in the joy of all these strangers. The man's face was white as a sheet, his beard straggled wildly, a limp, injured arm dangled from the stretcher. His eyes were closed, his lips pale. Ferdinand shivered. Gently, he raised the dangling arm and placed it carefully on the sick man's breast. Then the stranger opened his eyes, looked at Ferdinand, and out of distant regions of unknown torment the man formed a grateful smile of greeting.

It came to Ferdinand like a flash as he stood, still trembling: was he to do such things himself? Injure people like this, look his fellow men in the eye with no emotion but hatred, take part in this terrible crime of his own free will? The truth of what he felt revived strongly again, breaking the mechanism inside him. Freedom rose up, great and blessed freedom, destroying obedience. Never, never! something in him cried in a primal, mighty, unknown voice. It struck him down. Sobbing, he collapsed beside the stretcher.

People hurried to him, thinking he must have had an epileptic fit; the doctor came along. But he was already getting slowly to his feet and refused help. His face was calm and cheerful. He found his wallet, took out his last banknote and placed it on the wounded man's stretcher; then he took the call-up order and read it once more, slowly and deliberately. After that he tore it in two and scattered the scraps on the platform. People stared at him as if he were mad. But he was not ashamed any more. I am well again, he felt, and that was all. The music began once more. And his own heart drowned out all the musical notes with its resonant song.

*

Late that evening, he came home to his house. It was dark and closed, like a coffin. He knocked. Footsteps slowly made their way to the door; his wife opened it. When she saw him, she gave a start of surprise. But he gently took her arm and led her back to the doorway. They said nothing, just stood there, both of them trembling with happiness. He went into the living-room and saw his pictures in it. She had brought them all down from the studio so that she could be close to him through his work. He felt infinite love for her at this sign of her own for him, and realized how much he had just saved. In silence, he pressed her hand. The dog came racing out of the kitchen and jumped up at him; everything had been waiting for him, it seemed as if his real self had never left this place, and yet he felt like a man coming back from the dead.

Still they said nothing. But she took his hand gently and led him to the window. Outside, untouched by the self-inflicted torment of humanity run mad, lay the everlasting world, with endless stars shining for him under an endless sky. He looked up and saw, in a devout and solemn mood, that there was no law on earth for mankind except the law of humanity itself, that nothing unites men more truly than their own union. His wife's breath close to his lips was sweet and blessed, and sometimes their two bodies trembled slightly in the pleasure of holding each other close. But still they said nothing. Their hearts soared freely in the eternal freedom of things, released from the confusion of words and man-made laws.

TWENTY-FOUR HOURS IN THE LIFE OF A WOMAN

I N THE LITTLE GUEST HOUSE on the Riviera where I was staying at the time, ten years before the war, a heated discussion had broken out at our table and unexpectedly threatened to degenerate into frenzied argument, even rancour and recrimination. Most people have little imagination. If something doesn't affect them directly, does not drive a sharp wedge straight into their minds, it hardly excites them at all, but if an incident, however slight, takes place before their eyes, close enough for the senses to perceive it, it instantly rouses them to extremes of passion. They compensate for the infrequency of their sympathy, as it were, by exhibiting disproportionate and excessive vehemence.

Such was the case that day among our thoroughly bourgeois company at table, where on the whole we just made equable small talk and cracked mild little jokes, usually parting as soon as the meal was over: the German husband and wife to go on excursions and take snapshots, the portly Dane to set out on tedious fishing expeditions, the distinguished English lady to return to her books, the Italian married couple to indulge in escapades to Monte Carlo, and I to lounge in a garden chair or get some work done. This time, however, our irate discussion left us all still very much at odds, and if someone suddenly rose it was not, as usual, to take civil leave of the rest of us, but in a mood of heated irascibility that, as I have said, was assuming positively frenzied form.

The incident obsessing our little party, admittedly, was odd enough. From outside, the guest house where the seven of us were staying might have been an isolated villa—with a wonderful view of the rock-strewn beach from its windows—but in fact it was only the cheaper annexe of the Grand Palace Hotel to which it

STEFAN ZWEIG

was directly linked by the garden, so that we in the guest house were in constant touch with the hotel guests. And that same hotel had been the scene of an outright scandal the day before, when a young Frenchman had arrived by the midday train, at twenty-past twelve (I can't avoid giving the time so precisely because it was of importance to the incident itself, and indeed to the subject of our agitated conversation), and took a room with a view of the sea, opening straight on to the beach, which in itself indicated that he was in reasonably easy circumstances. Not only his discreet elegance but, most of all, his extraordinary and very appealing good looks made an attractive impression. A silky blond moustache surrounded sensuously warm lips in a slender, girlish face; soft, wavy brown hair curled over his pale forehead; every glance of his melting eyes was a caress—indeed everything about him was soft, endearing, charming, but without any artifice or affectation. At a distance he might at first remind you slightly of those pink wax dummies to be seen adopting dandified poses in the window displays of large fashion stores, walking-stick in hand and representing the ideal of male beauty, but closer inspection dispelled any impression of foppishness, for—most unusually—his charm was natural and innate, and seemed an inseparable part of him. He greeted everyone individually in passing, in a manner as warm as it was modest, and it was a pleasure to see his unfailingly graceful demeanour unaffectedly brought into play on every occasion. When a lady was going to the cloakroom he made haste to fetch her coat, he had a friendly glance or joke for every child, he was both affable and discreet—in short, he seemed to be one of those happy souls who, secure in the knowledge that their bright faces and youthful attractions are pleasing to others, transmute that security anew into yet more charm. His presence worked wonders among the hotel guests, most of whom were elderly and sickly, and he irresistibly won everyone's liking with the victorious bearing of youth, that flush of ease and liveliness with which charm so

178

delightfully endows some human beings. Only a couple of hours after his arrival he was playing tennis with the two daughters of the stout, thick-set manufacturer from Lyon—twelve-year-old Annette and thirteen-year-old Blanche—and their mother, the refined, delicate and reserved Madame Henriette, smiled slightly to see her inexperienced daughters unconsciously flirting with the young stranger. That evening he watched for an hour as we played chess, telling a few amusing anecdotes now and then in an unobtrusive style, strolled along the terrace again with Madame Henriette while her husband played dominoes with a business friend as usual; and late in the evening I saw him in suspiciously intimate conversation with the hotel secretary in the dim light of her office. Next morning he went fishing with my Danish chess partner, showing a remarkable knowledge of angling, and then held a long conversation about politics with the Lyon manufacturer in which he also proved himself an entertaining companion, for the stout Frenchman's hearty laughter could be heard above the sound of the breaking waves. After lunch he spent an hour alone with Madame Henriette in the garden again, drinking black coffee, played another game of tennis with her daughters and chatted in the lobby to the German couple. At six o'clock I met him at the railway station when I went to post a letter. He strode quickly towards me and said, as if apologetically, that he had been suddenly called away but would be back in two days' time. Sure enough, he was absent from the dining room that evening, but only in person, for he was the sole subject of conversation at every table, and all the guests praised his delightful, cheerful nature.

That night, I suppose at about eleven o'clock, I was sitting in my room finishing a book when I suddenly heard agitated shouts and cries from the garden coming in through my open window. Something was obviously going on over at the hotel. Feeling concerned rather than curious, I immediately hurried across—it was some fifty paces—and found the guests and staff milling around in great excitement. Madame Henriette, whose husband had been playing dominoes with his friend from Namur as usual, had not come back from her evening walk on the terrace by the beach, and it was feared that she had suffered an accident. The normally ponderous, slow-moving manufacturer kept charging down to the beach like a bull, and when he called: "Henriette! Henriette!" into the night, his voice breaking with fear, the sound conveyed something of the terror and the primeval nature of a gigantic animal wounded to death. The waiters and pageboys ran up and down the stairs in agitation, all the guests were woken and the police were called. The fat man, however, trampled and stumbled his way through all this, waistcoat unbuttoned, sobbing and shrieking as he pointlessly shouted the name "Henriette! Henriette!" into the darkness. By now the children were awake upstairs, and stood at the window in their night dresses, calling down for their mother. Their father hurried upstairs again to comfort them.

And then something so terrible happened that it almost defies retelling, for a violent strain on human nature, at moments of extremity, can often give such tragic expression to a man's bearing that no images or words can reproduce it with the same lightning force. Suddenly the big, heavy man came down the creaking stairs with a changed look on his face, very weary and yet grim. He had a letter in his hand. "Call them all back!" he told the hotel major-domo, in a barely audible voice. "Call everyone in again. There's no need. My wife has left me."

Mortally wounded as he was, the man showed composure, a tense, superhuman composure as he faced all the people standing around, looking at him curiously as they pressed close and then suddenly turned away again, each of them feeling alarmed, ashamed and confused. He had just enough strength left to make his way unsteadily past us, looking at no one, and switch off the light in the reading room. We heard the sound of his ponderous, massive body dropping heavily into an armchair, and then a wild, animal sobbing, the weeping of a man who has never wept before. That elemental pain had a kind of paralysing power over every one of us, even the least of those present. None of the waiters, none of the guests who had joined the throng out of curiosity, ventured either a smile or a word of condolence. Silently, one by one, as if put to shame by so shattering an emotional outburst, we crept back to our rooms, while that stricken specimen of mankind shook and sobbed alone with himself in the dark as the building slowly laid itself to rest, whispering, muttering, murmuring and sighing.

You will understand that such an event, striking like lightning before our very eyes and our perceptions, was likely to cause considerable turmoil in persons usually accustomed to an easygoing existence and carefree pastimes. But while this extraordinary incident was certainly the point of departure for the discussion that broke out so vehemently at our table, almost bringing us to blows, in essence the dispute was more fundamental, an angry conflict between two warring concepts of life. For it soon became known from the indiscretion of a chambermaid who had read the letter—in his helpless fury, the devastated husband had crumpled it up and dropped it on the floor somewhere—that Madame Henriette had not left alone but, by mutual agreement, with the young Frenchman (for whom most people's liking now swiftly began to evaporate). At first glance, of course, it might seem perfectly understandable for this minor Madame Bovary to exchange her stout, provincial husband for an elegant and handsome young fellow. But what aroused so much indignation in all present was the circumstance that neither the manufacturer nor his daughters, nor even Madame Henriette herself, had ever set eyes on this Lovelace before, and consequently their evening conversation for a couple of hours on the terrace, and the one-hour session in the garden over black coffee, seemed to have sufficed to make a woman about thirty-three years old and of blameless reputation abandon her husband and two children overnight, following a young dandy previously unknown to her without a second thought. This apparently evident fact was unanimously condemned at our table as perfidious deceit and a cunning manoeuvre on the part of the two lovers: of course Madame Henriette must have been conducting a clandestine affair with the young man long before, and he had come here, Pied Piper that he was, only to settle the final details of their flight, for—so our company deduced—it was out of the question for a decent woman who had known a man a mere couple of hours to run off just like that when he first whistled her up. It amused me to take a different view, and I energetically defended such an eventuality as possible, even probable in a woman who at heart had perhaps been ready to take some decisive action through all the years of a tedious, disappointing marriage. My unexpected opposition quickly made the discussion more general, and it became particularly agitated when both married couples, the Germans and the Italians alike, denied the existence of the *coup de foudre* with positively scornful indignation, condemning it as folly and tasteless romantic fantasy.

Well, it's of no importance here to go back in every detail over the stormy course of an argument conducted between soup and dessert: only professionals of the table d'hôte are witty, and points made in the heat of a chance dispute at table are usually banal, since the speakers resort to them clumsily and in haste. It is also difficult to explain how our discussion came to assume the form of insulting remarks so quickly; I think it grew so vehement in the first place because of the instinctive wish of both husbands to reassure themselves that their own wives were incapable of such shallow inconstancy. Unfortunately they could find no better way of expressing their feelings than to tell me that no one could speak as I did except a man who judged the feminine psyche by a bachelor's random conquests, which came only too cheap. This accusation rather annoyed me, and when the German lady added her mite by remarking instructively that there were real women on the one hand and 'natural-born tarts' on the other, and in her opinion Madame Henriette must have been one of the latter, I lost patience entirely and became aggressive myself. Such a denial of the obvious fact that at certain times in her life a woman is delivered up to mysterious powers beyond her own will and judgement, I said, merely concealed fear of our own instincts, of the demonic element in our nature, and many people seemed to take pleasure in feeling themselves stronger, purer and more moral than those who are 'easily led astray'. Personally, I added, I thought it more honourable for a woman to follow her instincts freely and passionately than to betray her husband in his own arms with her eyes closed, as so many did. Such, roughly, was the gist of my remarks, and the more the others attacked poor Madame Henriette in a conversation now rising to fever pitch, the more passionately I defended her (going far beyond what I actually felt in the case). My enthusiasm amounted to what in student circles might have been described as a challenge to the two married couples, and as a not very harmonious quartet they went for me with such indignant solidarity that the old Dane, who was sitting there with a jovial expression, much like the referee at a football match with stopwatch in hand, had to tap his knuckles on the table from time to time in admonishment. "Gentlemen, please!" But it never worked for long. One of the husbands had jumped up from the table three times already, red in the face, and could be calmed by his wife only with difficulty—in short, a dozen minutes more and our discussion would have ended in violence, had not Mrs C suddenly poured oil on the stormy waters of the conversation.

Mrs C, the white-haired, distinguished old English lady, presided over our table as unofficial arbiter. Sitting very upright in her place, turning to everyone with the same uniform friendliness, saying little and yet listening with the most gratifying interest, she was a pleasing sight from the purely physical viewpoint, and an air of wonderfully calm composure emanated from her aristocratically reserved nature. Up to a certain point she kept her distance from the rest of us, although she could also show special kindness with tactful delicacy: she spent most of her time in the garden reading books, and sometimes played the piano, but she was seldom to be seen in company or deep in conversation. You scarcely noticed her, yet she exerted a curious influence over us all, for no sooner did she now, for the first time, intervene in our discussion than we all felt, with embarrassment, that we had been too loud and intemperate.

Mrs C had made use of the awkward pause when the German gentleman jumped brusquely up and was then induced to sit quietly down again. Unexpectedly, she raised her clear, grey eyes, looked at me indecisively for a moment, and then, with almost objective clarity, took up the subject in her own way.

"So you think, if I understand you correctly, that Madame Henriette—that a woman can be cast unwittingly into a sudden adventure, can do things that she herself would have thought impossible an hour earlier, and for which she can hardly be held responsible?"

"I feel sure of it, ma'am."

"But then all moral judgements would be meaningless, and any kind of vicious excess could be justified. If you really think that a *crime passionnel*, as the French call it, is no crime at all, then what is the state judiciary for? It doesn't take a great deal of good will—and you yourself have a remarkable amount of that," she added, with a slight smile, "to see passion in every crime, and use that passion to excuse it."

The clear yet almost humorous tone of her words did me good, and instinctively adopting her objective stance I answered half in jest, half in earnest myself: "I'm sure that the state judiciary takes a more severe view of such things than I do; its duty is to protect morality and convention without regard for pity, so it is obliged to judge and make no excuses. But as a private person I don't see why I should voluntarily assume the role of public prosecutor. I'd prefer to appear for the defence. Personally, I'd rather understand others than condemn them."

Mrs C looked straight at me for a while with her clear grey eyes, and hesitated. I began to fear she had failed to understand what I said, and was preparing to repeat it in English. But with a curious gravity, as if conducting an examination, she continued with her questions.

"Don't you think it contemptible or shocking, though, for a woman to leave her husband and her children to follow some chance-met man, when she can't even know if he is worth her love? Can you really excuse such reckless, promiscuous conduct in a woman who is no longer in her first youth, and should have disciplined herself to preserve her self-respect, if only for the sake of her children?"

"I repeat, ma'am," I persisted, "that I decline to judge or condemn her in this case. To you, I can readily admit that I was exaggerating a little just now—poor Madame Henriette is certainly no heroine, not even an adventuress by nature, let alone a *grande amoureuse*. So far as I know her, she seems to me just an average, fallible woman. I do feel a little respect for her because she bravely followed the dictates of her own will, but even more pity, since tomorrow, if not today, she is sure to be deeply unhappy. She may have acted unwisely and certainly too hastily, but her conduct was not base or mean, and I still challenge anyone's right to despise the poor unfortunate woman."

"And what about you yourself; do you still feel exactly the same respect and esteem for her? Don't you see any difference between the woman you knew the day before yesterday as a respectable wife, and the woman who ran off with a perfect stranger a day later?"

"None at all. Not the slightest, not the least difference."

"*Is that so?*" She instinctively spoke those words in English; the whole conversation seemed to be occupying her mind to a remarkable degree. After a brief moment's thought, she raised her clear eyes to me again, with a question in them.

"And suppose you were to meet Madame Henriette tomorrow, let's say in Nice on the young man's arm, would you still greet her?"

"Of course."

"And speak to her?"

"Of course."

"If… if you were married, would you introduce such a woman to your wife as if nothing had happened?"

"Of course."

"*Would you really?*" she said, in English again, speaking in tones of incredulous astonishment.

"*Indeed I would,*" I answered, unconsciously falling into English too.

Mrs C was silent. She still seemed to be thinking hard, and suddenly, looking at me as if amazed at her own courage, she said: "I don't know if I would. Perhaps I might." And with the indefinable and peculiarly English ability to end a conversation firmly but without brusque discourtesy, she rose and offered me her hand in a friendly gesture. Her intervention had restored peace, and we were all privately grateful to her for ensuring that although we had been at daggers drawn a moment ago, we could speak to each other with tolerable civility again. The dangerously charged atmosphere was relieved by a few light remarks.

Although our discussion seemed to have been courteously resolved, its irate bitterness had none the less left a faint, lingering sense of estrangement between me and my opponents in argument. The German couple behaved with reserve, while over the next few days the two Italians enjoyed asking me ironically, at frequent intervals, whether I had heard anything of '*la cara signora Henrietta*'. Urbane as our manners might appear, something of the equable, friendly good fellowship of our table had been irrevocably destroyed.

The chilly sarcasm of my adversaries was made all the more obvious by the particular friendliness Mrs C had shown me since our discussion. Although she was usually very reserved, and hardly ever seemed to invite conversation with her table companions outside meal times, she now on several occasions found an opportunity to speak to me in the garden and—I might almost say—distinguish me by her attention, for her upper-class reserve made a private talk with her seem a special favour. To be honest, in fact, I must say she positively sought me out and took every opportunity of entering into conversation with me, in so marked a way that had she not been a white-haired elderly lady I might have entertained some strange, conceited ideas. But when we talked our conversation inevitably and without fail came back to the same point of departure, to Madame Henriette: it seemed to give her some mysterious pleasure to accuse the errant wife of weakness of character and irresponsibility. At the same time, however, she seemed to enjoy my steadfast defence of that refined and delicate woman, and my insistence that nothing could ever make me deny my sympathy for her. She constantly steered our conversation the same way, and in the end I hardly knew what to make of her strange, almost eccentric obsession with the subject.

This went on for a few days, maybe five or six, and she never said a word to suggest why this kind of conversation had assumed importance for her. But I could not help realising that it had when I happened to mention, during a walk, that my stay here would soon be over, and I thought of leaving the day after tomorrow. At this her usually serene face suddenly assumed a curiously intense expression, and something like the shadow of a cloud came into her clear grey eyes. "Oh, what a pity! There's still so much I'd have liked to discuss with you." And from then on a certain uneasy restlessness showed that while she spoke she was thinking of something else, something that occupied and distracted her mind a great deal. At last she herself seemed disturbed by this mental distraction, for in the middle of a silence that had suddenly fallen between us she unexpectedly offered me her hand.

"I see that I can't put what I really want to say to you clearly. I'd rather write it down." And walking faster than I was used to seeing her move, she went towards the house.

I did indeed find a letter in her energetic, frank handwriting in my room just before dinner that evening. I now greatly regret my carelessness with written documents in my youth, which means that I cannot reproduce her note word for word, and can give only the gist of her request: might she, she asked, tell me about an episode in her life? It lay so far back in the past, she wrote, that it was hardly a part of her present existence any more, and the fact that I was leaving the day after tomorrow made it easier for her to speak of something that had occupied and preyed on her mind for over twenty years. If I did not feel such a conversation was an importunity, she would like to ask me for an hour of my time.

The letter—I merely outline its contents here—fascinated me to an extraordinary degree: its English style alone lent it great clarity and resolution. Yet I did not find it easy to answer. I tore up three drafts before I replied:

I am honoured by your showing such confidence in me, and I promise you an honest response should you require one. Of course I cannot ask you to tell me more than your heart dictates. But whatever you tell, tell yourself and me the truth. Please believe me: I feel your confidence a special honour.

The note made its way to her room that evening, and I received the answer next morning:

You are quite right: half the truth is useless, only the whole truth is worth telling. I shall do my best to hide nothing from myself or from you. Please come to my room after dinner—at the age of sixty-seven, I need fear no misinterpretation, but I cannot speak freely in the garden, or with other people near by. Believe me, I did not find it easy to make my mind up to take this step.

During the day we met again at table and discussed indifferent matters in the conventional way. But when we encountered each other in the garden she avoided me in obvious confusion, and I felt it both painful and moving to see this white-haired old lady fleeing from me down an avenue lined with pine trees, as shy as a young girl.

At the appointed time that evening I knocked on her door, and it was immediately opened; the room was bathed in soft twilight, with only the little reading lamp on the table casting a circle of yellow light in the dusk. Mrs C came towards me without any self-consciousness, offered me an armchair and sat down opposite me. I sensed that she had prepared mentally for each of these movements, but then came a pause, obviously unplanned, a pause that grew longer and longer as she came to a difficult decision. I dared not inject any remark into this pause, for I sensed a strong will wrestling with great resistance here. Sometimes the faint notes of a waltz drifted up from the drawing room below, and I listened intently, as if to relieve the silence of some of its oppressive quality. She too seemed to feel the unnatural tension of the silence awkward, for she suddenly pulled herself together to take the plunge, and began.

"It's only the first few words that are so difficult. For the last two days I have been preparing to be perfectly clear and truthful; I hope I shall succeed. Perhaps you don't yet understand why I am telling all this to you, a stranger, but not a day, scarcely an hour goes by when I do not think of this particular incident, and you can believe me, an old woman now, when I say it is intolerable to spend one's whole life staring at a single point in it, a single day. Everything I am about to tell you, you see, happened within the space of just twenty-four hours in my sixty-seven years of life, and I have often asked myself, I have wondered to the point of madness, why a moment's foolish action on a single occasion should matter. But we cannot shake off what we so vaguely call conscience, and when I heard you speak so objectively of Madame Henriette's case I thought that perhaps there might be an end to my senseless dwelling on the past, my constant self-accusation, if I could bring myself to speak freely to someone, anyone, about that single day in my life. If I were not an Anglican but a Catholic, the confessional would long ago have offered me an opportunity of release by putting what I have kept silent into words—but that comfort is denied us, and so I make this strange attempt to absolve myself by speaking to you today. I know all this sounds very odd, but you agreed unhesitatingly to my suggestion, and I am grateful.

As I said, I would like to tell you about just one day in my life—all the rest of it seems to me insignificant and would be tedious listening for anyone else. There was nothing in the least out of the ordinary in the course of it until my forty-second year. My parents were rich landlords in Scotland, we owned large factories and leased out land, and in the usual way of the gentry in my country we spent most of the year on our estates but went to London for the season. I met my future husband at a party when I was eighteen. He was a second son of the well-known R family, and had served with the army in India for ten years. We soon married, and led the carefree life of our social circle: three months of the year in London, three months on our estates, and the rest of the time in hotels in Italy, Spain and France. Not the slightest shadow ever clouded our marriage, and we had two sons who are now grown up. When I was forty my husband suddenly died. He had returned from his years in the tropics with a liver complaint, and I lost him within the space of two terrible weeks. My elder son was already in the army, my younger son at university—so I was left entirely alone overnight, and used as I was to affectionate companionship, that loneliness was a torment to me. I felt I could not stay a day longer in the desolate house where every object reminded me of the tragic loss of my beloved husband, and so I decided that while my sons were still unmarried, I would spend much of the next few years travelling.

In essence, I regarded my life from that moment on as entirely pointless and useless. The man with whom I had shared every hour and every thought for twenty-three years was dead, my children did not need me, I was afraid of casting a cloud over their youth with my sadness and melancholy—but I wished and desired nothing any more for myself. I went first to Paris, where I visited shops and museums out of sheer boredom, but the city and everything else were strange to me, and I avoided company because I could not bear the polite sympathy in other people's eyes when they saw that I was in mourning. How those months of aimless, apathetic wandering passed I can hardly say now; all I know is that I had a constant wish to die, but not the strength to hasten the end I longed for so ardently.

In my second year of mourning, that is to say my forty-second year, I had come to Monte Carlo at the end of March in my unacknowledged flight from time that had become worthless and was more than I could deal with. To be honest, I came there out of tedium, out of the painful emptiness of the heart that wells up like nausea, and at least tries to nourish itself on small external stimulations. The less I felt in myself, the more strongly I was drawn to those places where the whirligig of life spins most rapidly. If you are experiencing nothing yourself, the passionate restlessness of others stimulates the nervous system like music or drama.

That was why I quite often went to the casino. I was intrigued to see the tide of delight or dismay ebbing and flowing in other people's faces, while my own heart lay at such a low ebb. In addition my husband, although never frivolous, had enjoyed visiting such places now and then, and with a certain unintentional piety I remained faithful to his old habits. And there in the casino began those twenty-four hours that were more thrilling than any game, and disturbed my life for years.

I had dined at midday with the Duchess of M, a relation of my family, and after supper I didn't feel tired enough to go to bed yet. So I went to the gaming hall, strolled among the tables without playing myself, and watched the mingled company in my own special way. I repeat, in my own special way, the way my dead husband had once taught me when, tired of watching, I complained of the tedium of looking at the same faces all the time: the wizened old women who sat for hours before venturing a single jetton, the cunning professionals, the *demi-mondaines* of the card table, all that dubious chance-met company which, as you'll know, is considerably less picturesque and romantic than it is always painted in silly novels, where you might think it the *fleur d'élégance* and aristocracy of Europe. Yet the casino of twenty years ago, when real money, visible and tangible, was staked and crackling banknotes, gold Napoleons and pert little five-franc pieces rained down, was far more attractive than it is today, with a solid set of folk on Cook's Tours tediously frittering their characterless gaming chips away in the grand, fashionably renovated citadel of gambling. Even then, however, I found little to stimulate me in the similarity of so many indifferent faces, until one day my husband, whose private passion was for chiromancy—that's to say, divination by means of the hand—showed me an unusual method of observation which proved much more interesting, exciting and fascinating than standing casually around. In this method you never look at a face, only at the rectangle of the table, and on the table only at the hands of the players and the way they move. I don't know if you yourself ever happen to have looked at the green table, just that green square with the ball in the middle of it tumbling drunkenly from number to number, while fluttering scraps of paper, round silver and gold coins fall like seedcorn on the spaces of the board, to be raked briskly away by the croupier or shovelled over to the winner like harvest bounty. If you watch from that angle, only the hands change—all those pale, moving, waiting hands around the green table, all emerging from the ever-different caverns of the players' sleeves, each a beast of prey ready to leap, each varying in shape and colour, some bare, others laden with rings and clinking bracelets, some hairy like wild beasts, some damp and writhing like eels, but all of them tense, vibrating with a vast impatience. I could never help thinking of a racecourse where the excited horses are held back with difficulty on the starting line in case they gallop away too soon; they quiver and buck and rear in just the same way. You can tell everything from those hands, from the way they wait, they grab, they falter; you can see an avaricious character in a claw-like hand and a spendthrift in a relaxed one, a calculating man in a steady hand and a desperate man in a trembling wrist; hundreds of characters betray themselves instantly in their way of handling money, crumpling or nervously creasing notes, or letting it lie as the ball goes round, their hands now weary and exhausted. Human beings give themselves away in play—a cliché, I know, but I would say their own hands give them away even more clearly in gambling. Almost all gamblers soon learn to control their faces—from the neck up, they wear the cold mask of impassivity; they force away the lines around their mouths and hide their agitation behind clenched teeth, they refuse to let their eyes show uneasiness, they smooth the twitching muscles of the face into an artificial indifference, obeying the dictates of polite conduct. But just because their whole attention is concentrated on controlling the face, the most visible part of the body, they forget their hands, they forget that some people are watching nothing but those hands, guessing from them what the lips curved in a smile, the intentionally indifferent glances wish to conceal. Meanwhile, however, their hands shamelessly reveal their innermost secrets. For a moment inevitably comes when all those carefully controlled, apparently relaxed fingers drop their elegant negligence. In the pregnant moment when the roulette ball drops into its shallow compartment and the winning number is called, in that second every one of those hundred or five hundred hands spontaneously makes a very personal, very individual movement of primitive instinct. And if an observer like me, particularly well-informed as I was because of my husband's hobby, is used to watching the hands perform in this arena, it is more exciting even than music or drama to see so many different temperaments suddenly erupt. I simply cannot tell you how many thousands of varieties of hands there are: wild beasts with hairy, crooked fingers raking in the money like spiders; nervous, trembling hands with pale nails that scarcely dare to touch it; hands noble and vulgar, hands brutal and shy, cunning hands, hands that seem to be stammering—but each of these pairs of hands is different, the expression of an individual life, with the exception of the four or five pairs of hands belonging to the croupiers. Those hands are entirely mechanical, and with their objective, businesslike, totally detached precision function like the clicking metal mechanism of a gas meter by comparison with the extreme liveliness of the gamblers' hands. But even those sober hands produce a surprising effect when contrasted with their racing, passionate fellows; you might say they were wearing a different uniform, like policemen in the middle of a surging, agitated riot. And then there is the personal incentive of getting to know the many different habits and passions of individual pairs of hands within a few days; by then I had always made acquaintances among them and divided them, as if they were human beings, into those I liked and those I did not. I found the greed and incivility of some so repulsive that I would always avert my gaze from them, as if from some impropriety. Every new pair of hands to appear on the table, however, was a fresh experience and a source of curiosity to me; I often quite forgot to look at the face which, surrounded by a collar high above them, was set impassively on top of an evening shirt or a glittering décolletage, a cold social mask.

When I entered the gaming hall that evening, passed two crowded tables, reached a third, and was taking out a few coins, I was surprised to hear a very strange sound directly opposite me in the wordless, tense pause that seems to echo with silence and always sets in as the ball, moving sluggishly, hesitates between two numbers. It was a cracking, clicking sound like the snapping of joints. I looked across the table in amazement. And then I saw—I was truly startled!—I saw two hands such as I had never seen before, left and right clutching each other like doggedly determined animals, bracing and extending together and against one another with such heightened tension that the fingers' joints cracked with a dry sound like a nut cracking open. They were hands of rare beauty, unusually long, unusually slender, yet taut and muscular—very white, the nails pale at their tips, gently curving and the colour of mother-of-pearl. I kept watching them all evening, indeed I kept marvelling at those extraordinary, those positively unique hands—but what surprised and alarmed me so much at first was the passion in them, their crazily impassioned expressiveness, the convulsive way they wrestled with and supported each other. I knew at once that I was seeing a human being overflowing with emotion, forcing his passion into his fingertips lest it tear him apart. And then—just as the ball, with a dry click, fell into place in the wheel and the croupier called out the number—at that very moment the two hands suddenly fell apart like a pair of animals struck by a single bullet. They dropped, both of them, truly dead and not just exhausted; they dropped with so graphic an expression of lethargy, disappointment, instant extinction, as if all was finally over, that I can find no words to describe it. For never before or since have I seen such speaking hands, hands in which every muscle was eloquent and passion broke almost tangibly from the pores of the skin. They lay on the green table for a moment like jellyfish cast up by the sea, flat and dead. Then one of them, the right hand, began laboriously raising itself again, beginning with the fingertips;

it quivered, drew back, turned on itself, swayed, circled, and suddenly reached nervously for a jetton, rolling the token uncertainly like a little wheel between the tips of thumb and middle finger. And suddenly it arched, like a panther arching its back, and shot forwards, positively spitting the hundred-franc jetton out on the middle of the black space. At once, as if at a signal, the inactive, slumbering left hand was seized by excitement too; it rose, slunk, crawled over to its companion hand, which was trembling now as if exhausted by throwing down the jetton, and both hands lay there together trembling, the joints of their fingers working away soundlessly on the table, tapping slightly together like teeth chattering in a fever—no, I had never seen hands of such expressive eloquence, or such spasmodic agitation and tension. Everything else in this vaulted room, the hum from the other halls around it, the calls of the croupiers crying their wares like market traders, the movement of people and of the ball itself which now, dropped from above, was leaping like a thing possessed around the circular cage that was smooth as parquet flooring—all this diversity of whirling, swirling impressions flitting across the nerves suddenly seemed to me dead and dull compared to those two trembling, breathing, gasping, waiting, freezing hands, that extraordinary pair of hands which somehow held me spellbound.

But finally I could no longer refrain; I had to see the human being, the face to which those magical hands belonged, and fearfully—yes, I do mean fearfully, for I was afraid of those hands!—my gaze slowly travelled up the gambler's sleeves and narrow shoulders. And once again I had a shock, for his face spoke the same fantastically extravagant language of extremes as the hands, shared the same terrible grimness of expression and delicate, almost feminine beauty. I had never seen such a face before, a face so transported and utterly beside itself, and I had plenty of opportunity to observe it at leisure as if it were a mask, an unseeing sculpture: those possessed eyes did not turn to right or left for so much as a second, their pupils were fixed and black beneath the widely opened lids, dead glass balls reflecting that other mahogany-coloured ball rolling and leaping about the roulette wheel in such foolish high spirits. Never, I repeat, had I seen so intense or so fascinating a face. It belonged to a young man of perhaps twenty-four, it was fine-drawn, delicate, rather long and very expressive. Like the hands, it did not seem entirely masculine, but resembled the face of a boy passionately absorbed in a game—although I noticed none of that until later, for now the face was entirely veiled by an expression of greed and of madness breaking out. The thin mouth, thirsting and open, partly revealed the teeth: you could see them ten paces away, grinding feverishly while the parted lips remained rigid. A light-blond lock of hair clung damply to his forehead, tumbling forwards like the hair of a man falling, and a tic fluttered constantly around his nostrils as if little waves were invisibly rippling beneath the skin. The bowed head was moving instinctively further and further forwards; you felt it was being swept away with the whirling of the little ball, and now, for the first time, I understood the convulsive pressure of the hands. Only by the intense strain of pressing them together did the body, falling from its central axis, contrive to keep its balance. I had never—I must repeat it yet again—I had never seen a face in which passion showed so openly, with such shamelessly naked animal feeling, and I stared at that face, as fascinated and spellbound by its obsession as was its own gaze by the leaping, twitching movement of the circling ball. From that moment on I noticed nothing else in the room, everything seemed to me dull, dim and blurred, dark by comparison with the flashing fire of that face, and disregarding everyone else present I spent perhaps an hour watching that one man and every movement he made: the bright light that sparkled in his eyes, the convulsive knot of his hands loosening as if blown apart by an explosion, the parting of the shaking fingers as the croupier pushed twenty gold coins towards their eager grasp. At that moment the face looked suddenly bright and very young, the lines in it smoothed out, the eyes began to gleam, the convulsively bowed body straightened lightly, easily—he suddenly sat there as relaxed as a horseman, borne up by the sense of triumph, fingers toying lovingly, idly with the round coins, clinking them together, making them dance and jingle playfully. Then he turned his head restlessly again, surveyed the green table as if with the flaring nostrils of a young hound seeking the right scent, and suddenly, with one quick movement, placed all the coins on one rectangular space. At once the watchfulness, the tension returned. Once more the little waves, rippling galvanically, spread out from his lips, once again his hands were clasped, the boyish face disappeared behind greedy expectation until the spasmodic tension exploded and fell apart in disappointment: the face that had just looked boyish turned faded, wan and old, light disappeared from the burnt-out eyes, and all this within the space of a second as the ball came to rest on the wrong number. He had lost; he stared at the ball for a few seconds almost like an idiot, as if he did not understand, but as the croupier began calling to whip up interest, his fingers took out a few coins again. But his certainty was gone; first he put the coins on one space, then, thinking better of it, on another, and when the ball had begun to roll his trembling hand, on a sudden impulse, quickly added two crumpled banknotes.

This alternation of up and down, loss and gain, continued without a break for about an hour, and during that hour I did not, even for a moment, take my fascinated gaze from that ever-changing face and all the passions ebbing and flowing over it. I kept my eyes fixed on those magical hands, their every muscle graphically reflecting the whole range of the man's feelings as they rose and fell like a fountain. I had never watched the face of an actor in the theatre as intently as I watched this one, seeing the constant, changing shades of emotion flitting over it like light and shade moving over a landscape. I had never immersed myself so wholeheartedly in a game as I did in the reflection of this stranger's excitement. If someone had been observing me at that moment he would surely have taken my steely gaze for a state of hypnosis, and indeed my benumbed perception was something like that—I simply could not look away from the play of those features, and everything else in the room, the lights, the laughter, the company and its glances, merely drifted vaguely around me, a yellow mist with that face in the middle of it, a flame among flames. I heard nothing, I felt nothing, I did not notice people coming forwards beside me, other hands suddenly reaching out like feelers, putting down money or picking it up; I did not see the ball or hear the croupier's voice, yet I saw it all as if I were dreaming, exaggerated as in a concave mirror by the excitement and extravagance of those moving hands. For I did not have to look at the roulette wheel to know whether the ball had come to rest on red or black, whether it was still rolling or beginning to falter. Every stage of the game, loss and gain, hope and disappointment, was fierily reflected in the nerves and movements of that passionate face.

But then came a terrible moment—something that I had been vaguely fearing all this time, something that had weighed like a gathering thunderstorm on my tense nerves, and now suddenly ripped through them. Yet again the ball had fallen back into the shallow depression with that dry little click, yet again came the tense moment when two hundred lips held their breath until the croupier's voice announced the winning number—this time it was zero—while he zealously raked in the clinking coins and crackling notes from all sides. At that moment those two convulsively clasped hands made a particularly terrifying movement, leaping up as if to catch something that wasn't there and then dropping to the table again exhausted, with no strength in them, only the force of gravity flooding back. Then, however, they suddenly came to life yet again, feverishly retreating from the table to the man's own body, clambering up his torso like wild cats, up and down, left and right, nervously trying all his pockets to see if some forgotten coin might not have slipped into one of them. But they always came back empty, and the pointless, useless search began again ever more frantically, while the roulette wheel went on circling and others continued playing, while coins clinked, chairs were shifted on the floor, and all the small sounds, put together a hundredfold, filled the room with a humming note. I trembled, shaking with horror; I felt it all as clearly as if my own fingers were rummaging desperately for a coin in the pockets and folds of my creased garments. And suddenly, with a single abrupt movement, the man rose to his feet opposite me, like a man standing up when he suddenly feels unwell and must rise if he is not to suffocate. His chair crashed to the floor behind him. Without even noticing, without paying any attention to his surprised and abashed neighbours as they avoided his swaying figure, he stumbled away from the table.

The sight petrified me. For I knew at once where the man was going: to his death. A man getting to his feet like that was not on his way back to an inn, a wine bar, a wife, a railway carriage, to any form of life at all, he was plunging straight into the abyss. Even the most hardened spectator in that hellish gaming hall could surely have seen that the man had nothing to fall back on, not at home or in a bank or with a family, but had been sitting here with the last of his money, staking his life, and was now staggering away somewhere else, anywhere, but undoubtedly out of that life. I had feared all along, I had sensed from the first moment, as if by magic, that more than loss or gain was staked on the game, yet now it struck me like a bolt of dark lightning to see the life suddenly go out of his eyes and death cast its pale shadow over his still living face. Instinctively—affected as I was by his own graphic gestures—I clutched at myself while the man tore himself away from his place and staggered out, for his own uncertain gait was now transferred to my own body just as his tension had entered my veins and nerves. Then I was positively wrenched away, I had to follow him; my feet moved without my own volition. It was entirely unconscious, I did not do it of my own accord, it was something happening to me when, taking no notice of anyone, feeling nothing myself, I went out into the corridor leading to the doors.

He was standing at the cloakroom counter, and the attendant had brought him his coat. But his arms would no longer obey him, so the helpful attendant laboriously eased them into the sleeves, as if he were paralysed. I saw him automatically put his hand in his waistcoat pocket to give the man a tip, but his fingers emerged empty. Then he suddenly seemed to remember everything, awkwardly stammered something to the cloakroom attendant, and as before moved forwards abruptly and then stumbled like a drunk down the casino steps, where the attendant stood briefly watching him go, with a smile that was at first contemptuous and then understanding.

His bearing shook me so much that I felt ashamed to have seen it. Involuntarily I turned aside, embarrassed to have watched a stranger's despair as if I were in a theatre—but then that vague fear suddenly took me out of myself once again. Quickly, I retrieved my coat, and thinking nothing very definite, purely mechanically and compulsively I hurried out into the dark after the stranger."

Mrs C interrupted her story for a moment. She had been sitting calmly opposite me, speaking almost without a break with her characteristic tranquil objectivity, as only someone who had prepared and carefully organised the events of her tale in advance could speak. Now, for the first time, she stopped, hesitated, and then suddenly broke off and turned directly to me.

"I promised you and myself," she began, rather unevenly, "to tell you all the facts with perfect honesty. Now I must ask you to believe in my honesty, and not assume that my conduct had any ulterior motives. I might not be ashamed of them today, but in this case such suspicions would be entirely unfounded. And I must emphasise that, when I hurried after that ruined gambler in the street, I had certainly not fallen in love with him—I did not think of him as a man at all, and indeed I was over forty myself at the time and had never looked at another man since my husband's death. All that part of my life was finally over; I tell you this explicitly, and I must, or you would not understand the full horror of what happened later. On the other hand, it's true that I would find it difficult to give a clear name to the feeling that drew me so compulsively after the unfortunate man; there was curiosity in it, but above all a dreadful fear, or rather a fear of something dreadful, something I had felt invisibly enveloping the young man like a miasma from the first moment. But such feelings can't be dissected and taken apart, if only because they come over one too compulsively, too fast, too spontaneously—very likely mine expressed nothing but the instinct to help with which one snatches back a child about to run into the road in front of a motor car. How else can we explain why non-swimmers will jump off a bridge to help a drowning man? They are simply impelled to do it as if by magic, some other will pushes them off the bridge before they have time to consider the pointless bravery of their conduct properly; and in just the same way, without thinking, without conscious reflection, I hurried after the unfortunate young man out of the gaming room, to the casino doors, out of the doors and on to the terrace.

And I am sure that neither you nor any other feeling human being with his eyes open could have withstood that fearful curiosity, for a more disturbing sight can hardly be imagined than the way the gambler, who must have been twenty-four at the most but moved as laboriously as an old man and was swaying like a drunk, dragged himself shakily and disjointedly down the steps to the terrace beside the road. Once there, his body dropped on to a bench, limp as a sack. Again I shuddered as I sensed, from that movement, that the man had reached the end of his tether.

Only a dead man or one with nothing left to keep him alive drops like that. His head, fallen to one side, leant back over the bench, his arms hung limp and shapeless to the ground, and in the dim illumination of the faintly flickering street lights any passer-by would have thought he had been shot. And it was like that—I can't explain why the vision suddenly came into my mind, but all of a sudden it was there, real enough to touch, terrifying and terrible—it was like that, as a man who had been shot, that I saw him before me at that moment, and I knew for certain that he had a revolver in his pocket, and tomorrow he would be found lying lifeless and covered with blood on this or some other bench. For he had dropped like a stone falling into a deep chasm, never to stop until it reaches the bottom: I never saw such a physical expression of exhaustion and despair.

So now, consider my situation: I was standing twenty or thirty paces from the bench and the motionless, broken man on it, with no idea what to do, on the one hand wishing to help, on the other restrained by my innate and inbred reluctance to speak to a strange man in the street. The gaslights flickered dimly in the overcast sky, few figures hurried past, for it was nearly midnight and I was almost entirely alone in the park with this suicidal figure. Five or ten times I had already pulled myself together and approached him, but shame or perhaps that deeper premonitory instinct, the idea that falling men are likely to pull those who come to their aid down with them, made me withdraw—and in the midst of this indecision I was clearly aware of the pointless, ridiculous aspect of the situation. Nonetheless, I could neither speak nor turn away, I could not do anything but I could not leave him. And I hope you will believe me when I say that for perhaps an hour, an endless hour, I walked indecisively up and down that terrace, while time was divided up by thousands of little sounds from the breaking waves of the invisible sea—so shaken and transfixed was I by the idea of the annihilation of a human being.

Yet I could not summon up the courage to say a word or make a move, and I would have waited like that half the night, or perhaps in the end my wiser self-interest would have prevailed on me to go home, and indeed I think I had already made up my mind to leave that helpless bundle of misery lying there—when a superior force put an end to my indecision. It began to rain. All evening the wind had been piling up heavy spring clouds full of moisture above the sea, lungs and heart felt the pressure of the lowering sky, and now drops suddenly began to splash down. Soon a heavy rain was falling in wet torrents blown about by the wind. I instinctively sheltered under the projecting roof of a kiosk, but although I put up my umbrella gusts of wind kept blowing the rain on my dress. I felt the cold mist thrown up by the falling raindrops spray my face and hands.

But—and it was such a terrible sight that even now, two decades later, the memory still constricts my throat—but in the middle of this cloudburst the unfortunate man stayed perfectly still on his bench, never moving. Water was gurgling and dripping from all the eaves; you could hear the rumble of carriages from the city; people with their coat collars turned up hurried past to right and to left; all living creatures ducked in alarm, fled, ran, sought shelter; man and beast felt universal fear of the torrential element—but that black heap of humanity on the bench did not stir or move. I told you before that he had the magical gift of graphically expressing everything he felt in movement and gesture. But nothing, nothing on earth could convey despair, total self-surrender, death in the midst of life to such shattering effect as his immobility, the way he sat there in the falling rain, not moving, feeling nothing, too tired to rise and walk the few steps to the shelter of the projecting roof, utterly indifferent to his own existence. No sculptor, no poet, not Michelangelo or Dante has ever brought that sense of ultimate despair, of ultimate human misery so feelingly to my mind as the sight of that living figure letting the watery element drench him, too weary and uncaring to make a single move to protect himself.

That made me act; I couldn't help it. Pulling myself together, I ran the gauntlet of the lashing rain and shook the dripping bundle of humanity to make him get up from the bench. 'Come along!' I seized his arm. Something stared up at me, with difficulty. Something in him seemed to be slowly preparing to move, but he did not understand. 'Come along!' Once again, almost angry now, I tugged at his wet sleeve. Then he slowly stood up, devoid of will and swaying. 'What do you want?' he asked, and I could not reply, for I myself had no idea where to take him—just away from the cold downpour where he had been sitting so senselessly, suicidally, in the grip of deep despair. I did not let go of his arm but dragged the man on, since he had no will of his own, to the sales kiosk where the narrow, projecting roof at least partly sheltered him from the raging attack of the stormy rain as the wind tossed it wildly back and forth. That was all I wanted, I had nothing else in mind, just to get him somewhere dry, under a roof. As yet I had thought no further.

So we stood side by side on that narrow strip of dry ground, the wall of the kiosk behind us and above us only the roof, which was not large enough, for the insatiable rain insidiously came in under it as sudden gusts of wind flung wet, chilly showers over our clothes and into our faces. The situation became intolerable. I could hardly stand there any longer beside this dripping wet stranger. On the other hand, having dragged him over here I couldn't just leave him and walk away without a word. Something had to be done, and gradually I forced myself to think clearly. It would be best, I thought, to send him home in a cab and then go home myself; he would be able to look after himself tomorrow. So as he stood beside me gazing fixedly out at the turbulent night I asked, 'Where do you live?'

'I'm not staying anywhere... I only arrived from Nice this morning... we can't go to my place.'

I did not immediately understand this last remark. Only later did I realise that the man took me for... for a *demi-mondaine*, one of the many women who haunt the casino by night, hoping to extract a little money from lucky gamblers or drunks. After all, what else was he to think, for only now that I tell you about it do I feel all the improbability, indeed the fantastic nature of my situation—what else was he to think of me? The way I had pulled him off the bench and dragged him away as if it were perfectly natural was certainly not the conduct of a lady. But this idea did not occur to me at once. Only later, only too late did his terrible misapprehension dawn upon me, or I would never have said what I did next, in words that were bound to reinforce his impression. 'Then we'll just take a room in a hotel. You can't stay here. You must get under cover somewhere.'

Now I understood his painful misunderstanding, for he did not turn towards me but merely rejected the idea with a certain contempt in his voice: 'I don't need a room; I don't need anything now. Don't bother, you won't get anything out of me. You've picked the wrong man. I have no money.'

This too was said in a dreadful tone, with shattering indifference, and the way he stood there dripping wet and leaning against the wall, slack and exhausted to the bone, shook me so much that I had no time to waste on taking petty offence. I merely sensed, as I had from the first moment when I saw him stagger from the gaming hall, as I had felt all through this improbable hour, that here was a human being, a young, living, breathing human being on the very brink of death, and I must save him. I came closer.

'Never mind money, come along! You can't stay here. I'll get you under cover. Don't worry about anything, just come with me.'

He turned his head and I felt, while the rain drummed round us with a hollow sound and the eaves cast water down to splash at our feet, that for the first time he was trying to make out my face in the dark. His body seemed to be slowly shaking off its lethargy too.

'As you like,' he said, giving in. 'It's all one to me... after all, why not? Let's go.' I put up my umbrella, he moved to my side and took my arm. I felt this sudden intimacy uncomfortable; indeed, it horrified me. I was alarmed to the depths of my heart. But I did not feel bold enough to ask him to refrain, for if I rejected him now he would fall into the bottomless abyss, and everything I had tried to do so far would be in vain. We walked the few steps back to the casino, and only now did it strike me that I had no idea what to do with him. I had better take him to a hotel, I thought quickly, and give him money to spend the night there and go home in the morning. I was not thinking beyond that. And as the carriages were now rapidly drawing up outside the casino I hailed a cab and we got in. When the driver asked where to, I couldn't think what to say at first. But realising that the drenched, dripping man beside me would not be welcome in any of the best hotels—on the other hand, genuinely inexperienced as I was, with nothing else in mind—I just told the cabby, 'Some simple hotel, anywhere!'

The driver, indifferent, and wet with rain himself, drove his horses on. The stranger beside me said not a word, the wheels rattled, the rain splashed heavily against the windows, and I felt as if I were travelling with a corpse in that dark, lightless rectangular space, in a vehicle like a coffin. I tried to think of something to say to relieve the strange, silent horror of our presence there together, but I could think of nothing. After a few minutes the cab stopped. I got out first and paid the driver, who shut the door after us as if drunk with sleep. We were at the door of a small hotel that was unknown to me, with a glass porch above us providing a tiny area of shelter from the rain, which was still lashing the impenetrable night around us with ghastly monotony.

The stranger, giving way to his inertia, had instinctively leant against the wall, and water was dripping from his wet hat and crumpled garments. He stood there like a drunk who has been fished out of the river, still dazed, and a channel of water trickling down from him formed around the small patch of ground where he stood. But he made not the slightest effort to shake himself or take off the hat from which raindrops kept running over his forehead and face. He stood there entirely apathetically, and I cannot tell you how his broken demeanour moved me.

But something had to be done. I put my hand into my bag. 'Here are a hundred francs,' I said. 'Take a room and go back to Nice tomorrow.'

He looked up in astonishment.

'I was watching you in the gaming hall,' I continued urgently, noticing his hesitation. 'I know you've lost everything, and I fear you're well on the way to doing something stupid. There's no shame in accepting help—here, take it!'

But he pushed away my hand with an energy I wouldn't have expected in him. 'You are very good,' he said, 'but don't waste your money. There's no help for me now. Whether I sleep tonight or not makes not the slightest difference. It will all be over tomorrow anyway. There's no help for me.'

'No, you must take it,' I urged. 'You'll see things differently tomorrow. Go upstairs and sleep on it. Everything will look different in daylight.'

But when I tried to press the money on him again he pushed my hand away almost violently. 'Don't,' he repeated dully. 'There's no point in it. Better to do it out of doors than leave blood all over their room here. A hundred or even a thousand francs won't help me. I'd just go to the gaming hall again tomorrow with the last few francs, and I wouldn't stop until they were all gone. Why begin again? I've had enough.'

You have no idea how that dull tone of voice went to my heart, but think of it: a couple of inches from you stands a young, bright, living, breathing human being, and you know that if you don't do your utmost, then in a few hours time this thinking, speaking, breathing specimen of youth will be a corpse. And now I felt a desire like rage, like fury, to overcome his senseless resistance. I grasped his arm. 'That's enough stupid talk. You go up these steps now and take a room, and I'll come in the morning and take you to the station. You must get away from here, you must go home tomorrow, and I won't rest until I've seen you sitting in the train with a ticket. You can't throw your life away so young just because you've lost a couple of hundred francs, or a couple of thousand. That's cowardice, silly hysteria concocted from anger and bitterness. You'll see that I'm right tomorrow!'

'Tomorrow!' he repeated in a curiously gloomy, ironic tone. 'Tomorrow! If you knew where I'd be tomorrow! I wish I knew myself—I'm mildly curious to find out. No, go home, my dear, don't bother about me and don't waste your money.'

But I wasn't giving up now. It had become like a mania obsessing me. I took his hand by force and pressed the banknote into it. 'You will take this money and go in at once!' And so saying I stepped firmly up to the door and rang the bell. 'There, now I've rung, and the porter will be here in a minute. Go in and lie down. I'll be outside here at nine tomorrow to take you straight to the station. Don't worry about anything, I'll see to what's necessary to get you home. But now go to bed, have a good sleep, and don't think of anything else!'

At that moment the key turned inside the door and the porter opened it.

'Come on, then!' said my companion suddenly, in a harsh, firm embittered voice, and I felt his fingers span my wrist in an iron grip. I was alarmed... so greatly alarmed, so paralysed, struck as if by lightning, that all my composure vanished. I wanted to resist, tear myself away, but my will seemed numbed, and I... well, you will understand... I was ashamed to struggle with a stranger in front of the porter, who stood there waiting impatiently. And so, suddenly, I was inside the hotel. I wanted to speak, say something, but my throat would not obey me... and his hand lay heavy and commanding on my arm. I vaguely felt it draw me as if unawares up a flight of steps—a key clicked in a lock. And suddenly I was alone with this stranger in a strange room, in some hotel whose name I do not know to this day."

Mrs C stopped again, and suddenly rose to her feet. It seemed that her voice would not obey her any more. She went over to the window and looked out in silence for some minutes, or perhaps she was just resting her forehead on the cold pane; I did not have the courage to look closely, for I found it painful to see the old lady so agitated. So I sat quite still, asking no questions, making no sound, and waited until she came back, stepping firmly, and sat down opposite me.

"Well—now the most difficult part is told. And I hope you will believe me when I assure you yet again, when I swear by all that is sacred to me, by my honour and my children, that up to that moment no idea of any... any relationship with the stranger had entered my mind, that I really had been suddenly plunged into this situation against my own will, indeed entirely unawares, as if I had fallen through a trapdoor from the level path of my existence. I have promised to be honest with you and with myself, so I repeat again that I embarked on this tragic venture merely through a rather overwrought desire to help, not through any other, any personal feeling, quite without any wishes or forebodings.

You must spare me the tale of what happened in that room that night; I myself have forgotten not a moment of it, and I never will. I spent it wrestling with another human being for his life, and I repeat, it was a battle of life and death. I felt only too clearly, with every fibre of my being, that this stranger, already half-lost, was clutching at his last chance with all the avid passion of a man threatened by death. He clung to me like one who already feels the abyss yawning beneath him. For my part, I summoned everything in me to save him by all the means at my command. A human being may know such an hour perhaps only once in his life, and out of millions, again, perhaps only one will know it—but for that terrible chance I myself would never have guessed how ardently, desperately, with what boundless greed a man given up for lost will still suck at every red drop of life. Kept safe for twenty years from all the demonic forces of existence, I would never have understood how magnificently, how fantastically Nature can merge hot and cold, life and death, delight and despair together in a few brief moments. And that night was so full of conflict and of talk, of passion and anger and hatred, with tears of entreaty and intoxication, that it seemed to me to last a thousand years, and we two human beings who fell entwined into its chasm, one of us in frenzy, the other unsuspecting, emerged from that mortal tumult changed, completely transformed, senses and emotions transmuted.

But I don't want to talk about that. I cannot and will not describe it. However, I must just tell you of the extraordinary moment when I woke in the morning from a leaden sleep, from nocturnal depths such as I had never known before. It took me a long time to open my eyes, and the first thing I saw was a strange ceiling over me, and then, looking further an entirely strange, unknown, ugly room. I had no idea how I came to be there. At first I told myself I must still be dreaming, an unusually lucid, transparent dream into which I had passed from my dull, confused slumber—but the sparkling bright sunshine outside the windows was unmistakably genuine, the light of morning, and the sounds of the street echoed from below, the rattle of carriages, the ringing of tram bells, the noise of people—so now I knew that I was awake and not dreaming. I instinctively sat up to get my bearings, and then—as my glance moved sideways—then I saw, and I can never describe my alarm to you, I saw a stranger sleeping in the broad bed beside me... a strange, perfectly strange, half-naked, unknown man... oh, I know there's no real way to describe the awful realisation; it struck me with such terrible force that I sank back powerless. But not in a kindly faint, not falling unconscious, far from it: with lightning speed, everything became as clear to me as it was inexplicable, and all I wanted was to die of revulsion and shame at suddenly finding myself in an unfamiliar bed in a decidedly shady hotel, with a complete stranger beside me. I still remember how my heart missed a beat, how I held my breath as if that would extinguish my life and above all my consciousness, which grasped everything yet understood none of it.

I shall never know how long I lay like that, all my limbs icy cold: the dead must lie rigid in their coffins in much the same way. All I know is that I had closed my eyes and was praying to God, to some heavenly power, that this might not be true, might not be real. But my sharpened senses would not let me deceive myself, I could hear people talking in the next room, water running, footsteps shuffling along the corridor outside, and each of these signs mercilessly proved that my senses were terribly alert.

How long this dreadful condition lasted I cannot say: such moments are outside the measured time of ordinary life. But suddenly another fear came over me, swift and terrible: the stranger whose name I did not know might wake up and speak to me. And I knew at once there was only one thing to do: I must get dressed and make my escape before he woke. I must not let him set eyes on me again, I must not speak to him again. I must save myself before it was too late, go away, away, away, back to some kind of life of my own, to my hotel, I must leave this pernicious place, leave this country, never meet him again, never look him in the eye, have no witnesses, no accusers, no one who knew. The idea dispelled my faintness: very cautiously, with the furtive movements of a thief, I inched out of bed (for I was desperate to make no noise) and groped my way over to my clothes. I dressed very carefully, trembling all the time lest he might wake up, and then I had finished, I had done it.

Only my hat lay at the foot of the bed on the far side of the room, and then, as I tiptoed over to pick it up—I couldn't help it, at that moment I had to cast another glance at the face of the stranger who had fallen into my life like a stone dropping off a window sill. I meant it to be just one glance, but it was curious—the strange young man who lay sleeping there really was a stranger to me. At first I did not recognise his face from yesterday. The impassioned, tense, desperately distressed features of the mortally agitated man might have been entirely extinguished—this man's face was not the same, but was an utterly childlike, utterly boyish face that positively radiated purity and cheerfulness. The lips, so grim yesterday as he clenched his teeth on them, were dreaming, had fallen softly apart, half-curving in a smile; the fair hair curled gently over the smooth forehead, the breath passed from his chest over his body at repose like the mild rippling of waves.

Perhaps you may remember that I told you earlier I had never before seen greed and passion expressed with such outrageous extravagance by any human being as by that stranger at the gaming table. And I tell you now that I had never, even in children whose baby slumbers sometimes cast an angelic aura of cheerfulness around them, seen such an expression of brightness, of truly blissful sleep. The uniquely graphic nature of that face showed all its feelings, at present the paradisaical easing of all internal heaviness, a sense of freedom and salvation. At this surprising sight all my own fear and horror fell from me like a heavy black cloak—I was no longer ashamed, no, I was almost glad. The terrible and incomprehensible thing that had happened suddenly made sense to me; I was happy, I was proud to think that but for my dedicated efforts the beautiful, delicate young man lying here carefree and quiet as a flower would have been found somewhere on a rocky slope, his body shattered and bloody, his face ruined, lifeless, with staring eyes. I had saved him; he was safe. And now I looked—I cannot put it any other way—I looked with maternal feeling at the man I had reborn into life more painfully than I bore my own children. In the middle of that shabby, threadbare room in a distasteful, grubby house of assignation, I was overcome by the kind of emotion—ridiculous as you may find it put into words—the kind of emotion one might have in church, a rapturous sense of wonder and sanctification. From the most dreadful moment of a whole life there now grew a second life, amazing and overwhelming, coming in sisterly fashion to meet me.

Had I made too much noise moving about? Had I involuntarily exclaimed out loud? I don't know, but suddenly the sleeping man opened his eyes. I flinched back in alarm. He looked round in surprise—just as I had done before earlier, and now he in his own turn seemed to be emerging with difficulty from great depths of confusion. His gaze wandered intently round the strange, unfamiliar room and then fell on me in amazement. But before he spoke, or could quite pull himself together, I had control of myself. I did not let him say a word, I allowed no questions, no confidences; nothing of yesterday or of last night was to be explained, discussed or mulled over again.

'I have to go now,' I told him quickly. 'You stay here and get dressed. I'll meet you at twelve at the entrance to the casino, and I'll take care of everything else.'

And before he could say a word in reply I fled, to be rid of the sight of the room, and without turning back left the hotel whose name I did not know, any more than I knew the name of the stranger with whom I had just spent the night."

Mrs C interrupted her narrative for a moment again, but all the strain and distress had gone from her voice: like a carriage that toils uphill with difficulty but then, having reached the top, rolls swiftly and smoothly down the other side, her account now proceeded more easily:

"Well—so I made haste to my hotel through the morning light of the streets. The drop in the temperature had driven all the hazy mists from the sky above, just as my own distress had been dispelled. For remember what I told you earlier: I had given up my own life entirely after my husband's death. My children did not need me, I didn't care for my own company, and there's no point in a life lived aimlessly. Now, for the first time, a task had suddenly come my way: I had saved a human being, I had exerted all my powers to snatch him back from destruction. There was only a little left to do—for my task must be completed to the end. So I entered my hotel, ignoring the porter's surprise when he saw me returning at nine in the morning—no shame and chagrin over last night's events oppressed me now, I felt my will to live suddenly revive, and an unexpectedly new sense of the point of my existence flowed warmly through my veins. Once in my room I quickly changed my clothes, putting my mourning aside without thinking (as I noticed only later) and choosing a lighter colour instead, went to the bank to withdraw money, and made haste to the station to find out train times. With a determination that surprised me I also made a few other arrangements. Now there was nothing left to do but ensure the departure from Monte Carlo and ultimate salvation of the man whom fate had cast in my way.

It is true that I needed strength to face him personally. Everything yesterday had taken place in the dark, in a vortex; we had been like two stones thrown out of a torrential stream suddenly striking together; we scarcely knew each other face to face, and I wasn't even sure whether the stranger would recognise me again. Yesterday had been chance, frenzy, a case of two confused people possessed; today I must be more open with him, since I must now confront him in the pitiless light of day with myself, my own face, as a living human being.

But it all turned out much easier than I expected. No sooner had I approached the casino at the appointed hour than a young man jumped up from a bench and made haste towards me. There was something so spontaneous, so childlike, unplanned and happy in his surprise and in each of his eloquent movements; he almost flew to me, the radiance of a joy that was both grateful and deferential in his eyes, which were lowered humbly as soon as they felt my confusion in his presence. Gratitude is so seldom found, and those who are most grateful cannot express it, are silent in their confusion, or ashamed, or sometimes seem ungracious just to conceal their feelings. But in this man, the expression of whose every feeling God, like a mysterious sculptor, had made sensual, beautiful, graphic, his gratitude glowed with radiant passion right through his body. He bent over my hand and remained like that for a moment, the narrow line of his boyish head reverently bowed, respectfully brushing kisses on my fingers; only then did he step back, ask how I was, and look at me most movingly. There was such courtesy in everything he said that within a few minutes the last of my anxiety had gone. As if reflecting the lightening of my own feelings, the landscape around was shining, the spell on it broken: the sea that had been disturbed and angry yesterday lay so calm and bright that every pebble beneath the gently breaking surf gleamed white, and the casino, that den of iniquity, looked up with Moorish brightness to the damask sky that was now swept clean. The kiosk with the projecting roof beneath which the pouring rain had forced us to shelter yesterday proved to be a flower stall; great bunches of flowers and foliage lay there in motley confusion, in white, red, other bright colours and green, and a young girl in a colourful blouse was offering them for sale.

I invited him to lunch with me in a small restaurant, and there the young stranger told me the story of his tragic venture. It confirmed my first presentiment when I had seen his trembling, nervously shaking hands on the green table. He came from an old aristocratic family in the Austrian part of Poland, was destined for a diplomatic career, had studied in Vienna and passed his first examination with great success a month ago. As a reward, and to celebrate the occasion, his uncle, a high-ranking general-staff officer, had taken him to the Prater in a cab, and they went to the races. His uncle was lucky with his bets and won three times running; then they ate supper in an elegant restaurant on the strength of the fat wad of banknotes that were the uncle's gains. Next day, again to mark his success in the examinations, the budding diplomat received a sum of money from his father which was as much as his usual monthly allowance. Two days earlier this would have seemed to him a large sum, but now, seeing how easily his uncle had won money, it struck him as trifling and left him indifferent. Directly after dinner, therefore, he went to the races again, laid wild, frenzied bets, and fortune—or rather misfortune—would have it that he left the Prater after the last race with three times the sum he had brought there. Now a mania for gambling infected him; sometimes he went to the races, sometimes to play in coffee houses and clubs, exhausting his time, his studies, his nerves, and above all his money. He was no longer able to think or to sleep peacefully, and he was quite unable to control himself; one night, coming home from a club where he had lost everything, he found a crumpled banknote forgotten in his waistcoat pocket as he was undressing. There was no holding him; he got dressed again and walked the streets until he found a few people playing dominoes in a coffee house, and sat with them until dawn. On one occasion his married sister came to his aid, paying his debts to moneylenders who were very ready to give credit to the heir of a great and noble name. For a while he was lucky at play again—but then matters went inexorably downhill, and the more he lost, the more urgently did unsecured obligations and fixed-term IOUs require him to find relief by winning. He had long ago pawned his watch and his clothes, and at last a terrible thing happened: he stole two large pearl earrings that she seldom wore from his old aunt's dressing table. He pawned one of the pearls for a large sum, which his gambling quadrupled that evening. But instead of redeeming the pearl he staked all his winnings and lost. At the time when he left Vienna the theft had not yet been discovered, so he pawned the second pearl and on a sudden impulse travelled by train to Monte Carlo to win the fortune he dreamt of at roulette. On arrival he had sold his suitcase, his clothes, his umbrella; he had nothing left but a revolver with four cartridges, and a small cross set with jewels given him by his godmother, Princess X. He did not want to part with the cross, but it too had been sold for fifty francs that afternoon, just to let him try to satisfy his urge by playing for life or death one last time that evening.

He told me all this with the captivating charm of his original and lively nature. And I listened shaken, gripped and much moved, but not for a moment did it occur to me to feel horror that the man at my table was in sober fact a thief. Yesterday, if someone had so much as suggested to me that I, a woman with a blameless past who expected the company she kept to be strictly and conventionally virtuous, would be sitting here on familiar terms with a perfectly strange young man, not much older than my son, who had stolen a pair of pearl earrings, I would have thought he had taken leave of his senses and such a thing was impossible. But I felt no horror at all as he told his tale, for he spoke so naturally and passionately that it seemed more like the account of a fever or illness than a crime. Moreover, the word 'impossible' had suddenly lost its meaning for a woman who had known such an unexpected, torrential experience as I had the night before. In those ten hours, I had come to know immeasurably more about reality than in my preceding forty respectable years of life.

Yet something else about his confession did alarm me, and that was the feverish glint in his eyes, which made all the nerves of his face twitch galvanically as he talked about his passion for gambling. Even speaking of it aroused him, and his face graphically and with terrible clarity illustrated that tension between pleasure and torment. His hands, those beautiful, nervous, slender-jointed hands, instinctively began to turn into preying, hunting, fleeing animal creatures again, just as they did at the gaming table. As he spoke I saw them suddenly trembling, beginning at the wrists, arching and clenching into fists, then opening up to intertwine their fingers once more. And when he confessed to the theft of the pearl earrings they suddenly performed a swift, leaping, quick, thieving movement—I involuntarily jumped. I could see his fingers pouncing on the jewels and swiftly stowing them away in the hollow of his clenched hand. And with nameless horror, I recognised that the very last drop of this man's blood was poisoned by his addiction.

That was the one thing that so shattered and horrified me about his tale, the pitiful enslavement of a young, light-hearted, naturally carefree man to a mad passion. I considered it my prime duty to persuade my unexpected protégé, in friendly fashion, that he must leave Monte Carlo, where the temptation was most dangerous, without delay, he must return to his family this very day, before anyone noticed that the pearl earrings were gone and his future was ruined for ever. I promised him money for his journey and to redeem the jewellery, though only on condition that he left today and swore to me, on his honour, never to touch a card or play any other game of chance again.

I shall never forget the passion of gratitude, humble at first, then gradually more ardent, with which that lost stranger listened to me, how he positively drank in my words as I promised him help, and then he suddenly reached both hands over the table to take mine in a gesture I can never forget, a gesture of what one might call adoration and sacred promise. There were tears in his bright but slightly confused eyes; his whole body was trembling nervously with happy excitement. I have tried to describe the uniquely expressive quality of his gestures to you several times already, but I cannot depict this one, for it conveyed ecstatic, supernal delight such as a human countenance seldom turns on us, comparable only to that white shade in which, waking from a dream, we think we see the countenance of an angel vanishing.

Why conceal it? I could not withstand that glance. Gratitude is delightful because it is so seldom found, tender feeling does one good, and such exuberance was delightfully new and heart-warming to me, sober, cool woman that I was. And with that crushed, distressed young man, the landscape itself had revived as if by magic after last night's rain. The sea, calm as a millpond, lay shining blue beneath the sky as we came out of the restaurant, and the only white to be seen was the white of seagulls swooping in that other, celestial blue. You know the Riviera landscape. It is always beautiful, but offers its rich colours to the eye in leisurely fashion, flat as a picture postcard, a lethargic sleeping beauty who admits all glances, imperturbable and almost oriental in her ever-opulent willingness. But sometimes, very occasionally, there are days when this beauty rises up, breaks out, cries out loud, you might say, with gaudy, fanatically sparkling colours, triumphantly flinging her flower-like brightness in your face, glowing, burning with sensuality. And the stormy chaos of the night before had turned to such a lively day, the road was washed white, the sky was turquoise, and everywhere bushes ignited like colourful torches among the lush, drenched green foliage. The mountains seemed suddenly lighter and closer in the cooler, sunny air, as if they were crowding towards the gleaming, polished little town out of curios-ity. Stepping outside, you sensed at every glance the challenging, cheering aspect of Nature spontaneously drawing your heart to her. 'Let's hire a carriage and drive along the Corniche,' I said.

The young man nodded enthusiastically: he seemed to be really seeing and noticing the landscape for the first time since his arrival. All he had seen so far was the dank casino hall with its sultry, sweaty smell, its crowds of ugly visitors with their twisted features, and a rough, grey, clamorous sea outside. But now the sunny beach lay spread out before us like a huge fan, and the eye leapt with pleasure from one distant point to another. We drove along the beautiful road in a slow carriage (this was before the days of the motor car), past many villas and many fine views; a hundred times, seeing every house, every villa in the green shade of the pine trees, one felt a secret wish to live there, quiet and content, away from the world!

Was I ever happier in my life than in that hour? I don't know. Beside me in the carriage sat the young man who had been a prey to death and disaster yesterday and now, in amazement, stood in the spray of the sparkling white dome of the sun above; years seemed to have dropped away from him. He had become all boy, a handsome, sportive child with a playful yet respectful look in his eyes, and nothing about him delighted me more than his considerate attentiveness. If the carriage was going up a steep climb which the horses found arduous, he jumped nimbly down to push from behind. If I named a flower or pointed to one by the roadside, he hurried to pluck it. He picked up a little toad that was hopping with difficulty along the road, lured out by last night's rain, and carried it carefully over to the green grass, where it would not be crushed as the carriage went by; and from time to time, in great high spirits, he would say the most delightful and amusing things; I believe he found laughter of that kind a safety valve, and without it he would have had to sing or dance or fool around in some way, so happily inebriated was the expression of his sudden exuberance.

As we were driving slowly through a tiny village high up on the road, he suddenly raised his hat politely. I was surprised and asked who he was greeting, since he was a stranger among strangers here. He flushed slightly at my question and explained, almost apologetically, that we had just passed a church, and at home in Poland, as in all strict Catholic countries, it was usual from childhood on to raise your hat outside any church or other place of worship. I was deeply moved by this exquisite respect for religion, and remembering the cross he had mentioned, I asked if he was a devout believer. When he modestly confessed, with a touch of embarrassment, that he hoped to be granted God's grace, an idea suddenly came to me. 'Stop!' I told the driver, and quickly climbed out of the carriage. He followed me in surprise, asking, 'Where are we going?' I said only, 'Come with me.'

In his company I went back to the church, a small country church built of brick. The interior looked chalky, grey and empty; the door stood open, so that a yellow beam of light cut sharply through the dark, where blue shadows surrounded a small altar. Two candles, like veiled eyes, looked out of the warm, incense-scented twilight. We entered, he took off his hat, dipped his hand in the basin of holy water, crossed himself and genuflected. When he was standing again I took his arm. 'Go and find an altar or some image here that is holy to you,' I urged him, 'and swear the oath I will recite to you.' He looked at me in surprise, almost in alarm. But quickly understanding, he went over to a niche, made the sign of the cross and obediently knelt down. 'Say after me,' I said, trembling with excitement myself, 'say after me: I swear… '—'I swear,' he repeated, and I continued, 'that I will never play for money again, whatever the game may be, I swear that I will never again expose my life and my honour to the dangers of that passion.'

He repeated the words, trembling: they lingered loud and clear in the empty interior. Then it was quiet for a moment, so quiet that you could hear the faint rustling of the trees outside as the wind blew through their leaves. Suddenly he threw himself down like a penitent and, in tones of ecstasy such as I had never heard before, poured out a flood of rapid, confused words in Polish. I did not understand what he was saying, but it was obviously an ecstatic prayer, a prayer of gratitude and remorse, for in his stormy confession he kept bowing his head humbly down on the prayer desk, repeating the strange sounds ever more passionately, and uttering the same word more and more violently and with extraordinary ardour. I have never heard prayer like that before or since, in any church in the world. As he prayed his hands clung convulsively to the wooden prayer desk, his whole body shaken by an internal storm that sometimes caught him up and sometimes cast him down again. He saw and felt nothing else: his whole being seemed to exist in another world, in a purgatorial fire of transmutation, or rising to a holier sphere. At last he slowly stood up, made the sign of the cross, and turned with an effort. His knees were trembling, his countenance was pale as the face of a man exhausted. But when he saw me his eyes beamed, a pure, a truly devout smile lit up his ecstatic face; he came closer, bowed low in the Russian manner, took both my hands and touched them reverently with his lips. 'God has sent you to me. I was thanking him.' I did not know what to say, but I could have wished the organ to crash out suddenly above the low pews, for I felt that I had succeeded: I had saved this man for ever.

We emerged from the church into the radiant, flooding light of that May-like day; the world had never before seemed to me more beautiful. Then we drove slowly on in the carriage for another two hours, taking the panoramic road over the hills which offers a new view at every turn. But we spoke no more. After so much emotion, any other words would have seemed an anti-climax. And when by chance my eyes met his, I had to turn them away as if ashamed, so shaken was I by the sight of my own miracle.

We returned to Monte Carlo at about five in the afternoon. I had an appointment with relatives which I could not cancel at this late date. And in fact I secretly wished for a pause in which to recover from feelings that had been too violently aroused. For this was too much happiness. I felt that I must rest from my overheated, ecstatic condition. I had never known anything like it in my life before. So I asked my protégé to come into my hotel with me for a moment, and there in my room I gave him the money for his journey and to redeem the jewellery. We agreed that while I kept my appointment he would go and buy his ticket, and then we would meet at seven in the entrance hall of the station, half-an-hour before the departure of the train taking him home by way of Genoa. When I was about to give him the five banknotes his lips turned curiously pale. 'No... no money... I beg you, not money!' he uttered through his teeth, while his agitated fingers quivered nervously. 'No money... not money... I can't stand the sight of it!' he repeated, as if physically overcome by nausea or fear. But I soothed him, saying it was only a loan, and if he felt troubled by it then he could give me a receipt. 'Yes, yes... a receipt,' he murmured, looking away, cramming the crumpled notes into his pocket without looking at them, like something sticky that soiled his fingers, and he scribbled a couple of words on a piece of paper in swift, flying characters. When he looked up damp sweat was standing out on his brow; something within seemed to be choking him, and no sooner had he given me the note than an impulse seemed to pass through him and suddenly—I was so startled that I instinctively flinched back—suddenly he fell on his knees and kissed the hem of my dress. It was an indescribable gesture; its overwhelming violence made me tremble all over. A strange shuddering came over me; I was confused, and could only stammer, 'Thank you for showing your gratitude—but do please go now! We'll say goodbye at seven in the station hall.'

He looked at me with a gleam of emotion moistening his eye; for a moment I thought he was going to say something, for a moment it seemed as if he were coming towards me. But then he suddenly bowed deeply again, very deeply, and left the room."

Once again Mrs C interrupted her story. She had risen and gone to the window to look out, and she stood there motionless for a long time. Watching the silhouette of her back, I saw it shiver slightly, and she swayed. All at once she turned back to me with determination, and her hands, until now calm and at rest, suddenly made a violent, tearing movement as if to rip something apart. Then she looked at me with a hard, almost defiant glance, and abruptly began again.

"I promised to be completely honest with you, and now I see how necessary that promise was. For only now that, for the first time, I make myself describe the whole course of those hours exactly as they happened, seeking words for what was a very complicated, confused feeling, only now do I clearly understand much that I did not know at the time, or perhaps would not acknowledge. So I will be firm and will not spare myself, and I will tell you the truth too: then, at the moment when the young man left the room and I remained there alone, I felt—it was a dazed sensation, like swooning—I felt a hard blow strike my heart. Something had hurt me mortally, but I did not know, or refused to know, what, after all, it was in my protégé's touchingly respectful conduct that wounded me so painfully.

But now that I force myself to bring up all the past unsparingly, in proper order, as if it were strange to me, and your presence as a witness allows no pretence, no craven concealment of a feeling which shames me, I clearly see that what hurt so much at the time was disappointment... my disappointment that... that the young man had gone away so obediently... that he did not try to detain me, to stay with me. It was because he humbly and respectfully fell in with my first attempt to persuade him to leave, instead... instead of trying to take me in his arms. It was because he merely revered me as a saint who had appeared to him along his way and did not... did not feel for me as a woman.

That was the disappointment I felt, a disappointment I did not admit to myself either then or later, but a woman's feelings know everything without words, without conscious awareness. For—and now I will deceive myself no longer—for if he had embraced me then, if he had asked me then, I would have gone to the ends of the earth with him, I would have dishonoured my name and the name

225

of my children—I would have eloped with him, caring nothing for what people would say or the dictates of my own reason, just as Madame Henriette ran off with the young Frenchman whom she hadn't even met the day before. I wouldn't have asked where we were going, or how long it would last, I wouldn't have turned to look back at my previous life—I would have sacrificed my money, my name, my fortune and my honour to him, I would have begged in the street for him, there is probably no base conduct in the world to which he could not have brought me. I would have thrown away all that we call modesty and reason if he had only spoken one word, taken one step towards me, if he had tried to touch me—so lost in him was I at that moment. But... as I told you... the young man, in his strangely dazed condition, did not spare another glance for me and the woman in me... and I knew how much, how fervently I longed for him only when I was alone again, when the passion that had just been lighting up his radiant, his positively seraphic face was cast darkly back on me and now lingered in the void of an abandoned breast. With difficulty, I pulled myself together. My appointment was a doubly unwelcome burden. I felt as if a heavy iron helmet were weighing down on my brow and I was swaying under its weight; my thoughts were as disjointed as my footsteps as I at last went over to the other hotel to see my relatives. I sat there in a daze, amidst lively chatter, and was startled whenever I happened to look up and see their unmoved faces, which seemed to me frozen like masks by comparison with that face of his, enlivened as if by the play of light and shade as clouds cross the sky. I found the cheerful company as dreadfully inert as if I were among the dead, and while I put sugar in my cup and joined absently in the conversation, that one face kept coming before my mind's eye, as if summoned up by the surging of the blood. It had become a fervent joy to me to watch that face, and—terrible thought!—in an hour or so I would have seen it for the last time. I must involuntarily have sighed or groaned gently, for my husband's cousin leant over to me: what was the matter, she asked, didn't I feel well? I looked so pale and sad. This unexpected question gave me a quick, easy excuse; I said I did indeed have a migraine, and perhaps she would allow me to slip away.

Thus restored to my own company, I hurried straight to my hotel. No sooner was I alone there than the sense of emptiness and abandonment came over me again, feverishly combined with a longing for the young man I was to leave today for ever. I paced up and down the room, opened shutters for no good reason, changed my dress and my ribbon, suddenly found myself in front of the looking glass again, wondering whether, thus adorned, I might not be able to attract him after all. And I abruptly understood myself: I would do anything not to lose him! Within the space of a violent moment, my wish turned to determination. I ran down to the porter and told him I was leaving today by the night train. Now I had to hurry: I rang for the maid to help me pack—time was pressing—and as we stowed dresses and small items into my suitcases I dreamt of the coming surprise: I would accompany him to the train, and then, at the very last moment, when he was giving me his hand in farewell, I would suddenly get into the carriage with my astonished companion, I would spend that night with him, and the next night—as long as he wanted me. A kind of enchanted, wild frenzy whirled through my blood, sometimes, to the maid's surprise, I unexpectedly laughed aloud as I flung clothes into the suitcases. My senses, I felt from time to time, were all in disorder. And when the man came to take the cases down I stared at him strangely at first: it was too difficult to think of ordinary matters while I was in the grip of such inner excitement.

Time was short; it must be nearly seven, leaving me at most twenty minutes before the train left—but of course, I consoled myself, my arrival would not be a farewell now, since I had decided to accompany him on his journey as long and as far as he would have me. The hotel manservant carried the cases on ahead while

I made haste to the reception desk to settle my bill. The manager was already giving me change, I was about to go on my way, when a hand gently touched my shoulder. I gave a start. It was my cousin; concerned by my apparent illness, she had come to see how I was. Everything went dark before my eyes. I did not want her here; every second I was detained meant disastrous delay, yet courtesy obliged me at least to fall into conversation with her briefly. 'You must go to bed,' she was urging me. 'I'm sure you have a temperature.' And she could well have been right, for the blood was pounding at my temples, and sometimes I felt the blue haze of approaching faintness come over my eyes. But I fended off her suggestions and took pains to seem grateful, while every word burned me, and I would have liked to thrust her ill-timed concern roughly away. However, she stayed and stayed and stayed with her unwanted solicitude, offered me eau de Cologne, would not be dissuaded from dabbing the cool perfume on my temples herself. Meanwhile I was counting the minutes, thinking both of him and of how to find an excuse to escape the torment of her sympathy. And the more restless I became, the more alarming did my condition seem to her; finally she was trying, almost by force, to make me go to my room and lie down. Then—in the middle of her urging—I suddenly saw the clock in the hotel lobby: it was two minutes before seven-thirty, and the train left at seven thirty-five. Brusquely, abruptly, with the brutal indifference of a desperate woman I simply stuck my hand out to my cousin—'Goodbye, I must go!'—and without a moment's thought for her frozen glance, without looking round, I rushed past the surprised hotel staff and out of the door, into the street and down it to the station. From the agitated gesticulating of the hotel manservant standing waiting there with my luggage I saw, well before I got there, that time must be very short. Frantically I ran to the barrier, but there the conductor turned me back—I had forgotten to buy a ticket. And as I almost forcibly tried to persuade him to let me on the platform all the same, the train began to move. I stared at it, trembling all over, hoping at least to catch a glimpse of him at the window of one of the carriages, a wave, a greeting. But in the middle of the hurrying throng I could not see his face. The carriages rolled past faster and faster, and after a minute nothing was left before my darkened eyes but black clouds of steam.

I must have stood there as if turned to stone, for God knows how long; the hotel servant had probably spoken to me in vain several times before he ventured to touch my arm. Only then did I start and come to myself. Should he take my luggage back to the hotel, he asked. It took me a few minutes to think; no, that was impossible, after this ridiculous, frantic departure I couldn't go back there, and I never wanted to again; so I told him, impatient to be alone, to take my cases to the left luggage office. Only then, in the middle of the constantly renewed crush of people flowing clamorously into the hall and then ebbing away again, did I try to think, to think clearly, to save myself from my desperate, painful, choking sense of fury, remorse and despair, for—why not admit it?—the idea that I had missed our last meeting through my own fault was like a knife turning pitilessly within me, burning and sharp. I could have screamed aloud: that red-hot blade, penetrating ever more mercilessly, hurt so much. Perhaps only those who are strangers to passion know such sudden outbursts of emotion in their few passionate moments, moments of emotion like an avalanche or a hurricane; whole years fall from one's own breast with the fury of powers left unused. Never before or after have I felt anything like the astonishment and raging impotence of that moment when, prepared to take the boldest of steps—prepared to throw away my whole carefully conserved, collected, controlled life all at once—I suddenly found myself facing a wall of senselessness against which my passion could only beat its head helplessly.

As for what I did then, how could it be anything but equally senseless? It was foolish, even stupid, and I am almost ashamed to tell you—but I have promised myself and you to keep nothing back. I… well, I went in search of him again. That is to say, I went in search of every moment I had spent with him. I felt irresistibly drawn to everywhere we had been together the day before, the bench in the casino grounds from which I had made him rise, the gaming hall where I had first seen him—yes, even that den of vice, just to relive the past once more, only once more. And tomorrow I would go along the Corniche in a carriage, retracing our path, so that every word and gesture would revive in my mind again—so senseless and childish was my state of confusion. But you must take into account the lightning speed with which these events overwhelmed me—I had felt little more than a single numbing blow, but now, woken too abruptly from that tumult of feeling, I wanted to go back over what I had so fleetingly experienced step by step, relishing it in retrospect by virtue of that magical self-deception we call memory. Well, some things we either do or do not understand. Perhaps you need a burning heart to comprehend them fully.

So I went first to the gaming hall to seek out the table where he had been sitting, and think of his hands among all the others there. I went in: I remembered that I had first seen him at the left-hand table in the second room. Every one of his movements was still clear before my mind's eye: I could have found his place sleepwalking, with my eyes closed and my hands outstretched. So I went in and crossed the hall. And then… as I looked at the crowd from the doorway… then something strange happened. There, in the very place where I dreamt of him, there sat—ah, the hallucinations of fever!—there sat the man himself. He looked exactly as I had seen him in my daydream just now—exactly as he had been yesterday, his eyes fixed on the ball, pale as a ghost—but he it unmistakably was.

I was so shocked that I felt as if I must cry out. But I controlled my alarm at this ridiculous vision and closed my eyes. 'You're mad—dreaming—feverish,' I told myself. 'It's impossible. You're hallucinating. He left half-an-hour ago.' Only then did I open my eyes again. But terrible to relate, he was still sitting there exactly as he had been sitting just now, in the flesh and unmistakable. I would have known those hands among millions... no, I wasn't dreaming, he was real. He had not left as he had promised he would, the madman was sitting there, he had taken the money I gave him for his journey and brought it here, to the green table, gambling it on his passion, oblivious of all else, while I was desperately eating my heart out for him.

I abruptly moved forwards: fury blurred my vision, a frenzied, red-eyed, raging desire to take the perjurer who had so shamefully abused my confidence, my feelings, my devotion by the throat. But I controlled myself. With a deliberately slow step (and how much strength that cost me!) I went up to the table to sit directly opposite him. A gentleman courteously made way for me. Two metres of green cloth stood between us, and as if looking down from a balcony at a play on stage I could watch his face, the same face that I had seen two hours ago radiant with gratitude, illuminated by the aura of divine grace, and now entirely absorbed in the infernal fires of his passion again. The hands, those same hands that I had seen clinging to the wood of the prayer desk as he swore a most sacred oath, were now clutching at the money again like the claws of lustful vampires. For he had been winning, he must have won a very great deal: in front of him shone a jumbled pile of jettons and louis d'ors and banknotes, a disordered medley in which his quivering, nervous fingers were stretching and bathing with delight. I saw them pick up separate notes, stroke and fold them, I saw them turn and caress coins, then suddenly and abruptly catch up a fistful and put them down on one of the spaces. And immediately that spasmodic tic around his nostrils began again, the call of the croupier tore his greedily blazing eyes away from the money to the spinning ball, he seemed to be flowing out of himself, as it were, while his elbows might have been nailed to the green table. His total addiction was revealed as even more dreadful, more terrible than the evening before, for every move he made murdered that other image within me, the image shining as if on a golden ground that I had credulously swallowed.

So we sat there two metres away from each other; I was staring at him, but he was unaware of me. He was not looking at me or anyone else, his glance merely moved to the money, flickering unsteadily with the ball as it rolled back to rest: all his senses were contained, chasing back and forth, in that one racing green circle. To this obsessive gambler the whole world, the whole human race had shrunk to a rectangular patch of cloth. And I knew that I could stand here for hours and hours, and he would not have the faintest idea of my presence.

But I could stand it no longer. Coming to a sudden decision, I walked round the table, stepped behind him and firmly grasped his shoulder with my hand. His gaze swung upwards, for a second he stared strangely at me, glassy-eyed, like a drunk being laboriously shaken awake, eyes still vague and drowsy, clouded by inner fumes. Then he seemed to recognise me, his mouth opened, quivering, he looked happily up at me and stammered quietly, in a confused tone of mysterious confidentiality, 'It's going well... I knew it would as soon as I came in and saw that he was here... ' I did not understand what he meant. All I saw was that this madman was intoxicated by the game and had forgotten everything else, his promise, his appointment at the station, me and the whole world besides. But even when he was in this obsessive mood I found his ecstasy so captivating that instinctively I went along with him and asked, taken aback, who was here?

'Over there, the one-armed old Russian general,' he whispered, pressing close to me so that no one else would overhear the magic secret. 'Over there, with the white sideboards and the servant behind him. He always wins, I was watching him yesterday, he must have a system, and I always pick the same number... He was winning yesterday too, but I made the mistake of playing on when he had left… that was my error… he must have won twenty thousand francs yesterday, he's winning every time now too, and I just keep following his lead. Now—'

He broke off in mid-sentence, for the hoarse-voiced croupier was calling his '*Faites votre jeu!*' and his glance was already moving away, looking greedily at the place where the white-whiskered Russian sat, nonchalant and grave, thoughtfully putting first one gold coin and then, hesitantly, another on the fourth space. Immediately the fevered hands before me dug into the pile of money and put down a handful of coins on the same place. And when, after a minute, the croupier cried '*Zéro!*' and his rake swept the whole table bare with a single movement, he stared at the money streaming away as if at some marvel. But do you think he turned to me? No he had forgotten all about me; I had dropped out of his life, I was lost and gone from it, his whole being was intent only on the Russian general who, with complete indifference, was hefting two more gold coins in his hand, not yet sure what number to put them on.

I cannot describe my bitterness and despair. But think of my feelings: to be no more than a fly brushed carelessly aside by a man to whom one has offered one's whole life. Once again that surge of fury came over me. I seized his arm with all my strength. He started.

'You will get up at once!' I whispered to him in a soft but commanding tone. 'Remember what you swore in church today, you miserable perjurer.'

He stared at me, perplexed and pale. His eyes suddenly took on the expression of a beaten dog, his lips quivered. All at once he seemed to be remembering the past, and a horror of himself appeared to come over him.

'Yes, yes… ' he stammered. 'Oh, my God, my God… yes, I'm coming, oh, forgive me… '

And his hand was already sweeping the money together, fast at first, gathering it all up with a vehement gesture, but then gradually slowing down, as if coming up against some opposing force. His eyes had fallen once more on the Russian general, who had just made his bet.

'Just a moment,' he said, quickly throwing five gold coins on the same square. 'Just this one more time... I promise you I'll come then—just this one more game... just... '

And again his voice fell silent. The ball had begun to roll and was carrying him away with it. Once again the addict had slipped away from me, from himself, flung round with the tiny ball circling in the smooth hollow of the wheel where it leapt and sprang. Once again the croupier called out the number, once again the rake carried his five coins away from him; he had lost. But he did not turn round. He had forgotten me, just like his oath in the church and the promise he had given me a minute ago. His greedy hand was moving spasmodically towards the dwindling pile of money again, and his intoxicated gaze moved only to the magnet of his will, the man opposite who brought good luck.

My patience was at an end. I shook him again, hard this time. 'Get up at once! Immediately! You said one more game... '

But then something unexpected happened. He suddenly swung round, but the face looking at me was no longer that of a humbled and confused man, it was the face of a man in a frenzy, all anger, with burning eyes and furiously trembling lips. 'Leave me alone!' he spat. 'Go away! You bring me bad luck. Whenever you're here I lose. You brought bad luck yesterday and you're bringing bad luck now. Go away!'

I momentarily froze, but now my own anger was whipped up beyond restraint by his folly.

'I am bringing you bad luck?' I snapped at him. 'You liar, you thief—you promised me... ' But I got no further, for the maniac leapt up from his seat and, indifferent to the turmoil around him, thrust me away. 'Leave me alone,' he cried, losing all control. 'I'm not under your control… here, take your money.' And he threw me a few hundred-franc notes. 'Now leave me alone!'

He had been shouting out loud like a madman, ignoring the hundred or so people around us. They were all staring, whispering, pointing, laughing—other curious onlookers even crowded in from the hall next door. I felt as if my clothes were being torn from my body, leaving me naked before all these prying eyes. '*Silence, madame, s'il vous plaît,*' said the croupier in commanding tones, tapping his rake on the table. He meant me, the wretched creature meant me. Humiliated, overcome by shame, I stood there before the hissing, whispering curious folk like a prostitute whose customer has just thrown money at her. Two hundred, three hundred shameless eyes were turned on my face, and then—then, as I turned my gaze evasively aside, overwhelmed by this filthy deluge of humiliation and shame, my own eyes met two others, piercing and astonished—it was my cousin looking at me appalled, her mouth open, one hand raised as if in horror.

That struck home; before she could stir or recover from her surprise I stormed out of the hall. I got as far as the bench outside, the same bench on which the gambling addict had collapsed yesterday. I dropped to the hard, pitiless wood, as powerless, exhausted and shattered as he had been.

All that is twenty-four years ago, yet when I remember the moment when I stood there before a thousand strangers, lashed by their scorn, the blood freezes in my veins. And once again I feel, in horror, how weak, poor and flabby a substance whatever we call by the names of soul, spirit or feeling must be after all, not to mention what we describe as pain, since all this, even to the utmost degree, is insufficient to destroy the suffering flesh of the tormented body entirely—for we do survive such hours and our blood continues to pulse, instead of dying and falling like a tree struck by lightning. Only for a sudden moment, for an instant, did this pain tear through my joints so hard that I dropped on the bench breathless and dazed, with a positively voluptuous premonition that I must die. But as I was saying, pain is cowardly, it gives way before the overpowering will to live which seems to cling more strongly to our flesh than all the mortal suffering of the spirit. Even to myself, I cannot explain my feelings after such a shattering blow, but I did rise to my feet, although I did not know what to do. Suddenly it occurred to me that my suitcases were already at the station, and I thought suddenly that I must get away, away from here, away from this accursed, this infernal building. Taking no notice of anyone, I made haste to the station and asked when the next train for Paris left. At ten o'clock, the porter told me, and I immediately retrieved my luggage. Ten o'clock—so exactly twenty-four hours had passed since that terrible meeting, twenty-four hours so full of changeable, contradictory feelings that my inner world was shattered for ever. At first, however, I felt nothing but that one word in the constantly hammering, pounding rhythm: away, away, away! The pulses behind my brow kept driving it into my temples like a wedge: away, away, away! Away from this town, away from myself, home to my own people, to my own old life! I travelled through the night to Paris, changed from one station to another and travelled direct to Boulogne, from Boulogne to Dover, from Dover to London, from London to my son's house—all in one headlong flight, without stopping to think or consider, forty-eight hours without sleep, without speaking to anyone, without eating, forty-eight hours during which the wheels of all the trains rattled out that one word: away, away, away! When at last I arrived unexpectedly at my son's country house, everyone was alarmed; there must have been something in my bearing and my eyes that gave me away. My son came to embrace and kiss me, but I shrank away: I could not bear the thought of his touching lips that I felt were disgraced. I avoided all questions, asked only for a bath, because I needed to wash not only the dirt of the journey from my body but all of the passion of that obsessed, unworthy man that seemed to cling to it. Then I dragged myself up to my room and slept a benumbed and stony sleep for twelve or fourteen hours, a sleep such as I have never slept before or since, and after it I know what it must be like to lie dead in a coffin. My family cared for me as for a sick woman, but their affection only hurt me, I was ashamed of their respect, and had to keep preventing myself from suddenly screaming out loud how I had betrayed, forgotten and abandoned them all for the sake of a foolish, crazy passion.

Then, aimless again, I went back to France and a little town where I knew no one, for I was pursued by the delusion that at the very first glance everyone could see my shame and my changed nature from the outside, I felt so betrayed, so soiled to the depths of my soul. Sometimes, when I woke in my bed in the morning, I felt a dreadful fear of opening my eyes. Once again I would be overcome by the memory of that night when I suddenly woke beside a half-naked stranger, and then, as I had before, all I wanted was to die immediately.

But after all, time is strong, and age has the curious power of devaluing all our feelings. You feel death coming closer, its shadow falls black across your path, and things seem less brightly coloured, they do not go to the heart so much, they lose much of their dangerous violence. Gradually I recovered from the shock, and when, many years later, I met a young Pole who was an attaché of the Austrian Embassy at a party, and in answer to my enquiry about that family he told me that one of his cousin's sons had shot himself ten years before in Monte Carlo, I did not even tremble. It hardly hurt any more; perhaps—why deny one's egotism?—I was even glad of it, for now my last fear of ever meeting him again was gone. I had no witness against me left but my own memory. Since then I have become calmer. Growing old, after all, means that one no longer fears the past.

And now you will understand why I suddenly brought myself to tell you about my own experience. When you defended Madame Henriette and said, so passionately, that twenty-four hours could determine a woman's whole life, I felt that you meant me; I was grateful to you, since for the first time I felt myself, as it were, confirmed in my existence. And then I thought it would be good to unburden myself of it all for once, and perhaps then the spell on me would be broken, the eternal looking back; perhaps I can go to Monte Carlo tomorrow and enter the same hall where I met my fate without feeling hatred for him or myself. Then the stone will roll off my soul, laying its full weight over the past and preventing it from ever rising again. It has done me good to tell you all this. I feel easier in my mind now and almost light at heart... thank you for that."

With these words she had suddenly risen, and I felt that she had reached the end. Rather awkwardly, I sought for something to say. But she must have felt my emotion, and quickly waved it away.

"No, please, don't speak... I'd rather you didn't reply or say anything to me. Accept my thanks for listening, and I wish you a good journey."

She stood opposite me, holding out her hand in farewell. Instinctively I looked at her face, and the countenance of this old woman who stood before me with a kindly yet slightly ashamed expression seemed to me wonderfully touching. Whether it was the reflection of past passion or mere confusion that suddenly dyed her cheeks with red, the colour rising to her white hair, she stood there just like a girl, in a bridal confusion of memories and ashamed of her own confession. Involuntarily moved, I very much wanted to say something to express my respect for her, but my throat was too constricted. So I leant down and respectfully kissed the faded hand that trembled slightly like an autumn leaf.

INCIDENT
ON LAKE GENEVA

O N THE BANKS OF LAKE GENEVA, close to the small Swiss resort of Villeneuve, a fisherman who had rowed his boat out into the lake one summer night in the year 1918 noticed a strange object in the middle of the water. When he came closer, he saw that it was a raft made of loosely assembled wooden planks which a naked man was clumsily trying to propel forward, using a piece of board as an oar. In astonishment, the fisherman steered his boat that way, helped the exhausted man into it, used some fishing nets as a makeshift covering for his nakedness, and then tried questioning the shivering figure huddling nervously into the corner of the boat. But he replied in a strange language, not a word of which was anything like the fisherman's, so the rescuer soon gave up any further attempts, pulled in his nets, and rowed back to the bank, plying his oars faster than before.

As the early light of dawn showed the outline of the bank, the naked man's face too began to clear. A childlike smile appeared through the tangled beard around his broad mouth, he raised one hand, pointing, and kept stammering out a single word over and over again: a question that was half a statement. It sounded like "*Rossiya*", and he repeated it more and more happily the closer the keel came to the bank of the lake. At last the boat crunched on the beach; the fisherman's womenfolk, who were waiting for him to land his dripping catch, scattered screeching, like Nausicaa's maids in the days of old, when they caught sight of the naked man covered by fishing nets, and only gradually, on hearing the strange news, did several men from the village appear. They were soon joined by that local worthy the courthouse usher, eagerly

officious and very much on his dignity. He knew at once, from
various instructions that he had received and a wealth of wartime
experience, that this must be a deserter who had swum over the lake
from the French bank, and he was preparing to interrogate him
officially, but any such elaborate process was quickly deprived of
any dignity or usefulness by the fact that the naked man (to whom
some of the locals had now thrown a jacket and a pair of cotton
drill trousers) responded to all questions with his questioning cry
of *"Rossiya? Rossiya?"* sounding ever more anxious and doubtful.
Slightly irked by his failure, the usher ordered the stranger to follow
him by means of gestures that could not be misunderstood, and
the wet, barefoot figure, his jacket and trousers flapping around
him, was escorted to the courthouse, surrounded by the vociferous
youths of the village who had now come along, and was taken
into custody there. He did not protest, he said not a word, but his
bright eyes had darkened with disappointment, and his shoulders
were hunched as if expecting blows.

By now news of this human catch had reached the nearby hotel,
and several ladies and gentlemen, glad of this intriguing episode
to relieve the monotonous course of the day's events, came over
to look at the wild man. One lady gave him some confectionery,
which he eyed as suspiciously as a monkey might, and did not touch.
A gentleman took a photograph. They all chattered and talked
vivaciously as they swarmed around him, until at last the manager
of the large hotel, who had lived abroad for a long time and knew
several languages, spoke to the terrified man first in German, then
in Italian and English, and finally in Russian. No sooner did he
hear the first sound of his native tongue than the frightened man
started violently, a broad smile split his good-natured face from
ear to ear, and suddenly he was telling his whole story frankly and
with self-assurance. It was very long and very confused, and the
chance-come interpreter could not always understand every detail,
but in essentials the man's history was as follows:

He had been fighting in Russia, and then one day he and a thousand others were packed into railway trucks and taken a very long way, they were transferred to ships and had travelled in those for even longer, through regions where it was so hot that, as he put it, the bones were baked soft inside your body. Finally they were landed again somewhere or other, packed into more railway trucks, and then they were suddenly told to storm a hill, but he knew no more about that, because a bullet had hit him in the leg as soon as the attack began. The audience, for whom the interpreter translated his questions and the man's answers, immediately realised that this fugitive was a member of one of those Russian divisions fighting in France who had been sent half-way round the world, from Siberia and Vladivostok to the French front, and as well as feeling a certain pity they were all moved at the same time by curiosity: what could have induced him to make this strange attempt at flight? With a smile that was half-good-natured, half-crafty, the Russian readily explained that as soon as he was better he had asked the orderlies where Russia was, and they had pointed to show him the way. He had roughly remembered the direction by noting the position of the sun and the stars, and so he had escaped in secret, walking by night and hiding in haystacks from patrols by day. He had eaten fruit and begged for bread for ten days, until at last he reached this lake. Now his account became less clear. Apparently he himself came from Lake Baikal, and seeing the undulating curves of the opposite bank ahead of him in the evening light, he had thought that Russia must lie over there. At any rate, he had stolen a couple of planks from a hut, and lying face downwards over them, had used a piece of old board as a paddle to make his way far out into the lake, where the fisherman found him. As soon as the hotel manager had translated the anxious question which concluded his confused explanation—could he get home tomorrow?—its naivety at first aroused loud laughter, but that soon turned to pity, and everyone

STEFAN ZWEIG

found a few coins or banknotes to give the poor man, who was now looking around him with miserable uncertainty.

By this time a telephone call to Montreux had brought the arrival of a senior police officer to take down an account of the case, rather an arduous task. For not only was the amateur interpreter's command of Russian inadequate, it was soon obvious that the man was uneducated to a degree scarcely comprehensible to Westerners. All he knew about himself was his own first name of Boris, and he was able to give only the most confused accounts of his native village, for instance that the people there were serfs of Prince Metchersky (he used the word serfs although serfdom had been abolished long ago), and that he lived fifty versts from the great lake with his wife and three children. Now a discussion of what was to be done with him began, while he stood amidst the disputants dull-eyed and hunching his shoulders. Some thought he ought to be handed over to the Russian embassy in Berne, others feared that such a measure would get him sent back to France; the police officer explained all the difficulty of deciding whether he should be treated as a deserter or a foreigner without papers; the local courthouse usher rejected out of hand any suggestion that the stranger should be fed and accommodated in Villeneuve itself. A Frenchman protested that there was no need to make such a fuss about a miserable runaway; he had better either work or be sent back. Two women objected strongly to this remark, saying that his misfortune wasn't his own fault, and it was a crime to send people away from their homes to a foreign country. It began to look as if this chance incident would lead to political strife when suddenly an old Danish gentleman intervened, saying in firm tones that he would pay for the man's board and lodging for a week, and meanwhile the authorities could come to some agreement with the embassy. This unexpected solution satisfied both the officials and the private parties.

During the increasingly agitated discussion the fugitive's timid gaze had gradually lifted, and his eyes were now fixed on the lips of

244

the hotel manager, the only person in all this turmoil who, he knew, could tell him his fate in terms that he was able to understand. He seemed to be vaguely aware of the turmoil caused by his presence, and as the noisy argument died down he spontaneously raised both hands in the silence, and reached them out to the manager with the pleading look of women at prayer before a holy picture. This moving gesture had an irresistible effect on all present. The manager went up to the man and reassured him warmly, saying that he had nothing to fear, he could stay here and come to no harm, he would have accommodation for the immediate future. The Russian tried to kiss his hand, but the other man withdrew it and quickly stepped back. Then he pointed out the house next door, a small village inn where the Russian would have bed and board, said a few more words of reassurance to him, and then, with another friendly wave, went up the beach to his hotel.

The motionless fugitive stared after him, and as the only person who understood his language dwindled in the distance, his face, which had brightened, grew gloomy again. His avid glances followed the figure of the manager as he went away, going up to the hotel above the bank of the lake, and he took no notice of the others present who were smiling at his strange demeanour. When a sympathetic bystander touched him and pointed to the inn, his heavy shoulders seemed to slump, and he went to the doorway with his head bowed. The bar was opened for him. He sat down at the table, where the barmaid brought him a glass of brandy by way of welcome, and stayed there without moving all afternoon, his eyes clouded. The village children kept looking in at the windows, laughing and shouting something at him—he never raised his head. Customers coming in looked at him curiously, but he sat where he was, back bowed, eyes staring at the table, shy and bashful. And when a crowd of guests came in to eat at midday and filled the room with their laughter, while hundreds of words he did not understand swirled around him and he himself, horribly aware of being a foreigner here, sat deaf and mute amidst the general liveliness, his hands trembled so badly that he could hardly raise the spoon from his soup. Suddenly a large tear ran down his cheek and dropped heavily on the table. He looked timidly around him. The others present had noticed the tear, and suddenly fell silent. And he felt ashamed; his large, shaggy head sank closer and closer to the black wood of the table.

He sat like that until evening. People came and went; he did not notice them, and they had stopped noticing him. He sat in the shadow of the stove like a shadow himself, his hands resting heavily on the table. He was forgotten, and no one saw him suddenly rise when twilight came and go up the path to the hotel, plodding lethargically like an animal. He stood for an hour at the door there, cap humbly in his hand, and then for another hour, not looking at anyone. At last this strange figure, standing still and black as a tree stump outside the sparkling lights of the hotel entrance as if he had put down roots there, attracted the attention of one of the pageboys, who fetched the manager. Once again his dark face lightened a little when he heard his own language.

"What do you want, Boris?" asked the manager kindly.

"Forgive me," stammered the fugitive, "I only wanted… I wanted to know if I can go home."

"Of course, Boris, to be sure you can go home," smiled the manager.

"Tomorrow?"

Now the other man looked grave too. The words had been spoken in so pleading a tone that the smile vanished from his face.

"No, Boris… not just yet. Not until the war is over."

"When is that? When will the war be over?"

"God only knows. We humans don't."

"But before that? Can't I go before that?"

"No, Boris."

"Is it so far to go?"

"Yes."

"Many more days' journey?"

"Many more days."

"I'll go all the same, sir. I'm strong. I don't tire easily."

"But you can't, Boris. There's a border between here and your home."

"A border?" He looked blank. The word was new to him. Then he said again, with his extraordinary obstinacy, "I'll swim over it."

The manager almost smiled. But he was painfully moved, and explained gently, "No, Boris, that's impossible. A border means there's a foreign country on the other side. People won't let you through."

"But I won't hurt them! I threw my rifle away. Why wouldn't they let me go back to my wife, if I ask them in Christ's name?"

The manager was feeling increasingly heavy at heart. Bitterness rose in him. "No," he said, "they won't let you through, Boris. People don't take any notice of the word of Christ any more."

"But what am I to do, sir? I can't stay here! The people that live here don't understand me, and I don't understand them."

"You'll soon learn, Boris."

"No, sir." The Russian bowed his head. "I can't learn things. I can only work in the fields, that's all I know how to do. What would I do here? I want to go home! Show me the way!"

"There isn't any way at the moment, Boris."

"But sir, they can't forbid me to go home to my wife and my children! I'm not a soldier any more."

"Oh yes, they can, Boris."

"What about the Tsar?" He asked the question very suddenly, trembling with expectation and awe.

"There's no Tsar any more, Boris. He's been deposed."

"No Tsar any more?" He stared dully at the other man, the last glimmer of light went out in his eyes, and then he said very wearily, "So I can't go home?"

"Not yet. You'll have to wait, Boris."

The face in the dark grew ever gloomier. "I've waited so long already! I can't wait any more. Show me the way to go! I want to try!"

"There's no way, Boris. They'd arrest you at the border. Stay here and we'll find you work."

"People here don't understand me, and I don't understand them," he obstinately repeated. "I can't live here! Help me, sir!"

"I can't, Boris."

"Help me, sir, for the sake of Christ! Help me, I can't bear it any more!"

"I can't, Boris. There's no way anyone can help anyone else these days."

They faced each other in silence. Boris was twisting his cap in his hands. "Then why did they take me away from home? They said I had to fight for Russia and the Tsar. But Russia is far away from here, and the Tsar... what do you say they did to the Tsar?"

"They deposed him."

"Deposed." He repeated the word without understanding it. "What am I to do, sir? I have to go home! My children are crying for me. I can't live here. Help me, sir, help me!"

"I just can't, Boris."

"Can no one help me?"

"Not at the moment."

The Russian bent his head even further, and then said abruptly, in hollow tones, "Thank you, sir," and turned away.

He went down the path very slowly. The hotel manager watched him for a long time, and was surprised when he did not go to the inn, but on down the steps to the lake. He sighed deeply and went back to his work in the hotel.

As chance would have it, it was the same fisherman who found the drowned man's naked body next morning. He had carefully placed the trousers, cap and jacket that he had been given on the bank, and went into the water just as he had come out of it. A statement was taken about the incident, and since no one knew the stranger's full name, a cheap wooden cross was put on the place where he was buried, one of those little crosses planted over the graves of unknown soldiers that now cover the continent of Europe from end to end.

MENDEL
THE BIBLIOPHILE

B ACK IN VIENNA AGAIN, on my way home from a visit to
the outer districts of the city, I was unexpectedly caught in a
heavy shower of rain that sent people running from its wet whiplash
to take refuge in such shelter as the entrances of buildings, and I
myself quickly looked round for a place where I could keep dry.
Luckily Vienna has a coffee house on every street corner, so with
my hat dripping and my shoulders drenched, I hurried into one
that stood directly opposite. Inside, it proved to be a suburban café
of the traditional kind, almost a stereotype of a Viennese café,
with none of the newfangled features that imitate the inner-city
music halls of Germany. It was in the old Viennese bourgeois
style, full of ordinary people partaking more lavishly of the free
newspapers than the pastries on sale. At this evening hour the air
in the café, which would always be stuffy anyway, was thick with
ornate blue smoke rings, yet the place looked clean, with velour
sofas that were obviously new and a shiny aluminium till. In my
haste I hadn't even taken the trouble to read its name outside, and
indeed, what would have been the point? Now I was sitting in the
warm, looking impatiently through window panes veiled by blue
smoke, and wondering when it would suit the vexatious shower
to move a few kilometres further on.

So there I sat, with nothing to do, and began to fall under the
spell of the passive lethargy that invisibly emanates, with narcotic
effect, from every true Viennese coffee house. In that empty, idle
mood I looked individually at the customers, to whom the artificial
light of the smoke-filled room lent an unhealthy touch of grey
shadow round the eyes, and studied the young woman at the till
mechanically setting out sugar and a spoon for every cup of coffee

served by the waiter; drowsily and without really noticing them I read the posters on the walls, to which I was wholly indifferent, and found myself almost enjoying this kind of apathy. But suddenly, and in a curious way, I was brought out of my drowsy state as a vague impulse began to stir within me. It was like the beginning of a slight toothache, when you don't know yet if it is on the right or the left, if it is starting in the upper or the lower jaw; there was just a certain tension, a mental uneasiness. For all at once—I couldn't have said how—I was aware that I must have been here once before, years ago, and that a memory of some kind was connected with these walls, these chairs, these tables, this smoky room, apparently strange to me.

But the more I tried to pin down that memory, the more refractory and slippery it was as it eluded me—like a luminous jellyfish unconsciously glowing on the lowest level of my mind, yet not to be seized and scrutinized at close quarters. In vain I stared at every item of furnishing; certainly much of it was new to me, for instance the till with the clinking of its automatic calculations, and the brown wallpaper imitating Brazilian rosewood. All that must have been imported later. Nonetheless, I knew I had been here once before, twenty years or more ago, and something of my own old self, long since overgrown, lingered here invisibly, like a nail hidden in wood. I reached out into the room, straining all my senses, and at the same time I searched myself—yet damn it all, I couldn't place that lost memory, drowned in the recesses of my mind.

I was annoyed with myself, as you always are when a failure of some kind makes you aware of the inadequacy and imperfection of your intellectual powers. But I did not give up hope of retrieving the memory after all. I knew I just had to lay hands on some tiny hook, for my memory is an odd one, good and bad at the same time: on the one hand defiant and stubborn, on the other incredibly faithful. It often swallows up what is most important, both incidents and faces, what I read and what I experience, engulfing it entirely in darkness, and will not give anything back from that underworld merely at the call of my will, only under duress. However, I need just some small thing to jog my memory, a picture postcard, a few lines of handwriting on an envelope, a sheet of newsprint faded by smoke, and at once what is forgotten will rise again like a fish on the line from the darkly streaming surface, as large as life. Then I remember every detail about someone, his mouth and the gap between the teeth in it on the left that shows when he laughs, the brittle sound of that laughter, how it makes his moustache twitch, and how another and new face emerges from that laughter—I see all that at once in detail, and I remember over the years every word the man ever said to me. But to see and feel the past so graphically I need some stimulus provided by my senses, a tiny aid from the world of reality. So I closed my eyes to allow me to think harder, to visualize and seize that mysterious hook at the end of the fishing line. Nothing, however, still nothing! All lost and forgotten. And I felt so embittered by the stubborn apparatus of memory between my temples that I could have struck myself on the forehead with my fists, as you might shake a malfunctioning automatic device that is unjustly refusing to do as you ask. No, I couldn't sit calmly here any longer, I was so upset by the failure of my memory, and in my annoyance I stood up to get some air.

But here was a strange thing: I had hardly taken a couple of steps across the room before the first phosphorescent glimmers of light began to dawn in my mind, swirling and sparkling. To the right of the cash desk, I remembered, there would be a way into a windowless room illuminated only by artificial light. And sure enough, I was right. There it was, not with the wallpaper I had known before, but the proportions of that rectangular back room, its contours still indistinct in my memory, were exactly the same. This was the card room. I instinctively looked for individual details, my nerves already joyfully vibrating (soon, I felt, I would remember it all). Two billiard tables stood idle, like silent ponds of green mud; in the corners of the room there were card tables, with two men who looked like civil servants or professors playing chess at one of them. And in the corner, close to the iron stove, where you went to use the telephone, stood a small, square table. Suddenly the realization flashed right through my entire mind. I knew at once, instantly, with a single, warm impulse jogging my memory: my God, that was where Mendel used to sit, Jakob Mendel, Mendel the bibliophile, and after twenty years here I was again in the Café Gluck at the upper end of Alserstrasse, to which he habitually resorted. Jakob Mendel—how could I have forgotten him for such an incredibly long time? That strangest of characters, a legendary man, that esoteric wonder of the world, famous at the university and in a small, eminent circle—how could I have lost my memory of him, the magician who traded in books and sat here from morning to evening every day, a symbol of the knowledge, fame and honour of the Café Gluck?

I had only to turn my vision inwards for that one second, and already his unmistakable figure, in three dimensions, was conjured up by my creatively enlightened blood. I saw him at once as he had been, always sitting at that rectangular table, its dingy grey marble top heaped high at all times with books and other writings. I saw the way he persistently sat there, imperturbable, his eyes behind his glasses hypnotically fixed on a book, humming and muttering as he read, rocking his body and his inadequately polished, freckled bald patch back and forth, a habit acquired in the *cheder*, his Jewish primary school in eastern Europe. He pored over his catalogues and books here, at that table, never sitting anywhere else, singing and swaying quietly, a dark, rocking cradle. For just as a child falls into sleep and is lost to the world by that rhythmically hypnotic rocking movement, in the opinion of pious Jews the spirit passes more easily into the grace of contemplation if one's own idle body rocks and sways at the same time. And indeed, Jakob Mendel saw and heard none of what went on around him. Beside him, the billiards players talked in loud voices, making a great deal of noise; the markers scurried about, the telephone rang, people came to scour the floor and heat the stove—he noticed none of it. Once a hot coal had fallen out of the stove, and was already burning and smoking on the wooden floor two paces away from him; only then did the infernal smell alert another of the guests in the café to the danger, and he made haste to extinguish the smoke. Jakob Mendel himself, however, only a couple of inches away and already affected by the fumes, had noticed nothing. For he read as other people pray, as gamblers gamble, as drunks stare into space, their senses numbed; he read with such touching absorption that the reading of all other persons had always seemed to me profane by comparison. As a young man, I had seen the great mystery of total concentration for the first time in this little Galician book dealer, Jakob Mendel, a kind of concentration in which the artist resembles the scholar, the truly wise resembles the totally deranged. It is the tragic happiness and unhappiness of total obsession.

An older colleague of mine from the university had taken me to see him. At the time I was engaged on research into Mesmer, the Paracelsian doctor and practitioner of magnetism, still too little known today, but I was not having much luck. The standard works on Mesmer proved to be unobtainable, and the librarian to whom I, as a guileless newcomer to the place, applied for information, replied in a surly tone that literary references were my business, not his. That was the occasion when my colleague first mentioned the man's name to me. "I'll go and see Mendel with you," he promised. "He knows everything, he can get hold of anything. He'll find you the most obscure book from the most forgotten of German second-hand bookshops. The ablest man in Vienna, and an original into the bargain, a bibliophilic dinosaur, the last survivor of a dying race from the prehistoric world."

So the two of us went to the Café Gluck, and lo and behold there sat Mendel the bibliophile, bespectacled, sporting a beard that needed trimming, clad in black, and rocking back and forth as he read like a dark bush blown in the wind. We went up to him, and he didn't even notice. He just sat there reading, his torso swaying over the table like a mandarin, and hanging on a hook behind him was his decrepit black overcoat, its pockets stuffed with notes and journals. My friend coughed loudly by way of announcing us. But Mendel, his thick glasses close to his book, still didn't notice us. Finally my friend knocked on the tabletop as loudly and energetically as you might knock at a door—and at last Mendel looked up, automatically pushed his clumsy steel-rimmed glasses up on his forehead, and from under his bushy, ashen grey brows two remarkable eyes gazed keenly at us. They were small, black, watchful eyes, as nimble and sharp as the darting tongue of a snake. My friend introduced me, and I explained my business, first—a trick expressly recommended by my friend—complaining with pretended anger of the librarian who, I said, wouldn't give me any information. Mendel leant back and spat carefully. Then he just laughed, and said with a strong eastern European accent, "Wouldn't, eh? Not him—couldn't is more like it! He's an igno-ramus, a poor old grey-haired ass. I've known him, heaven help me, these twenty years, and in all that time he still hasn't learnt anything. He can pocket his salary, yes, that's all he and his like can do! Those learned doctors—they'd do better to carry bricks than sit over their books."

This forceful venting of his grievances broke the ice, and with a good-natured wave of his hand he invited me, for the first time, to sit at the square marble-topped table covered with notes, that altar of bibliophilic revelations as yet unknown to me. I quickly explained what I wanted: works contemporary with Mesmer himself on magnetism, as well as all later books and polemics for and against his theories. As soon as I had finished, Mendel closed his left eye for a second, just like a marksman before he fires his gun. It was truly for no more than a second that this moment of concentrated attention lasted, and then, as if reading from an invisible catalogue, he fluently enumerated two or three dozen books, each with its place and date of publication and an estimate of its price. I was astonished. Although prepared for it in advance, this was more than I had expected. But my bafflement seemed to please him, for on the keyboard of his memory he immediately played the most wonderful variations on my theme that any librarian could imagine. Did I also want to know about the somnambulists and the first experiments with hypnosis? And about Gassner's exorcisms, and Christian Science, and Madame Blavatsky? Once again names came tumbling out of him, titles and descriptions; only now did I realize what a unique marvel of memory I had found in Jakob Mendel, in truth an encyclopaedia, a universal catalogue on two legs. Absolutely dazed, I stared at this bibliographical phenomenon, washed up here in the shape of an unprepossessing, even slightly grubby little Galician second-hand book dealer who, after reciting some eighty names to me full pelt, apparently without taking much thought, but inwardly pleased to have played his trump card, polished his glasses on what might once have been a white handkerchief. To hide my astonishment a little, I hesitantly asked which of those books he could, if need be, get hold of for me.

"Well, we'll see what can be done," he growled. "You come back here tomorrow, by then old Mendel will have found you a little something, and what can't be found here will turn up elsewhere. A man who knows his way around will have luck."

I thanked him courteously, and in all this civility I stumbled into a great act of folly by suggesting that I could write down the titles of books I wanted on a piece of paper. At the same moment I felt a warning nudge in the ribs from my friend's elbow. But too late! Mendel had already cast me a glance—what a glance!—that was both triumphant and injured, a scornful and superior, a positively regal glance, the Shakespearian glance of Macbeth when Macduff

suggests to that invincible hero that he yield without a fight. Then
he laughed again, briefly, the big Adam's apple in his throat rolling
back and forth in an odd way. Apparently he had bitten back a sharp
rejoinder with some difficulty. And good Mendel the bibliophile
would have been right to make every imaginable sharp remark, for
only a stranger, an ignoramus (*amhorez* is the Yiddish word he used
for it) could offer such an insult as to write down the title of a book
for him, Jakob Mendel, as if he were a bookseller's apprentice or a
servant in a library, as if that incomparable, diamantine bibliophilic
brain would ever have needed such a crude aid to his memory. Only
later did I realize how much my civil offer must have injured the
feelings of such an esoteric genius, for this small, squat Galician
Jew, entirely enveloped in his own beard and hunchbacked into the
bargain, was a Titan of memory. Behind that chalky, grubby brow,
which looked as if it were overgrown by grey moss, there stood in
an invisible company, as if stamped in steel, every name and title
that had ever been printed on the title page of a book. Whether
a work had first been published yesterday or two hundred years
ago, he knew at once its exact place of publication, its publisher
and the price, both new and second-hand, and at the same time
he unfailingly recollected the binding, illustrations and facsimile
editions of every book. He saw every work, whether he had held
it in his own hands or had only seen it once from a distance, in
a window display or a library, with the same optical precision as
the creative artist sees the still-invisible forms of his inner world
and those of other people. If, say, a book was offered for six marks
in the catalogue of a second-hand bookseller in Regensburg, he
immediately remembered that another copy of the same book
could have been bought for four crowns in an auction in Vienna
two years ago, and he also knew who had bought it; indeed, Jakob
Mendel never forgot a title or a number, he knew every plant, every
micro-organism, every star in the eternally oscillating, constantly
changing cosmos of the universe of books. He knew more in every

field than the experts in that field, he was more knowledgeable about libraries than the librarians themselves, he knew the stocks of most firms by heart better than their owners, for all their lists and their card indexes, although he had nothing at his command but the magic of memory, nothing but his incomparable faculty of recollection, which could only be truly explained and analysed by citing a hundred separate examples. It was clear that his memory could have been trained and formed to show such demonic infallibility only by the eternal mystery of all perfection: by concentration. This remarkable man knew nothing about the world outside books, for to his mind all the phenomena of existence began to seem truly real to him only when they were cast as letters and assembled as print in a book, a process that, so to speak, had sterilized them. But he read even the books themselves not for their meaning, for their intellectual and narrative content: his sole passion was for their names, prices, forms of publication and original title pages. Unproductive and uncreative in that last point, nothing but a list of hundreds of thousands of titles and names, stamped on the soft cortex of a mammalian brain as if written in a catalogue of books, Jakob Mendel's specifically bibliophilic memory was still, in its unique perfection, no less a phenomenon than Napoleon's memory for faces, Mezzofanti's for languages, the memory of a chess champion like Lasker for opening gambits or of a composer like Busoni for music. In a public place in the context of a seminar, that brain would have instructed and amazed thousands, hundreds of thousands of students and scholars, with results fertile for the sciences, an incomparable gain for those public treasuries that we call libraries. But that higher world was for ever closed to this small, uneducated Galician dealer in books, who had mastered little more than what he was taught in his studies of the Talmud, and consequently his fantastic abilities could take effect only as the secret knowledge shown when he sat at that marble-topped table in the Café Gluck. But some day, when there is a great psychologist

who, with patience and persistence equal to Buffon's in arranging
and classifying the entire animal kingdom, can do the same for
all varieties, species and original forms of the magical power that
we call memory, describing them separately and presenting their
variants (a work as yet absent from our intellectual world)—then
he would be bound to think of Jakob Mendel, that genius of prices
and titles, that nameless master of the science of antiquarian books.

By trade, to be sure, Jakob Mendel was known to the ignorant
only as a little dealer in second-hand books. Every Sunday the same
standard advertisement appeared in the *Neue Freie Presse* and the
Neues Wiener Tagblatt: "Old books bought, best prices paid, apply to
Mendel, Obere Alserstrasse", and then a telephone number which
in fact was the number of the Café Gluck. He would search through
stockrooms, and every week, with an old servant bearded like the
Emperor Joseph, brought back new booty to his headquarters and
conveyed it on from there, since he had no licence for a proper
bookshop. So he remained a dealer in a small way, not a very
lucrative occupation. Students sold him their textbooks, and his
hands passed them on from one academic year to the next, while
in addition he sought out and acquired any particular work that
was wanted, asking a small extra charge. He was free with good
advice. But money had no place within his world, for he had never
been seen in anything but the same shabby coat, consuming milk
and two rolls in the morning, the afternoon and the evening, and
at mid-day eating some small dish that they fetched him from the
restaurant. He didn't smoke, he didn't gamble, you might even
say he didn't live, but the two lively eyes behind his glasses were
constantly feeding words, titles and names to this strange being's
brain. And the soft, fertile substance of that brain absorbed this
wealth of words greedily, like a meadow soaking up thousands
upon thousands of raindrops. Human beings did not interest
him, and of all the human passions perhaps he knew only one,
although that, for sure, is the most human of them all: vanity. If

someone came to him for information, after laboriously searching for it elsewhere to no avail, and he could provide it at once, that alone made him feel satisfaction, pleasure; and so too perhaps did the fact that a few dozen people who respected and needed his knowledge lived in and outside Vienna. Every one of those massive conglomerations of millions of people, a place that we would call a metropolis, is sprinkled here and there with several small facets reflecting one and the same universe in miniature, invisible to most and valuable only to the expert, who is related to another expert by virtue of the same passion. And these bibliophiles all knew Jakob Mendel. Just as if you wanted advice on sheet music you turned to Eusebius Mandyczewski at the Viennese Music Association, a friendly presence sitting there in his grey cap among his files and his scores, and he would solve the most difficult problem with a smile as he first looked up at you; just as today everyone wanting to know about the Altwiener Theater and its culture would still turn infallibly to Karl Glossy, who knows all about the subject—so a few devout Viennese bibliophiles, when they had a tough nut to crack, made their pilgrimage to the Café Gluck and Jakob Mendel.

Watching Mendel during one of these conversations gave me, as a young man full of curiosity, a particular kind of pleasure. If you put an inferior book in front of him he would close it scornfully, muttering only, "Two crowns"; but faced with some rarity, or a unique specimen, he would lean respectfully back, place a sheet of paper under it, and you could see that he was suddenly ashamed of his grubby, inky fingers with their black-rimmed nails. Then he would begin leafing tenderly, cautiously and with immense reverence through the rare volume, page by page. No one could disturb him at a moment like that, as little as you can disturb a devout believer at prayer; and indeed that looking, touching, smelling and assessing, each of those single acts, had about it something of the succession of rituals in a religious ceremony. His hunched back shifted to and fro, meanwhile he muttered and growled, scratched his head, uttered curious vowel sounds, a long-drawn-out, almost awe-stricken, "Ah" or "Oh" of captivated admiration, or then again a swift and alarmed, "Oy!" or "Oy vey!" if a page turned out to be missing, or had been nibbled by a woodworm. Finally he would weigh up the thick tome respectfully in his hands, sniff at the large rectangle and absorb its smell with half-closed eyes, as delighted as a sentimental girl enjoying the scent of tuberose. During this rather elaborate procedure, the owner of the book of course had to possess his soul in patience. Having ended his examination, however, Mendel was very happy, indeed positively delighted to give any information, which infallibly came with wide-ranging anecdotes and dramatic accounts of the prices of similar copies. At these moments he seemed to become brighter, younger, livelier, and only one thing could embitter him beyond all measure: that was if a novice tried to offer him money for his opinion. Then he would draw back with an air of injury, for all the world like the distinguished curator of a gallery when an American tourist passing through the city tries to press a tip into his hand.

Holding a precious book meant to Mendel what an assignment with a woman might to another man. These moments were his platonic nights of love. Books had power over him; money never did. Great collectors, including the founder of a collection in Princeton University Library, tried in vain to recruit him as an adviser and buyer for their libraries—Jakob Mendel declined; no one could imagine him anywhere but in the Café Gluck. Thirty-three years ago, when his beard was still soft and black and he had ringlets over his forehead, he had come from the east to Vienna, a crook-backed lad, to study for the rabbinate, but he had soon abandoned Jehovah the harsh One God to give himself up to idolatry in the form of the brilliant, thousand-fold polytheism of books. That was when he had first found his way to the Café Gluck, and gradually it became his workplace, his headquarters, his post office, his world.

Like an astronomer alone in his observatory, studying myriads of stars every night through the tiny round lens of the telescope, observing their mysterious courses, their wandering multitude as they are extinguished and then appear again, so Jakob Mendel looked through his glasses out from that rectangular table into the other universe of books, also eternally circling and being reborn in that world above our own.

Of course he was highly esteemed in the Café Gluck, the fame of which was linked, so far as we were concerned, with Mendel at his invisible teacher's lectern rather than with the nominal patronage of that great magician Christoph Willibald Gluck, the composer of *Alceste* and *Iphigénie*. Mendel was as much a part of the fixtures and fittings as the old cherrywood cash desk, the two badly mended cues and the copper coffee pot, and his table was protected like a shrine—for his many customers and seekers after information were always urged by the staff, in a friendly manner, to place an order of some kind, thus ensuring that most of the profits of his knowledge disappeared into the broad leather bag worn at his hip by Deubler the head waiter. In return, Mendel the bibliophile enjoyed many privileges. He was free to use the telephone, his letters were fetched and anything he ordered from the restaurant brought in, the good old lady who looked after the toilets brushed his coat and sewed on buttons, and every week she took a little bundle of washing to the laundry for him. Lunch could be brought over from the nearby restaurant for him alone, and every day Herr Standhartner, the owner of the café, came to his table in person and said good morning (although usually Jakob Mendel, deep in his books, failed to notice the greeting). He arrived promptly at seven-thirty in the morning, and he left the café only when the lights were switched off. He never spoke to the other customers, and when Herr Standhartner once asked him courteously if he didn't find reading better by electric light than in the pallid, fitful illumination from the old Auer gas lamps, he gazed in surprise at the electric light bulbs; in spite of the noise and hammering of an installation lasting several days, this change had entirely passed him by. Only through the twin circles of his glasses, only through those two sparkling lenses that sucked everything in, did the billions of tiny organisms formed by the letters filter into his brain; everything else streamed over him as meaningless noise. In fact he had spent over thirty years, the entire waking part of his life, here at his rectangular table reading, comparing and calculating, in a continual daydream interrupted only by sleep.

So I was overcome by a kind of horror when I saw that the marble-topped table where Jakob Mendel made his oracular utterances now stood in this room as empty as a gravestone. Only now that I was older did I understand how much dies with such a man, first because anything unique is more and more valuable in a world now becoming hopelessly uniform. And then because, out of a deep sense of premonition, the young, inexperienced man I once was had been very fond of Jakob Mendel. In him, I had come close for the first time to the great mystery of the way what is special and overwhelming in our existence is achieved only by an inner concentration of powers, a sublime monomania akin to madness. And I had seen that a pure life of the mind, total abstraction in a single idea, can still be found even today, an immersion no less than that of an Indian yogi or a medieval monk in his cell, and indeed can be found in a café illuminated by electric light and next to a telephone—as a young man, I had sensed it far more in that entirely anonymous little book dealer than in any of our contemporary writers. Yet I had been able to forget him—admittedly in the war years, and in an absorption in my own work not unlike his. Now, however, looking at that empty table, I felt a kind of shame, and at the same time a renewed curiosity.

For where had he gone, what had happened to him? I called the waiter over and asked. No, he was sorry, he didn't know a Herr Mendel, no gentleman of that name frequented the café. But perhaps the head waiter would know. The head waiter ponderously steered his pot belly towards me, hesitated, thought it over. No, he didn't know any Herr Mendel either. But maybe I meant Mandl, Herr Mandl from the haberdashery shop in Florianigasse? A bitter taste rose to my mouth, the taste of transience: what do we live for, if the wind carries away the last trace of us from beneath our feet? For thirty years, perhaps forty, a man had breathed, read, thought and talked in this room of a few square metres, and only three or four years had to pass before there arose up a new king over Egypt, which knew not Joseph. No one in the Café Gluck knew anything now about Jakob Mendel, Mendel the bibliophile! Almost angrily I asked the head waiter if I could speak to Herr Standhartner, or was there anyone else from the old staff left in the house? Oh, Herr Standhartner, oh, dear God, he had sold the café long ago, he had died, and the old head waiter was living on his little property in the town of Krems. No, there was no one from the old staff here now... or yes! Yes, there was—Frau Sporschil was still here, the toilet lady (known in vulgar parlance as the chocolate lady). But he was sure she wouldn't be able to remember individual customers now. I thought at once, you don't forget a man like Jakob Mendel, and I asked her to come and see me.

She came, Frau Sporschil with her untidy white hair, her dropsical feet taking the few steps from her area of responsibility in the background to the front of the café and still hastily rubbing her red hands on a cloth; obviously she had just been sweeping or cleaning the windows of her dismal domain. From her uncertain manner I noticed at once that she felt uneasy to be summoned so suddenly into the smarter part of the café, under the large electric lights—in Vienna ordinary people suspect detectives and the police everywhere, as soon as anyone wants to ask them questions. So she looked at me suspiciously at first, glancing at me from under her brows, a very cautious, surreptitious glance. What good could I want of her? But as soon as I asked about Jakob Mendel she stared at me with full, positively streaming eyes, and her shoulders began to shake.

"Oh, my God, poor Herr Mendel—to think of anyone remembering him now! Yes, poor Herr Mendel"—she was almost weeping, she was so moved in the way of old people when they are reminded of their youth, of some good, forgotten acquaintanceship. I asked if he was still alive.

"Oh, my God, poor Herr Mendel, it must be five or six years he's been dead, no, seven years. Such a kind, good man, and when I think how long I knew him, more than twenty-five years, he was already coming here when I joined the staff. And it was a shame, a real shame, the way they let him die." She was growing more and more agitated, and asked if I was a relation. Because no one had ever troubled about him, she said, no one had ever asked after him—didn't I know what had happened to him?

No, I assured her, I knew nothing, and please would she tell me all about it? The good woman looked shy and embarrassed, and kept wiping her damp hands again and again. I realized that as the toilet lady she felt awkward standing here in the middle of the café, with her untidy white hair and stained apron. In addition, she kept looking anxiously to left and right in case one of the waiters was listening.

So I suggested that we might go into the card room, to Mendel's old table, and she could tell me all about it there. Moved, she nodded to me, grateful for my understanding, and the old lady, already a little unsteady on her feet, went ahead while I followed her. The two waiters stared after us in surprise, sensing some connection, and some of the customers also seemed to be wondering about the unlikely couple we made.

Over at Mendel's table, she told me (another account, at a later date, filled in some of the details for me) about the downfall of Jakob Mendel, Mendel the bibliophile.

Well then, she said, he had gone on coming here even after the beginning of the war, day after day, arriving at seven-thirty in the morning, and he sat there just the same and studied all day, as usual; the fact was they'd all felt, and often said so, that he wasn't even aware there was a war going on. I'd remember, she said, that he never looked at a newspaper and never talked to anyone else, but even when the newsboys were making their murderous racket, announcing special editions, and all the others ran to buy, he never got to his feet or even listened. He didn't so much as notice that Franz the waiter was missing (Franz had fallen at Gorlice), and he didn't know that Herr Standhartner's son had been taken prisoner at Przemyśl, he never said a word when the bread got worse and worse, and they had to serve him fig coffee instead of his usual milk, nasty stuff it was. Just once he did seem surprised because so few students came in now, that was all. "My God, the poor man, nothing gave him pleasure or grief except those books of his."

But then, one day, the worst happened. At eleven in the morning, in broad daylight, a policeman had come in with an officer of the secret police, who had shown the rosette badge in his buttonhole and asked if a man called Jakob Mendel came in here. Then they went straight over to Mendel's table, and he thought, suspecting nothing, they wanted to sell him books or ask for information. But they told him to his face to go with them, and they took him away. It had brought shame on the café; everyone gathered round poor Herr Mendel as he stood there between the two police officers, his glasses pushed up on his forehead, looking back and forth from one to the other of them, not knowing what they really wanted.

Frau Sporschil, however, said that she had instantly told the uniformed policeman this must be a mistake. A man like Herr Mendel wouldn't hurt a fly, but then the secret police officer shouted at her not to interfere in official business. And then, she added, they had taken him away, and it was a long time before he came back, two years. To this day she didn't really know what they'd wanted from him back then. "But I give you my oath," said the old woman, much upset, "Herr Mendel can't have done anything wrong. They made a mistake, I'd swear to it. It was a crime against that poor, innocent man, a real crime!"

And good, kind-hearted Frau Sporschil was right. Our friend Jakob Mendel really had not done anything wrong, only something stupid (and as I said, not until later did I learn all the details)—he had committed a headlong, touching and even in those crazy times entirely improbable act of stupidity, to be explained only by his total self-absorption, the oddity of his unique nature.

This was what had happened. One day the military censor-ship office, where it was the duty of the officials to supervise all correspondence sent abroad, had intercepted a postcard written and signed by one Jakob Mendel, properly stamped with suf-ficient postage for a country outside Austria, but—incredible to relate—sent to an enemy nation. The postcard was addressed to Jean Labourdaire, Bookseller, Paris, Quai de Grenelle, and on it the sender, Jakob Mendel, complained that he had not received the last eight numbers of the monthly *Bulletin bibliographique de la France*, in spite of having paid a year's subscription in advance. The junior censorship official who found it, in civil life a high-school teacher by profession and a scholar of Romance languages and literature by private inclination, who now wore the blue uniform of the territorial reserves, was astonished to have such a document in his hands. He thought it must be a silly joke. Among the 2,000 letters that he scanned every week, searching them for dubious comments and turns of phrase that might indicate espionage, he had never come across anything so absurd as someone in Austria addressing a letter to France without another thought, simply posting a card to the enemy country as if the borders had not been fortified by barbed wire since 1914, and as if, on every new day created by God, France, Germany, Austria and Russia were not killing a few thousand of each other's male populations. So at first he put the postcard in his desk drawer as a curio, and did not mention the absurdity to anyone else.

However, a few weeks later another card from the same Jakob Mendel was sent to a bookseller called John Aldridge, at Holborn Square in London, asking if he could procure the latest numbers of *The Antiquarian* for him; and once again it was signed by the same strange individual, Jakob Mendel, who with touching naiveté gave his full address. Now the high-school teacher felt a little uncomfortable in the uniform coat that he was obliged to wear. Was there, after all, some mysteriously coded meaning behind this idiotic joke? Anyway, he stood up, clicked his heels and put the two cards on the major's desk. The major shrugged his shoulders: what an odd case! First he asked the police to find out whether this Jakob Mendel actually existed, and an hour later Jakob Mendel was under arrest and, still stunned with surprise, was brought before the major. The major placed the mysterious postcards in front of him and asked whether he admitted to sending them. Agitated by the major's stern tone, and particularly upset because the police had tracked him down just when he was reading an important catalogue, Mendel said, almost impatiently, that of course he had written those postcards. He supposed a man still had a right to claim value for money paid as an advance subscription. The major turned in his chair and leant over to the lieutenant at the next desk. The two of them exchanged meaningful glances: what an utter idiot! Then the major wondered whether he should just tell this simpleton off in no uncertain terms and send him packing, or whether he ought to take the case seriously. In such difficult circumstances, almost any office will decide that the first thing to do is to write a record of the incident. A record is always a good idea. If it does no great good, it will do no harm either, and one more meaningless sheet of paper among millions will be covered with words.

This time, however, it unfortunately did do harm to a poor, unsuspecting man, for something very fateful emerged in answer to the major's third question. First the man was asked his name: Jakob, originally Jainkeff Mendel. Profession: pedlar (for he had no bookseller's licence, only a certificate allowing him to trade from door to door). The third question was the catastrophe: his place of birth. Jakob Mendel named a small village in Petrikau. The major raised his eyebrows. Petrikau, wasn't that in the Russian part of Poland, near the border? Suspicious! Very suspicious! So he asked more sternly when Mendel had acquired Austrian citizenship. Mendel's glasses stared at him darkly and in surprise: he didn't understand the question. For heaven's sake, asked the major, did he have his papers, his documents, and if so where were they? The only document he had was his permit to trade from door to door. The major's eyebrows rose ever higher. Then would he kindly explain how he came to be an Austrian citizen? What had his father been, Austrian or Russian? Jakob Mendel calmly replied: Russian, of course. And he himself? Oh, to avoid having to serve in the army, he had smuggled himself over the Russian border thirty-three years ago, and he had been living in Vienna ever since. The major was getting increasingly impatient. When, he repeated, had he acquired Austrian citizenship? Why would he bother with that, asked Mendel, he'd never troubled about such things. So he was still a Russian citizen? And Mendel, who was finding all this pointless questioning tedious, replied with indifference, "Yes, I suppose so."

Shocked, the major sat back so brusquely that his chair creaked. To think of such a thing! In Vienna, the capital of Austria, right in the middle of the war at the end of 1915, after Tarnów and the great offensive, here was a Russian walking around with impunity, writing letters to France and England, and the police did nothing about it! And then those fools in the newspapers are surprised that Conrad von Hötzendorf didn't advance directly to Warsaw, and on the general staff they are amazed that all troop movements are reported to Russia by spies. The lieutenant too had risen to his feet and was standing at his desk: the conversation abruptly became an interrogation. Why hadn't he immediately reported to the authorities as a foreigner? Mendel, still unsuspecting, replied in his sing-song Jewish tones, "Why would I want to go and report all of a sudden?" The major saw this reversal of his question as a challenge and asked, menacingly, whether he hadn't read the announcements? No! And didn't he read the newspapers either? Again, no.

The two of them stared at Mendel, who was sweating slightly in his uncertainty, as if the moon had fallen to earth in their office. Then the telephone rang, typewriters tapped busily, orderlies ran back and forth and Jakob Mendel was consigned to the garrison cells, to be moved on to a concentration camp. When he was told to follow two soldiers he stared uncertainly. He didn't understand what they wanted from him, but really he had no great anxiety. What ill, after all, could the man with the gold braid on his collar and the rough voice have in store for him? In his elevated world of books there was no war, no misunderstanding, only eternal knowledge and the desire to know more about numbers and words, titles and names. So he good-naturedly went down the steps with the two soldiers. Only when all the books in his coat pockets were confiscated at the police station, and he had to hand over his briefcase, where he had put a hundred important notes and customers' addresses, did he begin to strike out angrily around him. They had to overcome him, but in the process unfortunately his glasses fell to the floor, and that magic spyglass of his that looked into the intellectual world broke into a thousand pieces. Two days later he was sent, in his thin summer coat, to a concentration camp for civilian Russian prisoners at Komorn.

As for Jakob Mendel's experience of mental horror in those two years in a concentration camp, living without books—his beloved books—without money, with indifferent, coarse and mostly illiterate companions in the midst of this gigantic human dunghill, as for all he suffered there, cut off from his sublime and unique world of books as an eagle with its wings clipped is separated from its ethereal element—there is no testimony to any of it. But the world, waking soberly from its folly, has gradually come to know that of all the cruelties and criminal encroachments of that war, none was more senseless, unnecessary and therefore more morally inexcusable than capturing and imprisoning behind barbed wire unsuspecting civilians long past the age for military service, who had become used to living in a foreign land as if it were their own, and in their belief in the laws of hospitality, which are sacred even to Tungus and Araucanian tribesmen, had neglected to flee in time. It was a crime committed equally unthinkingly in France, Germany and England, in every part of a Europe run mad. And perhaps Jakob Mendel, like hundreds of other innocents penned up in a camp, would have succumbed miserably to madness or dysentery, debility or a mental breakdown, had not a coincidence of a truly Austrian nature brought him back to his own world just in time.

After his disappearance, several letters from distinguished customers had been delivered to his address. Those customers included Count Schönberg, the former governor of Styria and a fanatical collector of heraldic works; the former dean of the theological faculty at the university, Siegenfeld, who was working on a commentary on St Augustine; and the eighty-year-old retired Admiral the Honourable von Pisek, who was still tinkering with his memoirs—all of them, his faithful customers, had repeatedly written to Jakob Mendel at the Café Gluck, and a few of these letters were forwarded to the missing man in the concentration camp. There they fell into the hands of a captain who happened to have his heart in the right place, and who was surprised to discover the names of the distinguished acquaintances of this little half-blind, dirty Jew, who had huddled in a corner like a mole, grey, eyeless and silent, ever since his glasses had been broken (he had no money to buy a new pair). There must, after all, be something special about a man with friends like that. So he allowed Mendel to answer the letters and ask his patrons to put in a good word for him, which they did. With the fervent solidarity of all collectors, His Excellency and the Dean powerfully cranked up their connections, and their united support brought Mendel the bibliophile back to Vienna in the year 1917, after more than two years of confinement, although on condition that he reported daily to the police. However, he could return to the free world, to his old, cramped little attic room, he could walk past the window displays of books again, and above all he could go back to the Café Gluck.

Good Frau Sporschil was able to give me a first-hand account of Mendel's return to the café from an infernal underworld. "One day—Jesus, Mary and Joseph, thinks I, I can't believe my eyes!—one day the door's pushed open, you know what it's like, just a little way, he always came in like that, and there he is stumbling into the café, poor Herr Mendel. He was wearing a much-mended military coat, and something on his head that might once have been a hat someone had thrown away. He didn't have a collar, and he looked like death, grey in the face, grey-haired and pitifully thin. But in he comes, like nothing had happened, he doesn't ask no questions, he doesn't say nothing, he goes to the table over there and takes off his coat, but not so quickly and easily as before, it takes him an effort. And no books with him now, like he always brought—he just sits down there and don't say nothing, he just stares ahead of him with empty, worn-out eyes. It was only little by little, when we'd brought him all the written stuff that had come from Germany for him, he went back to reading. But he was never the same again."

No, he was not the same, he was no longer that *miraculum mundi*, a magical catalogue of all the books in the world. Everyone who saw him at that time sadly told me the same. Something in his otherwise still eyes, eyes that read only as if in his sleep, seemed to be destroyed beyond redemption. Something in him was broken; the terrible red comet of blood must, in its headlong career, have smashed destructively into the remote, peaceful, halcyon star that was his world of books. His eyes, used for decades to the tender, soundless, insect-like letters making up print, must have seen terrible things in that barbed-wire pen into which human beings were herded, for his eyelids cast heavy shadows over his once-swift and ironically sparkling pupils; sleepy and red-rimmed, they shed twilight on his formerly lively eyes as they peered through his glasses, now repaired by being laboriously tied together with thin string. And even more terrible: in the fantastic and elaborate structure of his memory, some prop must have given way, bringing the rest of it down in confusion, for the human brain, that control centre made of the most delicate of substances, a precision instrument in the mechanics of our knowledge, is so finely adjusted that a blocked blood vessel, even a small one, a shattered nerve, an exhausted cell or the shift of a molecule is enough to silence the heavenly harmony of the most magnificently comprehensive mind. And in Mendel's memory, that unique keyboard of knowledge, the keys themselves jammed now that he was back. If someone came in search of information now and then, Mendel would look wearily at him, no longer fully understanding; he heard things wrongly, and forgot what was said to him. Mendel was not Mendel any more, just as the world was no longer the world. Total immersion in reading no longer rocked him back and forth, but he usually sat there perfectly still, his glasses turned only automatically on a book, and you could not tell whether he was reading or only daydreaming. Several times, Frau Sporschil told me, his head dropped heavily on the book and he fell asleep in broad daylight; or he sometimes stared for hours on end at the strange and smelly light of the acetylene lamp they had put on his desk at this time when coal was in short supply. No, Mendel was not the old Mendel, no longer a wonder of the world but a useless collection of beard and clothes, breathing wearily, pointlessly sitting in his once-oracular chair, he was no longer the glory of the Café Gluck but a disgrace, a dirty mark, ill-smelling, a revolting sight, an uncomfortable and unnecessary parasite.

That was how the new owner of the café saw him. This man, Florian Gurtner by name, came from Retz, had made a fortune from shady deals in flour and butter during the starvation year of 1919, and had talked the unsuspecting Herr Standhartner into selling him the Café Gluck for 80,000 crowns in paper money, which swiftly depreciated in value. He set about the place with his firm rustic hands, renovating the old-established café to smarten it up, buying new armchairs for bad money at the right time, installing a marble porch, and he was already negotiating to buy the bar next door and turn it into a dance hall. Naturally enough, the odd little Galician parasite who kept a table occupied all day, and in that time consumed nothing but two cups of coffee and five rolls, was very much in the way of his hastily undertaken project to smarten up the café. Standhartner had, to be sure, specially commended his old customer to the new owner, and had tried to explain what an important man Jakob Mendel was; indeed he had, so to speak, transferred him along with the café's fixtures and fittings as someone with a claim on his goodwill. But along with the new furniture and the shiny aluminium cash register, Florian Gurtner had introduced the approach of a man out to earn all he could, and he was only waiting for an excuse to banish this last, annoying remnant of suburban shabbiness from his now-elegant café.

And a good reason to do so quite soon arose, for Jakob Mendel was in a bad way. The last banknotes he had saved had been pulverized in the paper mill of inflation, and his customers had disappeared. These days he was so exhausted that he lacked the strength to start climbing steps and going from door to door selling books again. There were a hundred little signs of his poverty. He seldom had something for lunch brought in from the restaurant now, and he was behind with paying the small sums he owed for coffee and rolls, once as much as three weeks behind. At that point the head waiter wanted to turn him out into the street. But good Frau Sporschil, the toilet lady, was sorry for Mendel and said she would pay his debt.

Next month, however, a great misfortune happened. The new head waiter had already noticed, several times, that when he was settling up accounts the money for the baked goods never worked out quite right. More rolls proved to be missing than had been ordered and paid for. His suspicions, naturally, went straight to Mendel, for the decrepit old servant at the café had come to complain, several times, that Mendel had owed him money for six months, and he couldn't get it out of him. So the head waiter kept his eyes open, and two days later, hiding behind the fire screen, he succeeded in catching Jakob Mendel secretly getting up from his table, going into the other front room, quickly taking two rolls from a bread basket and devouring them greedily. When it came to paying for what he had had that day, he denied eating any rolls at all. So that explained the disappearance of the baked goods. The waiter reported the incident at once to Herr Gurtner who, glad of the excuse he had been seeking for so long, shouted at Mendel in front of everyone, accused him of theft and made a great show of magnanimity in not calling the police at once. But he told Mendel to get out of his café immediately and never come back. Jakob Mendel only trembled and said nothing; he got up from where he sat, tottering, and went away.

"Oh, it was a real shame," said Frau Sporschil, describing this departure. "I'll never forget it, the way he stood there, his glasses pushed up on his forehead, white as a sheet. He didn't even take the time to put on his coat, although it was January, and you know what a cold year it was. And in his fright he left his book lying on the table, I didn't notice that until later, and I was going to follow him with it. But he'd already stumbled to the door, and I didn't dare follow him out into the streets, because there was Herr Gurtner himself standing by the door shouting after him so loud that people stopped and crowded together. Yes, I call it a shame, I felt shamed to the heart myself! Such a thing could never have happened when old Herr Standhartner was here, fancy chasing a man away just for a few rolls, with old Herr Standhartner he could have eaten them for free all his life. But folk these days, they've got no hearts. Driving away a man who sat here day after day for over thirty years—a shame, it really was, and I wouldn't like to have to answer to the Lord God for it, not me."

The good woman was greatly agitated, and with the passionate volubility of old age she repeated again and again that it was a real shame, and nothing like it would have happened in Herr Standhartner's day. So finally I had to ask her what had become of our friend Mendel, and whether she had seen him again. At that she pulled herself together, and then went on in even more distress.

"Every day when I passed his table, every time, believe you me, I felt a pang. I always wondered where he might be now, poor Herr Mendel, and if I'd known where he lived I'd have gone there, brought him something hot to eat, because where would he get the money to heat his room and feed himself? And so far as I know he didn't have any family, not a soul in the world. But in the end, when I still never heard a thing, I thought to myself it must all be over, and I'd never see him again. And I was wondering whether I wouldn't get a Mass read for him, because he was a good man, Herr Mendel, and we'd known each other more than twenty-five years.

"But then one day early, half past seven in the morning in February, I'm just polishing up the brass rails at the windows, and suddenly—I mean suddenly, believe you me—the door opens and in comes Herr Mendel. You know the way he always came in, kind of crooked and confused-looking, but this time he was somehow different. I can see it at once, he's torn this way and that, his eyes all glazed, and my God, the way he looked, all beard and bones! I think right away, he don't remember nothing, here he is sleepwalking in broad daylight, he's forgot it all, all about the rolls and Herr Gurtner and how shamefully they threw him out, he don't know nothing about himself. Thank God for it, Herr Gurtner wasn't there yet, and the head waiter had just had his own coffee. So I put my oar in quickly, I tell him he'd better not stay here and get thrown out again by that nasty fellow" (and here she looked timidly around and quickly corrected herself) "I mean by Herr Gurtner. So I call out to him. 'Herr Mendel,' I say. He stares at me. And at that moment, oh my God, terrible it was, at that moment it must all have come back to him, because he gives a start at once and he begins to tremble, but not just his fingers, no, he's trembling all over, you can see it, shoulders and all, and he's stumbling back to the door, he's hurrying, and then he collapsed. We telephoned for the emergency service and they took him away, all feverish like he was. He died that evening. Pneumonia, a bad case, the doctor said, and he said he hadn't really known anything about it, not how he came back to us. It just kind of drove him on, it was like he was sleepwalking. My God, when a man has sat at a table like that every day for thirty-six years, the table is kind of his home."

We talked about him for some time longer; we were the last two to have known that strange man—I, to whom in my youth, despite the minute scope of his own existence, little more than that of a microbe, he had conveyed my first inklings of a perfectly enclosed life of the mind, and she, the poor worn-out toilet lady who had never read a book, and felt bound to this comrade of her poverty-stricken world only because she had brushed his coat and sewn on his buttons for twenty-five years. And yet we understood one another wonderfully well as we sat at his old table, now abandoned, in the company of the shades we had conjured up between us, for memory is always a bond, and every loving memory is a bond twice over. Suddenly, in the midst of her talk, she thought of something. "Jesus, how forgetful I am—I still have that book, the one he left lying on the table here. Where was I to go to take it back to him? And afterwards, when nobody came for it, afterwards I thought I could keep it a memento. There wasn't anything wrong in that, was there?"

She hastily produced it from her cubby hole at the back of the café. And I had difficulty in suppressing a small smile, for the spirit of comedy, always playful and sometimes ironic, likes to mingle maliciously in the most shattering of events. The book was the second volume of Hayn's *Bibliotheca Germanorum Erotica et Curiosa*, the well-known compendium of gallant literature known to every book collector. And this scabrous catalogue—*habent sua fata libelli*—had fallen as the dead magician's last legacy into those work-worn, red and cracked, ignorant hands that had probably never held any other book but her prayer book. As I say, I had difficulty in keeping my lips firmly closed to the smile involuntarily trying to make its way out, and my moment of hesitation confused the good woman. Was it valuable after all, or did I think she could keep it?

I shook her hand with heartfelt goodwill. "Keep it and welcome. Our old friend Mendel would be glad to think that at least one of the many thousands who had him to thank for a book still remembers him." And then I went, feeling ashamed in front of this good old woman, who had remained faithful to the dead man in her simple and yet very human way. For she, unschooled as she was, had at least kept a book so that she could remember him better, whereas I had forgotten Mendel the bibliophile years ago, and I was the one who ought to know that you create books solely to forge links with others even after your own death, thus defending yourself against the inexorable adversary of all life, transience and oblivion.

THE DEBT
PAID LATE

M Y DEAR ELLEN,
I know you will be surprised to receive a letter from me after so long; it must be five or perhaps even six years since I last wrote to you. I believe that then it was a letter of congratulations on your youngest daughter's marriage. This time the occasion is not so festive, and perhaps my need to confide the details of a strange encounter to you, rather than anyone else, may strike you as odd. But I can't tell anyone else what happened to me a few days ago. You are the only person who would understand.

My pen involuntarily hesitates as I write these words, and I have to smile at myself a little. Didn't we exchange the very same "You are the only person who would understand" a thousand times when we were fifteen or sixteen years old—immature, excitable girls telling each other our childish secrets at school or on the way home? And didn't we solemnly swear, long ago in our salad days, to tell each other everything, in detail, concerning a certain person? All that is more than a quarter of a century ago; but a promise, once made, must be kept. And as you will see, I am faithfully keeping my word, if rather late in the day.

This was how it all happened. I have had a difficult and strenuous time of things this year. My husband was appointed medical director of the big hospital in R., so I had all the complications of moving house to deal with; meanwhile my son-in-law went to Brazil on business, taking my daughter with him, and they left their three children in our house. The children promptly contracted scarlet fever one after the other, and I had to nurse them… and that wasn't all, because then my mother-in-law died. Everything was happening at once. I thought at first that I had survived all these headlong events pretty well, but somehow they must have taken more out of me than I knew, because one day my husband said, after looking at me in silence for some time, "Margaret, I think that now the children, thank goodness, are better again you ought to do something about your own health. You look overtired, you've been well and truly overdoing things. Two or three weeks at a sanatorium in the country, and you'll be your old self again."

My husband was right. I was exhausted, more so than I admitted to myself. I became aware of it when I realized that in company— and since my husband took up his post here, there have been many functions to host and many calls to be paid—after an hour I couldn't concentrate properly on what people were saying, while I forgot the simplest things more and more often in the daily running of the household, and had to force myself to get up in the morning. With his observant and medically trained eye, my husband had diagnosed my physical and mental weariness correctly. All I really needed was two weeks to recover. Fourteen days without thinking about the meals, the laundry, paying calls, doing all the everyday business—fourteen days on my own to be myself, not a mother, grandmother, housekeeper and wife of the medical director of a hospital all the time. It so happened that my widowed sister was available to come and stay, so everything was prepared for my absence; and I had no further scruples in following my husband's advice and going away by myself for the first time in twenty-five years. Indeed, I was actually looking forward quite impatiently to being invigorated by my holiday. I rejected my husband's suggestion only in one point: his idea that I should spend it at a sanatorium, although he had thoughtfully found one whose owner had been a friend of his from their youth. But there would have been other people whom I knew there, and I would have had to go on being sociable and mixing in company. All I really wanted was to be on my own for fourteen days with books, walks, time to dream and sleep undisturbed, fourteen days without the telephone and the radio, fourteen days of silence at peace with myself, if I may put it like that. Unconsciously, I hadn't wanted anything so much for years as this time set aside for silence and rest.

And then I remembered that in the first years of my marriage, when my husband was practising as an assistant doctor in Bolzano, I had once spent three hours walking up to an isolated little village high in the mountains. In its tiny marketplace, opposite the church, stood one of those rural inns of the kind so often to be found in the Tyrol, its ground floor built of massive stones, the first floor under the wide, overhanging wooden roof opening on to a spacious veranda, and the whole place surrounded by vine leaves that in autumn, the season when I saw it, glowed around the whole house like a red fire gradually cooling. Small outbuildings and big barns huddled to the right and left of it, but the house itself stood on its own under soft autumnal clouds drifting across the sky, and looked down at the endless panorama of the mountains.

At the time I had felt almost spellbound outside that little inn, and I wanted to go in. I'm sure you know what it's like to see a house from the train or on a walk, and think all of a sudden: oh, why don't I live here? I could be happy in this place. I think such an idea occurs to everyone sometimes, and when you have looked at a house for a long time secretly wishing to live happily in it, everything about it is imprinted on your memory. For years I remembered the red and yellow flowers growing in window boxes, the wooden first-floor gallery, where laundry was fluttering like colourful banners the day I saw it, the painted shutters at the windows, yellow on a blue background with little heart-shapes cut out of the middle of them, and the roof ridge with a stork's nest on the gable. When my heart felt restless I sometimes thought of that house. How nice it would be to go there for a day, I would think, in the dreamy, half-unconscious way that you think of something impossible. And now wasn't this my best chance to make my old, and by this time almost forgotten, wish come true? Wasn't the

STEFAN ZWEIG

prettily painted house on the mountainside, an inn without the
tiresome amenities of our modern world, with no telephone or
radio, the very thing for overtired nerves? I would have no visitors
there, and there would be no formalities. As I called it to mind
again, I thought I was breathing in the strong, aromatic mountain air, and hearing the far-off ringing of rustic cowbells. Even
remembering it gave me fresh courage and made me feel better.
It was one of those ideas that take us by surprise apparently for
no reason at all, although in reality they express wishes that we
have cherished for a long time, waiting in the unconscious mind.
My husband, who didn't know how often I had dreamt of that
little house, seen only once years ago, smiled a little at first but
promised to make enquiries. The proprietors replied that all of
their three guest rooms were vacant at the moment, and I could
choose whichever I liked. All the better, I thought, no neighbours,
no conversations; and I went on the night train. Next morning,
a little country one-horse trap took me and my small suitcase up
the mountain at a slow trot.

It was all as delightful as I could have hoped for. The room
was bright and neat, with its simple, pale pine furniture, and
from the veranda, which was all mine in the absence of any other
guests, I had a view into the endless distance. A glance at the well-
scoured kitchen, shining with cleanliness, showed me, experienced
housewife that I am, that I would be very well looked after here.
The landlady, a thin, friendly, grey-haired Tyrolean, assured me
again that I need not fear being disturbed or pestered by visitors.
True, the parish clerk, the local policeman and a few of the other
neighbours came to the inn every evening to drink a glass or so,
play cards and talk. But they were all quiet folk, and at eleven they
went home again. On Sunday after church, and sometimes in the
afternoon, the place was rather livelier, because the locals came
to the inn from their farms or the mountains; but I would hear
hardly any of that in my room.

The day was too bright and fine, however, for me to stay indoors for long. I unpacked the few things I had brought, asked for a piece of good brown country bread and a couple of slices of cold meat to take out with me, and went walking over the meadows, climbing higher and higher. The landscape lay before me, the valley with its fast-flowing river, the surrounding snow-crowned peaks, as free as I was myself. I felt the sun on every pore of my skin, and I walked and walked and walked for an hour, two hours, three hours until I reached the highest Alpine meadows. There I lay down to rest, stretched out on the soft, warm moss, and felt a wonderful sense of peace come over me, together with the buzzing of the bees, the light and rhythmic sound of the wind—it was exactly what I had been longing for. I closed my eyes pleasurably, fell to dreaming, and didn't even notice when at some point I dropped off to sleep. I was woken only by a chill in the air on my limbs. Evening was coming on, and I must have slept for five hours. Only now did I realize how tired I had been. But I had good, fresh air in my nerves and in my bloodstream. It took me only two hours to walk back to the little inn with a strong, firm, steady step.

The landlady was standing at the door. She had been slightly anxious, fearing I might have lost my way, and offered to prepare my supper at once. I had a hearty appetite and was hungrier than I could remember feeling for years, so I was very happy to follow her into the main room of the inn. It was not large—a dark, low-ceilinged room with wood-panelled walls, very comfortable with its red-and-blue check tablecloths, the chamois horns and crossed shotguns on the walls. And although the big blue-tiled stove was not heated this warm autumn day, there was a comfortable natural warmth inside the room. I liked the guests as well. At one of the four tables the local policeman, the customs officer and the parish clerk sat playing cards together, each with a glass of beer beside him. A few farmers with strong, sun-browned faces sat at their ease at another, propping their elbows on it. Like all Tyroleans, they said little, and merely puffed at their long-stemmed porcelain pipes. You could see that they had worked hard all day and were relaxing now, too tired to think, too tired to talk—honest, upright men; it did one good to look at their faces, as strongly outlined as woodcuts. A couple of carters occupied the third table, drinking strong grain schnapps in small sips, and they too were tired and silent. The fourth table was laid for me, and soon bore a portion of roast meat so huge that normally I wouldn't have managed to eat half of it; but I had a healthy, even ravenous appetite after walking in the fresh mountain air.

I had brought a book down, meaning to read, but it was pleasant sitting here in this quiet room, among friendly people whose proximity was neither oppressive nor a nuisance. Sometimes the door opened, a fair-haired child came to fetch a jug of beer for his parents, or a farmer dropped in and emptied a glass standing at the bar. A woman came for a quiet chat with the landlady, who sat behind the bar darning socks for her children or grandchildren. There was a wonderful quiet rhythm to all this coming and going, which offered something for my eyes to see and was no burden on my heart, and I felt very well in such a comfortable atmosphere.

I had been sitting dreamily like that for a while, thinking of nothing in particular, when—it will have been about nine o'clock—the door was opened again, but not this time in the slow, unhurried way of the locals. It was suddenly flung wide, and the man who came in stood for a moment on the threshold filling the doorway, as if not quite sure whether to come in. Only then did he let the door latch behind him, much more loudly than the other guests, look around the room and greet all present with a deep-voiced and resonant, "A very good evening to you one and all, gentlemen!" I was immediately struck by his rather ornate and artificial vocabulary. In a Tyrolean village inn, people do not usually greet the "gentlemen" with such ceremony, and in fact this rather ostentatious form of address seemed to meet with an unenthusiastic response from the other guests in the room. No one looked up, the landlady went on darning grey woollen socks, and one of the carters was the only person to grunt an indifferent "Evening" in return, but in a tone of voice suggesting, "And to the devil with you!" No one seemed surprised by the strange guest's manner, but he was not to be deterred by this unforthcoming reception. Slowly and gravely, he hung up his broad hat with its well-worn brim—not a rustic item of headgear—on one of the chamois horns, and then looked from table to table, not sure where to sit down. Not a word of welcome came from any of them. The three card-players immersed themselves with conspicuous concentration in their game, the farmers on their benches gave not the slightest sign of moving closer to make room, and I myself, made to feel rather uncomfortable by the stranger's manner and fearing that he might turn out to be talkative, was quick to open my book.

So the stranger had no choice but to go over to the bar with a noticeably heavy, awkward step. "A beer, if mine hostess pleases, as fresh and delicious as your lovely self," he ordered in quite a loud voice. Once again I was struck by his dramatically emotional tone. In a Tyrolean village inn, such an elaborately turned compliment seemed out of place, and there was nothing whatsoever about that kindly old grandmother the landlady to justify it. As was to be expected, such a form of address failed to impress her. Without replying, she picked up one of the sturdy stoneware tankards, rinsed it out with water, dried it with a cloth, filled it from the barrel and pushed it to the newcomer over the bar, in a manner that was not exactly discourteous but was entirely indifferent.

Since the round paraffin lamp hung from its chains above him, right in front of the bar, I had a chance to take a better look at this unusual guest. He was about sixty-five years old, was very stout, and with the experience I had gained as a doctor's wife I immediately saw the reason for the dragging, heavy gait that I had noticed as soon as he came into the room. A stroke must have affected one side of his body to some extent, for his mouth also turned down on that side, and the lid of his left eye visibly drooped lower than his right eyelid. His clothes were out of place for an Alpine village; instead of the countryman's rustic jacket and lederhosen, he wore baggy yellow trousers that might once have been white, with a coat that had obviously grown too tight for him over the years and was alarmingly shiny at the elbows; his tie, carelessly arranged, hung from his fleshy, fat neck like a piece of black string. There was something run-down about his appearance in general, and yet it was possible that this man had once cut an imposing figure. His brow, curved and high, with thick, untidy white hair above it, had something of a commanding look, but just below his bushy eyebrows the decline set in: his eyes swam under reddened lids; his slack, wrinkled cheeks merged with his soft, thick neck. I was instinctively reminded of the mask of a late Roman emperor that I had once seen in Italy, one of those who presided over the fall of Rome. At first I did not know what it was that made me observe him so attentively, but I realized at once that I must take care not to show my curiosity, for it was obvious that he was already impatient to strike up a conversation with someone. It was as if he were under some compulsion to talk. As soon as he had raised his glass in a slightly shaky hand and taken a sip, he exclaimed in a loud voice, "Ah, wonderful, wonderful!" and looked around him. No one responded. The card-players shuffled and dealt the pack, the others smoked their pipes; they all seemed to know the new arrival and yet, for some reason of which I was unaware, not to feel any curiosity about him.

Finally there was no restraining him any longer. Picking up his glass of beer, he carried it over to the table where the farmers were sitting. "Will you gentlemen make a little room for my old bones?" The farmers moved together slightly and took no further notice of him. For a while he said nothing, pushing the half-full glass alternately forwards and backwards. Once again, I saw that his fingers trembled. Finally he leant back and began talking, in quite a loud voice. It was not really obvious whom he was addressing, for the two rustics sitting next to him had clearly shown that they were disinclined to embark on any conversation. He was, in fact, addressing everyone at large. He spoke—I sensed that at once—in order to speak and to hear himself speaking.

"Well, what a business that was today!" he began. "Well-meant of the Count, well-meant, I grant you. Meets me while he's driving along the road and stops his car, yes, indeed, he stops it specially for me. He's taking his children down to Bolzano to go to the cinema, says he, how would I like to go with them? Well, he's a distinguished man, a cultured, educated man, the Count knows where respect is due, and you don't say no lightly to such a man, not if you know what's right. So I go along with them, in the back seat of course, with his lordship the Count—after all, it's an honour, a man like that, and I let him take me into that magic-lantern show they've opened in the high street with such a fuss, advertisements and lights fit for a church festival. Well, I think, why shouldn't I see what those gentlemen the British and Americans are churning out over there, selling the stuff to us for good money? It's said to be quite an art, this cinema acting. Shame on them, say I"—and here he spat copiously—"shame on them for the rubbish they show on that screen of theirs! It's a disgrace to art, a disgrace to a world that has a Shakespeare and a Goethe in it! First came all that coloured nonsense with comical animals—well, I'll say nothing about that, it may be fun for children, it does no one any harm. But then they make a film of *Romeo and Juliet*—now that ought to be forbidden, forbidden in the name of art! The lines sound as if someone was croaking them into a stovepipe, those sacred lines of Shakespeare's, and all so sugary and sentimental! I'd have got up and walked out if I hadn't been there with his lordship the Count, on his invitation. Making such rubbish out of pure refined gold! And to think that we live in times like these!"

He grasped his glass of beer, took a large draught and put it down with a loud bang. His voice was very loud now, he was almost shouting. "And that's what actors do these days—they spit out Shakespearian lines into machines for money, filthy lucre, dragging their art in the dirt! Give me any tart in the street—I have more respect for her than for those apes with their smooth faces metres wide on the posters, raking in millions for committing a crime against art! Mutilating the word, the living word, shouting Shakespeare's verse into a funnel instead of edifying the public, instead of educating young people. A moral institution, that's what Schiller called the theatre, but that doesn't hold good any more. Nothing holds good any more but money, filthy money, and the spectacle they make of themselves. And anyone who doesn't know how to do that will die. Better die, say I—in my eyes, those who sell themselves to that sink of iniquity, Hollywood, should go to the gallows. To the gallows with them, I say, to the gallows!"

He had been shouting at the top of his voice and thumping the table with his fist. One of the trio at the card-players' table growled, "Keep quiet, can't you? We can't tell what cards we're playing through your stupid gabbling!"

The old man gave a start, as if to reply. For a moment there was strength and vigour in his dull gaze, but then he merely made a contemptuous gesture, as much as to imply that it was beneath him to answer. The two farmers beside him puffed at their pipes, and he stared silently ahead with glazed eyes, saying nothing, his expression sombre. You could tell it was not the first time he had forced himself to hold his tongue.

I was deeply shaken, and felt a pang. Something stirred in me at the sight of this humiliated man, who I felt at once must have seen better days, and yet somehow had sunk so low, perhaps because of drink. I could hardly breathe for fear that he or the others might embark on a violent scene. From the first moment when he came in and I had heard his voice, something in him—I didn't know what—had made me uneasy. But nothing happened. He sat still, his head sinking lower, he stared ahead, and I felt as if he were muttering something quietly to himself. No one took any more notice of him.

Meanwhile, the landlady had got up from the bar to fetch something from the kitchen. I took that as a chance to follow her and ask who the man was. "Oh," she said, unruffled, "poor fellow, he lives in the poorhouse here, and I give him a beer every evening. He can't afford to pay for it himself. But we don't have an easy time with him. He used to be an actor once somewhere or other, and it hurts his feelings that people don't really believe he ever amounted to much and show him no respect. Sometimes they poke fun at him, asking him to put on a show for them. Then he stands up and spouts stuff that nobody understands for hours. Sometimes they give him some tobacco for his pains, or buy him another beer. Sometimes they just laugh at him, and then he loses his temper. You have to go carefully with him, but he wouldn't hurt a fly. Two or three beers if someone will pay for them, and then he's happy—yes, poor devil, there's no harm in old Peter."

"What—what is his name?" I asked, startled without knowing why.

"Peter Sturzentaler. His father was a woodcutter in the village here, so they took him in at the poorhouse."

Well, my dear, you can imagine what had startled me so much. For at once I understood what might seem unimaginable. This Peter Sturzentaler, this down-at-heel, drunk, sick old man from the poorhouse, could be none other than the idol of our young days, the master of our dreams; the man who as Peter Sturz the actor, the male lead in our city theatre, had been the quintessence of all that was elevated and sublime, whom as you will remember, both of us—young girls who were still half children—had admired so madly, loved to such distraction. And now I also knew why something in the first words he spoke on entering the inn had troubled me. I had not recognized him—how could I have recognized him behind this mask of debasement, in such a state of change and decay?—but there had been something in his voice that found its way to my long-buried memory. Do you remember when we first saw him? He had come from some provincial city when our municipal theatre in Innsbruck offered him an engagement, and it so happened that our parents said we could go to the performance introducing him to Innsbruck audiences because it was a classic play, Grillparzer's *Sappho*, and he was playing the part of Phaon, the handsome young man who creates turmoil in Sappho's heart. But remember how he captured ours when he came on stage, in Greek costume, a wreath in his thick, dark hair, a new Apollo! He had hardly spoken his first lines before we were both trembling with excitement and holding hands with each other. We had never seen a man like this in our dull, sedate city of Innsbruck, and the young provincial actor, whose stage make-up and the artifice of whose presentation could not be seen from the gallery, seemed to us a divine symbol of all that was noble and sublime. Our foolish little hearts beat fast in our young breasts; we were different girls when we left the theatre, enchanted, and as we were close friends and did not want to endanger our friendship, we swore to each other to love and venerate him together. That was the moment when our madness began. Nothing mattered to us except him. All that happened at school, at home, in town was mysteriously linked with him, everything else paled beside him; we gave up loving books, and the only music we wanted to hear was in his voice. I think we talked of nothing else for months on end. Every day began with him; we hurried downstairs to get to the newspaper before our parents, to know what new part he had been given, to read the reviews; and none of them was enthusiastic enough for us. If there was a critical remark about him we were in despair, we hated any other actor who won praise. Oh, we committed too many follies for me to be able to remember a thousandth part of them today.

We knew when he went out, and where he was going, we knew whom he spoke to, and envied everyone who could stroll down the street with him. We knew the ties he wore, the stick he carried; we hid photographs of him not only at home but inside the covers of our school textbooks, so that we could take a secret look at him in the middle of lessons; we had invented our own secret language so that at school we could signal, from desk to desk, that he was in our thoughts. A finger raised to the forehead meant, "I'm thinking of him now." When we had to read poems aloud, we instinctively imitated his voice, and to this day I can hardly see many of the plays in which I first saw him without hearing the lines spoken in his voice. We waited for him at the stage door and followed him, we stood in the entrance of a building opposite the café that he patronized, and watched endlessly as he read the newspaper there. But our veneration for him was so great that in those two years we never dared to speak to him or try to get to know him personally. Other, more uninhibited girls who also admired him would beg for his autograph, and even dared to address him in the street. We never summoned up the courage for that. But once, when he had thrown away a cigarette end, we picked it up as if it were a holy relic and divided it in two, half for you and half for me. And this childish idolatry was transferred to everything that had any connection with him. His old housekeeper, whom we envied greatly because she could serve him and look after him, was an object of our veneration too. Once, when she was shopping in the market, we offered to carry her basket for her, and were glad of the kind words she gave us in return. Ah, what folly wouldn't we have committed for Peter Sturz, who neither knew nor guessed anything about it?

Today, now that we have become middle-aged and therefore sensible people, it may be easy for us to smile scornfully at our folly as the usual rapturous fantasy of a girlish adolescent crush. And yet I cannot conceal from myself that in our case it had already become dangerous. I think that our infatuation took such absurd, exaggerated shape only because, silly children that we were, we had sworn to love him together. That meant that each of us tried to outdo the other in her flights of fancy, and we egged each other on further every day, thinking of more and more new evidence to prove that we had not for a moment forgotten the idol of our dreams. We were not like other girls, who by now were swooning over smooth-cheeked boys and playing silly games; to us, all emotion and enthusiasm was bent on this one man. For those two passionate years, all our thoughts were of him alone. Sometimes I am surprised that after this early obsession we could still love our husbands and children later with a clear-minded, sound and healthy love, and we did not waste all our emotional strength in those senseless excesses. But in spite of everything, we need not be ashamed of that time. For, thanks to the object of our love, we also lived with a passion for his art, and in our folly there was still a mysterious urge towards higher, purer, better things; they acquired, purely by coincidence, personification in him.

All this already seemed so very far away, overgrown by another life and other feelings; and yet when the landlady told me his name, it gave me such a shock that it is a miracle she didn't notice it. It was so startling to meet the man whom we had seen only surrounded by the aura of our infatuation, had loved so wholeheartedly as the very emblem of youth and beauty, and to find that he was a beggar now, the recipient of anonymous charity, a butt of the mockery of simple-minded peasants and already too old and tired to feel ashamed of his decline—so startling that it was impossible for me to go back into the main room of the inn. I might not have been able to restrain my tears at the sight of him, or I might have given myself away to him by some other means. I had to regain my composure first. So I went up to my room to think, to recollect clearly what this man had meant to me in my youth. The human heart is strange: for years and years I had not given him a single thought, although he had once dominated all my thoughts and filled my whole soul. I could have died and never asked what had become of him; he could have died and I would not have known.

I did not light a lamp in my room, I sat in the dark, trying to remember both the beginning and the end of it all; and all at once I seemed to be back in that old, lost time. I felt as if my own body, which had borne children many years ago, was a slender, immature girl's body again, and I was the girl who used to sit on her bed with her heart beating fast, thinking of him before she went to sleep. Involuntarily, I felt my hands turn hot, and then something happened that alarmed me, something that I can hardly describe to you. A shudder suddenly ran through me, and at first I did not know why. Something shook me severely. A thought, a certain thought, a certain memory had come back to me; it was one that I had shut out of my mind for years and years. At the very second when the landlady told me his name, I felt something within me lying heavily on my mind, demanding expression, something that I didn't want to remember, something that, as that Professor Freud in Vienna says, I "had suppressed"—had suppressed at such a deep level that I really had forgotten it for years on end, one of those profound secrets that one defiantly keeps even from oneself. I also kept it from you at the time, even after swearing to tell you everything I knew about him. I had hidden it from myself for years. Now it had been roused and was close to the surface of my mind again; and only now that it is for our children, and soon our grandchildren, to commit their own follies, can I confess to you what happened between me and that man at the time.

And now I can tell you my most intimate secret openly. This stranger, this old, broken, down-at-heel actor who would now deliver lines of verse in front of the local rustics for a glass of beer, and was the object of their laughter and contempt—this man, Ellen, held my whole life in his hands for the space of a dangerous minute. If he had taken advantage of that moment—and it was in his power to do so—my children would never have been born, and I do not know where or what I would have been today. The friend who is writing you this letter today would probably have been an unhappy woman, and might have been as crushed and downtrodden by life as he was himself. Please don't think that I exaggerate. At the time, I myself did not understand the danger I was in, but today I see and understand clearly what I did not understand at the time. Only today do I know how deeply indebted I was to that stranger, a man I had forgotten.

I will tell you about it as well as I can. You will remember that at the time, just before your sixteenth birthday, your father was suddenly transferred from Innsbruck, and I can still see you in my mind's eye weeping stormily in my room, sobbing out the news that you would have to leave me—and leave *him*. I don't know which was harder for you. I am inclined to believe that it was the fact that you would lose sight of him, the idol of our youth, without whom life seemed to you not worth living. You made me swear to tell you everything about him, write you a letter every week, no, every day, write a whole diary—and for some time I faithfully did it. It was hard for me to lose you, too, because whom could I confide in now, to whom could I describe the emotional high flights and blissful folly of my exuberant feelings? However, I still had him, I could see him, he was mine and only mine now; and in the midst of my pain there was a little pleasure in that. But soon afterwards—as you may have heard—there was an incident that we knew only in vague outline. It was said that Sturz had made advances to the wife of the manager of the theatre—at least, so I was told later—and after a violent scene he had been forced to accept dismissal. He was allowed one final benefit performance. He was to tread the boards of our theatre once more, and then I too would have seen him for the last time.

Thinking back to it today, I don't believe that any other day in my life was unhappier than the one when it was announced that

Peter Sturz would be on stage in Innsbruck for the last time. I felt
ill. I had no one to share my desperation with, no one to confide
in. At school the teachers noticed how distracted and disturbed I
looked; at home I was so violent and frantic that my father, guessing
nothing, lost his temper and forbade me, on pain of punishment,
to go to the theatre. I pleaded with him—perhaps too hard and too
passionately—and only made matters worse, because my mother
too now spoke against me, saying all that theatre-going had been
a strain on my nerves and I must stay at home. At that moment I
hated my parents—yes, I was so confused and deranged that day
that I hated them and couldn't bear the sight of them. I locked
myself into my room. I wanted to die. One of those sudden fits
of melancholy that can actually endanger young people now
and then overcame me; I sat rigid in my chair, I did not shed any
tears—I was too desperate for that. Sometimes all was cold as ice
inside me, and then I would suddenly feel feverish and go from
room to room. I flung the window up and stared down at the yard
three storeys below, assessing how far I would fall if I jumped out.
And again and again my eyes went to my watch: it was only three
in the afternoon, and the performance began at seven. He was
going to act in our theatre for the last time, and I wouldn't hear
him; everyone else would cheer him to the echo, and I wouldn't be
there. Suddenly I couldn't bear it any more. I ignored my parents'
prohibition on my leaving the house. I went out without a word to
anyone, downstairs and out into the street—I don't know where
I thought I was going. I believe I had some confused notion of
drowning myself or doing something else senseless. I just didn't
want to live any more without him, and I did not know how to put
an end to my life. And so I went up and down the streets, ignoring
friends when they hailed me. I was indifferent to everything, no one
else in the world existed for me, he was the only one. Suddenly, I
don't know how it happened, I was standing outside the building
where he lived. You and I had often waited in the entrance to the

building opposite to see if he might come home, or we looked up at his windows, and perhaps that vague hope of meeting him by chance some time had unconsciously driven me here. But he did not appear. Dozens of unimportant people, the postman, a carpenter, a fat woman from the market, left the building or went into it, hundreds and hundreds of people who didn't matter to me hurried past in the street; but he never put in an appearance.

I don't remember how the next part happened, but suddenly I felt drawn there. I crossed the road, went up the stairs to the second floor without stopping to get my breath back, and then went to the door of his apartment; I just had to be close to him, nearer to him! I had to say something to him, although I didn't know what. I really was in a state of possession by a madness that I couldn't account for to myself, and perhaps I ran up the stairs so fast in order to outrun any kind of circumspect thought. I was already—still without stopping for breath—pressing the doorbell. I can hear its high, shrill note to this day, and then there was a long wait in total silence, broken suddenly by the sound of my awakening heart. At last I heard footsteps inside: the firm, heavy tread I knew from his appearances at the theatre. And at that moment sober reflection returned to me. I wanted to run away from the door again, but everything in me was frozen in alarm. My feet felt paralysed, and my little heart stood still.

He opened the door and looked at me in surprise. I don't know if he knew or recognized me at all. Out in the street there were always dozens of his immature admirers, boys and girls alike, flocking around him. But the two of us who loved him most had been too shy, we had always fled rather than meet his eyes. And this time, too, I stood before him with my head bent, and dared not look up. He waited to hear what I had to say to him—he obviously thought I was an errand girl from one of the shops in town bringing him a message. "Well, my child, what is it?" he finally encouraged me in his deep, sonorous voice.

I stammered, "I only wanted to... but I can't say it here..."
And I stopped again.

He said in a kindly tone, "Well, come in, then, child. What's
it about?"

I followed him into his room. It was a large, simple place, rather
untidy; the pictures had already been taken down from the walls,
cases were standing around half-packed. "There now, tell me...
who sent you here?" he asked again.

And suddenly it came bursting out of me in a torrent of burning tears. "Please stay here... please, please don't go away... stay
here with us."

He instinctively took a step back. His brows shot up, and his
mouth tightened in a sharp line. He had realized that I was another
of those importunate admirers who kept pestering him, and I was
afraid he would say something angry. But there must have been
something about me that made him take pity on my childish
despair. He came up to me and gently patted my arm: "My dear
child,"—he spoke like a teacher addressing a pupil—"it's not my
own doing that I am leaving this place, and it can't be altered now.
It is very nice of you to come and ask me to stay. Who do we actors
perform for if not the young? It has always been a particular joy
to me if young people applaud us. But the die is cast, and I can't
do anything about that. Well, as I said,"—and he stepped back
again—"it was very, very nice of you to come and tell me what
you have, and I thank you. Be a good girl, and I hope you will all
think of me kindly."

I realized that he had said goodbye, but that only increased my
desperation. "No, stay here," I exclaimed, sobbing, "for God's sake,
stay here... I... I can't live without you."

"My dear child," he said soothingly, but I clung to him, clung
to him with both arms—I who had never before had the courage
even to brush against his coat. "No, don't go away," I went on, still
sobbing in despair, "don't leave me alone! Take me with you. I'll

go anywhere you like with you… anywhere… do what you like to me… only don't leave me."

I don't know what other nonsensical stuff I poured out in my despair. I pressed close to him as if I could keep him there like that, with no idea at all of the dangerous situation my passionate outburst was inviting. You know how naive we still were at the time, and what a strange and unknown idea physical love was to us. But I was a young girl and—I can say so today—a strikingly pretty girl; men were already turning in the street to look at me, and he was a man, thirty-seven or thirty-eight years old at the time. He could have done anything he liked to me; I really would have followed him, and whatever he had tried I would have offered no resistance. It would have been easy for him to take advantage of my ignorance there in his apartment. At that moment my fate was in his hands. Who knows what would have become of me if he had improperly abused my childish persistence, if he had given way to his vanity, and perhaps his own desires and the strength of temptation? Only now do I understand what danger I was in. There was a moment at which, I now feel, he was not sure of himself, when he sensed my body pressed to his, and my quivering lips were very close. But he controlled himself and slowly pushed me away. "Just a moment," he said, breaking free of me almost by force, and he turned to the other door. "Frau Kilcher!"

I was horrified. Instinctively, I wanted to run away. Was he going to hold me up to ridicule in front of his old housekeeper? Make fun of me in front of her? Then she came in, and he turned to her. "What do you think, Frau Kilcher," he said to her, "this young lady has come to bring me warm farewell wishes in the name of her whole school. Isn't that touching?" He turned to me again. "Please tell your friends I am very grateful. I have always felt that the beauty of our profession is having youth, and thus the very best thing there is on earth, on our side. Only young people appreciate the finer points of the stage, I assure you, only they. You have given me great pleasure, my dear young lady, and"——here he clasped my hands——"I will never forget it."

My tears dried up. He had not shamed me, he had not humiliated me. But his concern for me went even further, because he turned to his housekeeper again: "Well, if we didn't have so much to do, I would very much have liked to talk to this charming young lady for a little while. However, you will escort her down to the door, Frau Kilcher, won't you? My very good wishes to you, my very good wishes."

Only later did I realize how thoughtful of him it was to spare and protect me by sending the housekeeper down to the door of the building with me. After all, I was well known in the little city of Innsbruck, and some ill-disposed person might have seen me, a young girl, stealing out of the famous actor's apartment all by myself, and could have spread gossip. Although he was a stranger to me, he understood better than I, still a child, what endangered me. He had protected me from my own ignorant youth——how clear that was to me now, more than twenty-five years later.

Isn't it strange, my dear friend, doesn't it put me to shame that I had forgotten all that for years and years, because I was so ashamed that I *wanted* to forget it? That I had never felt truly grateful to this man, never asked after him, when he had held my life, my fate in his hands that afternoon? And now the same man was sitting downstairs over his glass of beer, a wreck of a failure, a beggar, despised by everyone; no one knew who he was and who he had been except for me. I was the only one aware of it. Perhaps I was the only person on earth who still remembered his name, and I was indebted to him. Now I might be able to repay my debt. All at once I felt very calm. I was no longer upset, only a little ashamed of my injustice in forgetting, for so long, that this stranger had once been generous to me at a crucial moment in my life.

I went downstairs and back into the main room of the inn. I suppose that only some ten minutes in all had passed. Nothing had changed. The card game was still going on, the landlady was at the bar, doing her mending, the local rustics were sleepily puffing their pipes. He too was still sitting in his place, with his empty glass in front of him, staring ahead. Only now did I see how much sorrow there was in that wreck of a face, his eyes dull under their heavy lids, his mouth grim and bitter, distorted by the stroke. He sat there gloomily with his elbows on the table so that he could prop his bowed head in his hands, warding off his weariness. It was not the weariness of sleep; he was tired of life. No one spoke to him, no one troubled about him. He sat there like a great grey bird with tattered feathers, crouching in its cage, perhaps dreaming of its former freedom when it could still spread its wings and fly through the air.

The door opened again and three more of the locals came in, with heavy, dragging footsteps, ordered their beer and then looked around for somewhere to sit. "Move up, you," one of them ordered him rather brusquely. Poor Sturz looked up. I could see that the rough contempt with which they treated him hurt his feelings. But he was too tired and humiliated by now to defend himself or dispute the point. He moved aside in silence, pushing his empty beer glass along with him. The landlady brought full tankards for the newcomers. He looked at them, I noticed, with an avid, thirsty glance, but the landlady ignored his silent plea with composure. He had already had his charity for that evening, and if he didn't leave then that was his fault. I saw he no longer had the strength of mind to stand up for himself, and how much more humiliation awaited him in his old age!

At that moment the liberating idea occurred to me at last. I couldn't really help him, I knew that. I couldn't make a broken, worn-out man young again. But perhaps I could give him a little protection against the pain of such contempt, retrieve a little esteem for him in this village at the back of beyond for the few months he had left to live, already marked as he was by the finger of Death.

So I stood up and walked over, making something of a show of it, to the table where he was sitting squeezed between the locals, who looked up in surprise at my arrival, and addressed him. "Do I by any chance have the honour of speaking to Herr Sturz, leading man at the Court Theatre?"

He started in surprise. It was like an electric shock going right through him; even the heavy lid over his left eye opened. He stared at me. Someone had called him by his old name, known to no one here, by the name that all except for him had long ago forgotten, and I had even described him as leading man at the Court Theatre, which in fact he never had been. The surprise was too great for him to summon up the strength to get to his feet. Gradually, his gaze became uncertain; perhaps this was another joke thought up by someone in advance.

"Well, yes... that is... that was my name."

I offered him my hand. "Oh, this is a great pleasure for me... and a really great honour." I was intentionally raising my voice, because I must now tell outright lies to get him some respect in this company. "I must admit that I have never had the good fortune of admiring you on stage myself, but my husband has told me about you again and again. He often saw you at the theatre when he was a schoolboy. I think it was in Innsbruck..."

"Yes, Innsbruck. I was there for two years." His face suddenly began coming to life. He realized that I was not setting out to make fun of him.

"You have no idea, Herr Sturz, how much he has told me, how much I know about you! He will be so envious when I write tomorrow to tell him that I was lucky enough to meet you here in person. You can't imagine how much he still reveres you. No other actor, not even Kainz, could equal you, he has often told me, in the parts of Schiller's Marquis of Posa and Max Piccolomini, or as Grillparzer's Leander; and I believe that later he went to Leipzig just to see you on stage there. But he couldn't pluck up the courage to speak to you. However, he has kept all your photographs from those days, and I wish you could visit our house and see how carefully they are treasured. He would be delighted to hear more about you, and perhaps you can help me by telling me something more about yourself that I can pass on to him... I don't know whether I am disturbing you, or whether I might ask you to join me at my table."

The rustics beside him stared, and instinctively moved respectfully aside. I saw that they were feeling both uneasy and ashamed. They had always treated this old man as a beggar to be given a beer now and then and used as a laughing stock. But observing the respectful manner that I, a total stranger, adopted towards him, they were overcome for the first time by the unsettling suspicion that he was well known and even honoured out in the wider world. The deliberately humble tone that I assumed in requesting the favour of a conversation with him was beginning to take effect. "Off you go, then," the farmer next to him urged.

He stood up, still swaying, as you might stand up on waking from a dream. "By all means... happily," he stammered. I realized that he had difficulty in restraining his delight, and that as a former actor he was now wrestling with himself in an effort not to show the others present how surprised he was, and taking great pains, if awkwardly, to behave as if such requests, accompanied by such admiration, were everyday matters to be taken for granted. With the dignity acquired in the theatre, he strode slowly over to my table.

"A bottle of wine," I ordered, "the best you have in the house, in honour of Herr Sturz of the Court Theatre." Now the card-players also looked up from their game and began to whisper. Their old acquaintance Sturzentaler a famous man who used to act at the Court Theatre? There must be something about him if this strange woman from the big city showed him such respect. And it was in a different manner that the landlady now set a glass down in front of him.

Then he and I passed a wonderful hour. I told him everything I knew about him by pretending that I had heard it from my husband. He could hardly contain his amazement at finding that I could enumerate every one of the parts he had taken at Innsbruck, the name of the theatre critic there, and every word that critic had written about him. And then I quoted the incident when Moissi, the famous actor Moissi, after giving a guest performance, had declined to come out to the front of the stage to receive the applause alone, but had made Sturz join him, addressing him in fraternal fashion. Again and again, he expressed his astonishment as if in a dream. "You know about that, too!" He had thought his memory dead and buried long ago, and now here came a hand knocking on its coffin, taking it out, and conjuring up for him fame of a kind that he never really had. But the heart is always happy to lie to itself, and so he believed in that fame of his in the world at large, and suspected nothing. "You even know that... why, I had forgotten it myself," he kept stammering, and I noticed that he had difficulty in not showing his emotion; two or three times he took a large and rather grubby handkerchief out of his coat pocket and turned away as if to blow his nose, but really to wipe away the tears running down his wrinkled cheeks. I saw that, and my heart shook to see that I could make him happy, I could give this sick old man one more taste of happiness before his death.

So we sat together in a kind of rapture until eleven o'clock. At that point the police officer came deferentially up to the table to point out courteously that by law it was closing time. The old man was visibly startled; was this heaven-sent miracle coming to an end? He would obviously have liked to sit here for hours hearing about himself, dreaming of himself. But I was glad of the official warning, for I kept fearing that he must finally guess the truth of the matter. So I asked the other men, "I hope you gentlemen will be kind enough to see Herr Sturz of the Court Theatre safely home."

"With the greatest pleasure," they all said at the same time; one of them respectfully fetched him his shabby hat, another helped him up, and I knew that from now on they would not make fun of him, laugh at him or hurt the feelings of this poor old man who had once been such a joy to us, such a necessity in our youth.

As we said goodbye, however, the dignity he had maintained at some expense of effort deserted him, emotion overwhelmed him, and he could not preserve his composure. Large tears suddenly streamed from his tired old eyes, and his fingers trembled as he clasped my hand. "Ah, you good, kind, gracious lady," he said, "give your husband my regards, and tell him old Sturz is still alive. Maybe I can return to the theatre some day. Who knows, who knows, I may yet recover my health."

The two men supported him on his right and left, but he was walking almost upright; a new pride had straightened the broken man's back, and I heard a different note in his voice. I had been able to help him at the end of his life, as he had helped me at the beginning of mine. I had paid my debt.

Next morning I made my excuses to the landlady, saying that I could not stay any longer; the mountain air was too strong for me. I tried to leave her money to give the poor old man a second and third glass of beer whenever he wanted it, instead of that single tankard. But here I came up against her own native pride. No, she would do that herself anyway. They hadn't known in the village that Sturzentaler had been such a great man. It was an honour to the village as a whole, the mayor had already decided that he should be paid a monthly allowance, and she herself would vouch for it that they would all take good care of him. So I merely left a letter for him, a letter of effusive thanks for his kindness in devoting an evening to me. I knew he would read it a thousand times before his death, and show the letter to everyone; he would blissfully dream the false dream of his own fame again and again before his end.

My husband was greatly surprised to see me back from my holiday so soon, and even more surprised to find how happy and reinvigorated those two days away had left me. He described it as a miracle cure. But I see nothing miraculous about it. Nothing makes one as healthy as happiness, and there is no greater happiness than making someone else happy.

There—and now I have also paid my debt to you from the days when we were girls. Now you know all about Peter Sturz, our idol, and you know the last, long-kept secret of

Your old friend

Margaret.

MOONBEAM
ALLEY

T HE SHIP, delayed by a storm, could not land at the small French seaport until late in the evening, and I missed the night train to Germany. So I had an unexpected day to spend in this foreign town, and an evening which offered nothing more alluring than the melancholy music of a ladies' ensemble in a suburban nightclub, or a tedious conversation with my chance-met travelling companions. The air in the small hotel dining-room seemed to me intolerable, greasy with oil, stifling with smoke, and I suffered doubly from its murky impurity because I still tasted the pure breath of the sea on my lips, cool and salty. So I went out and walked down the broad, brightly lit street, going nowhere in particular, until I reached a square where an outdoor band was playing. I went on amidst the casually flowing tide of people who were out for a stroll. At first it did me good to be carried passively away by this current of provincially dressed persons who meant nothing to me, but soon I could no longer tolerate the company of strangers surging up close to me with their disconnected laughter, their eyes resting on me in surprise, with odd looks or a grin, the touches that imperceptibly urged me on, the light coming from a thousand small sources, the constant sound of footsteps. The sea voyage had been turbulent, and I still felt a reeling, slightly intoxicated sensation in my blood, a rocking and gliding beneath my feet, the earth seemed to move as if it were breathing and the street to rise to the sky. All this loud confusion suddenly made me dizzy, and to save myself I turned into a side street without looking at its name, and then into a yet smaller street, where the senseless noise gradually ebbed away. I walked aimlessly on through the tangle of alleys branching off each other

315

like veins, and becoming darker and darker the further I went from the main square. The large electrical arc lamps that lit the broad avenues like moons did not shine here, and the stars at last began coming into view again above the few street lamps, in a black and partly overcast sky.

I must have reached the sailors' quarter near the harbour. I could tell from the smell of rotting fish, from the sweetish aroma of seaweed and decay that bladderwrack gives off when the breakers wash it ashore, from the typical fumes of pollution and unaired rooms that linger dankly in these nooks and crannies until a great storm rises, bringing in fresh air. The nebulous darkness and unexpected solitude did me good. I slowed my pace, glancing down alley after alley now, each different from its neighbour, here a quiet alley, there an inviting one, but all dark, with the muted sound of music and voices rising so mysteriously from invisible vaults that one could scarcely guess at its underground sources. For the doors to all the cellars were closed, with only the light of a red or yellow lamp showing.

I liked such alleyways in foreign towns, places that are a disreputable marketplace for all the passions, a secret accumulation of temptations for the sailors who, after many lonely days on strange and dangerous seas, come here for just one night to fulfil all their many sensuous dreams within an hour. These little side-streets have to lurk somewhere in the poorer part of any big city, lying low, because they say so boldly and importunately things that are hidden beneath a hundred disguises in the brightly lit buildings with their shining window panes and distinguished denizens. Enticing music wafts from small rooms here, garish cinematograph posters promise unimaginable splendours, small, square lanterns hang under gateways, winking in very clear invitation, issuing an intimate greeting, and naked flesh glimpsed through a door left ajar shimmers under gilded fripperies. Drunks shout in the bars, gamblers argue in loud voices. The sailors grin when they meet each other here, their dull eyes glinting in anticipation, for they can find everything in such places, women and gaming, drink and a show to watch, adventures both grubby and great. But all this is hidden in modestly muted yet tell-tale fashion behind shutters lowered for the look of the thing, it all goes on behind closed doors, and that apparent seclusion is intriguing, is twice as seductive because it is both hidden and accessible. Such streets are the same in Hamburg and Colombo and Havana, similar in all seaports, just as the wide and luxurious avenues resemble each other, for the upper side and underside of life share the same form. These shady streets are the last fantastic remnants of a sensually unregulated world where instinct still has free rein, brutal and unbridled; they are a dark wood of passions, a thicket full of the animal kingdom, exciting visitors with what they reveal and enticing them with what they hide. One can weave them into dreams.

And the alley where I suddenly felt myself a captive was such a street. I had been idly following a couple of cuirassiers whose swords, dragging along after them, clinked on the uneven road surface. Women called to them from a bar, they laughed and shouted coarse jests back at the girls, one of the soldiers knocked at the window, then a voice somewhere swore at them and they went on. Their laughter faded in the distance, and soon they were out of my hearing. The alley was silent again; a couple of windows shone faintly, mistily reflecting the pale moon. I stood drinking in that silence, which struck me as a strange one because something behind it seemed to be murmuring words of mystery, lust and danger. I clearly felt that the silence was deceptive, and something of the world's decay shimmered in the murky haze. But I went on standing there, listening to the empty air. I was no longer aware of the town and the alley, of their names or my own, I just sensed that I was a stranger here, miraculously detached in the unknown, with no purpose in mind, no message to deliver, no links with anything, and yet I sensed all the dark life around me as fully as I felt the blood flowing beneath my own skin. I had only the impression that nothing here was for me and yet it all was all mine: it was the delightful sensation of an experience made deepest and most genuine because one is not personally involved. That sensation is one of the wellsprings of my inmost being, and in an unknown situation it always comes over me like desire. Then suddenly, as I stood listening in the lonely alley as if waiting for something that was bound to happen, something to urge me on, out of this somnambulistic sensation of listening to the void, I heard, muted by either distance or a wall between us, the very faint sound of a song in German coming from somewhere. It was that simple air from *Der Freischütz*, 'Fairest, greenest bridal wreath'. A woman's voice was singing it, very badly, but it was still a German tune, something German here in a foreign part of the world, and so it affected me in a way all its own. It was being sung some way off, but I felt it like a greeting, the first word I had heard in my native tongue for weeks. Who, I asked myself, speaks my language here, whose memory impels her to lift her voice from the heart in singing this poor little song here in this remote, disreputable alley? I followed the voice, going from house to house. They all stood half asleep, their shutters closed, but light shining behind the shutters gave their nature away, and sometimes a hand waved. Outside there were garish signs, screaming posters, and the words "Ale, Whisky, Beer" promised a hidden bar, but it all appeared sealed and uninviting, yet enticing at the same time. Now and then—and I heard a few footsteps in the distance—now and then the voice came again, singing the refrain more clearly this time, sounding closer and closer. I identified the house. For a moment I hesitated, and then pushed my foot against the inner door, which was heavily draped with white net curtains. However, as I stooped to go in, having made up my mind, something came to life in the shadow of the entrance and gave a start of alarm, a figure that had obviously been waiting there, its face pressed close to the pane. The lantern over the door cast red light on that face, yet it was pale with fright—a man was staring at me, wide-eyed. He muttered something like an apology and disappeared down the dimly lit alley. It was a strange greeting. I looked the way he had gone. Something still seemed to be moving in the vanishing shadows of the alley, but indistinctly. Inside the building the voice was still singing, and seemed to me even clearer now. That lured me on. I turned the door-handle and quickly stepped inside.

The last word of the song stopped short, as if cut off by a knife. And in some alarm I felt a void before me, a sense of silent hostility as if I had broken something. Only slowly did my eyes adjust to the room, which was almost empty: it contained a bar counter and a table, and the whole place was obviously just a means of access to other rooms behind it, whose real purpose was immediately made obvious by their opened doors, muted lamplight, and beds made up and ready. A girl sat at the table, leaning her elbows on it, her tired face made up, and behind her at the bar was the landlady, stout and dingy grey, with another girl who was not bad-looking. My greeting sounded harsh in the space, and a bored response came back with some delay. Finding that I had stepped into such a void, so tense and bleak a silence, I was ill at ease and would rather have left at once, but in my embarrassment I could think of no excuse, so I resigned myself to sitting down at the table in front of the bar. The girl, remembering her duties, asked what I would like to drink, and I recognised her as German at once from the harsh accent of her French. I ordered beer, she went out and came back again with the lethargic bearing that betrayed even more indifference than the empty look in her eyes, which glowed faintly under their lids like lights going out. Automatically, and in accordance with the custom of such places, she put a second glass down next to mine for herself. As she raised her glass she did not turn her blank gaze on me, so I was able to observe her. Her face was in fact still beautiful, with regular features, but inner weariness seemed to make it coarse, like a mask; everything about her drooped, her eyelids were heavy, her hair hung loose, her cheeks, badly made up and smudged, were already beginning to fall in, and broad lines ran down to her mouth. Her dress too was carelessly draped, her voice hoarse, roughened by smoke and beer. All things considered, I felt that this was an exhausted woman who went on living only out of habit and without feelings, so to speak. Self-consciously and with a sense of dread I asked a question. She replied with dull indifference, scarcely moving her lips, and without looking at me. I felt I was unwelcome. At the back of the room the landlady was yawning, and the other girl was sitting in a corner glancing in my direction, as if waiting for me to summon her. I would have liked to leave, but everything about me felt heavy, and I sat in that sated, smouldering air, swaying slightly as the sailors do, kept there by both distaste and curiosity, for this indifference was, in a way, intriguing.

Then I suddenly gave a start, alarmed by raucous laughter near me. At the same time the flame of the light wavered, and the draught told me that someone must have opened the door behind my back. "Oh, so here you are again, are you?" said the voice beside me shrilly, in German. "Slinking round the house again, you skinflint? Well, come along in, I won't hurt you."

I spun round, to look first at her as she uttered this greeting, in tones as piercing as if her body had suddenly caught fire, then at the door. Even before it was fully open I recognised the trembling figure and humble glance of the man who had been almost glued to the outside of the pane just now. Intimidated, he held his hat in his hand like a beggar, trembling at the sound of the raucous greeting and the laughter which suddenly seemed to shake her apathetic figure convulsively, and which was accompanied by the landlady's rapid whispering from the bar counter at the back of the room.

"Sit down there with Françoise, then," the woman beside me ordered the poor man as he came closer with a craven, shuffling step. "You can see I have a gentleman here."

She said this to him in German. The landlady and the other girl laughed out loud, although they couldn't understand her, but they seemed to know the new guest.

"Give him champagne, Françoise, the expensive brand, give him a bottle of it!" she called out, laughing, and turning to him again added with derision, "And if it's too expensive for you then you can stay outside, you miserable miser. I suppose you'd like to stare at me for free—you want everything for free, don't you?"

The tall figure seemed almost to collapse at the sound of this vicious laughter; he hunched his back as if his face were trying to creep away and hide like a dog, and his hand shook as he reached for the bottle and spilled some of the wine in pouring it. He was still trying to look up at her face, but he could not lift his gaze from the floor, where it wandered over the tiles. And only now, in the lamplight, did I clearly see that emaciated face, worn and pale, his hair damp and thin on his bony skull, his joints loose and looking as if they were broken, a pitiful creature without any strength, yet not devoid of malice. Everything about him was crooked, awry, cringing, and now, when he raised his eyes, though he immediately lowered them again in alarm, they had a gleam of ill will in them.

"Don't trouble yourself about him!" the girl told me in French, roughly taking my arm as if to turn me round. "This is old business between the two of us, it's nothing new." And again, baring her teeth as if ready to bite, she called out to him, "Listen to me, you old lynx! You just hear what I say. I said I'd rather jump into the sea than go with you, didn't I?"

Once again the landlady and the other girl laughed, loud and foolish laughter. It seemed to be a familiar joke to them, a daily jest. But I found it unpleasant to see that other girl, Françoise, suddenly press close to him with pretended affection, wheedling him with flattery from which he shrank, though he didn't have the courage to shake her off, and I was alarmed when his wandering gaze, awkward, anxious, abject, rested on me. And I felt dread of the woman beside me, who had suddenly been roused from her apathy and was full of such burning malice that her hands trembled. I threw some money on the table and was going to leave, but she wouldn't take it.

"If he annoys you I'll throw him out, the bastard. He must do as he's told. Come along, drink another glass with me!"

She pressed close to me with a wild, abrupt kind of tenderness which I knew at once was only pretended, to torment the other man. At every movement she quickly looked askance across the table, and it was dreadful to me to see how he began to wince whenever she paid me some little attention, as if he felt hot steel branding his flesh. Without paying any attention to her, I stared only at him, and shuddered to see something in the nature of anger, rage, envy and greed arising in him, yet he cringed again if she so much as turned her head. She now pressed very close to me, her body trembling with her vicious pleasure in this game, and I felt horror at her garishly painted face with its smell of cheap powder, at the fumes emanating from her slack flesh. I reached for a cigar to keep her away from my face, and while my eyes were searching the table for a match she ordered him, "Bring us a light!"

I was more horrified than he was at such an imposition, making him serve me, and quickly set about looking for a light myself. But he snapped to attention at her words as if at the crack of a whip, came over to us, reeling, with unsteady footsteps, and put his own lighter on the table quickly, as if he might burn up if he touched the tabletop. For a second I met his eyes: there was boundless shame in them, and crushing embitterment. That servile glance of his struck a chord in me as another man, a brother. I felt the force of his humiliation at the woman's hands and was ashamed for him.

"Thank you very much," I said in German—she started at that—"but you shouldn't have troubled." Then I offered him my hand. A hesitation, a long one, then I felt damp, bony fingers, and suddenly, convulsively, an abrupt pressure in thanks. For a second his eyes shone as they looked at mine, and then they were hidden again by those slack eyelids. In defiance of the woman, I was going to ask him to sit down with us, and I must already have begun to trace the gesture of invitation, for she quickly ordered him, "You sit down again and don't disturb us here."

All at once I was overcome by disgust at the sound of her caustic voice and this scene of torture. What did I care for this smoky bar, this unpleasant whore and the feeble man, these fumes of beer, smoke and cheap perfume? I craved fresh air. I pushed the money over to her, stood up and moved away with decision as she came flatteringly closer to me. It revolted me to help her humiliate another human being, and the determined manner of my withdrawal clearly showed how little she attracted me sensually. Her blood was up now, a line appeared around her mouth, but whatever word sprang to her lips she took care not to utter it, just turning on him and flouncing with undisguised hatred. But he was expecting the worst, and at this threatening movement he rapidly, with a hunted look, put his hand in his pocket and brought out a purse. It was obvious that he was afraid of being left alone with her now, and in his haste he had trouble untying the purse-strings—it was the kind of knitted purse adorned with glass beads that peasants and the lower classes carry. Anyone could see that he wasn't used to throwing his money about, unlike the sailors who produce the coins clinking in their pockets with a sweeping gesture and fling them down on the table; he was clearly in the habit of counting money carefully and weighing the coins up in his fingers. "How he trembles for his dear, sweet *pfennigs*! Are we going too slowly for you? Wait!" she mocked, and came a step closer. He shrank back, and seeing his alarm she said, shrugging her shoulders and with unspeakable revulsion in her eyes, "Oh, I won't take anything from you, I spit on your money. I know you've counted all your dear, nice little *pfennigs*. No one in the world must have too much money. And then of course," she added, suddenly tapping his chest, "there's the banknotes you've sewn in there so that no one will steal them!"

Sure enough, like a man with a weak heart suddenly clutching at his breast, he reached with a pale and trembling hand for a certain place on his coat, his fingers instinctively felt for the secret hiding-place and came away again, reassured. "Miser!" she spat. But then, suddenly, a flush rose to her victim's face; he threw the purse abruptly at the other girl, who first cried out in alarm, then laughed aloud, and he stormed past her and out of the door as if escaping from a fire.

For a moment she still stood there, eyes flashing with fury. Then her eyelids fell apathetically again, weariness relaxed her body from its tension. She seemed to grow old and tired within a moment. Something uncertain and lost blurred the gaze now resting on me. She stood there like a drunk waking up, feeling numb and empty with shame. "He'll be weeping and wailing for his money outside. Maybe he'll go to the police and say we stole it. And he'll be back tomorrow, but he won't have me all the same. Anyone else can, but not him!"

She went to the bar, threw coins down on it and swallowed a glass of brandy in a single draught. The vicious light was back in her eyes, but blurred as if by tears of rage and shame. I felt nauseated by her, and that destroyed pity. "Good evening," I said, and left. "*Bonsoir*," replied the landlady. She did not look round but just laughed, shrill and scornful laughter.

When I stepped outside there was nothing in the alley but night and the sky, a sultry darkness with the moonlight veiled and endlessly far away. I greedily took great breaths of the warm yet reviving air, my sense of dread turned to amazement at the diversity of human fate, and I felt again—it is a feeling that can make me happy to the point of tears—how fate is always waiting behind every window, every door opens on new experience, the wide variety of this world is omnipresent, and even its dirtiest corners swarm with predestined events as if with the iridescent gleam of beetles decomposing. Gone was the distasteful part of the encounter, and my tension was pleasantly resolved, turning to a sweet weariness that longed to turn all I had just seen and heard into a more attractive dream. Instinctively I looked around me, trying to work out my way back through this tangle of winding alleys. Then a shadow—he must have come close without making any noise—approached me.

"Forgive me,"—and I immediately recognised that humble tone of voice—"but I don't think you know your way around here. May I—may I show you which way to go? You are staying, sir, at…?"

I told him the name of my hotel.

"I'll go with you… if you'll permit me," he immediately added humbly.

Dread came over me again. This stealthy, spectral step, almost soundless yet close beside me, the darkness of the sailors' alley and the memory of what I had just witnessed all gradually turned to a dreamlike confusion of the emotions, leaving me devoid of judgement and unable to say no. I felt without seeing the subservience in his eyes, and noticed how his lips trembled; I knew that he wanted to talk to me, but in my daze, where the curiosity of my heart mingled uncertainly with physical numbness, I did nothing to encourage or discourage him. He cleared his throat several times, I noticed that he was trying and failing to speak, but some kind of cruelty which had, mysteriously, passed from the woman in the bar to me enjoyed watching him wrestle with shame and mental torment, and I did not help him, but let the silence lie black and heavy between us. And our steps, his quietly shuffling like an old man's, mine deliberately firm and decided, as if to escape this dirty world, sounded odd together. I felt the tension between us more strongly all the time; it was a shrill silence now, full of unheard cries, and it already resembled a violin string stretched too taut by the time he at last—and at first with dreadful hesitation—managed to bring out his words.

"You saw... you saw... sir, you saw a strange scene in there. Forgive me... forgive me if I mention it again... but it must seem strange to you... and I must look very ridiculous. That woman, you see..."

He stopped again. Something was constricting his throat. Then his voice sank very low, and he whispered rapidly, "That woman... she's my wife." I must have given a start of surprise, for he quickly went on as if to apologise. "That's to say, she was my wife... four or five years ago, it was in Geratzheim back in Hesse where I come from... sir, I wouldn't like you to think ill of her... perhaps it's my fault she's like that. She wasn't always... I... I tormented her. I took her although she was very poor, she didn't even have any household linen, nothing, nothing at all... and I'm rich, or that's to say well off... not rich... at least, I was then... and you see, sir, perhaps—she's right there—perhaps I was tight-fisted with money... but then I always was, sir, before this misfortune... and my father and mother before me, we all were... and I worked hard for every *pfennig*... and she was light-minded, she liked pretty things... but she was poor, and I was always reproaching her for it... I shouldn't have done it, I know that now, sir, for she is proud, very proud. You mustn't think she's really the way she makes out... that's a lie, and she does herself violence only... only to hurt me, to torment me... and... and because she's ashamed. Perhaps she's gone to the bad, but I... I don't think so, because, sir, she was very good, very good..."

He wiped his eyes in great agitation and stood still. Instinctively, I looked at him, and he suddenly no longer struck me as ridiculous. I found that I could even ignore his curiously servile manner of speech, the way he kept calling me "sir", as only the lower classes do in Germany. His face was greatly exercised by his internal struggle to put his story into words, and his eyes were fixed as he began walking unsteadily forward again, on the roadway itself, as if there, in the flickering light, he were laboriously reading the tale that so painfully tore its way out of his constricted throat.

"Yes, sir," he uttered now, breathing deeply, and in quite a different voice, a deep voice that seemed to come from a gentler world within him, "yes, she was very good... to me too, she was very grateful to me for saving her from poverty... and I knew that she was grateful, too, but... but I wanted to hear her say so... again and again, again and again... it did me good to hear her thank me... sir, it was so good, so very good, to feel... to feel that you are a better human being, when... when you know all the same that you're not... I'd have given all my money to hear it again and again... and she was very proud, so when she realised that I was insisting she must be grateful, she wanted to say so less and less. That's why... that, sir, is the only reason why I always made her ask... I never gave anything of my own free will... I felt good, making her come to beg for every dress, every ribbon... I tormented her like that for three years, I tormented her more and more... but it was only because I loved her, sir... I liked her pride, yet I still wanted to make her bow to me, madman that I was, and when she wanted something I was angry... but I wasn't really, sir... I was glad of any chance to humiliate her, for... for I didn't know how much I loved her..."

He stopped again. He was staggering as he walked now, and had obviously forgotten me. He spoke mechanically, as if in his sleep, in a louder and louder voice.

"And I didn't know... I didn't know it until that dreadful day when... when I'd refused to give her money for her mother, only a very little money... that is, I had it ready for her, but I wanted her to come and ask me once again... oh, what am I saying?... yes, I knew then, when I came home in the evening and she was gone, leaving just a note on the table... 'Keep your damned money, I want no more to do with you,' it said... nothing more... sir, I was like a lunatic for three days and three nights. I had the river searched and the woods, I gave the police large sums of money, I went to all the neighbours, but they just laughed and mocked me… there was no trace of her, nothing. At last a man came with news from the next village… he said he'd seen her… in the train with a soldier, she'd gone to Berlin. I followed her that very day… I neglected my business, I lost thousands… they stole from me, my servants, my manager, all of them… but I swear to you, sir, it was all the same to me… I stayed in Berlin, I stayed there a week until I found her among all those people… and went to her…" He was breathing heavily.

"Sir, I swear to you… I didn't say a harsh word to her… I wept, I went on my knees… I offered her money, all my fortune, said she should control it, because then I knew… I knew I couldn't live without her. I love every hair on her head… her mouth… her body, everything, everything… and I was the one who thrust her out, I alone… She was pale as death when I suddenly came in… I'd bribed the woman she was staying with… a procuress, a bad, vicious woman… she looked white as chalk standing there by the wall… she heard me out. Sir, I believe she was… yes, I think she was almost glad to see me, but when I mentioned the money… and I did so, I promise you, only to show her that I wasn't thinking of it any more… then she spat… and then… because I still wouldn't go… then she called her lover, and they both laughed at me… But, sir, I went back again day after day. The people of the house told me everything, I knew that the rascal had left her and she was in dire need, so I went once again… once again, sir, but she flew at me and tore up a banknote that I'd secretly left on the table, and when I next came back she was gone… What didn't I do, sir, to find her again? For a year, I swear to you, I didn't live, I just kept looking for her, I paid detective agencies until at last I found out that she was in Argentina… in… in a house of ill repute…" He hesitated a moment. The last words were spoken like a death rattle. And his voice grew deeper yet.

"I was horrified… at first… but then I remembered that it was I, no one else, who had sent her there… and I thought how she must be suffering, the poor creature… for more than anything else she's proud… I went to my lawyer, who wrote to the consul and sent money… not telling her who it came from… just so that she would come back. I received a telegram to say it had all succeeded… I knew what the ship was, and I waited to meet it in Amsterdam… I was there three days early, burning with impatience… at last it came in, I was so happy just to see the smoke of the steamer on the horizon, and I thought I couldn't wait for it to come in and tie up, so slowly, so slowly, and then the passengers came down the gangplank and at last, at last she was there… I didn't know her at first… she was different, her face painted… and as… as you saw her… and when she saw me waiting… she went pale. Two sailors had to hold her up or she'd have fallen off the gangplank. As soon as she was on shore I came up to her… I said nothing, my throat was too dry… She said nothing either, and didn't look at me… The porter carried her bags, we walked and walked… Then, suddenly, she stopped and said… oh, sir, how she said it… 'Do you still want me for your wife, even now?' I took her hand… she was trembling, but she said nothing. Yet I felt that everything was all right again… sir, how happy I was! I danced around her like a child when I had her in the room, I fell at her feet… I must have said foolish things… for she laughed through her tears and caressed me… very hesitantly, of course… but sir… it did me so much good. My heart was overflowing. I ran upstairs, downstairs, ordered a dinner in the hotel… our wedding feast… I helped her to dress… and we went down, we ate and drank and made merry… oh, she was so cheerful, like a child, so warm and good-hearted, and she talked of home… and how we would see to everything again… And then…" His voice suddenly roughened, and he made a movement with his hand as if to knock someone down. "There… there was a waiter… a bad, dishonest man… who thought I was drunk because I was raving and dancing and laughing madly… although it was just that I was happy, oh, so happy. And then, when

I paid him, he gave me back my change twenty francs short... I shouted at him and demanded the rest... he was embarrassed, and brought out the money... And then she began laughing aloud again. I stared at her, but her face was different... mocking, hard, hostile all at once. 'How pernickety you still are... even on our wedding day!' she said very coldly, so sharply, with such... such pity. I was horrified, and cursed myself for being so punctilious... I went to great pains to laugh again, but her merriment was gone, had died. She demanded a room of her own... what wouldn't I have given her?... and I lay alone all night, thinking of nothing but what I could buy her next morning... what I could give her... how to show her that I'm not miserly... would never be miserly with her again. And in the morning I went out, I bought a bracelet, very early, and when I went into her room... it... it was empty, just the same as before. And I knew there'd be a note on the table... I went away and prayed to God it wasn't true... but... but it was there... And it said..." Here he hesitated. Instinctively, I had stopped and was looking at him. He bent his head. Then he whispered, hoarsely:

"It said... 'Leave me alone. I find you repulsive.'"

We had reached the harbour, and suddenly the roar of the nearby breakers broke the silence. There lay the ships at anchor, near and far, lights winking like the eyes of large black animals, and from somewhere came the sound of singing. Nothing was distinct, yet there was so much to feel, an immensity of sleep, with the seaport dreaming deeply.

I sensed the man's shadow beside me, a flickering, spectral shape at my feet, now disintegrating, now coming together again as the light of the dim street lamps changed. I could say nothing, I could give no comfort and had no questions, but I felt his silence clinging to me, heavy and oppressive. Then, suddenly, he clutched my arm. He was trembling.

"But I won't leave this place without her... I've found her again, after months... She torments me, but I won't give up... I beg you, sir, talk to her... I must have her, tell her that, she won't listen to me... I can't go on living like this... I can't watch the men going in to her... and wait outside the house until they come down again, drunk and laughing... The whole alley knows me now, they laugh when they see me waiting... it drives me mad... and yet I go back again every evening. Sir, I beg you, speak to her... I don't know you, but do it for God's merciful sake... speak to her..."

Instinctively, and with horror, I tried to free my arm. But as he felt my resistance to his unhappiness, he suddenly fell on his knees in the middle of the road and embraced my feet.

"I beg you, sir... you must speak to her... you must, or... or something terrible will happen. I've spent all I have looking for her, and I won't... I won't leave her here alive. I've bought a knife... I have a knife, sir... I won't leave her here alive, I can't bear it... Speak to her, sir..."

He was rolling about on the ground in front of me like a madman. At that moment two police officers came down the street. I violently wrenched him up and to his feet. He stared at me for a moment, astonished. Then he said in a dry and very different voice, "Turn down that side-street, and you'll see your hotel." Once more he stared at me with eyes whose pupils seemed to have merged into something terribly white and empty. Then he walked away.

I wrapped my coat around me. I was shivering. I felt nothing but exhaustion, I was in a confused daze, black and devoid of any emotion, a darkly moving slumber. I wanted to think all this over, but that black wave of weariness kept rising inside me, carrying me away. I staggered into the hotel, fell into bed, and slept as soundly as a brute beast.

Next morning I didn't know how much of it all had been a dream and how much was real, and something in me didn't want to know. I had woken late, a stranger in a strange town, and I went to look at a church where there were said to be some very famous mosaics dating from the days of classical antiquity. But I stared blankly at them. Last night's encounter rose more and more clearly before my mind's eye, and I felt an irresistible urge to go in search of that alley and that house. But those strange alleys come to life only at night; by day they wear cold, grey disguises, and only those who know them well can recognise them. However hard I looked, I couldn't find the alley. I came back tired and disappointed, pursued by images of something that was either memory or delusion.

The time of my train was nine in the evening. I left the town with regret. A porter fetched my bags and carried them to the station for me. On our way, I suddenly turned at a crossing; I recognised the alley leading to the house, told the porter to wait, and—while he smiled first in surprise, then knowingly—went to look at the scene of my adventure once more.

There it lay in the dark, as dark as yesterday, and in the faint moonlight I saw the glass pane in the house door gleaming. Once again I was going closer when, with a rustling sound, a figure emerged from the darkness. With a shudder, I saw him waiting there in the doorway and beckoning me to approach. Dread took hold of me—I fled quickly, in cowardly fear of getting involved here and missing my train.

But then, just before I turned the corner of the alley, I looked back once again. When my gaze fell on him he pulled himself together and strode to the door. He quickly opened his hand, and I saw the glint of metal in it. From a distance, I couldn't tell whether the moonlight showed money or a knife gleaming there in his fingers...

LETTER FROM AN UNKNOWN WOMAN

W HEN R., *the famous novelist, returned to Vienna early in the morning, after a refreshing three-day excursion into the mountains, and bought a newspaper at the railway station, he was reminded as soon as his eye fell on the date that this was his birthday. His forty-first birthday, as he quickly reflected, an observation that neither pleased nor displeased him. He swiftly leafed through the crisp pages of the paper, and hailed a taxi to take him home to his apartment. His manservant told him that while he was away there had been two visitors as well as several telephone calls, and brought him the accumulated post on a tray. R. looked casually through it, opening a couple of envelopes because the names of their senders interested him; for the moment he set aside one letter, apparently of some length and addressed to him in writing that he did not recognize. Meanwhile the servant had brought him tea; he leant back in an armchair at his ease, skimmed the newspaper again, leafed through several other items of printed matter, then lit himself a cigar, and only now picked up the letter that he had put to one side.*

It consisted of about two dozen sheets, more of a manuscript than a letter and written hastily in an agitated, feminine hand that he did not know. He instinctively checked the envelope again in case he had missed an explanatory enclosure. But the envelope was empty, and like the letter itself bore no address or signature identifying the sender. Strange, he thought, and picked up the letter once more. It began, "To you, who never knew me," which was both a salutation and a challenge. He stopped for a moment in surprise: was this letter really addressed to him or to some imaginary person? Suddenly his curiosity was aroused. And he began to read:

My child died yesterday—for three days and three nights I wrestled with death for that tender little life, I sat for forty hours at his bedside while the influenza racked his poor, hot body with fever. I put cool compresses on his forehead, I held his restless little hands day and night. On the third evening I collapsed. My eyes would not stay open any longer; I was unaware of it when they closed. I slept, sitting on my hard chair, for three or four hours, and in that time death took him. Now the poor sweet boy lies there in his narrow child's bed, just as he died; only his eyes have been closed, his clever, dark eyes, and his hands are folded over his white shirt, while four candles burn at the four corners of his bed. I dare not look, I dare not stir from my chair, for when the candles flicker shadows flit over his face and his closed mouth, and then it seems as if his features were moving, so that I might think he was not dead after all, and will wake up and say something loving and childish to me in his clear voice. But I know that he is dead, I will arm myself against hope and further disappointment, I will not look at him again. I know it is true, I know my child died yesterday—so now all I have in the world is you, you who know nothing about me, you who are now amusing yourself without a care in the world, dallying with things and with people. I have only you, who never knew me, and whom I have always loved.

I have taken the fifth candle over to the table where I am writing to you now. For I cannot be alone with my dead child without weeping my heart out, and to whom am I to speak in this terrible hour if not to you, who were and are everything to me? Perhaps I shall not be able to speak to you entirely clearly, perhaps you will not understand me—my mind is dulled, my temples throb and hammer, my limbs hurt so much. I think I am feverish myself, perhaps I too have the influenza that is spreading fast in this part of town, and I would be glad of it, because then I could go with my child without having to do myself any violence. Sometimes everything turns dark before my eyes; perhaps I shall not even be able to finish writing this letter—but I am summoning up all my strength to speak to you once, just this one time, my beloved who never knew me.

I speak only to you; for the first time I will tell you everything, the whole story of my life, a life that has always been yours although you never knew it. But you shall know my secret only once I am dead, when you no longer have to answer me, when whatever is now sending hot and cold shudders through me really is the end. If I have to live on, I shall tear this letter up and go on preserving my silence as I have always preserved it. However, if you are holding it in your hands, you will know that in these pages a dead woman is telling you the story of her life, a life that was yours from her first to her last waking hour. Do not be afraid of my words; a dead woman wants nothing any more, neither love nor pity nor comfort. I want only one thing from you: I want you to believe everything that my pain tells you here, seeking refuge with you. Believe it all, that is the only thing I ask you: no one lies in the hour of an only child's death.

I will tell you the whole story of my life, and it is a life that truly began only on the day I met you. Before that, there was nothing but murky confusion into which my memory never dipped again, some kind of cellar full of dusty, cobwebbed, sombre objects and people. My heart knows nothing about them now. When you arrived I was thirteen years old, living in the apartment building where you live now, the same building in which you are holding my letter, my last living breath, in your hands. I lived in the same corridor, right opposite the door of your apartment. I am sure you will not remember us any more, an accountant's impoverished widow (my mother always wore mourning) and her thin teenage daughter; we had quietly become imbued, so to speak, with our life of needy respectability. Perhaps you never even heard our name, because we had no nameplate on the front door of our apartment, and no one came to visit us or asked after us. And it is all so long ago, fifteen or sixteen years; no, I am sure you don't remember anything about it, my beloved, but I—oh, I recollect every detail with passion. As if it were today, I remember the very day, no, the very hour when

I first heard your voice and set eyes on you for the first time, and how could I not? It was only then that the world began for me. Allow me, beloved, to tell you the whole story from the beginning. I beg you, do not tire of listening to me for a quarter of an hour, when I have never tired of loving you all my life.

Before you moved into our building a family of ugly, mean-minded, quarrelsome people lived behind the door of your apartment. Poor as they were, what they hated most was the poverty next door, ours, because we wanted nothing to do with their down-at-heel, vulgar, uncouth manners. The man was a drunk and beat his wife; we were often woken in the night by the noise of chairs falling over and plates breaking; and once the wife, bruised and bleeding, her hair all tangled, ran out onto the stairs with the drunk shouting abuse after her until the neighbours came out of their own doors and threatened him with the police. My mother avoided any contact with that couple from the first, and forbade me to speak to their children, who seized every opportunity of avenging themselves on me. When they met me in the street they called me dirty names, and once threw such hard snowballs at me that I was left with blood running from my forehead. By some common instinct, the whole building hated that family, and when something suddenly happened to them—I think the husband was jailed for theft—and they had to move out, bag and baggage, we all breathed a sigh of relief. A few days later the "To Let" notice was up at the entrance of the building, and then it was taken down; the caretaker let it be known—and word quickly went around—that a single, quiet gentleman, a writer, had taken the apartment. That was when I first heard your name.

In a few days' time painters and decorators, wallpaper-hangers and cleaners came to remove all trace of the apartment's previous grubby owners; there was much knocking and hammering, scraping and scrubbing, but my mother was glad of it. At last, she said, there would be an end to the sloppy housekeeping in that apartment. I still had not come face to face with you by the time you moved in; all this work was supervised by your manservant, that small, serious, grey-haired gentleman's gentleman, who directed operations in his quiet, objective, superior way. He impressed us all very much, first because a gentleman's gentleman was something entirely new in our suburban apartment building, and then because he was so extremely civil to everyone, but without placing himself on a par with the other servants and engaging them in conversation as one of themselves. From the very first day he addressed my mother with the respect due to a lady, and he was always gravely friendly even to me, little brat that I was. When he mentioned your name he did so with a kind of special esteem—anyone could tell at once that he thought far more of you than a servant usually does of his master. And I liked him so much for that, good old Johann, although I envied him for always being with you to serve you.

I am telling you all this, beloved, all these small and rather ridiculous things, so that you will understand how you could have such power, from the first, over the shy, diffident child I was at the time. Even before you yourself came into my life, there was an aura around you redolent of riches, of something out of the ordinary, of mystery—all of us in that little suburban apartment building were waiting impatiently for you to move in (those who live narrow lives are always curious about any novelty on their doorsteps). And how strongly I, above all, felt that curiosity to see you when I came home from school one afternoon and saw the removals van standing outside the building. The men had already taken in most of the furniture, the heavy pieces, and now they were carrying up a few smaller items; I stayed standing by the doorway so that I could marvel at everything, because all your possessions were so interestingly different from anything I had ever seen before. There were Indian idols, Italian sculptures, large pictures in very bright colours, and then, finally, came the books, so many of them, and more beautiful than I would ever have thought possible. They were stacked up by the front door of the apartment, where the manservant took charge of them, carefully knocking the dust off every single volume with a stick and a feather duster. I prowled curiously around the ever-growing pile, and the manservant did not tell me to go away, but he didn't encourage me either, so I dared not touch one, although I would have loved to feel the soft leather of many of their bindings. I only glanced shyly and surreptitiously at the titles; there were French and English books among them, and many in languages that I didn't know. I think I could have stood there for hours looking at them all, but then my mother called me in.

After that, I couldn't stop thinking of you all evening, and still I didn't know you. I myself owned only a dozen cheap books with shabby board covers, but I loved them more than anything and read them again and again. And now I couldn't help wondering what the man who owned and had read all these wonderful books must be like, a man who knew so many languages, who was so rich and at the same time so learned. There was a kind of supernatural awe in my mind when I thought of all those books. I tried to picture you: you were an old man with glasses and a long white beard, rather like our geography teacher, only much kinder, better-looking and better-tempered—I don't know why I already felt sure you must be good-looking, when I still thought of you as an old man. All those years ago, that was the first night I ever dreamt of you, and still I didn't know you.

You moved in yourself the next day, but for all my spying I hadn't managed to catch a glimpse of you yet—which only heightened my curiosity. At last, on the third day, I did see you, and what a surprise it was to find you so different, so wholly unrelated to my childish image of someone resembling God the Father. I had dreamt of a kindly, bespectacled old man, and now here you were—exactly the same as you are today. You are proof against change, the years slide off you! You wore a casual fawn suit, and ran upstairs

in your incomparably light, boyish way, always taking two steps
at a time. You were carrying your hat, so I saw, with indescribable amazement, your bright, lively face and youthful head of
hair; I was truly amazed to find how young, how handsome, how
supple, slender and elegant you were. And isn't it strange? In that
first second I clearly felt what I, like everyone else, am surprised
to find is a unique trait in your character: somehow you are two
men at once: one a hot-blooded young man who takes life easily,
delighting in games and adventure, but at the same time, in your
art, an implacably serious man, conscious of your duty, extremely
well read and highly educated. I unconsciously sensed, again like
everyone else, that you lead a double life, one side of it bright and
open to the world, the other very dark, known to you alone—my
thirteen-year-old self, magically attracted to you at first glance, was
aware of that profound duality, the secret of your nature.

Do you understand now, beloved, what a miracle, what an
enticing enigma you were bound to seem to me as a child? A man
whom I revered because he wrote books, because he was famous
in that other great world, and suddenly I found out that he was
an elegant, boyishly cheerful young man of twenty-five! Need I
tell you that from that day on nothing at home, nothing in my
entire impoverished childhood world interested me except for
you, that with all the doggedness, all the probing persistence of a
thirteen-year-old I thought only of you and your life. I observed
you, I observed your habits and the people who visited you, and
my curiosity about you was increased rather than satisfied, because
the duality of your nature was expressed in the wide variety of
those visitors. Young people came, friends of yours with whom
you laughed in high spirits, lively students, and then there were
ladies who drove up in cars, once the director of the opera house,
that great conductor whom I had only ever seen from a reverent
distance on his rostrum, then again young girls still at commercial
college who scurried shyly in through your door, and women visitors

in particular, very, very many women. I thought nothing special of that, not even when, on my way to school one morning, I saw a heavily veiled lady leave your apartment—I was only thirteen, after all, and the passionate curiosity with which I spied on your life and lay in wait for you did not, in the child, identify itself as love.

But I still remember, my beloved, the day and the hour when I lost my heart to you entirely and for ever. I had been for a walk with a school friend, and we two girls were standing at the entrance to the building, talking, when a car drove up, stopped—and you jumped off the running-board with the impatient, agile gait that still fascinates me in you. An instinctive urge came over me to open the door for you, and so I crossed your path and we almost collided. You looked at me with a warm, soft, all-enveloping gaze that was like a caress, smiled at me tenderly—yes, I can put it no other way—and said in a low and almost intimate tone of voice: "Thank you very much, Fräulein."

That was all, beloved, but from that moment on, after sensing that soft, tender look, I was your slave. I learnt later, in fact quite soon, that you look in the same way at every woman you encounter, every shop girl who sells you something, every housemaid who opens the door to you, with an all-embracing expression that surrounds and yet at the same time undresses a woman, the look of the born seducer; and that glance of yours is not a deliberate expression of will and inclination, but you are entirely unconscious that your tenderness to women makes them feel warm and soft when it is turned on them. However, I did not guess that at the age of thirteen, still a child; it was as if I had been immersed in fire. I thought the tenderness was only for me, for me alone, and in that one second the woman latent in my adolescent self awoke, and she was in thrall to you for ever.

"Who was that?" asked my friend. I couldn't answer her at once. It was impossible for me to utter your name; in that one single second it had become sacred to me, it was my secret. "Oh, a gentleman who lives in this building," I stammered awkwardly at last. "Then why did you blush like that when he looked at you?" my friend mocked me, with all the malice of an inquisitive child. And because I felt her touching on my secret with derision, the blood rose to my cheeks more warmly than ever. My embarrassment made me snap at her. "You silly goose!" I said angrily; I could have throttled her. But she just laughed even louder, yet more scornfully, until I felt the tears shoot to my eyes with helpless rage. I left her standing there and ran upstairs.

I loved you from that second on. I know that women have often said those words to you, spoilt as you are. But believe me, no one ever loved you as slavishly, with such dog-like devotion, as the creature I was then and have always remained, for there is nothing on earth like the love of a child that passes unnoticed in the dark because she has no hope: her love is so submissive, so much a servant's love, passionate and lying in wait, in a way that the avid yet unconsciously demanding love of a grown woman can never be. Only lonely children can keep a passion entirely to themselves; others talk about their feelings in company, wear them away in intimacy with friends, they have heard and read a great deal about love, and know that it is a common fate. They play with it as if it were a toy, they show it off like boys smoking their first cigarette. But as for me, I had no one I could take into my confidence, I was not taught or warned by anyone, I was inexperienced and naive; I flung myself into my fate as if into an abyss. Everything growing and emerging in me knew of nothing but you, the dream of you was my familiar friend. My father had died long ago, my mother was a stranger to me in her eternal sad depression, her anxious pensioner's worries; more knowing adolescent schoolgirls repelled me because they played so lightly with what to me was the ultimate passion—so with all the concentrated attention of my impatiently emergent nature I brought to bear, on you, everything that would otherwise have been splintered and dispersed. To me, you were—how can I put it? Any one comparison is too slight—you were everything to me, all that mattered. Nothing existed except in so far as it related to you, you were the only point of reference in my life. You changed it entirely. Before, I had been an indifferent pupil at school, and my work was only average; now I was suddenly top of the class, I read a thousand books until late into the night because I knew that you loved books; to my mother's amazement I suddenly began practising the piano with stubborn persistence because I thought you also loved music. I cleaned and mended my clothes solely to look pleasing and neat in front of you, and I hated the fact that my old school pinafore (a house dress of my mother's cut down to size) had a square patch on the left side of it. I was afraid you might notice the patch and despise me, so I always kept my school bag pressed over it as I ran up the stairs, trembling with fear in case you saw it. How foolish of me: you never, or almost never, looked at me again.

And yet I really did nothing all day but wait for you and look out for you. There was a small brass peephole in our door, and looking through its circular centre I could see your door opposite. This peephole—no, don't smile, beloved, even today I am still not ashamed of those hours!—was my eye on the world. I sat in the cold front room, afraid of my mother's suspicions, on the watch for whole afternoons in those months and years, with a book in my hand, tense as a musical string resounding in response to your presence. I was always looking out for you, always in a state of tension, but you felt it as little as the tension of the spring in the watch that you carry in your pocket, patiently counting and measuring your hours in the dark, accompanying your movements with its inaudible heartbeat, while you let your quick glance fall on it only once in a million ticking seconds. I knew everything about you, knew all your habits, every one of your suits and ties, I knew your various acquaintances and could soon tell them apart, dividing them into those whom I liked and those whom I didn't; from my thirteenth to my sixteenth year I lived every hour for you. Oh, what follies I committed! I kissed the door handle that your hand had touched; I stole a cigarette end that you had dropped before coming into the building, and it was sacred to me because your lips had touched it. In the evenings I would run down to the street a hundred times on some pretext or other to see which of your rooms had a light in it, so that I could feel more aware of your invisible presence. And in the weeks when you went away—my heart always missed a beat in anguish when I saw your good manservant Johann carrying your yellow travelling bag downstairs—in those weeks my life was dead and pointless. I went about feeling morose, bored and cross, and I always had to take care that my mother did not notice the despair in my red-rimmed eyes.

Even as I tell you all these things, I know that they were grotesquely extravagant and childish follies. I ought to have been ashamed of them, but I was not, for my love for you was never purer and more passionate than in those childish excesses. I could tell you for hours, days, how I lived with you at that time, and you hardly even knew me by sight, because if I met you on the stairs and there was no avoiding it, I would run past you with my head bent for fear of your burning gaze—like someone plunging into water—just to escape being scorched by its fire. For hours, days I could tell you about those long-gone years of yours, unrolling the whole calendar of your life, but I do not mean to bore you or torment you. I will tell you only about the best experience of my childhood, and I ask you not to mock me because it is something so slight, for to me as a child it was infinite. It must have been on a Sunday. You had gone away, and your servant was dragging the heavy carpets that he had been beating back through the open front door of the apartment. It was hard work for the good man, and in a suddenly bold moment I went up to him and asked if I could help him. He was surprised, but let me do as I suggested, and so I saw—if only I could tell you with what reverent, indeed devout veneration!—I saw your apartment from the inside, your world, the desk where you used to sit, on which a few flowers stood in a blue crystal vase. Your cupboards, your pictures, your books. It was only a fleeting, stolen glimpse of your life, for the faithful Johann would certainly not have let me look closely, but with that one glimpse I took in the whole atmosphere, and now I had nourishment for never-ending dreams of you both waking and sleeping.

That brief moment was the happiest of my childhood. I wanted to tell you about it so that even though you do not know me you may get some inkling of how my life depended on you. I wanted to tell you about that, and about the terrible moment that was, unfortunately, so close to it. I had—as I have already told you—forgotten everything but you, I took no notice of my mother any more, or indeed of anyone else. I hardly noticed an elderly gentleman, a businessman from Innsbruck who was distantly related to my mother by marriage, coming to visit us often and staying for some time; indeed, I welcomed his visits, because then he sometimes took Mama to the theatre, and I could be on my own, thinking of you, looking out for you, which was my greatest and only bliss. One day my mother called me into her room with a certain ceremony, saying she had something serious to discuss with me. I went pale and suddenly heard my heart thudding; did she suspect something, had she guessed? My first thought was of you, the secret that linked me to the world. But my mother herself was ill at ease; she kissed me affectionately once, and then again (as she never usually did), drew me down on the sofa beside her and began to tell me, hesitantly and bashfully, that her relation, who was a widower, had made her a proposal of marriage, and mainly for my sake she had decided to accept him. The hot blood rose to my heart: I had only one thought in answer to what she said, the thought of you.

"But we'll be staying here, won't we?" I just managed to stammer.

"No, we're moving to Innsbruck. Ferdinand has a lovely villa there."

I heard no more. Everything went black before my eyes. Later, I knew that I had fallen down in a faint; I heard my mother, her voice lowered, quietly telling my prospective stepfather, who had been waiting outside the door, that I had suddenly stepped back with my hands flung out, and then I fell to the floor like a lump of lead. I cannot tell you what happened in the next few days, how I, a powerless child, tried to resist my mother's all-powerful will; as I write, my hand still trembles when I think of it. I could not give my real secret away, so my resistance seemed like mere obstinacy, malice and defiance. No one spoke to me, it was all done behind my back. They used the hours when I was at school to arrange our move; when I came back, something else had always been cleared away or sold. I saw our home coming apart, and my life with it, and one day when I came in for lunch, the removals men had been to pack everything and take it all away. Our packed suitcases stood in the empty rooms, with two camp beds for my mother and me; we were to sleep there one more night, the last, and then travel to Innsbruck the next day.

On that last day I felt, with sudden resolution, that I could not live without being near you. I knew of nothing but you that could save me. I shall never be able to say what I was thinking of, or whether I was capable of thinking clearly at all in those hours of despair, but suddenly—my mother was out—I stood up in my school clothes, just as I was, and walked across the corridor to your apartment. Or rather, I did not so much walk; it was more as if, with my stiff legs and trembling joints, I was magnetically attracted to your door. As I have said before, I had no clear idea what I wanted. Perhaps to fall at your feet and beg you to keep me as a maidservant, a slave, and I am afraid you will smile at this innocent devotion on the part of a fifteen-year-old, but—beloved, you would not smile if you knew how I stood out in that ice-cold corridor, rigid with fear yet impelled by an incomprehensible power, and how I forced my trembling arm away from my body so that it rose and—after a struggle in an eternity of terrible seconds—placed a finger on the bell-push by the door handle and pressed it. To this day I can hear its shrill ringing in my ears, and then the silence afterwards when my blood seemed to stop flowing, and I listened to find out if you were coming.

But you did not come. No one came. You were obviously out that afternoon, and Johann must have gone shopping, so with the dying sound of the bell echoing in my ears I groped my way back to our destroyed, emptied apartment and threw myself down on a plaid rug, as exhausted by the four steps I had taken as if I had been trudging through deep snow for hours. But underneath that exhaustion my determination to see you, to speak to you before they tore me away, was still burning as brightly as ever. There was, I swear it, nothing sensual in my mind; I was still ignorant, for the very reason that I thought of nothing but you. I only wanted to see you, see you once more, cling to you. I waited for you all night, beloved, all that long and terrible night. As soon as my mother had got into bed and fallen asleep I slipped into the front room, to listen for your footsteps when you came home. I waited all night, and it was icy January weather. I was tired, my limbs hurt, and there was no armchair left in the room for me to sit in, so I lay down flat on the cold floor, in the draught that came in under the door. I lay on the painfully cold floor in nothing but my thin dress all night, for I took no blanket with me; I did not want to be warm for fear of falling asleep and failing to hear your step. It hurt; I got cramp in my feet, my arms were shaking; I had to keep standing up, it was so cold in that dreadful darkness. But I waited and waited and waited for you, as if for my fate.

At last—it must have been two or three in the morning—I heard the front door of the building being unlocked down below, and then footsteps coming upstairs. The cold had left me as if dropping away, heat shot through me; I quietly opened the door to rush towards you and fall at your feet... oh, I don't know what I would have done, such a foolish child as I was then. The steps came closer and closer, I saw the flicker of candlelight. Shaking, I clung to the door handle. Was it you coming?

Yes. It was you, beloved—but you were not alone. I heard a soft, provocative laugh, the rustle of a silk dress, and your lowered voice—you were coming home with a woman...

How I managed to survive that night I do not know. Next morning, at eight o'clock, they dragged me off to Innsbruck; I no longer had the strength to resist.

My child died last night—and now I shall be alone again, if I must really go on living. They will come tomorrow, strange, hulking, black-clad men bringing a coffin, and they will put him in it, my poor boy, my only child. Perhaps friends will come as well, bringing flowers, but what do flowers on a coffin mean? They will comfort me, and say this and that—words, words, how can they help me? I know that I must be alone again when they have gone. I felt it then, in those two endless years in Innsbruck, the years from my sixteenth to my eighteenth birthday, when I lived like a prisoner or an outcast in my family. My stepfather, a very placid, taciturn man, was kind to me; my mother seemed ready to grant all my wishes, as if atoning for her unwitting injustice to me; young people tried to make friends with me, but I rejected all their advances with passionate defiance. I didn't want to live happy and content away from you, I entrenched myself in a dark world of self-torment and loneliness. I didn't wear the brightly coloured new clothes they bought me, I refused to go to concerts or the theatre, or on outings in cheerful company. I hardly went out at all: would you believe it, beloved, I didn't come to know more than ten streets of the little town in the two years I lived there? I was in mourning, and I wanted to mourn, I became intoxicated by every privation that I imposed on myself over and beyond the loss of you. And I did not want to be distracted from my passion to live only for you. I stayed at home alone for hours, days, doing nothing but thinking of you again and again, always reviving my hundred little memories of you, every time I met you, every time I waited for you, staging those little incidents in my mind as if in a theatre. And that is why, because I went over every second of the past countless times, I retain such a vivid memory of my whole childhood that I feel every minute of those past years with as much heat and ardour as if they were only yesterday.

My life at the time was lived entirely through you. I bought all your books; when your name was in the newspaper it was a red-letter day. Would you believe that I know every line of your books by heart, I have read them so often? If anyone were to wake me from sleep at night and quote a random line from them, I could still, thirteen years later, go on reciting the text from there, as if in a dream: every word of yours was my Gospel and prayer book. The whole world existed only in relation to you; I read about concerts and premieres in the Viennese newspapers with the sole aim of wondering which of them might interest you, and when evening came I was with you, even though I was so far away: now he is going into the auditorium, now he is sitting down. I dreamt of that a thousand times because I had once seen you at a concert.

But why describe this raving, tragic, hopeless devotion on the part of an abandoned child feeling angry with herself, why describe it to a man who never guessed at it or knew about it? Yet was I really still a child at that time? I reached the age of seventeen, eighteen—young men turned to look at me in the street, but that only embittered me. To love, or even merely play at love with anyone but you was so inexplicable to me, so unimaginably strange an idea, that merely feeling tempted to indulge in it would have seemed to me a crime. My passion for you was the same as ever, except that my body was changing, and now that my senses were awakened it was more glowing, physical, womanly. And what the child with her sombre, untaught will, the child who had pressed your doorbell, could not guess at was now my only thought: to give myself to you, devote myself to you.

The people around me thought me timid, called me shy (I had kept my secret strictly to myself). But I was developing an iron will. All that I thought and did tended in one direction: back to Vienna, back to you. And I imposed my will by force, senseless and extraordinary as it might seem to anyone else. My stepfather was a prosperous man, and regarded me as his own child. But I insisted, with grim obstinacy, that I wanted to earn my own living, and at last I managed to get a position with a relation as an assistant in a large ready-to-wear dress shop.

Need I tell you where I went first when I arrived back in Vienna—at last, at last!—one misty autumn evening? I left my case at the station, boarded a tram—how slowly it seemed to be going, I bitterly resented every stop—and hurried to the apartment building. There was light in your windows; my whole heart sang. Only now did the city, strange to me these days with its pointless roar of traffic, come to life, only now did I come to life again myself, knowing that I was near you, you, my only dream. I did not guess that in reality I was as far from your mind now, when only the thin, bright glass pane stood between you and my radiant gaze, as if valleys, mountains and rivers separated us. I merely looked up and up; there was light there, here was the building, and there were you, the whole world to me. I had dreamt of this hour for two years, and now I was granted it. I stood outside your windows all that long, mild, cloudy evening, until the light in them went out. Only then did I go home to the place where I was staying.

Every evening after that I stood outside your building in the same way. I worked in the shop until six; it was hard, strenuous work, but I liked it, because all the activity there made me feel my own restlessness less painfully. And as soon as the iron shutters rolled down behind me I hurried to my desired destination. My will was set on seeing you just once, meeting you just once, so that my eyes could see your face again, if only from a distance. And after about a week it finally happened: I met you at a moment when I didn't expect it. Just as I was looking up at your windows, you came across the street. Suddenly I was that thirteen-year-old child again, and felt the blood rise to my cheeks. Instinctively, against my innermost urge to feel your eyes on me, I lowered my head and hurried past you, quick as lightning. Afterwards I was ashamed of my timid flight, the reaction of a schoolgirl, for now I knew very clearly what I wanted: I wanted to meet you, I was seeking you out, I wanted you to recognize me after all those years of weary longing, wanted you to take some notice of me, wanted you to love me.

But it was a long time before you really noticed me, although I stood out in your street every evening, even in flurries of snow and the keen, cutting wind of Vienna. I often waited in vain for hours, and often, in the end, you left the building in the company of friends. Twice I saw you with women, and now that I was an adult I sensed what was new and different about my feeling for you from the sudden tug at my heartstrings, wrenching them right apart, when I saw a strange woman walking so confidently arm in arm with you. I was not surprised. After all, I knew about your succession of women visitors from my childhood days, but now it hurt me physically, and I was torn between hostility and desire in the face of your obvious intimacy with someone else. One day, childishly proud as I was and perhaps still am, I stayed away from your building, but what a terrible, empty evening of defiance and rebellion I spent! Next evening, once again, I was standing humbly outside your building waiting, waiting, just as I had spent my whole life standing outside your life, which was closed to me.

And at last one evening you did notice me. I had already seen you coming in the distance, and I steeled my will not to avoid you.

As chance would have it, a cart waiting to be unloaded obstructed the street, and you had to pass close to me. Involuntarily your absent-minded gaze fell on me, and as soon as it met the attention of my own eyes—oh, what a shock the memory gave me!—it became that look you give women, the tender, all-enveloping, all-embracing gaze that also strips them, the look that, when I was a child, had made me into a loving woman for the first time. For one or two seconds that gaze held mine, which neither could nor wished to tear itself away—and then you had passed me. My heart was beating fast; instinctively I slowed my pace, and as I turned, out of a curiosity that I could not master, I saw that you too had stopped and were still looking at me. And the way you observed me, with such interest and curiosity, told me at once that you did not recognize me.

You did not recognize me, neither then nor ever, you never recognized me. How can I describe to you, beloved, the disappointment of that moment? That was the first time I suffered it, the disappointment of going unrecognized by you. I have lived with it all my life, I am dying with it, and still you do not recognize me. How can I make you understand my disappointment? During those two years in Innsbruck, when I thought of you every hour and did nothing but imagine our next meeting back in Vienna, I had dreamt of the wildest—or the most blissful—possibilities, depending on my mood at the time. I had dreamt, if I may so put it, of everything; in dark moments I had pictured you rejecting me, despising me for being too uninteresting, too ugly, too importunate. In passionate visions I had gone through all forms of your disfavour, your coldness, your indifference—but in no moment of dark emotion, not even in full awareness of my inferiority, had I ventured to envisage this, the worst thing of all: the fact that you had never even noticed my existence. Today I understand it—ah, you have taught me to understand it!—I realize that, to a man, a girl's or a woman's face must have something extraordinarily changeable in it, because it is usually only a mirror reflecting now passion, now childishness, now weariness, and passes by as a reflection does; so that a man can easily forget a woman's face because age changes its light and shade, and different clothes give her a new setting. Those who are resigned to their fate really know that. However, still a girl at the time, I could not yet grasp your forgetfulness, because somehow my immoderate, constant concern with you had made me feel—although it was a delusion—that you, too, must often think of me, you would be waiting for me; how could I have gone on breathing in the certainty that I was nothing to you, no memory of me ever touched you, however lightly? And this moment, when your eyes showed me that nothing in you recognized me, no thin gossamer line of memory reached from your life to mine, was my first fall into the depths of reality, my first inkling of my destiny.

You did not recognize me at that time. And when, two days later, we met again, your eyes rested on me with a certain familiarity, you still did not recognize me as the girl who loved you and whom you had woken to life, but only as the pretty eighteen-year-old who had met you in the same place two days earlier. You looked at me in surprise, but in a friendly manner, with a slight smile playing round your mouth. Once again you passed me, once again immediately slowing your pace; I trembled, I rejoiced, I prayed that you would speak to me. I felt that, for the first time, you saw me as a living woman; I myself slowed down and did not avoid you. And suddenly I sensed you behind me; without turning round I knew that now, for the first time, I would hear your beloved voice speaking directly to me. Expectation paralysed me; I feared I would have to stop where I was because my heart was thudding so violently—and then you were beside me. You spoke to me in your easy, cheerful way, as if we had been on friendly terms for a long time—oh, you had no idea about me, you have never had any idea of my life!—so captivatingly free and easy was the way you spoke to me that I was even able to answer you. We walked all down the street side by side. Then you suggested that we might go and have something to eat together. I agreed. What would I ever have dared to deny you?

We ate together in a small restaurant—do you still know where it was? No, I am sure you don't distinguish it now from other such evenings, for who was I to you? One among hundreds, one adventure in an ever-continuing chain. And what was there for you to remember about me? I said little, because it made me so infinitely happy to have you near me, to hear you speaking to me. I did not want to waste a moment of it by asking questions or saying something foolish. I shall never forget my gratitude to you for that hour, or how entirely you responded to my passionate reverence, how tender, light and tactful you were, entirely without making importunate advances, entirely without any hasty, caressing gestures of affection, and from the first moment striking a note of such certain and friendly familiarity that you would have won my heart even if it had not been yours long ago, given with all my goodwill. Ah, you have no idea what a wonderful thing you did in not disappointing my five years of childish expectation!

It was getting late; we left the restaurant. At the door you asked me whether I was in a hurry or still had time to spare. How could I have failed to show that I was ready for you? I said that I could indeed spare some time. Then you asked, quickly surmounting a slight hesitation, whether I would like to go to your apartment and talk. "Oh, most happily," I said, and it came out of the fullness of my feelings so naturally that I noticed at once how you reacted, in either embarrassment or pleasure, to my quick tongue—but you were also visibly surprised. Today I understand why you were astonished; I know it is usual for women, even when they long to give themselves, to deny that readiness, pretending to be alarmed or indignant, so that first they have to be reassured by urgent pleading, lies, vows and promises. I know that perhaps only prostitutes, the professionals of love, or perhaps very naive adolescents, respond to

such an invitation with such wholehearted, joyful consent as mine.
But in me—and how could you guess that?—it was only my will put
into words, the concentrated longing of a thousand days breaking
out. In any case, you were struck; I began to interest you. I sensed
that, as we were walking along, you glanced sideways at me with a
kind of astonishment while we talked. Your feelings, your magically
sure sense of all that is human, immediately scented something
unusual here, a secret in this pretty, compliant girl. Your curiosity
was awakened, and I noticed, from your circling, probing questions, that you wanted to discover the mystery. But I evaded you;
it would be better to seem foolish than to let you know my secret.

We went up to your apartment. Forgive me, beloved, when I tell
you that you cannot understand what that corridor, that staircase
meant to me—what turmoil and confusion there was in my mind,
what headlong, painful, almost mortal happiness. Even now I can
hardly think of it without tears, and I have none of those left. But
imagine that every object in the building was, so to speak, imbued
with my passion, each was a symbol of my childhood, my longing: the gate where I had waited for you thousands of times, the
stairs from which I always listened for your footsteps, and where I
had seen you for the first time, the peephole through which I had
stared my soul out, the doormat outside your door where I had
once knelt, the click of the key at which I had always leapt up from
where I was lying in wait. All my childhood, all my passion were
here in those few metres of space; this was my whole life, and now
it came over me like a storm, everything, everything was coming
true, and I was with you, going into your, into our apartment
building. Think of it—it sounds banal, but I can't put it any other
way—as if going only as far as your door had been my reality all
my life, my sombre everyday world, but beyond it a child's magic
realm began, the realm of Aladdin, remember that I had stared
a thousand times, with burning eyes, at the door through which I
now stepped, almost reeling, and you will guess—but only guess,

you can never entirely know, beloved!—what that tumultuous minute meant in my life.

I stayed with you all night. You did not realize that no man had ever touched me before, had ever felt or seen my body. But how could you guess that, beloved, when I offered no resistance, showed no bashful hesitancy, so that you could have no idea of my secret love for you? It would certainly have alarmed you, for you love only what is light and playful, weightless, you are afraid of intervening in someone else's life. You want to give of yourself to everyone, to the world, but you do not want sacrificial victims. If I tell you now, beloved, that I was a virgin when I gave myself to you, I beg you not to misunderstand me! I am not accusing you, you did not entice me, lie to me, seduce me—it was I who pressed myself on you, threw myself on your breast and into my own fate. I will never, never blame you for anything, I will only thank you for the richness of that night, sparkling with desire, hovering in bliss. When I opened my eyes in the dark and felt you at my side, I was surprised not to see the stars above me, I could feel heaven so close—no, I never regretted it, beloved, for the sake of that hour I never regretted it. I remember that when you were asleep and I heard your breathing, felt your body, while I was so close to you, I shed tears of happiness in the dark.

In the morning I was in a hurry to leave early. I had to go to the shop, and I also wanted to be gone before your manservant arrived; I couldn't have him seeing me. When I was dressed and stood in front of you, you took me in your arms and gave me a long look; was some dark and distant memory stirring in you, or did I merely seem to you beautiful, happy as indeed I was? Then you kissed me on the mouth. I gently drew away, about to go. "Won't you take a few flowers with you?" you asked, and I said yes. You took four white roses out of the blue crystal vase on the desk (which I knew from that one stolen childhood glance) and gave them to me. I was still kissing them days later.

We had arranged to meet again another evening. I went, and again it was wonderful. You gave me a third night. Then you said you had to go away—oh, how I hated those journeys of yours even in my childhood!—and promised to get in touch with me as soon as you were back. I gave you a poste restante address. I didn't want to tell you my name. I kept my secret. And again you gave me a few roses when you said goodbye—goodbye.

Every day for two whole months I went to ask if any post had come... but no, why describe the hellish torment of waiting, why describe my despair to you? I am not blaming you, I love you as the man you are, hot-blooded and forgetful, ardent and inconstant, I love you just as you always were and as you still are. You had come back long ago, I could tell that by the light in your windows, and you did not write to me. I have not had a line from you to this day and these last hours of mine, not a line from you to whom I gave my life. I waited, I waited in despair. But you did not get in touch with me, you never wrote me a line... not a line...

My child died yesterday—he was also yours. He was your child, beloved, conceived on one of those three nights, I swear it, and no one tells lies in the shadow of death. He was our child, and I swear it to you, because no man touched me between those hours when I gave myself to you and the time when he made his way out of my body. I was sacred to myself because of your touch; how could I have shared myself with you, who had been everything to me, and other men who passed by touching my life only slightly? He was our child, beloved, the child of my conscious love and your careless, passing, almost unconscious affection, our child, our son, our only child. You will ask—perhaps alarmed, perhaps only surprised—you will ask, beloved, why I kept the child secret all these long years, and mention him only today, now that he lies here sleeping in the dark, sleeping for ever, ready to leave and never return, never again? But how could I have told you? You would never have believed me, a stranger who showed herself only too willing on those three nights, who gave herself to you without resistance, indeed with desire, you would never have believed the anonymous woman of your fleeting encounter if she said she was keeping faith with you, the faithless—you would never have considered the child your own without suspicion! Even if what I said had seemed probable to you, you would never have been able to dismiss the secret suspicion that I was trying to palm off some other man's child on you because you were prosperous. You would have suspected me, a shadow would have remained, a fugitive, tentative shadow of distrust between us. I didn't want that. And then I know you; I know you rather better than you know yourself. I know that it would have been difficult for you, who love the carefree, light-hearted, playful aspect of love, suddenly to be a father, suddenly responsible for someone else's life. You can breathe only at liberty; you would have felt bound to me in some way. You would have hated me for that—I know that you would have done so, against your own conscious will. Perhaps only for hours, perhaps only for fleeting minutes I would have been a burden to you, a hated burden—but in my pride I wanted you to think of me all your life without any anxiety. I preferred to take it all on myself rather than burden you, I wanted to be the only one among all your women of whom you always thought with love and gratitude. But the fact is that you never thought of me at all, you forgot me.

I am not blaming you, my beloved, no, I am not blaming you. Forgive me if a touch of bitterness flows into my pen now and then, forgive me—my child, our child lies dead in the flickering candlelight; I clenched my fists against God and called him a murderer, my senses are confused and dulled. Forgive my lament, forgive me! I know that deep in your heart you are good and helpful, you help everyone, even a total stranger who asks for help.

But your kindness is so strange, it is open to all to take as much of it as they can hold, it is great, infinitely great, your kindness, but it is—forgive me—it is passive. It wants to be appealed to, to be taken. You help when you are called upon to help, when you are asked for help, you help out of shame, out of weakness, and not out of joy. You do not—let me say so openly—you do not like those who are in need and torment any better than their happier brothers. And it is hard to ask anything of people like you, even the kindest of them. Once, when I was still a child looking through the peephole in our door, I saw you give something to a beggar who had rung your bell. You gave him money readily before he asked you, even a good deal of it, but you gave it with a certain anxiety and in haste, wanting him to go away again quickly; it was as if you were afraid to look him in the face. I have never forgotten your uneasy, timid way of helping, fleeing from gratitude. And so I never turned to you. Certainly I know that you would have stood by me then, even without any certainty that the child was yours. You would have comforted me, you would have given me money, plenty of money, but never with anything but a secret impatience to push what was unwelcome away from you; yes, I believe you might even have asked me to do away with the child before its birth. And I feared that more than anything—because what would I not have done if you wanted it, how could I have denied you anything? However, that child meant everything to me, because it was yours, yourself again but no longer as a happy, carefree man whom I could not hold, yourself given to me for ever—so I thought—there in my body, a part of my own life. Now at last I had caught you, I could sense your life growing in my veins, I could give you food and drink, caress and kiss you when my heart burned for that. You see, beloved, that is why I was so blissfully happy when I knew that I was carrying a child of yours, that is why I never told you, because then you could not escape from me again.

To be sure, beloved, they were not such blissful months as I had anticipated in my mind, they were also months of horror and torment, of revulsion at the vileness of humanity. I did not have an easy time. I could not work in the shop during the final months, or my relative would have noticed and sent news home. I did not want to ask my mother for money—so I eked out an existence until the baby's birth by selling what little jewellery I had. A week before he was born, my last few crowns were stolen from a cupboard by a washerwoman, so I had to go to the maternity hospital where only very poor women, the outcasts and forgotten, drag themselves in their need. And the child—your child—was born there in the midst of misery. It was a deadly place: strange, everything was strange, we women lying there were strange to each other, lonely and hating one another out of misery, the same torment in that crowded ward full of chloroform and blood, screams and groans. I suffered the humiliation, the mental and physical shame that poverty has to bear from the company of prostitutes and the sick who made our common fate feel terrible, from the cynicism of young doctors who stripped back the sheets from defenceless women with an ironic smile and felt them with false medical expertise, from the greed of the nurses—in there, a woman's bashfulness was crucified with looks and scourged with words. The notice with your name in such a place is all that is left of you, for what lies in the bed is only a twitching piece of flesh felt by the curious, an object to be put on display and studied—the women who bear children at home to husbands waiting affectionately for the birth do not know what it means to give birth to a baby alone and defenceless, as if one were on the laboratory table! If I read the word "hell" in a book to this day, I suddenly and against my conscious will think of that crowded, steamy ward full of sighs, laughter, blood and screams, that slaughterhouse of shame where I suffered.

Forgive me, forgive me for telling you about it. I do so only this one time, never again, never. I have said nothing for eleven years, and I will soon be silent for all eternity; just once I must cry out and say what a high price I paid for my child, the child who was all my bliss and now lies there with no breath left in his body. I had forgotten those hours long ago in his smile and voice, in my happiness, but now he is dead the torment revives, and I had to scream out from my heart just this one time. But I do not accuse you—only God, only God, who made that torment pointless. I do not blame you, I swear it, and never did I rise against you in anger. Even in the hour when I was writhing in labour, when my body burned with shame under the inquisitive eyes of the students, even in the second when the pain tore my soul apart, I never accused you before God. I never regretted those nights or my love for you, I always blessed the day you met me. And if I had to go through the hell of those hours again and knew in advance what was waiting for me I would do it again, my beloved, I would do it again a thousand times over!

Our child died yesterday—you never knew him. Never, even in a fleeting encounter by chance, did your eyes fall on him in passing. I kept myself hidden away from you for a long time once I had my son; my longing for you had become less painful, indeed I think I loved you less passionately, or at least I did not suffer from my love so much now that I had been given the child. I did not want to divide myself between you and him, so I gave myself not to you, a happy man living without me, but to the son who needed me, whom I must nourish, whom I could kiss and embrace. I seemed to be saved from my restless desire for you, saved from my fate by that other self of yours who was really mine—only occasionally, very occasionally, did my feelings humbly send my thoughts out to where you lived. I did just one thing: on your birthday I always sent you a bunch of white roses, exactly the same as the roses you gave me after our first night of love. Have you ever wondered in these ten or eleven years who sent them? Did you perhaps remember the woman to whom you once gave such roses? I don't know, and I will never know your answer. Merely giving them to you out of the dark was enough for me, letting my memory of that moment flower again once a year.

You never knew our poor child—today I blame myself for keeping him from you, because you would have loved him. You never knew the poor boy, never saw him smile when he gently opened his eyelids and cast the clear, happy light of his clever, dark eyes—your eyes!—on me, on the whole world. Oh, he was so cheerful, such a dear; all the light-hearted nature of your being came out again in him in childish form, your quick, lively imagination was reborn. He could play with things for hours, entranced, just as you play with life, and then sit over his books, serious again, his eyebrows raised. He became more and more like you; the duality of gravity and playfulness that is so much your own was visibly beginning to develop in him, and the more like you he grew to be, the more I loved him. He studied hard at school, he could talk French like a little magpie, his exercise books were the neatest in the class, and he was so pretty too, so elegant in his black velvet suit or his white sailor jacket. Wherever he went he was the most elegant of all; when I took him to the Adriatic seaside resort of Grado, women stopped on the beach to stroke his long, fair hair; in Semmering, when he tobogganed downhill, everyone turned admiringly to look at him. He was so good-looking, so tender, so attractive; when he went to be a boarder at the Theresian Academy last year he wore his uniform and his little sword like an eighteenth-century pageboy—now he wears nothing but his nightshirt, poor boy, lying there with pale lips and folded hands.

You may perhaps be wondering how I could afford to bring the child up in such luxury, allowing him to live the cheerful, carefree life of the upper classes. Dearest, I speak to you out of the darkness; I am not ashamed, I will tell you, but do not alarm

yourself, beloved—I sold myself. I was not exactly what they call
a streetwalker, a common prostitute, but I sold myself. I had rich
friends, rich lovers; first I went in search of them, then they sought
me out, because I was—did you ever notice?—very beautiful.
Everyone to whom I gave myself grew fond of me, they all thanked
me and felt attached to me, they all loved me—except for you,
except for you, my beloved!

Do you despise me now for telling you that I sold myself? No,
I know you do not; you understand everything, and you will also
understand that I did it only for you, for your other self, your child.
Once, in that ward in the maternity hospital, I had touched the
worst aspect of poverty, I knew that the poor of this world are
always downtrodden, humiliated, victims, and I would not have
your child, your bright, beautiful son growing up deep down in
the scum of society, in the dark, mean streets, the polluted air of
a room at the back of an apartment building. I did not want his
tender mouth to know the language of the gutter, or his white body
to wear the fusty, shabby garments of the poor—your child was
to have everything, all the riches, all the ease on earth; he was to
rise to be your equal, in your own sphere of life.

That, my beloved, was my only reason for selling myself. It was
no sacrifice for me, since what people usually call honour and
dishonour meant nothing to me; you did not love me, and you were
the only one to whom my body truly belonged, so I felt indifferent to
anything else that happened to it. The caresses of those men, even
their most ardent passion did not touch me deeply at all, although
I had to go very carefully with many of them, and my sympathy
for their unrequited love often shook me when I remembered
what my own fate had been. All of them were good to me, all of
them indulged me, they all showed me respect. There was one in
particular, an older man, a widower who was an imperial count,
the same man who wore himself out going from door to door to
get my fatherless child, your child, accepted into the Theresian

Academy—he loved me as if I were his daughter. He asked me to marry him three or four times—I could be a countess today, mistress of an enchanting castle in the Tyrol, living a carefree life, because the child would have had a loving father who adored him, and I would have had a quiet, distinguished, kindly husband at my side—but I did not accept him, however often he urged me, and however much my refusals hurt him. Perhaps it was folly, for then I would be living somewhere safe and quiet now, and my beloved child with me, but—why should I not tell you?—I did not want to tie myself down, I wanted to be free for you at any time. In my inmost heart, the depths of my unconscious nature, my old childhood dream that one day you might yet summon me to you, if only for an hour, lived on. And for the possibility of that one hour I rejected all else, so that I would be free to answer your first call. What else had my whole life been since I grew past childhood but waiting, waiting to know your will?

And that hour really did come, but you do not know it. You have no inkling of it, beloved! Even then you did not recognize me—you never, never, never recognized me! I had met you a number of times, at the theatre, at concerts, in the Prater, in the street—every time my heart leapt up, but you looked past me; outwardly I was so different now, the shy child had become a woman, said to be beautiful, wearing expensive clothes, surrounded by admirers: how could you detect in me that shy girl in the dim light of your bedroom? Sometimes the man who was with me greeted you, you greeted him in return and looked at me, but your glance was that of a courteous stranger, appreciative but never recognizing me: strange, terribly strange. Once, I still remember, that failure to recognize me, although I was almost used to it, became a burning torment. I was sitting in a box at the Opera House with a lover and you were in the box next to ours. The lights dimmed during the overture, and I could no longer see your face, I only felt your breath as near to me as it had been that first night, and your hand, your fine and delicate hand lay on the velvet-upholstered partition between our boxes. And at last I was overcome by longing to bend down to that strange but beloved hand, the hand whose touch I had once felt holding me, and kiss it humbly. The music was rising tempestuously around me, my longing was more and more passionate, I had to exert all my self-control and force myself to sit there, so powerfully were my lips drawn to your beloved hand. After the first act I asked my lover to leave with me. I could not bear it any more, knowing that you were sitting beside me in the dark, so strange to me and yet so close.

But the hour did come, it came once more, one last time in my buried, secret life. It was almost exactly a year ago, on the day after your birthday. Strange: I had been thinking of you all those hours, because I always celebrated your birthday like a festival. I had gone out very early in the morning to buy the white roses that I asked the shop to send you, as I did every year, in memory of an hour that you had forgotten. In the afternoon I went out with my son, I took him to Demel's café and in the evening to the theatre; I wanted him, too, to feel from his early youth that this day, although he did not know its significance, was in some mystical fashion an occasion to be celebrated. Then next day I was out with my lover of the time, a rich young manufacturer from Brünn who adored and indulged me, and wanted to marry me like the rest of them—and whose proposals I had turned down apparently for no good reason, as with the rest of them, although he showered presents on me and the child, and was even endearing in his rather awkward, submissive way. We went together to a concert, where we met cheerful companions, had supper in a restaurant in the Ringstrasse, and there, amidst laughter and talking, I suggested going on to the Tabarin, a café with a dance floor. I normally disliked cafés of that kind, with their organized, alcoholic merriment, like all similar kinds of "fun", and usually objected to such suggestions, but this time—as if some unfathomable magical power in me suddenly and unconsciously caused me to suggest it in the midst of the others' cheerful excitement—I had a sudden, inexplicable wish to go, as if something special were waiting for me there. Since I was accustomed to getting my way, they all quickly stood up, we went to the Tabarin, drank champagne, and I fell suddenly into a fit of hectic, almost painful merriment, something unusual in me. I drank and drank, sang sentimental songs with the others, and almost felt an urge to dance or rejoice. But suddenly—I felt as if something either cold or blazing hot had been laid on my heart—I stopped short: you were sitting with some friends at the next table, looking admiringly at me, with an expression of desire, the expression that could always send my entire body into a state of turmoil. For the first time in ten years you were looking at me again with all the unconsciously passionate force of your being. I trembled, and the glass that I had raised almost fell from my hands. Fortunately my companions did not notice my confusion: it was lost in the noise of the laughter and music.

Your gaze was more and more ardent, immersing me entirely in fire. I did not know whether at last, at long last, you had recognized me, or you desired me again as someone else, a stranger. The blood shot into my cheeks, I answered my companions at our table distractedly. You must have noticed how confused your gaze made me. Then, unseen by the others, you signed to me with a movement of your head a request to go out of the café for a moment. You ostentatiously paid your bill, said goodbye to your friends and left, not without first indicating to me again that you would wait for me outside. I was trembling as if in frost, as if in a fever, I could not answer anyone, I could not control my own racing blood. As chance would have it, at that very moment a pair of black dancers launched into one of those newfangled modern dances with clattering heels and shrill cries; everyone was watching them, and I made use of that second. I stood up, told my lover that I would be back in a moment, and followed you.

You were standing outside the cloakroom, waiting for me; your expression brightened as I came out. Smiling, you hurried to meet me; I saw at once that you didn't recognize me, not as the child of the past or the young girl of a couple of years later. Once again you were approaching me as someone new to you, an unknown stranger.

"Would you have an hour to spare for me, too, sometime?" you asked in confidential tones—I sensed, from the assurance of your manner, that you took me for one of those women who can be bought for an evening.

"Yes," I said, the same tremulous yet of course compliant "Yes" that the girl had said to you in the twilit street over a decade ago.

"Then when can we meet?" you asked.

"Whenever you like," I replied—I had no shame in front of you. You looked at me in slight surprise, the same suspiciously curious surprise as you had shown all that time ago when my swift consent had startled you before.

"Could it be now?" you asked, a little hesitantly.

"Yes," I said. "Let's go."

I was going to the cloakroom to collect my coat. Then it occurred to me that my lover had the cloakroom ticket for both our coats. Going back to ask him for it would have been impossible without offering some elaborate reason, but on the other hand I was not going to give up the hour with you that I had longed for all these years. So I did not for a second hesitate; I just threw my shawl over my evening dress and went out into the damp, misty night without a thought for the coat, without a thought for the kindly, affectionate man who had been keeping me, although I was humiliating him in front of his friends, making him look like a fool whose lover runs away from him after years the first time a stranger whistles to her. Oh, I was entirely aware of the vile, shameful ingratitude of my conduct to an honest friend; I felt that I was being ridiculous, and mortally injuring a kind man for ever in my madness—but what was friendship to me, what was my whole life compared with my impatience to feel the touch of your lips again, to hear you speak softly close to me? I loved you so much, and now that it is all over and done with I can tell you so. And I believe that if you summoned me from my deathbed I would suddenly find the strength in myself to get up and go with you.

There was a car outside the entrance, and we drove to your apartment. I heard your voice again, I felt your tender presence close to me, and was as bemused, as childishly happy as before. As I climbed those stairs again after more than ten years—no, no, I cannot describe how I still felt everything doubly in those seconds, the past and the present, and in all of it only you mattered. Not much was different in your room, a few more pictures, more books, and here and there new pieces of furniture, but still it all looked familiar to me. And the vase of roses stood on the desk—my roses, sent to you the day before on your birthday, in memory of someone whom you did not remember, did not recognize even now that she was close to you, hand in hand and lips to lips. But all the same, it did me good to think that you looked after the flowers: it meant that a breath of my love and of myself did touch you.

You took me in your arms. Once again I spent a whole, wonderful night with you. But you did not even recognize my naked body. In bliss, I accepted your expert caresses and saw that your passion draws no distinction between someone you really love and a woman selling herself, that you give yourself up entirely to your desire, unthinkingly squandering the wealth of your nature. You were so gentle and affectionate with me, a woman picked up in the dance café, so warmly and sensitively respectful, yet at the same time enjoying possession of a woman so passionately; once more, dizzy with my old happiness, I felt your unique duality—a knowing, intellectual passion mingled with sensuality. It was what had already brought me under your spell when I was a child. I have never felt such concentration on the moment of the act of love in any other man, such an outburst and reflection of his deepest being—although then, of course, it was to be extinguished in endless, almost inhuman oblivion. But I also forgot myself; who was I, now, in the dark beside you? Was I the ardent child of the past, was I the mother of your child, was I a stranger? Oh, it was all so familiar, I had known it all before, and again it was all so intoxicatingly new on that passionate night. I prayed that it would never end.

But morning came, we got up late, you invited me to stay for breakfast with you. Together we drank the tea that an invisible servant had discreetly placed ready in the dining room, and we talked. Again, you spoke to me with the open, warm confidence of your nature, and again without any indiscreet questions or curiosity about myself. You did not ask my name or where I lived: once more I was just an adventure to you, an anonymous woman, an hour of heated passion dissolving without trace in the smoke of oblivion. You told me that you were about to go away for some time, you would be in North Africa for two or three months. I trembled in the midst of my happiness, for already words were hammering in my ears: all over, gone and forgotten! I wished I could fall at your feet and cry out, "Take me with you, recognize me at last, at long last, after so many years!" But I was so timid, so cowardly, so slavish and weak in front of you. I could only say, "What a pity!"

You looked at me with a smile. "Are you really sorry?"

Then a sudden wildness caught hold of me. I stood up and looked at you, a long, hard look. And then I said, "The man I loved was always going away too." I looked at you, I looked you right in the eye. Now, now he will recognize me, I thought urgently, trembling.

But you smiled at me and said consolingly, "People come back again."

"Yes," I said, "they come back, but then they have forgotten."

There must have been something odd, something passionate in the way I said that to you. For you rose to your feet as well and looked at me, affectionately and very surprised. You took me by the shoulders. "What's good is not forgotten; I will not forget you," you said, and as you did so you gazed intently at me as if to memorize my image. And as I felt your eyes on me, seeking, sensing, clinging to you with all my being, I thought that at last, at last the spell of blindness would be broken. He will recognize me now, I thought, he will recognize me now! My whole soul trembled in that thought.

But you did not recognize me. No, you did not know me again, and I had never been more of a stranger to you than at that moment, for otherwise—otherwise you could never have done what you did a few minutes later. You kissed me, kissed me passionately again. I had to tidy my hair, which was disarranged, and as I stood looking in the mirror, looking at what it reflected—I thought I would sink to the ground in shame and horror—I saw you discreetly tucking a couple of banknotes of a high denomination in my muff. How I managed not to cry out I do not know, how I managed not to strike you in the face at that moment—you were paying me, who had loved you from childhood, paying me, the mother of your child, for that night! I was a prostitute from the Tabarin to you, nothing more—you had paid me, you had actually paid me! It was not enough for you to forget me, I had to be humiliated as well.

I reached hastily for my things. I wanted to get away, quickly. It hurt too much. I picked up my hat, which was lying on the desk beside the vase of white roses, my roses. Then an irresistible idea came powerfully to my mind: I would make one more attempt to remind you. "Won't you give me one of your white roses?"

"Happily," you said, taking it out of the vase at once.

"But perhaps they were given to you by a woman—a woman who loves you?" I said.

"Perhaps," you said. "I don't know. They were sent to me, and I don't know who sent them; that's why I like them so much."

I looked at you. "Or perhaps they are from a woman you have forgotten."

You seemed surprised. I looked at you hard. Recognize me, my look screamed, recognize me at last! But your eyes returned a friendly, innocent smile. You kissed me once more. But you did not recognize me.

I went quickly to the door, for I could feel tears rising to my eyes, and I did not want you to see them. In the hall—I had run out in such a hurry—I almost collided with your manservant Johann. Diffident and quick to oblige, he moved aside, opened the front door to let me out, and then in that one second—do you hear?—in that one second as I looked at the old man, my eyes streaming with tears, a light suddenly came into his gaze. In that one second—do you hear?—in that one second the old man, who had not seen me since my childhood, knew who I was. I could have knelt to him and kissed his hands in gratitude for his recognition. As it was, I just quickly snatched the banknotes with which you had scourged me out of my muff and gave them to him. He trembled and looked at me in shock—I think he may have guessed more about me at that moment than you did in all your life. All, all the other men had indulged me, had been kind to me—only you, only you forgot me, only you, only you failed to recognize me!

My child is dead, our child—now I have no one left in the world to love but you. But who are you to me, who are you who never, never recognizes me, who passes me by as if I were no more than a stretch of water, stumbling upon me as if I were a stone, you who always goes away, forever leaving me to wait? Once I thought that, volatile as you are, I could keep you in the shape of the child. But he was your child too: overnight he cruelly went away from me on a journey, he has forgotten me and will never come back. I am alone again, more alone than ever, I have nothing, nothing of yours—no child now, not a word, not a line, you have no memory of me, and if someone were to mention my name in front of you, you would hear it as a stranger's. Why should I not wish to die since I am dead to you, why not move on as you moved on from me? No, beloved, I do not blame you, I will not hurl lamentations at you and your cheerful way of life. Do not fear that I shall pester you any more—forgive me, just this once I had to cry out what is in my heart, in this hour when my child lies there dead and abandoned. Just this once I had to speak to you—then I will go back into the darkness in silence again, as I have always been silent to you.

However, you will not hear my cries while I am still alive—only if I am dead will you receive this bequest from me, from one who loved you above all else and whom you never recognized, from one who always waited for you and whom you never summoned. Perhaps, perhaps you will summon me then, and I will fail to keep faith with you for the first time, because when I am dead I will not hear you. I leave you no picture and no sign, as you left me nothing; you will never recognize me, never. It was my fate in life, let it be my fate in death. I will not call for you in my last hour, I will leave and you will not know my name or my face. I die with an easy mind, since you will not feel it from afar. If my death were going to hurt you, I could not die.

I cannot write any more… my head feels so dulled… my limbs hurt, I am feverish. I think I shall have to lie down. Perhaps it will soon be over, perhaps fate has been kind to me for once, and I shall not have to see them take my child away… I cannot write any more. Goodbye, beloved, goodbye, and thank you… it was good as it was in spite of everything… I will thank you for that until my last breath. I am at ease: I have told you everything, and now you know—or no, you will only guess—how much I loved you, and you will not feel that love is any burden on you. You will not miss me—that consoles me. Nothing in your happy, delightful life will change—I am doing you no harm with my death, and that comforts me, my beloved.

But who... who will always send you white roses on your birthday now? The vase will be empty, the little breath of my life that blew around you once a year will die away as well! Beloved, listen, I beg you... it is the first and last thing I ask you... do it for me every year on your birthday, which is a day when people think of themselves—buy some roses and put them in that vase. Do it, beloved, in the same way as others have a Mass said once a year for someone now dead who was dear to them. I do not believe in God any more, however, and do not want a Mass—I believe only in you, I love only you, and I will live on only in you... oh, only for one day a year, very, very quietly, as I lived near you... I beg you, do that, beloved... it is the first thing that I have ever asked you to do, and the last... thank you... I love you, I love you... goodbye.

His shaking hands put the letter down. Then he thought for a long time. Some kind of confused memory emerged of a neighbour's child, of a young girl, of a woman in the dance café at night, but a vague and uncertain memory, like a stone seen shimmering and shapeless on the bed of a stream of flowing water. Shadows moved back and forth, but he could form no clear picture. He felt memories of emotion, yet did not really remember. It was as if he had dreamt of all these images, dreamt of them often and deeply, but they were only dreams.

Then his eye fell on the blue vase on the desk in front of him. It was empty, empty on his birthday for the first time in years. He shivered; he felt as if a door had suddenly and invisibly sprung open, and cold air from another world was streaming into his peaceful room. He sensed the presence of death, he sensed the presence of undying love: something broke open inside him, and he thought of the invisible woman, incorporeal and passionate, as one might think of distant music.

DATE OF FIRST
PUBLICATION IN GERMAN

FORGOTTEN DREAMS
Vergessene Träume 1900

IN THE SNOW
Im Schnee 1901

A SUMMER NOVELLA
Sommernovellette 1906

THE GOVERNESS
Die Gouvernante 1907

FANTASTIC NIGHT
Phantastische Nacht 1922

COMPULSION
Der Zwang 1920

MOONBEAM ALLEY
Die Mondscheingasse 1922

LETTER FROM AN UNKNOWN WOMAN
Brief einer Unbekannten 1922

TWENTY-FOUR HOURS IN THE LIFE OF A WOMAN
Vierundzwanzig Stunden aus dem Leben einer Frau 1927

INCIDENT ON LAKE GENEVA
Episode vom Genfer See 1927

MENDEL THE BIBLIOPHILE
Buchmendel 1929

THE DEBT PAID LATE
Die spät bezahlte Schuld 1951
[date of writing unknown, *c.*1940]

PUSHKIN PRESS

Pushkin Press was founded in 1997, and publishes novels, essays, memoirs, children's books—everything from timeless classics to the urgent and contemporary.

Our books represent exciting, high-quality writing from around the world: we publish some of the twentieth century's most widely acclaimed, brilliant authors such as Stefan Zweig, Marcel Aymé, Antal Szerb, Paul Morand and Yasushi Inoue, as well as compelling and award-winning contemporary writers, including Andrés Neuman, Edith Pearlman and Ryu Murakami.

Pushkin Press publishes the world's best stories, to be read and read again. Here are just some of the titles from our long and varied list. For more amazing stories, visit www.pushkinpress.com.

THE SPECTRE OF ALEXANDER WOLF
GAITO GAZDANOV

'A mesmerising work of literature' Antony Beevor

BINOCULAR VISION
EDITH PEARLMAN

'A genius of the short story' Mark Lawson, *Guardian*

TRAVELLER OF THE CENTURY
ANDRÉS NEUMAN

'A beautiful, accomplished novel: as ambitious as it is generous, as moving as it is smart' Juan Gabriel Vásquez, *Guardian*

BEWARE OF PITY
STEFAN ZWEIG

'Zweig's fictional masterpiece' *Guardian*

THE WORLD OF YESTERDAY
STEFAN ZWEIG

'*The World of Yesterday* is one of the greatest memoirs of the twentieth century, as perfect in its evocation of the world Zweig loved, as it is in its portrayal of how that world was destroyed' David Hare

JOURNEY BY MOONLIGHT
ANTAL SZERB

'Just divine… makes you imagine the author has had private access to your own soul' Nicholas Lezard, *Guardian*

BONITA AVENUE
PETER BUWALDA

'One wild ride: a swirling helix of a family saga… a new writer as toe-curling as early Roth, as roomy as Franzen and as caustic as Houellebecq' *Sunday Telegraph*

THE PARROTS
FILIPPO BOLOGNA

'A five-star satire on literary vanity… a wonderful, surprising novel' *Metro*

I WAS JACK MORTIMER
ALEXANDER LERNET–HOLENIA

'Terrific… a truly clever, rather wonderful book that both plays with and defies genre' Eileen Battersby, *Irish Times*

SONG FOR AN APPROACHING STORM
PETER FRÖBERG IDLING

'Beautifully evocative… a must-read novel' *Daily Mail*

THE RABBIT BACK LITERATURE SOCIETY
PASI ILMARI JÄÄSKELÄINEN

'Wonderfully knotty… a very grown-up fantasy masquerading as quirky fable. Unexpected, thrilling and absurd' *Sunday Telegraph*

RED LOVE: THE STORY OF AN EAST GERMAN FAMILY
MAXIM LEO

'Beautiful and supremely touching… an unbearably poignant description of a world that no longer exists' *Sunday Telegraph*

COIN LOCKER BABIES
RYU MURAKAMI

'A fascinating peek into the weirdness of contemporary Japan' Oliver Stone

TALKING TO OURSELVES
ANDRÉS NEUMAN

'This is writing of a quality rarely encountered... when you read Neuman's
beautiful novel, you realise a very high bar has been set' *Guardian*

CLOSE TO THE MACHINE
ELLEN ULLMAN

'Astonishing... impossible to put down' *San Francisco Chronicle*

MARCEL
ERWIN MORTIER

'Aspiring novelists will be hard pressed to achieve this quality' *Time Out*

JOURNEY INTO THE PAST
STEFAN ZWEIG

'Lucid, tender, powerful and compelling' *Independent*

POPULAR HITS OF THE SHOWA ERA
RYU MURAKAMI

'One of the funniest and strangest gang wars in recent literature' *Booklist*

LETTER FROM AN UNKNOWN WOMAN AND OTHER STORIES
STEFAN ZWEIG

'Zweig's time of oblivion is over for good... it's good
to have him back' Salman Rushdie

ONE NIGHT, MARKOVITCH
AYELET GUNDAR-GOSHEN

'A remarkable first novel, trenchant and full of love, highly
impressive in its maturity and wisdom' Eshkol Nevo

MY FELLOW SKIN
ERWIN MORTIER

'A Bildungsroman which is related to much European literature from Proust
and Mann onwards... peculiarly unforgettable' AS Byatt, *Guardian*